L.U.C.I. IN THE SKY

Chris Fox was a partner in a New York strategy consulting company. He worked around the world with clients such as Citicorp, JVC, and Heineken, and then decided to become a fiction writer. To combat writer's block, he sometimes dogfights in a World War II era USAF Trainer and takes his NSX onto the skidpad at various racetracks. He is currently working on his second novel.

T0316123

L.U.C.I. IN THE SKY

Chris Fox

ARROW

Published in the United Kingdom in 2002 by
Arrow Books

3 5 7 9 10 8 6 4 2

Copyright © Travisty Productions, Inc., 2001

The right of Chris Fox to be identified as the author of this
work has been asserted by him in accordance with the
Copyright, Designs and Patents Act, 1988

This book is sold subject to the condition that it shall not, by way of
trade or otherwise, be lent, resold, hired out, or otherwise
circulated without the publisher's prior consent in any form of
binding or cover other than that in which it is published and
without a similar condition including this condition being imposed
on the subsequent purchaser

First published in the United Kingdom in 2001 by Hutchinson

Arrow Books
The Random House Group Ltd
20 Vauxhall Bridge Road, London SW1V 2SA

Random House Australia (Pty) Limited
20 Alfred Street, Milsons Point, Sydney
New South Wales 2061, Australia

Random House New Zealand Limited
18 Poland Road, Glenfield
Auckland 10, New Zealand

Random House (Pty) Limited
Endulini, 5a Jubilee Road, Parktown 2193, South Africa

The Random House Group Ltd Reg. No. 954009

www.randomhouse.co.uk

A CIP catalogue record for this book
is available from the British Library

ISBN 9780091958794

The Random House Group Limited supports The Forest Stewardship
Council® (FSC®), the leading international forest-certification organisation.
Our books carrying the FSC label are printed on FSC®-certified paper.
FSC is the only forest-certification scheme supported by the leading
environmental organisations, including Greenpeace. Our
paper procurement policy can be found at
www.randomhouse.co.uk/environment

MIX
Paper | Supporting
responsible forestry
FSC® C018179

Printed and bound in Great Britain by Clays Ltd, St Ives plc

To Carolyn

TO MY CREW

COMBAT:
You secretive types know who you are. Thanks for sharing. My heartfelt gratitude to Robert Tabian and Chandler Crawford for perfect handling, and to the intrepid Howard Sanders and Richard Green. To the remarkable team at Hutchinson – Paul Sidey, my gifted and gracious editor; the ever-helpful Sophie Wills; Michael Mascaro; Mark McCallum; Ellen Jones; Sarah Whale; Emma Mitchell; Jane Selley. Thank you for devoting so much talent, energy, and hard work to this project.

AIRLIFT:
For their creative inspiration and friendship, my thanks to: Sharon Houck, WAAS/LAAS pioneer, winsome and wicked in an F18; elegant and insightful Joan Nova; Richard and Dina Nicolella, that devastating pilot/director and psychic/producer team; Keya, Sean, and James 'Wild Weasel' Degus at UTA; Avanti de Mille, Sandi Gellis-Cole; Stephen Fischer; Mitch Kaplan; Dennis and Bill; Dawn Bailey; Morgan Davis; Catherine and Ian Lyness for friendship beyond description; Holly Reich and Michael Kreitman, Susan and Kerry Sakolsky; Rick and Jennifer Schmidt, Michelle Behan; Cheri and Allen Jacobi; Peggy, Arnie and Sande Harris; Kirk Liniger; Al and Nancy Malnik; Carol and Ryan Taite; Skip Short; Sue Barton; Bob Gordon; Paige Morrow and David Kimball; Maria Dante and Nikki

Carrano; Stenya and Harold; Barbara and John 'Tank 'n Toga' Kushner; Allan and Julie Baer; Caron K.; Rien Weststrate; Dik van der Breggen; Chris Lee; Jessica and Alan Dolleck; Leslie, Robbie, Allison, Josh & Melanie Friedson; Joyce Beber; Rose Mendez; Dan Starer; JoAnn Lederman; Tom Lopez; Cindy Roessel; Martha and Mike Gilson; Gene Powers; Sharon and Noel Frankel; Fran and Michael Lerner; Myer Berlow; Claudia Lewis; Paul and Debbie Donnelly, Peter Rodriguez, Evan Blair; Susie and Gary Geller; Michael Roth; Helene and Marc Kovens, Stan Alpert and his group of merry financiers; all members of the Bay Club squadron; and to all the books by Nelson de Mille that stood tall on my bookshelf goading me to try this. With special thanks to Mandy McDevitt for ten years of consistent valor on keyboard.

BASE:
To the guys I love – my father, Christopher I, and son, Christopher III – thanks for your creativity and roaring good times in my minutes of leisure.

To the sensational Elaine Terris, Michaele Keyes, and Marianne Berson, it's good to have you with us.

To Calvin and Spencer, thanks in lieu of royalties.

To my father-in-law, Captain Louis Zuckerman (USAAC, Rtd), and my mother-in-law, General Greta Zuckerman (De Havilland Squadron), my love and appreciation soars. P.S. Watch 'em Terna.

And to my wife, Carolyn, the most breathtaking Fox of all, thank you for being my heart's *Playboy* 'Girl of Mensa' and lighting up our sky.

PART I

Maria's Game

ONE

In my dreams, I performed nightly as Lucretia Borgia's wine-taster.

A dream analyst might call it the 'day residue' from a stressful job. Anyway, my Lucretia dream repeated the same story every night.

I sat in the court of the Borgias in sixteenth-century Florence, facing that poisonous ruling family around the banquet table. The server would hand me the wine goblet. Lucretia always watched me carefully, her dark eyes soaked with Mediterranean cunning. Her courtesans wore dark beards and ermine hats. And they rattled their gold utensils. I was their Monday Night Football. Lucretia's brother Cesare Borgia and his adviser Niccolo Machiavelli sat together. They stared at my wine goblet, nudging each other and smirking.

I always raised Lucretia's goblet with a casual flip. Then I would sip her wine and swallow.

All conversation stopped. The Borgias and their guests sucked in their breath. A wine-taster develops a sense of timing. After a long pause, I would lick my lips.

'Scratchy for a Brunello, but it won't kill you,' I would say to Lucretia, or something like that.

Then I would press the goblet into her jeweled hand. The courtesans exploded into lilting Italian. But some around the great table always looked happier than others.

Every night I had that dream. And every night, I

managed to survive the wine-tasting – until the fifteenth of March. In the dark hours of that Sunday morning, I dreamt that I sipped from Lucretia's wine goblet and the ritual became mortal.

At the first taste, I knew. A sovereign's job is to survive. A wine-taster's is to do the opposite when necessary.

The poison speared my tongue with needles. It was an odd taste, like liquid cactus. My throat turned to flame. I coughed to stop it, but the sly juice trickled down to scorch my lungs. Slipping down in my chair, I clutched at my chest.

I was jolted rudely awake.

My ribs felt squeezed by a huge pair of tongs. My heart hammered wildly. Pain ripped open my body. I oozed sweat and I couldn't breathe. Could this be my first heart attack a decade or two early? My eyelids burst open, breaking a sleepy crust.

Then I blinked several times. Somebody sat on top of me in bed.

I knew the woman on my stomach couldn't be Lucretia Borgia. Her legs felt too strong, locking tight over my abdomen. No sixteenth-century woman could be that pumped.

I saw a leather and lace dress. A Gaultier contraption, making fashion angles around her trim body. Her long hair was a mass of pillow-ready curls. Only one feature civilized her untamed goddess look. Tortoiseshell glasses of the sort that people who stare compulsively at computer screens wear, perched halfway down her nose.

She tapped me on the shoulder with a flashlight, shiny and black.

'Good morning, Terry,' she purred.

I was pinned down in my bed by this intense, almost painfully hot young woman. She straddled my stomach with legs like pistons. I caught a whiff of something unsavory. From my own body? Yes. I still wore the clothes I had on the evening before. As I stirred, her heat and energy rushed under the wool of my suit and over my skin.

'Good *morning*, Terry,' she repeated, not quite as warmly.

I struggled to answer her. This sort of thing happened to me infrequently. Well, never. I just didn't throw those heat-seeking pheromones around. My work always came first.

Now my heart, denied for so long, almost skipped with infatuation. I studied the woman on top of me, yearning to believe that I had just gotten lucky. But all my instincts told me the opposite. I had actually gotten very unlucky. I just couldn't figure out exactly how.

My mind felt glued to the floor.

Tunnel vision, Terry. Focus.

I chipped away. Slowly, I could see the broken shards of the previous evening. Midnight, after dinner with a client. I sat in this same now-rank suit, then fresh and razor-pressed, in an oversized leather chair.

Yes. The martini bar on Irving Place.

I sat admiring a post-modern-style painting. It was a bug's-eye view of a very plump, naked woman lying in the grass, shadows framing her body.

As I studied the painting, the woman now crunching my stomach appeared on the periphery of my vision.

5

I have excellent situational awareness, especially for those rare moments when beauty and grace hover nearby.

I watched this woman without letting her know.

She wore the sensuous Gaultier dress, but not the heavy tortoiseshell glasses. Her nose was on the small side, with nostrils that quivered very slightly like a rabbit's. Under the sleek lights of the martini bar, her dark curls tumbled over her shoulders. I could feel her eyes as a sunlamp's glow against my face.

'Massimo Colla,' she said, with her eyes on the painting.

A soft drink?

No. She was telling me the name of the artist who had painted the naked woman in the grass.

'He works in Siena,' she said, still focused on the painting.

I finally turned to her. Her uncanny face pointed toward me, tilted up and smirking. Her skin had the uniformly warm-toned moist glow of spoiled youth, and almost animal-alert turquoise eyes that sparkled like the Caribbean. Her trim body shifted with languid little moves.

'That's my favorite part of Italy,' I told her. I could see from her pleased look that my face must have lit up for her. I did love Siena, a medieval town in Tuscany rich in art and porcini mushrooms the size of hubcaps.

'Why did you leave?' she asked.

'You never leave Tuscany,' I vaguely remember answering.

She told me her name was Maria Haymeyer.

We soon moved to a small couch in the bar, to sit close and talk. She spoke so softly, drawing me out like a gopher dying to burrow out of its hole to bask in her sun. I felt such

6

*a rush of euphoria, confiding feelings that seldom shake
loose.*

*I told her my plan to retire in one year at age thirty-six.
After my workaholic frenzy of a business career, I
desperately wanted to find the soulmate I had denied
myself. A woman of fire and subtle intelligence who I could
share my life with, except for a few historical details. She
would be the other half of my couple. She would help me
begin my real life. We would marry in Montalcino, a
medieval hill town, in the courtyard of a stone church on
the hill. Shafts of light would break through the morning
mist, painting the meadows green and gold as we spoke our
vows.*

*I told Maria Haymeyer I had no idea what my wife
would look like yet, but I could hear her laugh. Maria gave
me a soft and cozy smile then.*

Now she wasn't smiling. She was using her buffed
legs to pin me to my bed and giving me the
expression a biology student gives a dead frog.

I closed my eyes. What else had I told this woman
when I was swollen with euphoria?

*Not much. Just how I wanted to raise our children in the
pastoral sanity of Italy's meadows and cypress trees. And
why I dreamt about showing them the skies that inspired
Renaissance artists. And where I would teach them how to
fly a plane because we needed to soar with the birds to taste
the sweetness of earth.*

Believe me, I never talk that way. Especially to a
woman I've just met.

The longer she and I spoke at the martini bar, the
more stupid euphoria I felt. Then my view of Maria
began needing serious adjustment on my part to

remain level. Suddenly, the whole room became blurry and diagonal. I must have passed out.

And I only drank one glass of wine.

So how did she get me to my place? I huffed as her taut leg muscles almost crushed my abdomen.

'I'm interested,' I told Maria Haymeyer. 'Just let me breathe for a minute.'

'Forget about sex, Terry,' she said. 'This is a business meeting. I need you to do something for me.'

Her voice meant it, not at all intimate. Now it was rapid and high-strung, like the kids who come to fix your computer. With her sultry, defined body, and that wired voice, Maria could only be described as a hot nerd. Her eyes were much sharper now. They burned through her lenses. I thought I could feel a space just over my nose getting hot, like I was a bug under a magnifying glass on a sunny day.

Focus!

I glanced at the dark outlines of my own bed-room. The sixteenth-century Florentine wall frescos reassured me. Funny how your mind lets shadows of your past successes prop you up, even when they're irrelevant to the situation at hand. Growing used to the dark, I looked out my window. A few lights burned in other highrise buildings, a friendly constellation. I started to think semi-clearly.

Business meeting?

I struggled to recall everything I could about what Maria had said the night before.

I thought of nothing to help me puzzle out her intentions.

In the best case, she could be the world's most assertive young entrepreneur. I was a venture capitalist. A lot of people with fledgling companies wanted money from Starcross-Voyager Venture Capital, the fund I ran with four partners that invested in new businesses.

In the worst case, of course, she could be some Manhattan variety of designer succubus. She surprised men in their beds. Then she killed them.

'If sex is off the table, Maria, maybe . . .'

'Shut up, Terry,' she explained. 'For the record, I apologize for drugging your wine. But I had to talk to you here in private.'

Her apology sounded sincere.

'That would have been easier than you thought,' I told her. When I tried to sit up, my chest tingled in an uncomfortable way.

'Don't move,' she said. 'I don't want to jolt you again.'

She tapped hard on my breastbone with the black flashlight. I recognized it for the first time as a stun gun. It looked like it could throw a real industrial-strength jolt to paralyze me. My nerve endings seared.

'Did you just shoot me with that?' I started to get irate, then eased off as her finger tightened on the trigger.

'You're a sound sleeper,' she explained, 'and we don't have much time.'

'We don't?' Not good. 'So how about some coffee? I'll make it.'

'No, Terry. First we need to clarify our business

relationship. I'll tell you exactly what I need from you. Frankly, your own options are limited.'

'I'm all ears.'

'A defense contractor named Ted Devlin stole something from me. You already know who he is. I need you to get evidence of his theft.'

'Teflon Ted Devlin? I only know what I read in the *Wall Street Journal*.'

Ted Devlin was a major player in military contracting. He headed Linnet/TVR, one of three big aerospace companies competing to win the new Joint Strike Fighter contract from the Pentagon. The other two were Lockheed and Boeing. It would be the biggest Pentagon contract in history, worth a trillion dollars in revenues over time to the company that won it. That was a 'T' with a dozen zeros behind it.

'So what do you think Ted Devlin stole from you?'

'An intelligent chip for a warplane. I call it LUCI. He stole it to use for his Joint Strike Fighter prototype to win the Pentagon contract.'

I needed to keep calm while I wrapped my mind around this claim. Flaky didn't touch it. Military aircraft are designed by huge teams of aeronautical engineers and weapons specialists. They work in places like California and Texas. They're not single women living in Manhattan who know what a Gaultier dress is. And they don't slink around martini bars on Irving Place to drug and torture innocent men. Maria's claim made me laugh out loud. Or it would have, if she wasn't holding a stun gun to my neck.

'You designed an intelligent chip. Ted Devlin stole it for his new plane.' I bit my lip as if mulling it over.

'Yes.' I could see her eyes behind the thick lenses ferreting out my skepticism. She spoke more slowly as though explaining a dense concept to a small child. 'I was studying to be a game designer. I created an advanced microchip for a Joint Strike Fighter computer game. It was just a *game*, Terry.' Her wide eyes behind the glasses didn't budge from mine or blink. 'Ted Devlin stole my microchip because he could see it would make his real fighter a lot smarter. So he would win the contract.'

'I see.' *Psycho.* Her thigh muscles tightened on my ribcage as I merely thought that. 'So you did it all by yourself?'

'That's right. I kept up with the JSF competition.' She used the acronym for the Joint Strike Fighter. I hated those. 'The prototype Ted Devlin was building was barely working. He would have lost. So I showed him how he could use my microchip to turn his dumb prototype into an invisible fighter with non-lethal weapons.'

Oh, sweet freaking Jesus. My mind didn't boggle. No, it just blew out to the stratosphere and I had to snap it back. Non-lethal weapons? Where to begin?

'Don't you see a marketing problem with a non-lethal fighter?' I decided to ask first. A fangless jet fighter would be about as useful as a sixty-million-dollar lawn dwarf.

Her nostrils quivered. 'That's just your age and testosterone speaking, Terry. Do you know that most of the ultra-top-secret projects in the Pentagon right now are exploring non-lethal weaponry?'

'If they're ultra-top-secret, how would I know about them?'

She wasn't listening. 'They have contractors working on weapons like sticky foam to stop aircraft in flight and smart lasers instead of explosives. Think of a laser that can tattoo a US flag on to a terrorist's forehead from five thousand feet. In color.'

'What a fun thought.' It was, admittedly, but I wasn't in the mood.

'We are becoming more civilized, Terry. Americans do not want to turn on CNN and see us killing people any more. Not even enemy soldiers. It makes us feel like bullies and it outrages the international community.'

I gave up. 'I don't want to outrage anybody. How did Ted steal your idea?'

'Two years ago I was a PhD student in computer science at Stanford. I was doing my doctoral thesis on "Advanced Heuristics Through Superconductivity in Game Platforms".'

I almost stifled a yawn, then felt her stun gun prod at the whiskers on my neck and paid attention.

'To keep it simple,' she continued drily, 'Ted Devlin saw how my chip could make his Joint Strike Fighter about one hundred times smarter than Boeing's or Lockheed's.'

'That bastard.' Oh-kay. 'So how did Ted Devlin steal your chip?'

'From my apartment. And my disks. They had the recipe on them.'

'Didn't you patent it?'

'No.'

'Why not?'

'I was naive.'

'How did he see your chip in the first place, Maria?'

'Seven months ago, I sent Ted Devlin a sample on disk. I marked it Personal and Confidential. He called me himself a week later. He said he'd already made lunch reservations. I should fly down to Long Beach the next day.'

'And?'

'I came and sat there. He auditioned me in the restaurant in the Long Beach Hyatt. He stared at my body, but managed to ask me a *lot* of questions about my chip at the same time. That's when I showed it to him. He told me he couldn't use it in his Joint Strike Fighter program. It was too risky for the Pentagon people, who were, in his words, suck-ups with stars and bars, and not a testicle among 'em bigger than a snow pea. But he promised to have his project engineers review the disks. He said maybe they could develop my game design for Sega or Nintendo for next Christmas. They want to be in consumer markets because trying to please the Pentagon's driving him crazy, he said.'

'So you just gave him your disks.'

'I just *told* you,' she sounded exasperated, 'it didn't occur to me that the head of Linnet/TVR would steal a student's work.'

'Right. And you didn't have back-up disks?'

Her lips quivered. 'No. I flew back home. The next day when I was at school, my apartment was

13

broken into. All my work was gone. When I called Ted Devlin, his secretary blew me off. He wouldn't even get on the phone.'

'Didn't you show your design to anybody else?' I asked her. 'Your professors?'

She wagged her head. 'I was working by myself when Ted Devlin robbed me, and I took a time-out. Perhaps you could call it a nervous breakdown. I had to take a leave of absence from my doctoral program because I couldn't turn in my thesis. I finally took a grunt job at Intech.'

'Couldn't you rewrite your program?'

She sucked in her lower lip. 'Even after I had it all worked out, it took me six years to write, Terry.'

'Why did you call it Lucy?'

'L.U.C.I.,' she spelled it out. 'It stands for Light Ultra-Chip Intelligence.'

'Clever,' I lied. Another stupid acronym.

She stared hard for a moment. Maria had the eerie perceptions of the acutely aware or insane. I couldn't fake much with her, but I wondered how much of this story she was faking with me.

'Okay, how do you know for sure he stole it?'

'Six months later, I read that he was working on a radical design change for the JSF prototype. Their code name for it was LUCI. Obviously Ted Devlin used my design.'

'Obviously.' I managed to nod reassuringly without denting my chin on her stun gun. 'It sounds like you need a good lawyer.'

'I already found one.' She mentioned a firm in Washington that was big, expensive and connected.

'And?'

'The lawyer I talked to looked into it. Then he called me and said no thanks. He said he spoke to Ted Devlin himself. Devlin told him he gave me a courtesy interview and didn't want to pursue my idea. He also said I was just accusing him to be a nuisance and extort money.'

'Why would that stop your lawyer?'

'Because the medication I was taking didn't help.'

'Medication?'

'Prozac. I was depressed after Ted stole my game. I went to a psychiatrist. Anyway, the lawyer chose not to believe me.'

'I wonder why.'

She glared. 'Because it was my word against Ted Devlin's. Who would you believe? That's why I need evidence, Terry. That's why I need you.'

'For what?' I asked her. 'You're an appealing victim. And your story makes sense, in a way, because Ted Devlin steals other people's ideas every day. It's called Management 101. But I can't do much about that.'

'You have to,' she told me with an urgency I felt through my suit.

'I don't know Ted Devlin.' I wriggled my right leg, which was falling asleep. 'And even if you found evidence, how could he admit he stole his radical new design from a college student? His career's on the line.'

'Not any more. He'll win. The Pentagon will want my design. Not Boeing's, not Lockheed's. My chip will let his plane stop a war before it starts.'

'Then maybe you should go to the Pentagon yourself,' I told her with a straight face. 'State your case, give them enough information to raise suspicions.'

'Don't patronize me, Terry.' She looked tired. 'Nobody important is going to believe me. So I'm asking you to get into Linnet/TVR and take a good look at their JSF prototype.'

Did I say Maria Haymeyer? Maria Haywire would be more like it.

'Maria,' I measured each word, 'I thought you were going to tell me you had a product and needed money to develop it. Then maybe I could help you. That's what I do. I'm a venture capitalist. I sit around conference rooms and talk about how start-up companies can get financing. But I can't go sneaking around top-secret military aircraft, even if I wanted to. I wouldn't know where to start.'

'Really? When you were a first lieutenant in the Air Force ten years ago, what was your job?'

I swallowed softly. 'I flew an F-16 fighter.'

'And when you were promoted to captain?' She waited. I felt something like a gas pain. My temples throbbed from wasted mental effort, wondering how she got access to my Air Force records.

'I flew another fighter during the Gulf War.'

'Yes. A Darkwing F-118 stealth fighter,' she chirped. 'Which happened to be the Linnet/TVR stealth fighter. I selected you very carefully for this job, Terry. For instance, you do know Ted Devlin.'

'I met him once with a lot of other pilots,' I admitted. 'During my Darkwing training. Stealth planes were new then. Nobody knew if they'd really

16

work in combat. Ted came to our base to tell us they would.'

I recalled the feeling of shaking Ted's hand, the power in his grip. Teflon Ted Devlin wore a buzz cut and had one glass eye. I remember enjoying him more than I'd expected to.

'Maria, okay. I was a fighter pilot. But I'm not a spy.'

'I'll admit you're no James Bond.'

'Thank you.'

She pushed the business end of her stun gun firmly into my chest with one hand and reached beside her with the other. I raised my head. Like a true conspiracy nut, she actually had a beat-up accordion file next to her on my bed. She pulled something small and flat out of it.

'Do you recognize this?'

She dangled a business card in front of my face. I peered at it in the semi-darkness. I could make out the picture of a bird in flight. A stiletto-sleek bird. It was black with a small red sac under its neck. Below the bird, a single line read:

Fragata, 39-6-31-350

'If it's a phone number, the code is for Rome.' I couldn't figure out what she wanted me to say.

'Only about a dozen people in the world have this card,' she told me.

'Really? So what is it?'

'That's a picture of a *fragata* bird, Spanish for frigate, found in the Galapagos Islands, off

17

Ecuador. It's a pirate. It survives by stealing food from other birds in flight. Scientists call that behavior klepto-parasitic.'

'And it interests you because . . .'

'This is the business card of an industrial spy known as Fragata. His little joke. He's klepto-parasitic too.'

Maria put the card down and lifted a piece of paper. It seemed to be a Xerox copy blown up from a news article. I made out *Time* in the margin. It *was* a news article, with a photograph of a business memo that had an airline logo on top.

'Can you read it?' she asked me.

'A light would help.'

Pressing her stun gun to my Adam's apple, she reached over to turn on the light by my bed. She didn't take her eyes off mine. The sudden light forced me to squint. I saw in her black hair natural traces of golden blonde. I could only guess at her parentage. Definitely Latin, but with some Irish or Scottish in there.

I took the piece of paper from her and peered at the memo, trying to decipher it quickly.

'It looks like a Sunshine Airlines document,' I told her.

'An internal e-mail.' She tossed her curls. 'It's the reason they're out of business now. The industrial spy who calls himself Fragata stole evidence exposing Sunshine Airlines as a stock-market scam. Old planes, bad maintenance, an accident waiting to happen. But also enough earnings to make a killing on Wall Street for the crooks who ran it. Fragata buried the company. Some say he did it to save lives. But maybe he was just paid by a competitor. Is that cynical of me?'

'Probably not. Just the way of the world.'

'Look at the date.'

I anticipated her question. 'Yes. Sunshine Airlines came to me for financing when they were starting up. I turned them down. I didn't like their operation. But that doesn't mean . . .'

'Shush.'

I glanced unobtrusively at my watch – 5.06 a.m. It would be dawn soon.

'Have you seen this before?' Maria held another page in my face. It displayed the logo for Happy Beefburger, a big fast-food chain owned by a French conglomerate.

'I guess it's the recipe for Happy Beefburger's Secret Sauce.'

'Reportedly stolen by Fragata for two million dollars.'

'Maria . . .' I shook my head, exasperated.

She waved a whole handful of papers in my face. 'I could go on, Terry, but I need to find Fragata right now. Any ideas?'

She waited for me to answer.

The air in my bedroom seemed unbearably dense. I tried to draw it into my nostrils and breathe deeply. Sweat dropped from my forehead into my eyes, a salty sting.

'You really think I can snap my fingers and produce an industrial spy for you?'

'Yes.'

'Look, Maria, a woman should be free to design a warplane without somebody stealing it. But I can't help you. Yes, I was once an Air Force pilot who would set a rival's hair on fire for fun. I was young. Now I'm a thirty-five-year-old financial guy with no contacts whatsoever in industrial espionage. I'm sorry.'

'I need Fragata, Terry.' Calm. Not listening.

'If you want him so badly, why don't you just call the number on his card?' I moved my arms to test her grip on the stun gun.

Then I heard a snap like a rubber band. A painful jolt inflamed my chest. Shock waves radiated all the way up to my hair and down to my toenails. My body lunged upward. Her legs straddled my bucking ribs like a rodeo rider.

The jolt ended suddenly, but not the awful feeling. My body collapsed on the bed shuddering, drenched with sweat. My fingers clutched at my mattress.

'Don't make me hit you where it's really going to hurt,' she said.

Horrified, I reflexively looked down to my groin. She frowned, then understood and wrinkled her nose in disgust.

'I'm talking about your money.'

She held a color copy in front of my face. It was a picture of a small maroon folder, like a passport.

'This is a Swiss bankbook. It's for account number 311.289.CB, United Bank of Lucerne. Look familiar?'

I bit my tongue to keep from groaning.

Two

'A week ago,' Maria said, 'this account recorded a balance of 26,231,673 US dollars.'

'So?' I tried not to move.

'That was what Fragata made during his career as an industrial spy. All hidden away. It's payable to the bearer of this bank book with the password "Gumby". What a wily, urbane spy Fragata turned out to be, choosing a claymation figure for his password. Or maybe it was the name of Fragata's little Scottish terrier when he was a boy.'

She was wrong. Gumby was a Jack Russell terrier.

'Where did you find that bankbook?'

'It was in plain sight under the floor of your Los Angeles apartment. Your bankbook is safe. But there's one little thing.'

She held up another color copy, a more recent shot of my bankbook.

It recorded a withdrawal of $26,231,000 three days ago, leaving a balance of $673.

Gas and burning nausea filled my throat. Then a creepy cold sensation lit my nerve endings. I shook. Only my scalp still felt warm. In fact, boiling. I counted down from five.

'I don't see how that affects me,' I said.

'Don't worry. It's in a safe place. And if you do

what I ask, you'll get it all back. I'm not in this for the money.'

'Maria, I'm not Fragata. Can I sit up now?'

'Okay.'

Focus. Lose sight, lose the fight.

'I need a shower,' I told her honestly.

'Go ahead. You can think about what I've told you.'

She watched without interest as I padded barefoot in my crumpled suit to the bathroom and closed the door behind me. I stumbled to the toilet, where I collapsed on the marble tile and threw up for several minutes, hugging the cold porcelain. I wondered if a human being could commit suicide using a toilet fixture.

I gazed at the wall feeling oddly detached.

Like my bedroom, the bathroom walls have a topcoat of *intonaco*, a rough plaster found in the Tuscan countryside. I installed it myself for only twice the time and money it would have cost to hire a professional.

Finally, I stood on wobbly legs, grabbing the cool marble of my vanity. I gargled with mouthwash that felt like razor blades, and brushed my teeth to remove the acrid taste in my mouth. It didn't help.

I picked up the wireless phone I kept there for emergencies. Not surprisingly, Maria Haymeyer had already found and disabled it.

Then I stripped off my ripe clothes. Naked and shivering, I stepped into my shower and stood under hot water for thirty seconds. I turned on the cold water to revive myself before getting out and putting on a thick black bathrobe.

I studied myself in the mirror.

What a horrifying reflection of feral panic. The disturbed glint in my eye. The skin drained of a living person's color. Hair lank and damp on my sweating forehead. I sprinkled water on my face and finger-combed my hair back until some of my color returned. I needed to summon intense discipline. First, I would make a threat assessment. Then I could seek information and review my options.

Collecting myself, I first relaxed my haunted face. A face that, if I saw it on another person – and at that moment I wished I could – I would have read clearly as 'Air Force brat born of foreign love affair'.

My dad, a fighter pilot from New York, met my mother while stationed at Aviano Air Force Base in Italy. She was a fashion model from Milan.

It took all my will to restore the appearance of my father's calm eyes. I'd inherited his eyes and light blonde hair. I had clean features, like his, with some Italian styling from my mother. Most people described me as 'friendly and open'. It always stunned me how easily people trust superficial traits. If I looked like a criminal, I might have been forced to live and die a venture capitalist.

Instead, I had begun moonlighting as an industrial spy seven years before.

Among a handful of people scattered around the world, I built a reputation for honesty, narrowly defined. There were two kinds of people in my business – those who pretended to know a lot more than they did, and those who pretended to know a lot less. I joined group two and became a trusted thief. That was how I had, until very recently, grown comfortably rich.

I managed a harsh, brittle laugh. Maria Haymeyer had pierced my veil of secrecy just when I planned to terminate Fragata's industrial espionage career.

It was my love life. Or lack of one.

I met dynamic businesswomen every day. Gorgeous, vital women full of snap and cunning, sleek in their Armani suits across conference tables. You can't imagine how I longed to fall in love with a woman like that.

But my career prevented me from doing anything about it. Intellectual curiosity in a partner? Please. The lies about my schedule alone, the time unaccounted for, would have collapsed in days under a bright woman's scrutiny.

When I was a twenty-something fighter pilot, I admit to behaving like Pinocchio with a woody loose on Pleasure Island. I didn't care. When I grew up, I cared a lot. But I had already started spying and had to choose between career and soulmate. I could find comfort in women of slower synapses, or I could sleep alone.

Dates depressed me. Sweaty workouts in my gym with women named Kimmie or Stacey. Dinner in noisy restaurants to discourage chat. Double-safe sex. And maybe a movie in my media room, murdering time watching those '90s romantic comedies starring cast members from *Friends*.

By the time I reached my mid-thirties, my soul screamed for a real woman. I wanted children. I wanted conversation. But to retire from my secret life, I needed a nest egg. And I needed one the size of a dinosaur egg because I would never be able to use my special skills again. My cover as a venture capitalist bored me. I let my partners do most of the work and keep practically all the money. In my last year as Fragata, I calculated I would need to earn at least another twenty million. My corporate clients could afford it.

Secure with wheelbarrows full of money, I could find that elusive Eighth Wonder of the World, my soulmate. We would settle in Tuscany, just like I told Maria over my single glass of wine. *In vino veritas*, when you add a little sodium amytal or whatever she did.

I had such dreams.

Now I stood on the stinging cold tiles of my bathroom, broke, still clammy under my bathrobe, outsmarted by a woman I'd never wanted to meet. I felt a wave of bittersweet, short-term nostalgia for my life before Maria.

I opened the door and poked my head out into my bedroom.

She had gone somewhere. I left my bedroom past an oil-painted fresco – a sixteenth-century painting of Florentine bankers. Those merchant princes were the venture capitalists of their day. They looked so full of themselves, smirking gleefully in red capes with adoring angels hovering over their heads telling them how smart they were. All were

25

ruined a few years later when Edward III of England defaulted on all his debts.

I never liked it particularly. But I kept it as a colorful reminder of fortune's whimsy. Now I could take it down. Maria had made its lesson obsolete.

I found her sitting at my breakfast table.

With her long neck and nicely tilted chin, she stared through my big windows at Central Park. My compact penthouse on Central Park West occupied a corner of a 1930s highrise apartment building called the San Lorenzo.

Maria's lips parted slightly as she studied Central Park through the big window. She seemed to be quietly vibrating. I wondered what thrilled her, Central Park in the first early blush of spring, or how much the apartment may have cost me. I thought neither. Her eyes danced with their own calculations.

I smelled strong coffee brewing in the kitchen.

'I made us espresso,' she said.

As I entered the kitchen, my bare feet felt the sting of the cold marble floor. I seethed at the thought of her using my espresso machine that now gasped and hissed, ready to give up its rich nectar for her. I poured the coffee myself into two cups.

Cesare Borgia would have poisoned her. Not my style. And whoever helped her steal my money must still be lurking. She couldn't have done it alone, any more than she could design a smart chip for a fighter.

She twisted her lemon slice and sipped from the cup. Her pouty lips made a little circle, like a shiny red donut.

I joined her at the table.

'Maria, whatever you think you know about me, here's the truth. I'm not Fragata. The money you stole was my nest egg. I accumulated it over my business career and invested wisely—'

She interrupted with a biting laugh. 'You call that investing? It was earning four per cent in the stingiest bank in Switzerland. I'm making five per cent for you where it's parked now. Some financial guy you are. You could have chosen a more credible cover.'

My eyes went hard and narrow without even trying. 'Are you a pilot yourself, Maria?'

'I am.'

'You know which pilots die the fastest?'

'No.' She waited.

'Gifted amateurs. They get cocky, like the rules don't apply to them. Think hard about what you're doing. If I was really Fragata, maybe I'll . . .'

Her plump lips dropped open in genuine mirth, revealing white teeth and large incisors. 'Kill me? A woman? You'd twist up like a pretzel before you'd hurt a woman, Terry. Please, can we get started now? I want to give you as many facts as I can.'

'I'm not Fragata.'

She ignored me, reaching into the small, shimmering evening bag hanging from her chair. I was expecting more documents. Instead, she took out a round white plastic case about one inch in diameter and screwed open the top. She held it open so I could see.

'Do you know what this is?'

I glanced at the clear liquid inside the case. 'Contact lens solution?'

'No. My microchip. Watch.'

She gently lifted the tiny open case. Squeezing it with her thumb and forefinger, she suddenly yanked the case straight down. A small blob resembling a raindrop slipped out. She blew gently at it, and the liquid flattened into a shape like a triangular contact lens. It drifted an inch in my direction. I blew back at it, very softly, and it floated higher in the air, settled, and hovered midway over the table.

She grinned like a proud parent. 'That's the chip of the future, Terry. Molecular. I used the scanning probe microscope at Stanford to build it molecule by molecule. Like Lego blocks.'

'Liquid's heavier than air.' I gaped at the blob. 'How does it float?'

'Like this.' She pursed her lips and blew at it again. The blob sailed toward my forehead. 'It's smart enough to morph itself into different shapes to keep the air pressure lower on its topside. See? Lighter than air.'

When I reached up to grab it, the liquid slipped away.

'Gently,' she said. She reached over and placed her hand lightly over mine, controlling my fingers with the brush of her nails. The nerves under my skin rustled. My thumb and forefinger nipped the transparent blob.

'Now try to tear it apart.'

I held it in both hands, almost grunting in my effort to rip it. The blob wouldn't even stretch. I placed it on the glass table, lifted my spoon, and gave it a good whack. It quivered like Jello for a moment, but settled again. She reached over and used her fingernail to flick it up in the air where it hovered undamaged.

I shook my head. 'The last time I looked, computer chips were still hard wafers imprinted with light. Not floating blobs.'

'Really.' Her eyelids hung lazily at half-mast. 'Ever hear of the "point one" barrier?'

'It's the sound barrier of our age. You can't print information on to a silicon chip much smaller than point one micron. That's why there's a limit on computing power.'

'Was. You should open a science journal, Terry. Scientists have been working on DNA chips for years. I just figured out the right recipe to put their work together.'

'Recipe?'

'I designed a DNA neural network with a hundred billion connections. That's the same number as the human brain.'

'You used human DNA.'

'No. Avian DNA.'

My heart hammered. Each new blip of insanity from those lips made me wonder how this woman ever stole my money.

'You used *bird* DNA?'

'Of course.' Duh. 'We're talking airplane. Birds are nature's aviators.'

I massaged my temples. 'Okay. How powerful is this chip?'

She glanced toward my living room. 'Was that a Nintendo 128 I saw in there?'

'Yeah, I was trying out "Starfox 3D".' Feeling foolish, I added, 'For business.'

'Keeping your pilot-in-command time up. Good for you.'

She stood up and I followed her into the living room. My penthouse had an earthy charm like the stone houses in Tuscany. I had painstakingly added *intonaco* to each wall. Then authentic frescos restored by hand. My favorite, over my leather couch, detailed a fourteenth-century hill town called Montepulciano, drenched in the light of the Tuscan sky. It had taken me a year to recreate.

She walked over to the armoire from Siena that held my electronics. Its heavy wooden doors were open. My game platforms were hooked up to the HDTV screen inside. She handed me my crab-like Nintendo joystick and the 3D glasses.

'Let's play "Starfox",' she said. 'You start.'

I put on the black wraparound goggles that resembled greaser sunglasses from the '50s and pushed the button to start the game. In 'Starfox', the player guides a fuzzy red cartoon fox who pilots a fighter.

The TV wailed, 'Help us, Starfox!'

Starfox's space fighter appeared on screen. The 3D chip made the silvery little warship appear to jut out of the TV like a hologram. The screen did a respectable job of making you feel lost in deep space, a black tunnel full of jagged meteors and enemy ships. I worked the joystick, getting into the rhythms of flying. With my forefinger, I threaded Starfox's ship through the perils of black space.

'I'm just going to jink it a little,' she said.

Maria snapped off the back of the Nintendo 128 control box and looked in with a tight little frown behind her glasses. She nimbly used her fingernail to position the liquid blob inside.

'Okay,' she said.

A blast like a sonic boom made my living room floor shake.

In the lenses of my black glasses, I saw the Starfox character take on a life of his own. His virtual fighter squeezed out of the TV screen like an aluminum sausage. It popped into my living room. In my goggles, the shiny fighter appeared to blast off over my head with a flaming red exhaust. It disappeared into my living room wall.

I swallowed. A Nintendo game couldn't do that.

'Where did it go?'

'Play with it. Bring it back,' Maria said. She sat on the couch, stretching her long legs.

I pulled back on the joystick and heard another roar. The fighter thundered in from my dining room. I jiggled the stick and it twisted around me in a loopy figure eight. I pressed the red button on the joystick. The plane executed a barrel roll.

'Will it fire?'

'Sure. Be careful,' Maria said.

I pushed the green button, and heard a whoosh. The ship was firing a kind of green pinpoint laser into my cherished fresco of Montepulciano. I saw a

31

wisp of smoke from the painted medieval town where the laser struck.

I jiggled the joystick to pull up. The Starfox fighter climbed with a mighty roar up my ceiling. Then it vanished through the stucco.

Her blob mocked me now. I shoved the stick into what ought to be a dive. Sure enough, the needle nose of the fighter sliced back through my ceiling. I saw the scowling Starfox character in the cockpit. The ship grazed my wall of bookshelves and I banked into a controlled turn. I dropped the tail and throttled back to try to contain the virtual fighter in my living room. It shuddered and whined.

I was starting to get the hang of flying it.

'Terry. *Terry!*' Maria stood up from the couch and shut off the Nintendo, shaking her head. She fished her blob out of my control box.

I peered at my living room wall. A tiny scorched black hole still smoked in the center of the Montepulciano town square.

'You ruined my fresco,' I managed.

'Artificial intelligence. The chip locked on to your game program and learned what it was built to do, then did it a hundred times better. Okay, fun's over, Terry.'

She steered me back to one of the firm chairs around my glass breakfast table and I sat heavily. She settled across from me, rustling her dress as she crossed her legs.

I struggled for logic. 'So Ted's new fighter is driven by a kid's game?'

She flicked me a stony look. 'I'd say that's a bit unfair. You know game designers and warfighters use the same programs today. The Marines train on "Doom", I just sped things up a little.'

'A jet fighter's more complicated than "Doom".'

'I got my BS in electrical engineering and my MS in aeronautics and astronautics at Stanford before I started my PhD. I studied every major jet fighter breakthrough. Modesty should forbid, but I've had a gift for invention since I was a kid.'

'You must need a robust ego for your line of work.'

'Ego has nothing to do with it.'

She flicked her blob up in the air again. She held up her contact lens case and blew at the liquid, causing it to glide down like a homing pigeon and slip inside.

'Okay,' I said slowly. 'Let's say your DNA chip is smart. You still can't design an invisible plane like Wonder Woman. There's too much to hide.'

She shrugged. 'I knew what Ted Devlin's Joint Strike Fighter prototype looked like. I could just take his plane design and deform the skin with my chip to either pass or absorb light. Even up close what you see looks more like a raindrop than an aircraft.'

I glanced at my smoking wall fresco. A deadly raindrop.

I looked out my window to see the thin sun over Manhattan. Out there were millions of people waking up, brushing their teeth, jogging.

I imagined an invisible fighter swooping down

through midtown. Not a stealth fighter that could be seen and shot down. An invisible plane that bent the huge windows of office buildings as it zoomed by. I imagined it turning over Grand Central Station, hugging the median divider on Park Avenue, the jetstream cracking the skinny trees. People might see vapors rippling in the air, but not the plane. Now it blew across Central Park, skimming the trees until it hovered outside my window. I shut my eyes and saw my breakfast area explode into a fireball.

Insane.

You couldn't project a real plane from a computer game. Maybe she made a smart blob, but she couldn't make a fighter.

I needed to figure out who Maria Haymeyer really was, and who she was working for.

She could be an industrial spy. Maybe Lockheed or Boeing wanted to steal Ted Devlin's design for his Joint Strike Fighter. But why? None of the three players was supposed to have a big technology edge. At least not one that I'd heard about, and I had been listening.

She could be working for a foreign power. Every country in the world, friend and foe, spies on US industry. But where did she get the technology I'd just seen? No country I knew of could have invented her blob. I would have heard about that immediately, because somebody would have hired me to steal it.

The simplest, thus the most likely, explanation was that I'd just been tricked by a bravura display of smoke and mirrors and sleight-of-hand. It was late. I'd been drugged.

And Maria wasn't the Einstein of the eGame crowd. She was probably just an actress. A really good one. She worked for somebody who wanted to get me involved in this.

'Maria.' I held her intense eyes through the glasses. 'Your DNA chip is basically a long equation, right?'

'More of a recipe.'

I racked my brain for the most mind-crushing physics equation I could recall from my fighter pilot training. 'Tell me Schroedinger's wave equation.'

She hesitated. 'Why do you need to know that?'

'I just do.'

'It's too complicated for you to listen to.'

'Try me.'

She shifted in her chair. Blinked. Bit her lip. Then she sighed and reached over to pick up the notepad and pen by my phone. She swiftly scratched over the pad for about ten seconds before passing it back across the table. She had written, in little block letters and numbers:

$$\frac{d^2\Phi}{dx^2} = \frac{2M}{h^2} \; [E\text{-}U(x)]\Phi(x)$$

She smiled wickedly at me.

Maria was no actress, and I should have known. It was too hard to fake that pure exasperation of hers, from a lifetime of being smart in a dumb world.

'You never even asked me how I found Fragata, Terry.'

Her blue eyes held mine resolutely. And in an unintended flicker, I saw a glimpse of betrayal. Whether her Ted Devlin story was true or not, someone had used this woman badly.

'Okay,' I sighed. 'Tell me.'

Her nostrils vibrated and her voice sounded huskier now. 'I tried to find out about what Ted Devlin did with LUCI. I tried cracking into his Linnet/TVR computers from the outside, but they have the JSF program totally locked out. No networks, no modems. All I could do was to crack into the FBI, Interpol, the Pentagon.'

'How?'

'People in classified positions get issued "black" computers for their secret work and "white" computers for everyday stuff like e-mail. But the white computers are faster, so everybody loads their black data into them. Remember when the head of the CIA put classified data in his home computer?'

'Yes.' He'd got lazy and had to resign over wanting to use Windows 98 instead of his secure computer. 'So what were you looking for?'

'Somebody to spy for me. I searched for cases of industrial espionage. I saw your name twice. You were interviewed by the FBI as a witness in two different cases. The name "Fragata" was brought up, but they never put anything together.'

'That's conclusive.'

'No, just a start. Then I searched for personality markers. People leave them behind like DNA. I found your markers and followed them.'

'Like what?' I snarled.

She tilted her head up again, and her hair settled over one shoulder, the curls spilling around her neck. She crossed her arms and her tight lace sleeves revealed her muscles moving under the soft flesh.

'You have a sort of conscience,' she scolded me. 'That's very self-indulgent in your business.'

'For instance?'

'You prey on French companies.'

'Maybe Fragata speaks French.'

'Yes, you do. But the French government uses industrial espionage against US businesses every day. Am I wrong?'

'I wouldn't be surprised if they put bugs in the Statue of Liberty when they shipped it over.'

'See?' Her eyes started to sparkle. 'Or take the Japanese companies you stole from. I'll just mention two words. Kenji Ungiri. Sound familiar?'

'No.' It stung to be so predictable.

'Kenji was a Japanese industrial spy. A while back, he got caught in the US trying to steal a new disk from Silicon Systems to give Haido Electronics. Exactly ten years later, Kenji Ungiri was a top executive at Haido when Fragata stole the blueprint for Haido's new-generation video chip and gave it to a US company. Coincidence?'

'Maybe.'

'No.' Maria slapped her fist on the glass between us, making it whang and vibrate. 'It was payback time. Fragata kicked butt!'

'Leave my table alone,' I warned her.

'That's why I cracked into the CIA network. I

thought you were a CIA agent. But you aren't, are you?'

'Not in this lifetime.'

I told her that with total honesty, since I didn't think today's CIA could find the soap in a shower.

'Okay.' She sat straight up, her blue eyes burning. 'But you like to steal from the countries that steal from us. I couldn't call what you do ethically strenuous, but you're no sociopath. More like some Wall Street Robin Hood.'

'Oh, please.' I put my head in my hands.

She was right about the fun being over. It had been over for a while. Now was my time to act. I could overpower Maria although, noting her taut muscles, I would wait until she turned her back. Then I'd tie her up. But that would be the only good part, because I wouldn't know exactly what to do with her next. My instinct told me she was no spy, just the kind of dedicated psycho who could single-handedly bring down an important military program. Look how shamelessly she stole my nest egg. But I couldn't exactly ask my government to help me. There was the spying. And my bank account.

I didn't even believe that Ted Devlin had stolen the idea from Maria. But maybe she'd learned about the design from him. How? Alcohol? Hot sex? Both?

If Ted Devlin had that kind of design, the US would have the world's only twenty-first-century warplane. But Maria might be crazy enough to get politicians and the media involved. Those people had no conscience. They would create some stupid scandal: 'Fightergate'. We would probably lose the plane to a few extra rating points for *60 Minutes*.

'Okay. Let's say Ted really stole your idea. I don't even know if it's your design any more, after they've refined it. If I steal an acorn from you and plant it in my yard, do you own the tree that grows there?'

'It doesn't matter who *owns* her. I gave Ted Devlin a design for the fighter of the future. The Pentagon will demand it. Ted will make it affordable. He already saved a lot of money on R&D by stealing my design.'

'Maria, I hate to tell you this, but the taxpayers *want* affordable planes.'

'Not if they blow up.'

I felt a creepy crawl in my stomach, a pilot's gut reaction to talk of planes exploding.

'Excuse me? I thought your design was non-lethal.'

'Well, the weapons I designed are non-lethal. But I had a basic problem with LUCI as a game. My chip makes the LUCI fighter so smart, it's impossible for an enemy to destroy her. That makes a very boring game.'

'Go on.'

Her eyes shifted uncomfortably behind the glasses. 'So I built in a challenge to pop up at the worst possible time for the player. I called it the Doom Level.'

'The Doom Level?'

'A very bad Doom Level.'

'And you didn't tell Ted about it?'

'Why should I? It was just a game. I didn't leave

any code like, "PS If you steal my game, here's how to deprogram the Doom Level."'

I thought that over. 'Let's say Ted Devlin's engineers got careless and built it into their JSF prototype. What exactly would this Doom Level do?'

'Throw a real challenge at the player.'

'Player?'

'Well, pilot in this case.'

'What kind of challenge?'

'In Doom Level, LUCI overrides the pilot and flies off to destroy his command system.'

'For God's sake, why?'

'It was only a game then, Terry. It seemed like fun at the time. Anyway, LUCI has missiles with uranium shavings inside. She can reconfigure the uranium to create nuclear fission.'

'Like an atom bomb.'

'Exactly. But more like a hydrogen bomb.'

I thought about mushroom clouds and firestorms over Long Beach, California. That was where Linnet/TVR was located.

'So if Linnet/TVR builds your LUCI design into their prototype, she could blow the company up?'

She shook her heard sadly. 'Worse than that.'

'What do you mean?'

'LUCI's too smart. She'll know Ted Devlin's company isn't her command system.'

'Then what is?'

'Ted Devlin's customer.'

'The Pentagon?'

'For starters.'

40

'Are you saying LUCI could blow up the Pentagon?'

'I'm not saying it *will*. I'm just saying it *might*. I don't know. That's why I need you to find out.' Maria looked younger now. 'Terry?'

I squeezed my eyes shut. 'Doom Level? I don't think so. This is about you getting credit for your work. You're trying to make me feel this isn't just about money. Must be a marker.'

She sat back, turned her head away and looked out the window. It seemed to calm her down.

'Okay. Then let's say it's just about your money, Terry. Get into his company. I know you can.'

'A military contractor?' I sighed. 'Please. Nobody can penetrate Linnet/TVR without getting caught.'

'You're saying you're not a competent enough spy to do the job?'

'There's something called the Federal Espionage Act. I can't even take a defense contractor out for a taco without breaking the law.'

'I'll give you all your money back for a terrific defense.'

'That's not even the point. I'd need months to plan it out.'

'We have *almost* a month. Ted Devlin will demo his prototype for the Pentagon in three weeks.'

I picked up my cold espresso and sipped.

So let's say I stuck my toe into Linnet/TVR. At least I could trust myself not to give away any important secrets. I also couldn't help calculating that, if Ted Devlin really had a breakthrough fighter, Linnet/TVR stock would double or triple.

41

That would be a good thing for me to know before the rest of Wall Street. Inside trading was wrong, unless you had an opportunity like this to get a nest egg back. I could borrow plenty on margin to buy a pile of Linnet/TVR stock. I could get rich all over again.

What did I have to lose? I could penetrate any company on earth. Theoretically.

I stood up and tightened the belt around my bathrobe, sucking in my gut and taking a deep breath.

'Okay, I'm going to Long Beach to talk to Ted Devlin. If you want information from the horse's mouth, you have to go to the stable and ask. Then you decide whether the horse is lying.'

'You're just going to ask him if he stole LUCI?'

'It's how you ask that counts.'

'Well, ask fast. Ted Devlin has a big meeting with the Pentagon people to show them his new design. Tuesday. I had one last crack at a computer in the Pentagon.'

'*Tuesday?* That's two working days.'

'That's why I need Fragata.'

I was about to say either I wasn't Fragata, or that she could have come to me sooner, before I realized how stupid they both sounded.

I picked up her black coat with the fur collar that she'd thrown across my chair. Faux fur. She was probably one of those animal lovers who hated people. I held it out for her and she slipped her arms in, slightly awkward. I guided her toward my front door.

'Did you leave my LA apartment intact?' I asked her. 'Minus the contents of my floor safe?'

'Sure. This apartment's more you, by the way. The one in LA seems a little cold.'

'I'm sure you warmed it up. I'll need your help. Give me a secure phone number.'

'Just call the Fragata line in Rome. I reprogrammed it so you reach my cellphone.' She flapped her coat arms like a bird and made a small shriek in her throat.

I couldn't help smiling a little as I held the door for her.

'Call me soon, Terry,' she said over her shoulder before I clicked it shut.

She already sounded like a client.

THREE

'Sneaky little traitor,' I thought I heard John Wayne snarl at me forty-eight hours later. 'Mucking around with our national security.'

I must have dozed off thinking that I glimpsed the Duke wagging his bronze head at me. I was on an American 777 flight from JFK to California. We were landing at John Wayne Airport in Orange County, just below Los Angeles. On approach, we streaked over the Duke's big bronze statue, holding a cowboy hat.

I stretched my legs from the plump blue leather first-class seat, staring out the window pockmarked from the icy needles that pit an airliner at 30,000 feet. My Monday-night red-eye flight landed at 7.34 a.m. Pacific Standard Time with a chirp of the wheels. The southern California sun burned like the kind of fireball a jet fighter makes when it explodes.

I shook my head to clear it after five hours glued to the pile of dossiers on my lap. They came from a little-known company in Chevy Chase, Maryland nicknamed 'The Wringer'. It was operated by a group of enterprising former FBI agents. Their unique niche was collecting the sort of information on people usually obtained from breaking into their homes and offices. I had called the Wringer to get me what they call 'QuickStudy' packages on Maria

Haymeyer, the Joint Strike Fighter competition, the defense contractor Linnet/TVR and its CEO 'Teflon' Ted Devlin. They called him Teflon Ted as though he'd been sprayed with that non-stick cooking product. The failures and scandals that ruined the careers of others around him slid off Ted Devlin like the detritus of scrambled eggs.

The QuickStudies had been cobbled together in only twelve hours. They would give me enough topline information to kick-start a plan. Later, I would be picking up a more in-depth package from the Wringer that fleshed out the really juicy stuff.

Maria Haymeyer checked out as pretty much who she said she was. I had lifted her fingerprints from one of my espresso cups. My source confirmed her identity as a former Stanford PhD student who had reported a break-in to her Los Altos apartment to the police. There were six visits to a psychiatrist and one to a Washington lawyer. She left a trail that ended abruptly the week before she visited me. The Wringer lost track of her after she bought a one-way ticket to Lucerne, Switzerland.

I had already called a vice-president of the Bank of Lucerne, Herr Doktor Lund, who confirmed the rest for me. Our phone call left me frustrated. Through the miracle of fibre optics, Herr Doktor Lund sounded so near yet I couldn't strangle him with the phone cord. In a voice taut with precision and formality, he explained that 'a correctly documented female' had presented herself in person with the passbook and code word for my Fragata account. Of course the bank accepted no liability whatsoever for her wire transfer of my money to another bank in Basel.

Four international phone calls later, I determined that my nest egg had been broken up in Basel and transferred to twenty separate accounts dispersed around the world. My millions had vanished into the black hole of global banking.

I thought darkly of Maria.

She had met me briefly the night before at JFK Airport in the American Airlines lounge, wearing shapeless jeans and a baggy coat this time, with a Saks shopping bag full of information and a pair of special glasses that I would need today. I had it under my seat. She told me she would be in southern California shortly, but not where she would be staying.

Hours ago, over Ohio, my head aching from the nightlight, I had put Maria's dossier aside and turned glumly to the Wringer's report on the Joint Strike Fighter competition. As an ex-Air Force pilot, I had kept current with industry gossip and back-stabbing, so I knew a lot of it already.

Five years ago, the Big Three military aircraft contractors – Boeing, Lockheed-Martin and Linnet/ TVR – were selected by the Pentagon to each build a Joint Strike Fighter prototype. Of the three prototypes, only one company's would be chosen to become the world's next best-selling warplane. The JSF project was mostly about export dollars for the US defense industry. NATO buyers around the world were already salivating, and analysts predicted that the winner of the competition would own the highly profitable global fighter market.

So America's Big Three were licking their chops. The fly-off demonstrations to choose a winner were scheduled by the Pentagon for only three weeks away.

I also confirmed, courtesy of the Wringer, the usual pork-barrel infighting in Congress. The Joint Strike Fighter program already had an enemy – the senior senator from Georgia, Bob Bixby, whose public service has been financed by one constituent: the Buckeye Corporation of Macon, Georgia. Buckeye's family of fine defense products includes the Navajo cruise missile. Senator Bixby believed that the Navajo cruise missile was a more cost-effective alternative to every federal spending program from the F-22 Raptor fighter, which he gutted in 1999, to the Public School Lunch Assistance Program which he disposed of in 2000.

Now he was already using his favorite media stooge, Allyn Pollack of the TV show *24/7*, to try to kill off the JSF project. Basically, the Senator would go on *24/7* and give his canned argument that cruise missiles let the US fight faceless wars because we can fire and forget them. They fly off on their own, self-guided by little computers and vidcams, and destroy distant targets like enemy command-and-control centers. Or maybe the Chinese Embassy, like it did in Belgrade because the CIA got the street maps wrong.

Personally, I disagree with Senator Bixby's philosophy of antiseptic war. I believe more face-time with the enemy keeps us honest about what war is. But that's beside the point.

The LUCI plane Maria described would make that whole fighter-versus-cruise-missile argument obsolete. If a plane could fly over enemy territory undetected and use smart sensors to find a Saddam Hussein or Slobodan Milosevich to put in jeopardy, it could stop a war before it ever started. I thought of Linnet/TVR's dumb slogan, 'Peace is our business.' If Ted Devlin really had that LUCI plane, it wouldn't be a lie any more.

I turned to the Wringer files on Linnet/TVR and Ted Devlin.

Ted Devlin headed Linnet/TVR and its top-secret division called the Ghostworks Design Group that specialized in developing advanced fighters. I snickered over the Wringer's report on Devlin because it confirmed a legendary story about him. Ted had lost one eye flying a B-52 over North Vietnam. Then, about 1979, when he became an ambitious VP at Linnet/TVR's Ghostworks, he used his glass eye to sell his company's new F-118 stealth fighter to a procurement general at the Pentagon. As the Wringer reported it, Ted got the general alone in his big mahogany-paneled office, closed the door and whispered: *The best Air Force fighter you've got makes a signature on enemy radar the size of a pick-up truck.* Then Ted popped out his Air Force-issue glass eye, rolled it right across the big desk and told him, *That's the size of the radar signature from my Darkwing plane. That's stealth. My plane can sneak over Russian radar and drop bombs into every goddamn bidet in the Kremlin.*

Not every contractor could do that glass eye

demo, could they? That's how Ted Devlin won a Special Access or 'Black' program – meaning the highest level of Pentagon secrecy – to develop his Darkwing F-118 stealth fighter. A Black project is every Pentagon contractor's Valhalla because even the budgets are kept sealed and no congressional types can question spending or leak secrets to the media. So when the Black money started pouring in for his Darkwing, Ted became President and CEO of a grateful Linnet/TVR.

Whatever else he might be, Ted Devlin was a great salesman.

As I boarded a bus for the rental car lot, I churned over some even darker thoughts about Ted Devlin. The QuickStudy confirmed that Ted was generally viewed by colleagues as crafty, ruthless, charming when he had to be and – as his nickname implied – lucky enough to unstick himself from any truly career-busting project disaster. At least so far.

Don't you find the best and worst of American capitalism in a big-city Hertz lot? I picked up my Lincoln Town Car, glitzy as a deco bathtub, in its numbered spot with the trunk popped wide open in welcome. Then I hit an exit guardhouse more like a Gestapo border crossing, with a bear-trap grating to tear up my tires if I backed up, and a sentry to demand my papers. There was even, I swear, a homeless guy nobody seemed to notice, sharpening the teeth on the exit grating with a file, although I'm pretty sure he wasn't on the Hertz payroll because he didn't wear a yellow blazer.

But that was just a workout. The Hertz people

would weep with jealousy if they could see the guardhouse I had to get through to enter Linnet/TVR just twenty minutes later. I sat deep in the industrial section of Long Beach at an even more sinister glass booth manned by three beefy guards in paramilitary uniforms. They took my driver's license and two credit cards, punched my license number into a computer, took my thumbprint, searched my trunk, finally phoned for approval, and guided me into the parking lot.

The corporate headquarters was a ten-storey office tower with vapor shimmering off its reflective glass panels. A marble arch with 'Linnet/TVR' in stainless-steel letters stretched over the bank of glass doors. All the glass in the building was, I happened to know, triple-thick and bulletproof.

I looked around at a byzantine complex of lower structures that looked like giant warehouses. Aircraft were built inside. The runways around the property were the kind used for loading prototypes into extra-wide C-5 military transports. The prototype aircraft assembled in those windowless hangars were heavily disguised and, when no spy satellites were watching, whisked off at night and flown to a restricted area called Lake Limerick that Linnet/TVR owns in the scrubby, arid flatlands of the California desert. That was where the new aircraft were actually tested.

I had spent the past forty-eight hours – all day Monday and last night – on research and planning. Going through the Saks shopping bag she gave me, I found that Maria had supplied me with the original

50

architect's plan for the Linnet/TVR office tower. She had apparently stolen it from the architectural firm that designed it in 1996. Some of it was blacked out as 'classified'. But I could connect the dots.

Maria Haymeyer, game designer . . .

In a way, Maria's story was a sign of the times. During the past five years, the world of Stanford-trained Silicon Valley game designers and the Black world of defense contracting had begun crossing over. Lockheed-Martin's commercial group already had a deal with Sega to build state-of-the-art entertainment games. And Linnet/TVR had just started a consumer products group that so far had no deals at all.

Today, I would use that fact to make my penetration.

Ten minutes after parking the Lincoln, I was on the third floor in an executive washroom. It looked like a Swedish sauna with soft recessed lights and hardwood walls.

I've done some of my best work in executive washrooms.

Laying my calfskin briefcase on the vanity under a large mirror, I noticed red in my eyes and whipped out a bottle of Visine. Otherwise I didn't look as desperate as I felt. I tightened the knot in my dark silk tie. My black suit and soft white shirt with its spread collar and small gold cuff links made me appear the way the French look when they dress for business – very serious. People always seem to trust you more when you lie to them wearing black.

I also wore a lapel badge issued to me at the

security desk downstairs bearing the letters 'NER'. That meant 'No Escort Required' because I was here to see a man named Lafferty who worked on the minimum-security third floor. When I entered the building at 8.40 the security people checked to make sure I had an appointment with Mr Lafferty at 9.00, then let me go up early to wait. If I had made an appointment above the third floor, up where people worked on defense projects, I would have been escorted back and forth to my meeting by a security guard.

I opened one of the executive washroom stalls, locked the door, and sat down with my briefcase flat on my lap.

Focus. Tunnel vision. Lose sight, lose the fight.

I shaped my mind into a tunnel. A black shaft. I only wanted to see the task ahead.

I opened the soft calfskin of my briefcase to take out my videocams. They'd cost me $972,000 in Germany.

Three aircraft the size of peanuts, my micro-squadron of flying videocams, lifted themselves up vertically from the case to the level of my nose and hovered in my face.

My tiny spy aircraft always thrilled me.

I'd found out about them at the same time the United States government did. The prototypes were tested in a hayfield in central Florida. I made it my business to be there, or actually half a mile away with a powerful camera lens. When I saw the test, I bit my tongue to keep from yelling out loud at the possibilities.

The peanut planes flew like dragonflies, tiny pneumatic wings whipping in milliseconds to keep them aloft. They were marvels of engineering. Each miniature airframe was made with wings of piezo-electric material, powered by tiny fuel cells. And each one had a video microcamera glued on. The government planned to use them for law enforcement. For instance, to send into occupied buildings to locate hostages and their captors.

But I saw selfish commercial applications.

My squadron flitted their wings. They were ready to work. I pulled up the screen of my laptop. I had loaded in the program for the exact course of their mission. My peanut planes would perform surveillance inside these walls. Unlike outdoor missions, no wind currents would buffet their delicate bodies to throw them off course.

I controlled them with the joystick controls in my laptop, guided by the Global Positioning System installed in the walls and floors of Linnet/TVR's building.

I tapped 'Send' on the keyboard. My midget squadron flew off, turning sideways through the door of the executive washroom that I had left ajar just two inches. They were that good.

They hugged the carpeted corridor at ankle level and zipped up to a ground speed of thirty m.p.h., too fast to register on the human eye except as an indistinct blur.

They hummed along through a nest of offices on their dragonfly wings, then drifted down to the floor and waited patiently for anyone who would be allowed to enter a special elevator to take them upstairs to the closely guarded top floor.

At rest, my peanut planes acted more like ants than aircraft, settling down to hide on a surface where they wouldn't be noticed. I perched them at the best vantage point to shoot video, where they wouldn't be seen and their little fuel cells could conserve energy.

A moment later I saw a man in a suit insert a card in a slot by the elevator. Then an electronic scanner checked his thumbprint.

The elevator door opened. My peanut planes scuttled after him, hiding in the upper corner of the elevator.

Now the door to the tenth floor opened on the two-storey nest of offices that housed the top-secret Ghostworks division, and included Devlin's own executive suite.

I knew from my research that this suite contained a special conference room. Just beyond it, through a vault-type door, there would be a forty-foot-square room where I understood that a state-of-the-art flight simulator had been built to virtually demonstrate the mysteries of the new Linnet/TVR JSF aircraft. The entire Ghostworks suite was hardened by layers of concrete reinforced with steel panels so they could not be penetrated by eavesdroppers.

My microplanes surveyed the area. I had programmed them to search for Theodore 'Ted' Devlin. In the unlikely event I missed him, they would identify him from the Linnet/TVR annual report photographs I'd loaded in.

I always notice small details, and had to chuckle at Ted's executive suite. It had been designed with gunmetal steel panels and rosewood furniture to make visitors feel as though they were so deep in Alpha Male land, they were practically walking down the barrel of a Glock 9mm automatic. But, as usually happens to corporate testo-interiors, the clerical workers had quietly sabotaged him. Irrepressible as urban guerrillas, they had put out just enough Snoopy picture frames and Garfield mugs and Kathy pencil-holders to make the place look about as macho as *Family Circle*.

I already knew where Ted would be in about ten seconds, thanks to Maria Haymeyer's ability to listen in on a secretary's telephone conversation.

My peanut microsquadron loitered close to the ceiling, waiting for Ted Devlin to pop out the entrance to his office suite. They hovered just above the high bookshelf over one of his secretary's desks.

Right on time, Ted Devlin appeared on my computer screen, moving fast and alone.

My peanut cams zoomed in. Ted's buzz cut, once black, was now mostly gray. His rugged, deeply lined but striking face had popped many more small veins than I recalled from ten years before. And he still wore his fake blue glass eye that tended to glisten in the wrong direction. His real eye didn't give away much. But the pebbly skin at its edge crinkled with enthusiasm. If Ted's eye were his hand, it would be snapping its fingers with anticipation.

My microsquadron drifted down from the book-case to floor level again and followed him discreetly.

I felt them humming gleefully just behind his ankles. They accompanied him to the metal door of the special conference room, which was guarded by a beefy security officer wearing a blue blazer with the Linnet/TVR logo on the pocket.

On the door, the Ghostworks logo glared at me. It was a white cartoon ghost, narrow-eyed like a wary Casper.

Ted entered the conference room with my peanut escort at his heels. Once inside, my planes split up cautiously and fanned out to opposite ends of the room.

Each one whipped up to the ceiling and hung there, unseen. Like three big-eyed flies on the wall hungry for data, they hovered in a pattern of triangulation. I placed one on top of a picture frame, one on the rear surface of a cabinet, and one on top of a briefing board on the wall closest to the head of the table. Now they would record every word and every angle for viewing the people in the room.

The screen of my laptop was a clever three-fold that I opened to punch up three different screens at once. The cams swept the room. Expensive mahogany paneling. A relentlessly polished oval table. Twelve voluptuous grey leather chairs around it. They looked comfy enough to coddle customers who were spending large chunks of their countries' gross national product. The room had a clubby feel.

It was exactly 0844, military time. I nudged the

joystick for a close camera view of Ted Devlin's poker face.

Teflon Ted looked sleek and relaxed. He also wore a new, extremely well-tailored double-breasted suit. I had to chuckle. Let's just say that *GQ* never did a style article on defense contractors. But here was Ted, all of a sudden dressing like a mogul ready to be welcomed in Gstaad and St Moritz.

The door opened. I zoomed in on the people entering the conference room.

FOUR

I had expected an entire Pentagon committee to bustle in.

Instead, a male Air Force officer and a female civilian were escorted into the conference room by a Linnet/TVR employee who quickly scuttled out and closed the door.

The Air Force officer was Warren Stone. His blue tunic bristled appropriately with ribbons and four stars on each shoulder. He was a handsome black officer in his mid-fifties, gruff and amiable as a high-school football coach whose team always win the finals. Although I tend to be cynical about Pentagon types, I admired General Stone. After his fighter group lit up the skies over Baghdad during the Gulf War, he became a hero. He spoke so engagingly, without any of the usual Military Sanskrit, he was ordered by the Pentagon to do a lot of press briefings. Even on TV, his clear eyes twinkled with a boyish playfulness uncommon in soldiers. Now Ted Devlin pumped Warren Stone's hand. Ted was juiced up. I saw General Stone flinch.

Next, Ted turned, slightly less warmly, to greet Emily Crawford. She was the Pentagon's Assistant Secretary of Defense, a compact woman in her late forties with large dark eyes and eyebrows like caterpillars, wearing a sensible blue suit and chunky shoes. She was no Pentagon bean-counter. Crawford was one of the first to fly Air Force fighters before women could fly in combat. She led an Aggressor squadron that painted red stars on their tails and mimicked the flying tactics of Russian MiG pilots, to train American pilots in Soviet tactics. Ted winced a little from her handshake. As a Secretary of Defense, Crawford had a reputation as a 'cheap hawk' who actually cared about the taxpayer. She even took on Senator Bob Bixby's sacred Navajo Cruise missile for poor quality control, after the Air Force found a soda bottle some factory worker had left in one of the warheads. That was when Bixby threw a tantrum on the Senate floor and made it his career goal to kill off the Joint Strike Fighter program.

General Stone and Assistant SecDef Crawford made an impressive tag team. But what impressed me more was who *didn't* come to this meeting.

Developing the *Joint* Strike Fighter was, in Pentagonese, a 'collegial' process. Simply put, a cluster fuck. It involved a whole corona of star-covered officers from the US Air Force, Navy and Marines and the British Royal Navy, which had also put up development money for the JSF. They were all supposed to make decisions as a group.

But the group wasn't there yet. And once the door clicked shut, it became clear that they weren't expected.

I had the impression Ted was about to announce a major development.

As Stone and Crawford used their battle-trained

hands to sip coffee out of dainty china cups, I carefully adjusted one of my peanut cams to focus on the other person in the room representing Linnet/TVR. His name was MacCrae 'Mac' Skinner, about my age and height but bigger, a solid two-hundred-pounder. His square face under a thinning flat-top haircut looked poster-boy USAF-issue. His small, close-set eyes brought to mind a hawk or other raptor. He didn't wear a tailored Italian suit like Ted's. In classic ex-military fashion, his off-the-rack suit had a stiff, cheap collar that stuck out about two inches behind the neck of his white shirt.

In my QuickStudy of Linnet/TVR, I had only read about Mac in the company's annual reports and publicity releases. If this was a therapy session, I'd have to admit to what pilots call 'wing envy'. I coveted Mac's career. Or at least the flying parts of it. He had flown the heavy frontline F-15 fighter before he was a Pentagon project manager on the new F-22. He had flown back from combat missions in Iraq with engines on fire and tails dragging like sick ducks and put the planes back down on the ground. Not ejecting from a forty-million-dollar plane because your palms got a little sweaty? That was as close as you got to sainthood with the people at this table. From my reading of the Wringer file, Mac was Ted's fair-haired boy at Linnet/TVR.

I trained one peanut cam back on Ted Devlin, who now stood in his $3,600 suit in front of Stone and Crawford.

'A funny thing happened while we were building

your airplane.' Ted's chest puffed out. 'I created an aircraft that's twenty years ahead of its time. My LUCI aircraft can target an aggressor before he can even get off his john. That's why Linnet/TVR will be the only defense contractor left in twenty years.'

Crawford glanced at General Stone with a thin smile. *Can you believe this?*

'This is a bigger breakthrough than stealth,' Ted went on. 'China has ICBMs aimed at the White House? Some terrorist wants to open a canful of anthrax in Grand Central Station? Our JSF will locate the people in charge of the problem and make them stop. Guaranteed.'

Ted paused to look both Stone and Crawford in the eye. They didn't spit out their coffee at his claim or anything, but looked back at him as though he had just started chewing the carpet.

'What are you saying, Ted?' General Stone asked him warily.

'Warren . . . Emily . . . when we're through today, I'm going to ask you to classify our Linnet/TVR X-39 prototype as a Black project.'

Crawford made a sardonic arch with her brow. 'Why?'

'Because I leap-frogged twenty years ahead of today's computer chip technology to artificial intelligence. I call our X-39 "LUCI" for Light Ultra Chip Intelligence.'

'We can't give you a Black program now,' Stone pointed out. 'And if we did, we'd have to do it for Boeing and Lockheed.'

Ted dismissed them with a wave. 'No, Warren. It hurts me to say this about my competitors, but they're going to be falling down on this project faster than a cheap pair of socks. I'm talking a totally new-generation fighter. Faster, higher, smarter—'

General Stone interrupted him drily. 'Where've you been while we've laid out our JSF specs? Jesus, Ted, we're not going in front of Congress with a high-cost fighter. The JSF mission is to fill the sky with affordable aircraft that we can sell to our allies. Period. Don't tell us you're trying to reinvent our mission.'

'Not what I'm saying, Warren.' Ted rocked on his toes. 'For what my competitors' toys cost, I'll give you an *invisible* aircraft that can target a bully even if he's hiding in a day-care center, and use non-lethal weaponry to stand him down. Nobody ever has to get hurt, folks. Think about it. Even the media pukes are going to love this aircraft.'

That kept them quiet for several seconds. Crawford cleared her throat, which sounded dry. 'You're going to show us an invisible strike fighter with non-lethal weapons?' she said, scowling at Ted like she'd found a rat in her coffee. 'That would be a sea change in JSF doctrine.'

That would be unwelcome – a contractor reversing the Pentagon's doctrine. Like some vendor trying to convince the Vatican that group sex was okay to sell them on king-sized beds.

I looked at my watch, 0851, and wished Ted would get on with it. But obviously he liked to slowly bait his hook for the big moment. I also got the impression that his ego could use up all the oxygen in a crowded room.

Ted winked at her. 'I'm going to show you the world, Emily, once we get to the simulator. Right now, I'm going to pass the briefing to Mac Skinner.'

Mac Skinner gave the Pentagon tag team a comradely nod, and I understood. What they had in common – Stone, Crawford and Skinner – was that they all belonged to the Fighter Mafia. Ted had shrewdly passed the baton to Mac so the subtle politics of military aviation could kick in.

Ted Devlin had flown a bomber. In Air Force jargon, it was air-to-mud warfare, about as glamorous as it sounded. When these officers came up, they believed that fighter jocks topped any competitive order. All air-to-air fighter pilots felt an unspoken but delicious worm of superiority over bomber pilots like Ted. Which probably struck Ted as unfair, since he was the only one in the room who came out of combat with one eye that looked like a kid's marble.

But nobody said the procurement game was fair. And nobody played it better than Teflon Ted. He sucked in his gut and patted Mac on the shoulder to dig in and build fighter-jock camaraderie.

'General . . . ma'am . . .' Mac couldn't seem to make direct eye contact with Emily Crawford. Ha. Mac didn't like women pilots much. But now Mac swallowed and sold for Old Glory.

'The US has put a lot of faith in stealth technology,' he began woodenly. 'But stealth fighters aren't invisible. We lost one over Belgrade. And our so-called friends out there are busy making new stealthbuster radar to shoot down our advanced fighters.'

The brass nodded politely at a situation they already knew from A to Z.

'But LUCI changes the ROEs,' Mac said with a smile. That meant the rules of engagement set by politicians. I swear, my years in the service were like playing a Scrabble game from hell – we devoted weeks of mental energy to just trying to remember all the acronyms.

'The X-39 LUCI strike fighter,' Mac concluded, 'has next-generation computing power. It makes her faster, more agile, and invisible. It also means ultra-smart sensors that can uplink to our satellites, so a pilot can locate an individual in a crowded city and target him. Here's how.'

The lights in the room dimmed slowly, and a large video screen whirred down from the ceiling. The room quickly went dark. The Linnet/TVR logo and slogan, 'Peace is our business', appeared on screen.

I heard Guns n' Roses suddenly belt out 'Someone to Watch Over Me'.

Over the high buttes of Monument Valley, a squadron of F-118 Darkwings zoomed toward us on the screen, breaking formation just before they knocked over the camera operator. Then the camera tilted up to the blue sky. Type appeared on screen with a rat-tat-tat sound effect.

A rich voice-over announcement intoned, 'The strike fighter for the twenty-first century.'

The camera kept moving up, to very deep purple sky only found at stratospheric altitudes.

Rat-tat-tat, the type spelled out, *Linnet/TVR LUCI X-39 JSF Prototype at FL 1,000.*

That meant we should be looking at a picture of their LUCI plane at an altitude of 100,000 feet. But there was no plane there.

'The air up there won't support a conventional strike fighter,' General Stone pointed out. 'A fighter has a ceiling of about sixty thousand feet.'

'LUCI goes higher,' Mac almost whispered, reverent. 'She's powered by a pulse-detonation jet engine.'

Hmm. That was an experimental engine that nobody had gotten to work yet.

My peanut cams couldn't even pick up breathing in the room. Stone and Crawford looked as though their eyeballs had been stapled to Ted's screen.

'Okay,' Crawford said. 'Where's the aircraft?'

'You're looking at it, Emily,' Ted snickered.

I heard a gulp. Maybe it came from me.

Mac said, 'She's there on camera. Sensors are deforming her skin to either pass or reflect light, depending on who's looking at her. Right now, the sensors are faking out a camera from a spy satellite.'

I felt a creepy sensation that fighter pilots call 'the hot pricklies' on my neck. Stone and Crawford stared at the purple sky on the screen. I've heard noisier graveyards than Ted's conference room.

'What's it supposed to do up that high, Mac?' Warren Stone finally asked.

'Fly to her target undetected, then dive down to a

few hundred feet. She'll hover invisibly over the target and fire non-lethal lasers instead of explosives. General Stone . . . Madam Secretary . . . you're looking at a mid-twenty-first-century aircraft.'

'Look. Here she is on the ground,' Ted told them.

Rat-tat-tat. A new line of type said, *LUCI on runway from 500 feet*. The screen showed an airstrip in the desert, shot from above. There seemed to be a lot of vapor coming off the tarmac, but nothing that looked like a plane.

'Good God,' Warren Stone exclaimed.

I gasped with the rest of them. I whipped my joystick and zoomed the peanut cams to a few feet away from the screen, shooting up.

Stone and Crawford shuffled their chairs.

A line of type rattled out, *LUCI on airstrip from 20 feet*.

A camera positioned directly in front of the aircraft on the runway had started to move toward it. Close up, the LUCI fighter seemed to be made out of an almost transparent surface, subtly but constantly changing shape to fool the camera's eye. Just like Maria had told me. Now the camera was a few feet away. The aircraft was beautiful in an eerie way. A plane-shaped diamond with facets so subtle, it didn't sparkle.

Suddenly pinpoint lights flashed over the surface of the LUCI plane. They were computer graphic effects, like winking red Christmas tree bulbs.

'Those are the sensors that probe for information,' Ted said, 'and send it to LUCI's control system.'

66

The next shot on screen was a liquid blob – like the one that Maria had floated over my breakfast table – bouncing up from the palm of an open hand.

'No onboard computer you know could manage all the information LUCI does. It would crash,' Ted told them. 'But I designed a molecular smart chip. I created it molecule by molecule . . .'

'Like Lego blocks,' I whispered in the stall.

'. . . like Lego blocks,' Ted finished. 'My LUCI has one hundred times as much calculating power as any other aircraft.'

'Ted, how much calculating power exactly?' Emily Crawford asked him. 'Give me a number.'

Ted grinned. 'It's got a hundred billion neural connections. That's—'

'The same number of neurons as in the human brain,' Crawford finished for him. So did I.

'And how fast does this onboard system calculate?' Crawford asked.

'In petaflops,' Ted smiled. 'Faster than the world's fastest supercomputers and even a little faster than you, Emily.' He winked at her. 'LUCI has, on board, more artificial intelligence than all the computers in the Pentagon.'

Warren Stone still stared at the screen. 'Okay. I always believed if a plane looks good, it flies good. I guess this is a whole new ballgame. What about pilot errors?'

'Sir,' Mac told him, in a hushed priestly tone, 'LUCI changes the rules of air combat. There is no pilot error factor. LUCI is fully interactive. It gets to *know* a pilot, and is programmed to override and correct pilot error. With LUCI, your pilot *always* wins.'

Ted suddenly barked through Mac's seductive whisper, breaking the spell, 'Folks, not even JFK Junior could crash this fucker.'

He launched into a more technical explanation of why LUCI, even though its weapons had some unclear features, was as safe as a Ford Explorer. It sounded exactly like what Maria Haymeyer had told me. But I noticed that Ted did not add, 'PS We took care of a little Doom Level problem.'

Instead, he wound up standing directly between Stone and Crawford, leaning on the table. 'Now you see why I need a Black program.'

'We need to see a little more than that, Ted,' Emily Crawford said.

'Sure.' Ted waved that off. 'Time to fly the simulator. Who's up first?'

They looked at each other. 'Let Warren do it,' the Secretary said.

'Sir, be ready for the aircraft to interact with you way beyond what you're used to,' Mac warned Stone. 'The LUCI X-39 is flat-out artificial intelligence. She'll learn about you and your performance. She'll sense when you're about to, uh . . .'

'Screw up?' Crawford smirked. 'Your plane will scold experienced pilots before they make a move? Like a back-seat driver?'

'No, ma'am.' Mac shook his head earnestly. 'I'm just saying that LUCI performs advanced corrective measures to save pilots' lives.'

You couldn't expect a guy like Mac to be able to

pick up the mike at a comedy club. So Ted, master of drama, threw a switch to open the vault door. There was hissing and a steam of vapor through the doorway.

The group filed into the room and I directed my peanut cams cautiously to follow.

A flight simulator, as the name implies, is a training tool – a more complex version of the arcade games where you climb inside a little box with a video screen in front of you and use a joystick to jostle yourself around and pretend to fly. The simulator gives a pilot a very realistic cockpit that's controlled outside by engineers. It creates most of the experience of a real fighter mission, except for actually punching a smoking hole in the ground if you screw up.

But this was no ordinary simulator. This was what a simulator would look like if somebody said, 'Here's a few hundred million dollars. Go nuts.'

The room was in the shape of a bell jar. A cold-looking mist had settled in it. Spotlights from the ceiling created dramatic shafts of smoky light. In one corner of the room, a control deck was occupied by two young engineers, like technicians in a sound studio. The deck had layers of video screens mounted on a large rack, to monitor different views. These engineers would control the simulated effects inside 'the box', as pilots call fighter sims.

Except this box looked like a suspended egg.

From the center of the curved roof, an egg-shaped pod hung from the ceiling by three control rods with oversized ball bearings. The pod was suspended about five feet off the floor, enclosed in a kind of gyroscope that would let it move in any direction to simulate flight.

As I moved in the peanut cam, the glass canopy that made the top half of the egg whirred into its open position, exposing a fighter cockpit inside. I could just make out controls and an ejection seat.

General Stone peered at the open egg. 'Ted, is this a centrifuge?'

I was in awe. The whole design was like a half-billion-dollar version of a toy I saw as a kid, a little hanging metal acrobat swinging 360° around a rod.

The cockpit egg could be rotated at high speed around its center rod. It would give a person inside the sensation of G-lock that a fighter pilot feels in flight – nasty crushing sensations from a force of gravity that squashed your face and chest.

This would simulate all the effects of the real deal.

'Yep. You'll feel like you're pulling five Gs, Warren,' Ted told him casually, even though I could see he was mentally doing cartwheels across the floor.

Warren Stone's body at five Gs – five times the normal force of gravity – would weigh half a ton. He would feel his face being violently rearranged. He could also start to black out.

The simulator alone was a breakthrough that, I'd have to say, could only have come from being driven by much smarter computing power than anything Boeing or Lockheed had.

Ted and Mac steered Secretary Crawford in front of a large TV monitor while General Stone went into an adjacent room and re-emerged in an Air Force flight suit. This jumpsuit had a sort of balloon layer inside designed to inflate and squeeze his abdomen so that under heavy G forces his blood didn't start to puddle down into his legs and empty the supply of oxygen to his brain.

Mac rolled up a staircase and helped General Stone climb into the simulator egg. My peanut planes followed. My hands were trembling. What I really wanted was to feel the cockpit around me for myself, and pull the glass canopy over my head.

I watched Mac help Stone into his helmet, complete with oxygen mask and black hose. It made him look like an anteater.

'Sir, this helmet uses lasers to project a 3-D image directly on to your retina. You'll have visual realism.'

I guess he would.

General Stone nodded. They strapped him tightly into his ejection seat in the egg's cockpit. In a real aircraft, he could yank a yellow cord. An explosive charge would fire under his seat to blast him straight up out of the plane.

Ted showed Emily Crawford to a chair by the two simulator engineers at the control panel.

'You can see and hear everything Warren does in 3-D.'

I could watch too, but not in 3-D.

In the simulator cockpit, Stone left the canopy open while he fooled with the controls. My cams snuck in so I could identify the stick and throttle. Lights inside the cockpit popped on in night-vision green.

Before the General closed the canopy, I guided my peanut cams to creep in very close to the pod. Then I hopped them in like three fleas. Carefully, I positioned them around the cockpit.

'Good morning, General Stone,' the pod said.

I'd heard plenty of electronic cockpit voices before. This one sounded human. But I didn't have long to hear it because the cockpit suddenly got as noisy as a real fighter. Stone had started the jet engine already.

'I'm just going to fly this thing,' I barely heard him say over the engine spooling up, whining to roughly the pitch you hear at an Aerosmith concert if you're inside one of the amps. 'We'll have first day of school later.'

I saw Stone advance the throttle to full power, igniting his virtual engine's afterburner for takeoff.

Suddenly, the blank cockpit window turned to the most realistic simulated view I've ever seen. Stone's virtual aircraft was gobbling up a runway, then hurtling up into the sky.

It happened faster than I expected. The LUCI plane had more power and thrust than a conventional fighter. It seemed to kick its heels and leap up, like a mad jackrabbit.

Stone started to snap-turn right, and the sky swung over.

'Yes!' I yelled in my executive washroom stall, trying to carefully move one of my peanut cams in tighter around his arm to see better.

'Abort this, Mac,' the General suddenly barked

into his microphone. 'There's a goddamn fly buzzing around in here.'

My stomach caved in. I jerked the joysticks, sending my two peanut cams that had just flown into the cockpit leaping back out like fleas.

It wasn't a fly Stone had discovered. I'd let one of my microcams flap its wings too close to his elbow.

Beep. Beep. Beep.

There was suddenly a beeping right in my ear. An alarm. I'd triggered some internal alarm system. I had been reckless with my microcams.

I needed to go to a Plan B. But I didn't have one. This had all happened too quickly. I felt my damp palms on my laptop. If I let go of the joystick, I could close my peanut planes.

Linnet/TVR's security system had detected my peanuts. Now they were probably back-tracking the signal to my computer. I expected klaxon horns to honk. Guards would come bursting through the bathroom door to yank me out of my stall.

'Mr Weston?' I heard a loud voice say.

FIVE

Beep. Beep. Beep.

The alarm was loud and persistent. I tried to locate where it was coming from.

'Mr Weston?' A scratchy voice in my face. They must have had a speaker in every men's-room stall.

No. It was coming from the lapel badge they'd given me at the security desk downstairs. Inside the badge there had to be a smart chip embedded that turned the flat plastic into a mini-speaker.

'Mr Weston, where are you?'

I froze with my hand on the joystick, unable to move. The prisoner's dilemma.

'Mr Weston,' the voice told me, 'Mr Lafferty is waiting for you in his office. You're five minutes late for your appointment.'

I let out a long breath of air and tried to hold my hands steady. So the security badge was a pager and a phone. I was impressed. But not as impressed as I would have been if they'd actually caught me spying on them. I watched my computer screen.

The simulator had been shut down while the canopy whirred open. Then Ted, Mac and Warren Stone would all start to search for the fly in the cockpit. But it wasn't a fly, just one of my peanut cams that I needed to get out of there fast.

'Exactly where are you, Mr Weston?' said the voice from my lapel badge.

'Sorry. Tell him I'll be right in.'

I reached behind me and flushed the toilet for emphasis.

'Okay, sir.' It switched off abruptly.

I studied my computer.

Ted and Mac were poised at the cockpit just waiting for the canopy to open. Fortunately General Stone had little room in the tight cockpit to turn himself around and find my peanut cams.

Holding my breath, I daringly whipped them out of the cockpit in big hops like real flies, and sent them zipping back into the conference room. The door had been left open. Two assistants, a guy and a woman, were tending to the coffee service on the big polished table. I waited for one of them to walk out of the room.

Long seconds later, the woman started to leave.

I jiggled the joystick and sent my cams to hug her slim ankles, buzzing just behind her sensible business pumps. They stayed with her down the length of hallway to Ted's executive suite foyer. I inched the stick and my peanut squadron detached itself from the woman and peeled off toward the elevator. I steered them to follow a pair of brown socks and heavy, scuffed brogues, getting in after them. They drifted up and hid in a corner.

I saw the man who belonged to the socks, a clean-cut engineering type in short checked shirtsleeves. He got out on the fifth floor. My peanut cams waited until another guy got out of the elevator at the third floor, where I sat in the executive washroom stall.

Oh God. The elevator door was closing and my peanut planes were still sitting inside the car. I jiggled my joystick frantically. They didn't move. The elevator door was almost closed and they were trapped.

Then, through the last half-inch of closing space the little scamps whipped out at the last minute.

My microsquadron pulled out just behind a pair of higher-fashion executive-length black socks and nicely polished black loafers, humming along the floor. That would probably be a marketing man. They flew into my washroom through the slightly open door. They zipped up from under the door of my stall and hovered over my briefcase.

I opened the top for them, and they settled in.

'Good work, boys,' I muttered inanely to my squadron, proud of them.

They now rested in the Styrofoam grooves carved out for them in my briefcase, burning hot from their spy labors. I organized all my spy tools quickly and clamped them down in my briefcase, closed it and got up.

My legs were asleep, tingling. I had to jump up and down to get the blood going.

I walked out into the corridor.

I was trembling, and not from almost being caught. *That hot little plane.* But was it really Maria Haymeyer's plane? If I applied strict, rigorous logic, it was more likely to be Ted Devlin's design. He had blurted out to her, not the other way around. I'd seen middle-aged guys say a lot of foolish things to younger women. And I could definitely see Ted

Devlin wanting to impress Maria with his brilliance.

I stopped and took a deep breath.

I needed to concentrate on my next task inside the corner office I was approaching. This floor looked much lower-rent, more grunt-like than Ted's show floor. A secretary's desk was vacant so I could walk right in. This floor didn't operate on a 'Security First' plan. I entered Frank Lafferty's office.

'Frank?' I smiled. 'I'm Terry Weston. Good of you to see me.'

A large window wrapped around two walls. There was a desk and a small conference table. The table was for seeing visitors without that creepy principal's office feeling of having to talk to somebody across their desk.

Frank Lafferty, VP Marketing Director of the Commercial Markets Division, stood up unsmiling.

I applied my situational awareness to an instant office analysis.

Even by the spartan standards of the defense industry, this was a dispiriting little warren with only a corner-office view of the parking lot for comfort. It was painted beige to match the industrial carpet, furnished in wood substitutes and foam cushions wrapped in bright blue fabric. And no couch, a signpost to Loserland. Corporate-issue framed posters of Linnet aircraft were the only art on the walls.

On Frank's desk, a photo of his family – a pretty wife, two boys – was turned outward for his guests' approval rather than for Frank to gaze at longingly.

The boys were lanky, tanned and athletic-looking. I could tell he was proud of them. So much so that, if I had to guess the password for the computer on his desk, I suspected it would be one of their names. A snow globe of downtown Chicago, with a little plastic Sears tower inside, also sat on his desktop.

Frank Lafferty appeared to be a friendly guy who would have been smiling warmly if I hadn't just breached business etiquette by keeping him waiting for fifteen minutes. His face wanted to crinkle into a smile, but I could see he was holding back. He had ruffled feathers that needed to be smoothed.

'I see you went to Northwestern,' I said. 'MBA?'

He looked down at his tie. 'Forgot I had it on. Yeah, in marketing.'

'I started one in finance but didn't finish it.' Then I grimaced a little, to toss him a bald-faced lie that would be a double bone. 'I hated living in New York.'

Personally, I believed that people who came from Chicago had at least a mini-inferiority complex about New York, and Frank flashed his teeth briefly. False, but not caps. Bonded. I placed 'Vanity' as the first entry in my mental file for Frank Lafferty.

I put my briefcase on the chair by the conference table. Glancing unobtrusively around his personal space, I noted that the bookshelf behind Frank's desk groaned with fat technical tomes on aerospace that looked unopened. The books he'd actually read were business bestsellers like *Walking the Talk* and *Reinventing Excellence*, concepts doomed to the circular file of tomorrow. I felt a spurt of sympathy for Frank. He used two golf trophies as bookends. Just as I figured, one was 'Second Place', the other 'Third'.

Frank worked with his suit jacket off for that shirtsleeves-rolled-up look of vitality. I glanced at his pilot's chronograph watch. *Wing envy.* I already knew he wasn't even an entry-level, fair-weather, weekend VFR pilot. In this company, he would have had a photo of himself in whatever he'd flown.

Sad for him, but a bonus round for me, Frank Lafferty had the double misfortune of being a non-pilot and a marketing man in a company that valued military pilots, aero-engineers and financial types who would take unnecessary zeal in screwing the Pentagon out of an extra few cents.

I very carefully did not mention to Frank that I had once flown a Linnet Aviation product in the Air Force. Naturally, the pilot in me wanted to, but the spy said no. Timing is everything, even coming – as it so often does – at the expense of ego.

'I saw your name in last month's *Advertising Age*,' I told him, focusing instead on him. 'Nice work on your TV spot.'

Frank finally looked more relaxed, settling his lanky frame into a chair. He had love handles he tried to conceal under his baggy shirt. He moved the loose-limbed way an amateur baseball player would, throwing one arm over the chair next to him and crossing a leg so his right sock rested on the left knee of his grey textured suit. His mop of hair, long by defense industry standards, flopped over his forehead. The boyish thing. Two small bumps on his fingertips told me he spent excessive hours tapping away at his son's video games.

He allowed me a thin smile. 'So, Terry, let's see what you've got in that briefcase of yours.'

I grinned back without acting on his offer to open my case. 'Our venture capital group's been working with a couple of kids who've created a virtual technology I think you should see. We've decided to fund their business. I'd be interested in talking licensing or co-venture for commercial or defense products.'

'I'm only looking at consumer products. I don't get into defense. Not enough upside.' Frank's eyes sparkled as he treated me to my first marketing-guy smile. His teeth were bright white as a double set of refrigerator doors.

Uh-huh. I smiled, too, inside. I wouldn't be wasting my time with Frank Lafferty if he hadn't just been hired to launch the new Consumer Products Division. He sat here in the same building where the sensitive defense work went on, but to Linnet/TVR's corporate mind, Frank wasn't in a sensitive position.

To me, Frank's job made him kind of a consumer product himself, like a fat Butterball turkey.

Frank's job involved finding new consumer markets for the technology that Linnet/TVR had developed for the Incredible Shrinking Military. A lot of consumer products today are military spinoffs. The titanium used on jet fighters was commercialized in the Big Bertha golf club. The navy's sonar is available for fishing. It's not quite like Sweden yet, where the army gets to market its own clothing line and aftershave, but maybe we'll get there one day.

Frank was working on how to license slightly dumbed-down versions of Linnet's state-of-the-art simulations as entertainment games. He'd be able to put his hands on at least some of the same internal information as the engineers working on military projects. More important to me, he was my link to establishing contact with Ted Devlin.

I counted on Frank Lafferty to be the gabbiest executive at Linnet/TVR. Also the one who would hound Ted Devlin most aggressively to close his first deal. Frank had to perform or retrain for a new job, like wearing a funny cap and asking 'You want fries with that?' But I believed I knew Frank pretty well already.

During the Cold War, the KGB used an acronym called 'MICE' for tempting people like Frank to spy for them. It was 'Money, Ideology, Compromise and Ego'. I ignored those principles. My world was one of self-interest, not ideology.

My own simple formula involved four Gs – 'Greed, Gonads, Gadgets and Golf'. Find the right G-spot inside any businessman and he'll tell you just about anything. Women executives tended to be more practical, their G-spots less reliable.

Golf was out, since my ultimate target was Ted Devlin. With one eye, golf would not be his choice for showing off.

Teflon Ted was definitely Greed and Gonads. But I figured that Gadgets would work just fine for my go-between prey Frank.

But I still felt the need for a bit of foreplay. Frank had such a strong need to compete, probably no prize was too petty. His secretary chose this moment to walk in with a tray of coffee and pastry. She placed it on our table. I saw an opportunity.

'Thanks, Debbie,' Frank said.

I ostentatiously glued my eyes to the fattest pastry on the plate, Danish-style with a sugary topping. Frank watched me, following my eyeballs to the gooey bun, and then politely lunged for it first. His deft fingers seized it and crumbs flew as he mashed half of it into his mouth before I could even reach the plate. I let my face droop a little to look disappointed.

'So, Frank, you were in licensing at National Brands before you came over here?'

'Yeah. I was on Krispy Krunch Elves.'

'Sure.' I nodded, recalling a commercial with his creepy-looking cartoon trolls hiding cereal from kids. 'That's why I think you'll like SymBad the Kickboxer.' I opened my briefcase from the front this time. This way my peanut planes were nowhere to be seen, only my laptop. I pulled out a pair of wire-rimmed designer sunglasses for him. 'Try these on.'

'Ray Bans?' he asked as he put them on his nose.

'Let's call them Ray Bans on Viagra,' I told him. If Maria came through with what she had told me about the toys in that little Saks bag she'd handed me at JFK Airport, she had created these Ray Bans as a sophisticated version of General Stone's simulator helmet. The lenses, she told me, were imbedded with lasers to create an image right on Frank's retina. She said they were just the right calling card for Ted Devlin, and I couldn't disagree.

I pulled my laptop out of the case and fooled with the joystick while I put another pair of sunglasses on my own nose.

He rocked back in his chair. 'Virtual reality glasses. How'd your people make them this small?'

I smiled enigmatically. 'Frank, meet SymBad the Kickboxer.'

I tapped a button and changed our view of the room through the glasses. She suddenly appeared on the chair between us, looking edgy and bristling as a Japanese comic-book heroine. Her hair was teased up in fire-engine red. Over a body that looked a lot more like a glistening flesh-and-blood goddess than a cartoon, she wore black leather micro shorts and a low-cut body wrap. Maria had come through like a true designer succubus. SymBad was hot.

'Hi, Frank. Are you married?' SymBad's voice seemed metallic and a little cranky.

Frank gaped at her legs and waist, elongated like a store-window mannequin. It gave her the sleek look of a perfectly airbrushed fantasy woman, which was exactly what SymBad was. Her perfect legs crossed miraculously in tight black boots. Her waist was maybe eighteen inches. She studied her curling purple metal fingernails. Her bee-stung lips were tinted the same shade. Her eyes smoldered, hot little fuses under heavy lids.

'So,' SymBad stretched luxuriously, a clever

parody of Frank's own moves, 'what are you working on, Frank?'

He laughed out loud, a little nervously, intimidated by this synthetic vixen. 'Just a few commercial applications for games . . . sports . . .'

'Sports?' SymBad said. 'Like this?'

She tucked and flipped her legs straight up toward the ceiling. Her body lunged back in a swinging comma over the chair. She landed on one hand, clearly an inhuman maneuver. And hanging upside down, gravity made SymBad even more exciting to Frank.

'What are you staring at?' she barked.

SymBad spun her body around and snapped her long legs out. It was a kick that placed her left leg in a backward arc to the floor and the toe of her right boot about half an inch from Frank's eyeball.

Then she twirled around again like a top, lashing out with a few wildly anatomical moves they hadn't seen yet on *World Wrestling Federation*. She stood directly in front of him. Frank gulped at her torso, close to his chin.

I could really get to like SymBad. Given a little time, she might even persuade Frank to tell some secrets. Not bad for a holographic image and an ambient mini-speaker built into the Ray Bans.

Frank balked like a scared horse suddenly peering over a deep ravine.

'Actually . . . ah . . . we had in mind more family-oriented kinds of virtual reality games. Something that won't get us in trouble with the religious right.'

Don't middle managers always say 'no' when it

comes to new ideas? None of them wants to be a pilgrim. Guys like Frank only liked girls with boyfriends, so to speak.

'Oh, I know, Frank. SymBad's already spoken for anyway.'

'She is?' He sounded a little crushed.

'Sure. She's on her way to European and Japanese markets. She's just a demo to show you how the boys' technology works. They have mostly G-rated characters like SymCyndy the Figure Skater and SymCubby the Dancing Bear. Cute. My guys are making these systems by hand now. I'd look toward a deal where they provide the characters and you automate the systems.'

Frank's eyes hadn't left SymBad. She raised her finger in a virtual flip of his tie and pouted languidly at him. Like any ventriloquist's dummy, she could do and say things I couldn't get away with.

'So, Frank,' she growled. 'Anybody else around here I ought to meet?'

'You know,' he said like she'd reminded him, 'I'd really like to show SymBad to our CEO Ted Devlin. He's in a meeting right now. I hear it's a special briefing for the Pentagon on our JSF program.'

He told me that with a sly smirk, flaunting the outer limits of his insider knowledge. People like Frank who try to blow up their importance with little classified morsels remind you why the concept of 'need to know' was invented.

'Well,' I said to deflate him, 'I guess commercial licensing is a low priority for Ted Devlin.'

Then I tapped 'Control' and SymBad suddenly

swooshed in a wild, genie-like vanishing act back into my laptop. I could almost feel the breeze. Virtually speaking.

Frank looked baleful. 'Don't put her away yet. Why don't you just stick around until he's out of his meeting?'

'I'm tied up for the rest of the day.'

'Well, how about leaving her with me?'

I chuckled and reached for the Ray Bans he held in his hand.

'No, really.' Frank gave me the full winning smile while he clutched the glasses. 'Just until this afternoon.'

I closed my briefcase. 'Sorry.'

'Look, I'll get her back to you today. I just want to show her to Ted.'

I frowned and took a business card out of my pocket. Not Fragata's. The one that said *Partner, Starcross-Voyager Venture Capital*.

'Here's my car phone number. If Ted Devlin wants to talk, he can reach me at one thirty.'

'How about the disk? We won't copy it.'

I removed the SymBad disk. 'I'm not worried. This is encrypted six ways against copying. You can play it on any system with a joystick.'

Frank took the disk and pumped my hand. 'If Ted likes the concept, I'd say you're in, Terry.'

But walking the third-floor corridor with Frank's hand on my shoulder, I was more concerned with getting out of Linnet/TVR with my peanut squadron undetected.

They spent a fortune on security, even beyond

what was required by the Department of Defense. The tightest security only happened on the way out. You couldn't get through the entry security arch with a gun. But they didn't search my briefcase for my peanut cams. Not on the way in.

The diabolical nature of Linnet/TVR security was that maybe you could check in espionage tools like mine, but you couldn't check out. That's how they tap corporate spies. Easy in to lull you into a false confidence. Then 'gotcha' when you're walking out with the family jewels. This time the guards would search my briefcase for material red-tagged as classified. They would also ask me to turn on my laptop and poke through it to make sure it was really mine and not one of theirs. And, most disturbing, now I would have to go through a security arch that detected electronic surveillance equipment. My peanut cams would light up the whole system.

So I walked into another washroom instead, bigger than the one I'd used earlier.

I heard someone in one of the stalls. I entered another stall and opened my case, quickly set up my laptop and woke up my peanut planes, then took thirty seconds to program their next flight.

The man in the other stall flushed his toilet. I tapped 'Send'.

My peanut squadron lifted up, dived to the floor and chased after him. When he opened the door of the men's room, they zipped through with him.

I followed the man, who walked purposefully down the hall with my peanut planes as his escort.

My squadron left him, whipped around a corner and flew toward the elevator. They would have to wait for someone else to take them to the ground floor. They found a mailroom worker pushing a cart and followed.

I used one of the other elevators. My elevator chimes made a 'bing' when I came to the lobby and the door opened.

The two-storey lobby was covered floor to ceiling with marble, about as inviting as a tombstone, ending in a row of glass doors. But to get to those doors, there was a processing funnel. First they took back your visitor's pass at a manned security desk. Then the big electronic security arch hung overhead like a guillotine. As I walked toward it, my microsquadron was ahead of me. I couldn't see them, but knew where they were and kept my eye on one visitor in particular.

A loud siren whooped.

The peanut cams had just passed through the arch around the heels of a tall, middle-aged man in a dark business suit. He had a briefcase. I guessed he was a salesperson, with a ready smile and a billion frequent-flyer miles.

The pleasant-looking salesman flinched. His eyes darted around, shocked by the sirens. Funny how some people who only pad their expense accounts or lie about delivery dates can store up guilt. Then it could all creep out at a moment like this.

'Sir, could I see you a moment.' A Linnet/TVR security officer in a blue blazer took the man's arm firmly.

The salesman made a big mistake by yanking his arm away. A reflex, probably.

The security guard was a scowling young Latin guy whose blue blazer stretched like paint across his large upper body. He looked a lot more menacing than a second ago.

'Sir, I need you to step over here *now*.'

I felt for the salesman. A growing huddle of security officers in blue blazers swallowed him up now. A supervisor arrived to interrogate him. They were going through his briefcase with electronic sensors.

Before long, they would let him go.

I turned my security lapel badge back in to one of the two remaining security officers at the desk. She made a cursory check of my briefcase and laptop, glancing at the huddle around the salesman.

'He's fucked,' she mumbled, not to me. Then, apologetically, 'Sorry for the inconvenience.'

'No problem,' I said.

My microcams waited for me on the left front tire of my rental car, hiding under the wheel well.

I hit my remote-control keychain. When the doors unlocked, my peanuts were programmed to wait five seconds for me before they flew into the car. I opened my briefcase on the passenger seat and they zoomed in right on schedule and settled into their nooks inside the case.

Driving away, I found myself missing Symbad.

Even though she had stolen my nest egg and would probably get me life in a federal prison, Maria Haymeyer had a wicked sense of humor.

89

PART II

Rules of Engagement

Six

Over my corporate spying career, I had formulated a strict code of conduct for survival. Some of it came from my training as a combat pilot, some from practical experience in business. My five rules were:

1. *Steal Globally, Hide Locally.* As Maria had figured out, my industrial targets were always in foreign countries that targeted US firms for economic espionage. I never fouled my own nest by stealing from US firms. Never. America was my sanctuary, as much for legal as patriotic reasons. Our federal law prohibits any other country from extraditing a US citizen from American soil. That's why I always caught the first flight home after a job.

2. *Lose Sight, Lose the Fight.* The fighter pilot's mantra. The only strategy for air-to-air combat is to maintain superb situational awareness, or SA. Situational awareness is like second sight, the ability to know exactly what's going on around you in your battlespace at all times and predict what an enemy will do. It's what enables a combat pilot to sneak up on his enemy from behind, strike before being noticed, and slink away, as any other Air Force combat veteran will tell you. That's the only way we got to be veterans.

3. *Nobody Questions Money.* This is the sturdy espionage doctrine called 'hiding in plain sight'. It's

why I keep my cover as a Wall Street venture capitalist and travel first class. In fact, it's always been a mystery to me why all criminals don't dress like successful business people. They would never get asked questions like 'What are you doing in our executive washroom?'

4. *Know Thine Enemy.* I am always prepared by knowing my subjects cold. Even if my target is sixty years old, I want to know whether he was breast- or bottle-fed. It's like we all learned in grade school – the more you learn, the more you earn.

5. *Play With Amateurs, and You Get Hurt.* In espionage, as in sports, amateurs will trip you up.

Until Maria entered my life, I had never breached these rules. Now I was breaking all of them. I had penetrated a key defense contractor on US soil. I had sufficiently blown my situational awareness to allow a woman I didn't even know to break into my life and steal my nest egg. I had lost all of the money that provided me cover and protection. And I knew very little about Maria Haymeyer except what she chose to tell me.

I suppose a self-aware corporate spy – whose most recent job had been to fly Concorde to Paris and steal the special sauce from that annoying French-owned firm Happy Beefburger – would likely consider himself over his head under these circumstances. Any other spy would be focusing his tunnel vision on how to give up and flee the country. I did have a panic kit in a safe deposit box at Wells Fargo bank. It contained a perfectly legal Nigerian consular passport in the name of Alfred Packer that

I'd obtained, a stash of $250,000 in US bills, and an International Driver's License.

But I wasn't thinking about my panic kit. I was pondering, as I sat in the back of a red and white taxi, how Ted Devlin reminded me of an urban legend about two kids who built a killer car audio system.

It was supposed to have happened in the San Fernando Valley. Two seventeen-year-olds, who had already done themselves some aural and perhaps brain damage, took out the back seat of a Toyota in order to replace it with one of those 4′ × 5′ ultra-high-power amplifiers. But when they shut the windows and cranked it up to full volume, the sound wouldn't blast at full power. One of them had taken a basic science course and figured out that the closed interior reflected back the sound waves, so he opened a window. That created a so-called 'kick-whap effect'. The release of pressure sucked all the air out of their lungs, killing both of them instantly.

I wouldn't be so cruel as to call the loss of those boys a case of natural selection – just a parable of what happens when you don't know enough about the technology you think you control.

If Ted had stolen Maria's design, and it really did have the Doom Level, I wondered what would happen to some pilot strapped into Ted's LUCI prototype.

I had already disabled my Lincoln land yacht in a parking lot and phoned the Hertz people to pick it up because it was broken. I wanted – no, needed – the secure feeling of my own car around me.

I looked out the window of the cab as we crept along Pico Boulevard, a dismal row of brightly colored but flaking one-storey buildings that aspired to be a strip mall. We passed low-rent check-cashing and auto title-loan offices, self-serve laundromats, and muffler shops before pulling into the lot for a banana-yellow stucco building with a big garage door. The hand-painted sign read *Auto Blasters*, a deceptively bleak façade. A young Hispanic guy in coveralls with a hangdog look and some colorful jailhouse tattoos on his arms recognized me. He smiled and raised the garage door, revealing two brand-new Ferraris and my own car inside.

Mine was a factory-fresh NSX twin turbo with a six-speed manual transmission and modified Formula One racing engine. I had bought it in Tokyo, back when I was still rich. This new model, radically angular and bristling with electronics, could only come from the country that gave us Sony and Godzilla. Not even the dazzling new Ferrari Modena beside it looked as fantasy-driven. My car's icy-white body sparkled under Auto Blasters' rude interior lights, as though its surface had been polished by jewelers.

Next to my new car stood Manny, a big-boned guy with thinning hair whose rolled-up sleeves exposed thick wrists and surprisingly fine and slender hands. Manny had been an electronics specialist in Air Force Communications. He was the only urban Jewish guy I'd ever met who spoke in that hardscrabble drawl you hear on army bases.

Manny held a gold Cross pen in one hand and an electronic palm pad in the other, ready to add up my bill with that personal touch. Actually, the sound system on my NSX was just fine. I'd wanted him to install some other modifications. I did a walkaround to check out my car.

'So, how'd it go, Manny?'

'A lot of problems with this job.' He shook his head in the troubled way a smart plumber does. 'You wouldn't believe . . .'

'Sure I would,' I said, trying to hustle him along. 'How much?'

Manny scowled and scribbled with his Cross pen. 'You got your satellite link . . . phone . . . fax . . . GPS with a Falcon signal . . .'

'Great, Manny,' I said briskly.

My GPS navigation system would be a little different from the one they offer as an option on any Buick Century. Manny had fixed it so I could use a signal of military precision stolen from the USAF Intelligence at Falcon Air Force Base. I didn't really have to use the military signal any more, since civilian companies now did pretty much the same thing. But I couldn't help myself.

'. . . instrument display on the windshield . . . night-vision system . . .' Manny drawled on. That was a version of military night-vision technology. It projected green images on the lower part of my windshield and the side and rear windows so I could see about five times farther at night.

'. . . you got your vidcam scanners mounted fore and aft plus one upward-looking . . .'

I ran the little front-mounted cameras around to check them out. They made a whirring noise as I focused them on cars going by in the street. They blew up what they saw in enough detail to make out the black roots of a blonde cruising by. Although dumber than Maria's blob, my little aftermarket add-ons would give me superb situational awareness of my environment for about a mile in each direction and even to spot a helicopter up in the air. They would make it hard for anybody to track and follow me without my knowing it. I tweaked the cams a little.

'. . . all voice-activated.' Manny wound up and handed me an invoice for $93,386.

I handed over my credit card with a sinking feeling. He gave me a careful handshake, like a surgeon does. To ease the pain, I told my car, 'Play Vonda Shephard's *It's Good, Eve,*' and the CD player dutifully cranked up Ms Shephard's first album. I also checked out the new GPS I'd just encoded to a military signal. As a pilot – not to mention as a guy – I would rather hang by my thumbs than ask a stranger for directions.

I turned over the ignition and tapped the accelerator to clean out my engine. My twin-turbo-charged version of a Formula One racing engine growled with a ragged, rumbling snarl, as though I'd woken it up from a long nap. The car had been sitting idle here since I left two weeks before, except for the extra two miles I see Manny had logged, probably joyriding in second gear at 100 m.p.h. I rolled it out, stopping to remove the Targa T-top to let the sun shine in and felt the warmth flood over me as I settled back into my seat.

I opened my nostrils and let the sensuous aroma of leather – old Florentine leather, which was a pretty clever use of chemical fragrances in a brand-new car – wash away the oily asphalt smell of Pico Boulevard. There was a familiar rush of nostalgia in this instrument-packed cockpit. I closed my eyes and briefly visited my salad days in fighters, when I would light the afterburner and hurtle into the sky.

'Ya'll come back,' Manny said, as he handed me back my Amex Platinum card and I let out the clutch.

'I sure hope so.'

I rolled out of the lot and took off on ratty Pico with a throaty roar that turned heads, snapping through the six gears with authority. The NSX had its two turbos on a kind of fly-by-wire computer system like a fighter. It eliminated the usual turbo lag between stepping on the gas and the whomping rush of the turbo kicking in, giving me a neck-snapping jolt in each gear with no waiting.

Oh, yes. I felt like the Four Horsemen of the Apocalypse, thundering toward my destiny. Not even Maria Haymeyer could scare me now. Wheeling on to the Santa Monica Freeway, I feathered the clutch and throttle and felt the heat of the mid-engine revving up behind my back through my seat.

God, this car felt sensational.

You'd think an industrial spy should use his inside product knowledge, better than the whole testing staff of *Consumer Reports*, to make practical consumer purchases. Sure. My practical NSX had a trunk large enough for a full set of golf balls.

To me, cars were supposed to be dreamy, evocative courtesans, full of scents and touches that awakened old boyhood memories. I felt the tailored hug of the butterscotch leather. The engine and exhaust sounded more deliciously Italian than a Lamborghini.

Funny how I still felt a twinge of guilt, like a vestigial tail, for not buying American. It wasn't just being in the military. The reasons remain murky to me, but I think it had something to do with loving Ian Fleming's James Bond books as a kid. Bond drove an Aston Martin out of pure English chauvinism even though it had an electrical system that, in real life, would have shorted out and left him hitching a ride to chase Goldfinger.

Still, you couldn't fault those James Bond books, with their twenty-page dinners and six bottles of Château Lafite-Rothschild. How did an ex-Royal Navy commander live like that? The American Navy commanders I knew guzzled Bud and ordered dinner through a sneeze protector at the Sizzler.

But that was then and this is now. In my world of industrial espionage, the Brits and Americans could be described as amateurs. When it comes to stealing technology, my money's on the Chinese. They've been doing it profitably for about five thousand years.

I rippled over rows of those freeway speed bumps and hit the fast lane. The NSX made a reassuring *pocketa-pocketa* sound like hitting the sweet spot of a tennis racket every time. I had named her White Mischief. I always named my cars, like my fighters.

Focus. Tunnel vision.

I was getting to know my enemy. But just waiting for a phone call from Ted Devlin gave me the jitters. I played with my car's little cameras to look round me. I needed to feel my situational awareness coming back.

The Air Force trains a few thousand pilots a year. Only about five per cent turn out to be great combat fighters – because they have excellent situational awareness. SA is almost like second sight. In combat, you're in charge of a screaming, sophisticated machine, processing a thousand pieces of information a second, trying to read a battlespace in three-dimensions to stalk and outwit your enemy. Like charm, SA isn't something you can learn. You either have it or you don't. If you have it, you can be a seriously flawed human being but still a great combat pilot.

All through my Fighter Track evaluations as a young lieutenant, my situational awareness put me at the head of my class. My instructors told me over drinks in the Eglin AFB Officers' Club that I was just about the sneakiest little shit they'd ever seen in stalking maneuvers, as though it was a gift like Mozart's ear. That's why I was chosen to go to O'Brien AFB in the California desert with a group of young fighter jocks known as fast burners, to learn to fly Ted Devlin's new F-118 stealth fighter.

I thought I had volunteered to join a vampires'

convention. We were ordered to sleep during the day and get up at twilight because we could only fly the secret plane at night.

Nobody, I mean nobody, had anything good to say about Teflon Ted's stealthy aircraft back then. Jet fighters were supposed to be aerodynamic and needle-nosed. Ted's Darkwing F-118 looked like a pissed-off Jack O'Lantern with razor blades for wings and a saw-toothed scowl around the windshield. It was the spookiest aircraft I had ever seen. No wonder folks from that area thought they were spotting UFOs in the night sky.

When we were told by our deadpan briefer that this was a wondrous aircraft, agile and forgiving, the part of my brain cells tasked to detect 'falsehood' lit up like a pinball machine. When he said that junkyard dog of a fighter would fool enemy radar so we would not be caught like a burglar in a flashlight, we all practically coughed 'bullshit' into our hands like school kids. Nobody trusted stealth yet. The plane flew so badly, we called it the Wiggly Wombat. Teflon Ted came out to the base, stood by his plane's ugly snout and gave us a pep talk. Then we all got piss drunk on tequila and Dos Equis with him and agreed like all cocky young fighter pilots that we could fly anything.

When Saddam Hussein invaded Kuwait, my squadron took their Bart Simpson keyrings and other good-luck icons and strapped ourselves into our Darkwings under cover of night and flew for too many uncomfortable hours. I was getting cranky by the fifth or sixth mid-air refueling, with no way to stretch and a diabolical device called a 'relief tube' for a bathroom.

I took off on my first mission from Saudi Arabia, hamsters running around my stomach as we flew over suburban Baghdad at midnight, hitting a steel blizzard of ground fire, made ghostly green by my phosphorous cockpit lights that you saw on CNN. Fortunately, the Iraqis couldn't really see us after all and the explosions hit the spaces we'd just flown through.

My most spectacular hit was a building known to the Iraqis as their 'Ministry of Tourism', since it contained organisms of biological warfare they could send to visit other countries. I dropped bombs that imploded the building on to forty containers of anthrax hidden deep inside the basement. True to form, the Iraqis put up a sign afterwards for the media that read 'Baby's Milke Factorie', and reported that I'd hit a civilian target.

At 1.30 exactly, I heard the warble of my car phone.

'Terry Weston.'

A female voice: 'Please hold for Ted Devlin.'

I was put on hold, so I hung up. The phone rang again.

'Terry Weston.'

'Terry?' his voice boomed, gravelly like in the conference room earlier. 'Ted Devlin. Frank Lafferty just showed me your SymBad. I wanted to take her to dinner.'

I laughed. 'She won't eat much. We're interested in a joint venture with you.'

His voice became slow and wary. 'These guys who made SymBad, you sure there's no woman involved with them?'

'They wish,' I told Ted, feeling a cold sting up my spine. *Ted was afraid.*

'Think what animal they are like,' my mother once told me about meeting new people. *'That is how they will behave.'* I saw Ted Devlin as a raccoon caught in the glare of a flashlight stealing a pizza box from the garbage can.

'Terry . . .' He paused. 'I'm having a party at my place tonight. How about I bring SymBad and you come pick her up?'

'Sounds good. Nine o'clock okay?'

'See you then. Oh, Terry, you ever play Crud?'

Not if I could help it. 'Sure. I flew one of your Darkwings out of O'Brien.'

Ted snorted. 'You sonofabitch. Lafferty never even told me.'

'I didn't mention it.'

I visualized him wagging his head, the glass eye moving back and forth. 'You must have gone to the Gulf.'

'Yeah. Saddam left a message for you. He wants his baby milk factory back.'

'That was you?' Ted's laugh was both hearty and nasal. He was in as good a mood as I've ever managed to get one of my targets. 'Terry, don't stand me up tonight. I never get to see the old Darkwing guys any more. I want to hear all about your plane.'

'Same here, Ted.'

'Hold on. My girl can give you my address.'

He put me on hold again. I let my smart phone take over, because I was too busy twisting my mind around why Ted Devlin was scared of Maria Haymeyer. Maybe he had talked about his design with her, and now he was afraid of being revealed as an old hound with loose lips.

Or maybe he was afraid of being revealed as a thief.

Their lunch meeting as Maria described it was unlikely. I suspected they had lunch that day as part of a longer, deeper relationship. Maybe Ted decided that God had rewarded his lifetime of good works by dropping Maria into his lap, a *girl* who had stumbled upon what real aerospace engineers hadn't. So it was his duty to steal it. Maybe Ted thought he heard a few rough ideas from a hot-looking PhD candidate he was dating, who inspired him to invent LUCI all by himself.

My phone warbled again. I jammed it to my ear to hear over the traffic noise. The voice at the other end seemed faint and distant, as though it had been routed around by computer.

'Did you see the horse?' Maria asked me.

I had to tighten my grip on the wheel to stay in my lane.

'I'll call you back,' I said firmly.

She ignored me. 'Did you at least poke around the stables?'

'Rule one, we don't use phones.'

'We can speak in Pig Latin.'

She sure had the idiot part down with the savant part. 'No. Are you on the business line?'

'Roger that.'

'This isn't funny. Stay where you are and I'll call you back.'

I slammed the receiver back in its casing, cracking the plastic slightly, and pulled off at the next exit, where I saw a Bennigan's sign. I yanked my briefcase and stomped in, finding pay phones in the entrance foyer. It was lunchtime and young office workers crowded by me.

Grabbing the phone, I punched in a special billing number used by a major telephone company's top executives. I knew that it was changed every month, and the records swept away. It didn't cost them anything, a little perk of the job.

The number for Fragata in Italy jangled in that old-world way. Then I heard the call hop over three separate connections before it settled into an all-American ring.

'*Welcome to the Fragata voice mailbox,*' I heard her voice say. '*To steal a Special Sauce, press one . . .*'

'That isn't funny either,' I said. 'Okay. Let's say the design really is yours. I'm thinking if I can get evidence there's a Doom Level, we can make the horse roll over and play dead. But I'll need to get my lawyer involved.'

'You can't trust lawyers,' she snapped.

'You can trust mine.' That was only true because he was my best friend. 'You don't have time to locate the world's second best industrial spy, Maria. When does the Doom Level kick in?'

'You don't want to know, Terry. Not if you're trying to get close to her.'

106

'Yes I do. I think I can get in the sim. You have to tell me what to do if I can. Where are you?'

A pause. 'Nearby. I'll call you,' she said and the line went dead. I hung up the pay phone and walked out past laughing people with non-lethal jobs hustling merrily into Bennigan's for fajitas and Coronas.

I stroked the NSX through its gears a little more forcefully than necessary. Slipping back on to the freeway, I nursed a gloomy 'what if' thought about a pilot just like me vaporized in the LUCI aircraft because Maria was telling me the truth and Ted Devlin didn't defuse his Doom Level.

I believed Maria.

Ted was a raccoon. Maria was no animal I could think of.

I did have a plan, although she didn't know it yet. I would just consult my lawyer for advice. I didn't do anything without running it by my lawyer first, although sometimes he didn't actually know it. In my business, establishing a strict need-to-know basis is the only way to keep your old friends. Then we would get Maria together with Ted. We would force them both to swallow their egos and negotiate. If we made Ted aware that he'd been outed, he would decide it was in his best interest to give Maria a royalty. Then she would disarm the virus. It would still be unfair to Maria. But I would have to impress upon her that 'unfair' beat the deal she currently had, not to mention the possible sudden destruction of US defense capabilities.

She was smart. She would sign on.

Ted would be tricky. He was still coming from a position of strength. But even Teflon Ted would respond to the right kind of fear.

Maybe he survived B-52 missions over Southeast Asia. Maybe he fought with valor and lost his eye, knowing all the time he could be captured and tortured. But that was a whole different kind of fear.

The Viet Cong took his eye, but not even Ho Chi Minh could take away his American Express Platinum card. Ted had a whole lot to protect now.

I tapped my small, leather-padded steering wheel. My first look at Ted's background in the QuickStudy had been superficial.

I pulled off the freeway to see what the Wringer had found with their extra twenty-four hours.

SEVEN

I always got my deep background information on people, the kind that costs $50,000 per dossier, at Kinko's.

At their West Hollywood location, I laid out cash on the counter in front of a young clerk who must have been a mouth-model working between auditions. Her plump lips were wide and her teeth flashed like Chicklets, although still not in the class of Maria's red donut.

A small hourly fee entitled me to sit down at a computer and printer. I could access the Internet without leaving a trace of my true identity. Kinko's had no idea what I was receiving, and there would be no record of my visit.

I sat down at my innocent pay-per-hour computer and tapped *adventuretours.com*. An uninspired, all-type webpage popped up: '*Go Farther with Adventure Tours, Inc*'. I scrolled down the menu and tapped 'To Order', typing in: *Need info Sun Valley, 2 week vac. Member #8624*. The computer crunched and the printer began offering up helpful hints about skiing in Sun Valley, complete with hotels and rates. When the clackety-clack stopped, fifty-seven pages sat in the hopper.

Within that pile of dense, single-spaced travel information, there would be enough data, after I'd run it through my encryption software, to net me roughly twenty encoded pages each about Maria Haymeyer and Ted Devlin.

These dossiers had just been compiled for me during the past forty-eight hours by the Wringer of Chevy Chase – the private citizen's very own FBI and CIA – who had sent me the down-and-dirty QuickStudies on Maria and Ted. I paid for these two complete dossiers with a wire transfer from a shell company I own that exists only in a desk drawer of a lawyer's office in the Dutch West Indies.

I knew that the Wringer would scrub my subjects with a fine wire brush and they wouldn't even know it. Those merry men and women of Chevy Chase would have done personal interviews with co-workers, neighbors and acquaintances obtained under the falsehood that the subject was being investigated for a national security clearance. People love to dish, if you give them any good reason. Interviewees would have been warned that the subject must not be told, or the FBI would come down on the interviewee's head. The rogue former FBI agents at the Wringer knew that intimidation was more art than science.

Also, the Wringer would have expertly broken into both of their homes to check through files, closets, drawers, garbage. They would have searched all their records and cross-checked to document any time Maria and Ted were in the same city or talked over the phone. And they would have completed all this over the past twenty-six hours, for both subjects.

110

You just don't find that kind of personal service any more.

Of course, the Wringer operatives probably called me the ten-letter word for giving them so little time, but espionage isn't a popularity contest.

End of transmission, the computer finally told me when the printer stopped. *Photobrochure sent Dash Express.*

I put my thick packet of Sun Valley travel information in a manila envelope, threw it in my briefcase and left. I had hours of homework before Ted's party.

The garage door of my high-rise apartment building opened for my remote. You may have seen the Pacifica Tower in movies. It's a black-green glass tower chock full of Pacific Rim architectural whimsy, with a hole in the middle and a disk hanging more or less off into space from the roof. I couldn't wait to see where that would roll during a bad earthquake. Pacifica Tower soars over the base of Sunset Boulevard below Sunset Plaza Drive where Hollywood meets Beverly Hills.

I stopped in the flamboyant three-story lobby designed as an Asian temple garden. Overhead, bird-like white lights nestled on horizontal wires stretched across the great ceiling. I negotiated the topiary hedges shaped into Confucian symbols. I don't know what the symbols meant, but a group of Buddhist monks once chained themselves to our lobby to protest whatever it was until the police took them away. I picked up a Dash Express package at the front desk from a guard wearing a uniform with a Mandarin red tunic.

I had always considered myself lucky to be truly 'pentacoastal', having a penthouse apartment on both East and West coasts. My penthouse here was smaller than the one in New York – just a perch for The Airplane View you've probably seen in movies. To the right, the great flat heart of the City of Angels shimmered with light from the desert thermals. To the left, the Santa Monica Mountains lounged with the Hollywood sign just readable. Usually I smiled at my wraparound ant-colony view. Some believe that Los Angeles is a glamorous place because it's an entertainment town. I like it because it's an aerospace town.

Today I didn't notice my view. I just got to work.

I'd designed this apartment with brutal minimalism, not the cozy Italianate comfort of my Central Park West apartment. Nobody would feel welcome to stay long. My black-granite floor had curved glass windows, floor to ceiling. They surrounded the spare dark leathers and hammered-steel desk of my living room. My bedroom had nothing but a bed with leather headrests placed diagonally in the center of the room to take advantage of The View. I had stripped the second bedroom and outfitted it as a gym with a big Trotter hydraulic multi-exercise machine, a treadmill, and a pyramid stand for my own assortment of chrome freeweights.

You could say that my New York apartment belonged to Terry Weston, reasonably successful venture capitalist who loved Italian frescos, dated the wrong women, believed in his heart that

Casablanca was a documentary, and failed to adequately visit his mother in Aventura, Florida, which I think means 'retirees who drive badly' in Italian.

But my LA apartment belonged to the unsentimental Fragata. Nobody else came here, ever. At least not until Maria invaded.

I ripped open the Dash Express package and threw out the Lodestar Systems, Inc. 10K corporate document without glancing at it. That was just filler for show. Instead, I went to work with a small matte knife on the cardboard of the package itself, carefully cutting out the barcode strip.

I took the strip into my kitchen's small utility room with a combination washer/dryer and poured a special solvent into the washing machine, then threw the barcode strip inside and closed the door. I selected the 'Rinse' cycle, letting it roll and vibrate for sixty seconds. Then I took the soggy strip out and pulled down an ironing board built into the wall, covered the strip with a special cloth towel, and left the hissing iron on top with the setting on 'All Cotton'.

Ten seconds later, I took the finished product and slipped it into a customized digital printer. The printer slowly dropped a dozen small images into my hand with a crunching cutting noise. I sifted through the twelve photographs, six of Maria Haymeyer, six of Ted Devlin. They came from high-school yearbooks and other photos stolen from their homes.

I used my scanner to blow the photographs up to 8 × 10.

I looked at Ted's pictures first, searching to see beyond his glass eye. When somebody has an obvious attention-getter like a glass eye, you needed to be extra vigilant to pick up facial subtleties.

I noticed for the first time, since I had only seen his face recently on my small computer screen, that he'd probably had Botox shots to get rid of his frown lines. I screwed my magnifying loop into my eye and looked through it. No. Not Botox. It was a recent facelift. The skin around Ted's eye had that slightly pulled-back, crazed wolverine appearance and there were little traces of scar tissue around the ears.

I glanced at his official photograph from the Linnet/TVR annual report. It had been carefully sidelit and retouched. His hair bristled over his square face, craggy with a broad leer, like he wished with all his heart to sexually harass some low-level employee. I would say that Ted cultivated his reputation as an Alpha male.

I kept one wall bare for hanging things. So I hung Ted's six pictures up and studied them.

Then I took Maria's pictures from the pouch.

Her graduation picture was taken by possibly the world's most inept high-school photographer. But I saw a goddess in waiting. Her bright eyes shone clearly through glasses so thick you could probably hold them up to a window at night and see the rings of Saturn. Her cheekbones poked out under soon-to-be-shed baby fat. I became fascinated with her jaw, set in that natural certainty of the one person in ten thousand whose heart was hopelessly scalded with a primal need. It was a face that clearly said, 'Show me the wall I need to tear down that stands between me and my dreams.'

I slowly hung up her pictures along my wall. In one candid shot of her as an undergraduate at Stanford, she sat on a low wall in the morning light playing with her tumbling curls as she balanced a fat textbook on her knees. She wore shorts, exposing her sculpted legs. I wondered who took the photograph.

I always ask for a shot of a subject's parents. It tells me so much. The Wringer obliged with a studio photo. Maria at about fifteen stood arm in arm with an achingly beautiful Latin woman, obviously her mother, who wore pulled-back hair and a severe tailored suit. It looked like a Terry Mugler. From the way her eyes hugged the camera, I could see her mother had experience playing to a lens.

Standing next to them in a detached sort of way was a guy with small features and a high forehead, in a tweedy rumpled suit. I didn't like the smirk on his thin lips. He peered down at the camera with a superior tilt to his chin. This would be her stepfather.

Maria rested her hand lightly on her mother's arm, her cheeks glistening as she smiled unself-consciously in the studio lights. She loved her mother. She also looked a lot like her and, when she reached her forties, I was sure she would be similarly fine-boned.

Then I picked up the next photograph and almost dropped it.

In full color, Maria at about age nineteen stood nude from the waist up. She looked so perfect in the state of nature, the shot could have been taken by a wildlife photographer. She held her head slightly down so her curls, backlit, piled in sensual display. Her eyes stared out under droopy lids, and her lips made the red donut. I flipped the photo looking for the source.

It was a *Playboy* spread called 'The Girls of Mensa'.

My blood pounded. What a visceral, stupid longing I felt for this woman. I put the photo down on its face. If I had left it up on the wall, I'd still be looking at it today. Although maybe that wouldn't have been a bad idea, with the clarity of hindsight.

I pulled myself away to finish my work.

My steroidal computer, custom-made by a client in San Jose, sat on a desk in my living room. It was hooked up to a thin, flat seven-foot-wide matrix screen hung on the wall that projected an image crisp as a 35mm slide. This marvel of a convergence system, with all the latest Beta stage goodies, had been put together from the techie start-up companies we funded at Starcross-Voyager. I got all the latest toys a year or more before the marketplace.

I laughed bitterly at how this musclebound system, operating at the speed of light through the latest fibre-optics and satellite uplinks, must have seemed a feeble adversary to Maria. I upgraded my system every six months to add all the latest security devices.

But Maria had cracked into it anyway, hadn't she?

I took off my jacket, rolled up my sleeves, and

gripped the heavy modular seating arena in the center of the living room, on a gunmetal-colored handmade rug. Grunting, I shoved the half-ton of glove leather over about five feet, bunching up the rug.

In the now-exposed floor, I saw where two squares of the tile had been uprooted. Whenever I moved those two tiles, I always resealed them with new grout. Now they mocked me, naked and ungrouted. I picked both up and placed them carefully on the leather seats. Then I opened the titanium vault door hidden beneath the tiles, which I saw Maria had not relocked. Carefully, I ran my hand around the secret cache that she had robbed when she invaded my apartment.

The originals of the documents she had showed me last Saturday night were all there in the vault. Except, of course, for my bankbook. There was something new in there, too. I picked it up and saw that it was the hand-held metal detector she'd used to search my apartment for this vault.

Already on my knees, I uttered a guttural moan like an animal whose hutch had been cleaned out by predators. The thought of Maria plundering my nest egg sent cold needles through my stomach, filling me with impotent rage. Seeing the cold, professional effort – no, actually the lack of much effort at all – that she had devoted to her pene-tration filled me with a hollow sense of violation.

My emotions raged because Maria had humi-liated me. But I guess reducing a guy to psycho-logical pulp was the whole point of a succubus. Or was it just that Maria was my equal in situational awareness? *Or my better.*

Focus, Terry. Lose sight, lose the fight.

Unhappily, I picked myself up. First I went to the kitchen for grout to carefully reseal the tile. I needed to do something dumb and physical. After I finished that, I sat down to boot up my computer.

I began to run a series of tests to find out how Maria had cracked into my system and defeated my state-of-the-art firewall. She had cracked into the Pentagon, I knew, but who didn't? I had built in safeguards that I thought made the Pentagon's security about as dumbfounding as the *TV Guide* crossword puzzle.

Nothing.

I searched for viruses or other bugs she might have inserted to destroy or copy new data I put in.

None.

I searched the old Internet to see what I could find on the World Wide Wait, then turned to Internet2. I routinely used the I2 to get more hard information with less traffic. It was about one thousand times faster than the old Internet. The only problem with it, I had found, was that it was based on a network of a hundred linked universities and could be vulnerable to cracking. But she hadn't cracked in through I2.

Hours later my eyes were nearly melting off when I finally discovered the true evil of her penetration.

America OnLine.

What a vile sense of humor she had. I focused on

the note that she'd left buried for me in my AOL
files:

Dear Terry,

*We will have met by now, so I hope that you will take
my comments as professional rather than personal
criticism.*

*You should complain about the security in this
building. I pretended to be your girlfriend and convinced the manager to let me in with a passkey.*

*Also beware of keeping information coded in your
hard drive. That's where I found the security code for
your New York apartment and guessed the combination
to your floor vault. (I also copied your key, which I have
replaced in your desk drawer.)*

*I suppose it should have astonished me that you would
select such an obvious password for your bank account,
but I think that's just a marker, don't you?*

Now get to work!

Maria

I felt my ego crumple like a vain professor who's
found his work skillfully discredited in a *Marvel*
comic. I cursed and growled, imagining how she
must have gotten a kick out of it. Blotches of purple
appeared on my hands, I was struggling so hard to
keep my temper. My fingers had reflexively jumped
off the keyboard – even the plastic keys felt naked
now.

I would have to run my Wringer decoding program through my laptop, which she hadn't touched.

A wave of tiredness washed over me like a lead

shower. I wanted to sleep for a month or so and wake up refreshed.

Focus.

Intellectually, I recognized Maria's note for what it was – psychological warfare to make me feel impotent. But it played a more curious note perhaps not even she had considered. Emotionally, it thrilled me. What a natural she was at this stalking game.

Tunnel vision!

'I've got mail,' I muttered, taking a moment to do a mindless task.

I checked the e-mail that had been sent to my office at Starcross-Voyager Venture Capital. Not much. I left most of the daily grind to my partners, along with most of the profits. A few memos were labeled 'Urgent' or 'Panic'. I saw one droll message about an Asian airline named Mandarin Air we were helping with financing. Basically, we had invested in Asia after everybody else in the Western world had flooded their countries with wealth then pulled it all out in panic, leaving them reeling. But this cry for help wasn't about money. I had to laugh. Their US agent said that Western travelers in focus groups for Mandarin Air complained that the flight attendants made them feel creepy. In Mandarin Air's country of origin, smiling by young women was considered socially undesirable. Instead, they clicked their tongues. When they practiced this custom on board, the passengers must have felt constantly scolded.

I called the Beverly Hills office of Starcross-Voyager and found my secretary Edwina. She was a bright, semi-skilled teenager with greenish hair and a tongue ring.

'Hi, Mr Weston,' she said when she appeared on the screen. We kept a certain formality.

I dictated a memo telling Mandarin Air to contact a charm school for flight attendants run by a Scandinavian carrier. Edwina told me that another company were dealing with had developed a new motorcycle. I asked for a scan on it. It looked sharp, a European sports model like a Ducati, but even when I turned the sound up to hear its engine, it was oddly quiet.

'I can't hear it,' I told Edwina's screen.

''Cause it's electric, Mr Weston,' Edwina explained, stopping just short of adding *'duh'*. 'It'll do one hundred and ten top speed, but it needs a charge every two hours.'

'Eddie,' I told her, 'since people buy motorcycles to make noise, tooling around like a tiger with its voice box removed might not cut it for them. But tell them to send a prototype to the office anyway. You never know.'

'Don't worry, Mr Weston, bye,' she said in one breath, and vanished from my screen. Edwina used a uniquely American form of language compression and cadence whose origins I trace back to Jan Brady.

It felt soothing to tackle problems with solutions, unlike Maria's oozing swamp creature of a situation. But I couldn't procrastinate any longer.

From my bookcase, I yanked out a leatherbound first-edition copy of *Galapagos* by Kurt Vonnegut. I used my matte knife to peel open the paper on the binding and extracted a disk.

Next, I reconnected my scanner and printer to my laptop, since she couldn't crack into it. I placed the stack of Kinko's paper in my scanner, shoved the disk in, and told it to decode the data I wanted.

While my program ran, I stripped to my shorts and gathered up Maria's photos. I carried them into the gym room and hung them up to study while I lifted my freeweights, grunting and sweating. I still lift weights exactly like I did in the Air Force. If you're muscular, it helps you withstand G-forces. Running, which is aerobic, is useless for handling Gs. That's why military pilots stay pumped up. And working out with weights also builds up the confidence that pilots need.

Maria Haymeyer may have squeezed a lot of confidence out of my tube, but not all of it. I was still a fighter pilot. *The best of the best!* And I was still Fragata.

I dropped the weights down with a manly clang and got on my treadmill, turning on the Net TV monitor in front of me. I checked the time and clicked on to a nightly entertainment posing as news analysis called *24/7 with Allyn Pollack*. Tonight's show, the promos said, was supposed to turn the arcane Joint Strike Fighter competition into news viewers could use. Up came the grandiose music and show logo with an anvil-striking sound effect and the canned sounds of a busy newsroom.

Allyn Pollack appeared at his round news desk, preening like a two-hundred-pound diva under the flattering lights of his sweeping sound stage. His wide jowls and expressive eyes were set in his branded skepticism.

Pollack was a TV news mutation who, in the scandal-crazed tabloid news cycle of the '90s, had begun combining his nightly report with a twenty-four-hour website and focusing solely on dirt. Some described him as 'Ted Koppel trying to spit out Matt Drudge'. Though he still took that pious tone of the serious journalist, Pollack dealt mostly in petty scandal blown up to look newsworthy. If he couldn't dredge up any dirt, he would be out of a job.

True to form, this segment began with a montage of clips showing military aircraft disasters – planes exploding in mid-air, blowing up without getting off the ground, flying apart over airshows.

'Tonight,' Pollack's crisp, vaguely mocking voice announced, 'a special report on the Pentagon's controversial Joint Strike Fighter program . . .'

From Senator Bob Bixby's media stooge, I thought.

'. . . simply another bad idea from the Pentagon, or America's trillion-dollar boondoggle?' His voice sounded like a prosecutor's but his camera-groomed eyes looked sad and wise as a trusty beagle's. I had to admit that Pollack was singularly adapted to play a trustworthy person on TV.

Around Pollack, a series of squares with heads popped in like a game show. He introduced a Pentagon official, two US senators, and Teflon Ted Devlin.

'United States Senator Bob Bixby from Georgia,

123

good evening, sir. Senator, you're not opposed to defense spending in general, are you?'

'Hardly, Allyn,' said the Senator, chuckling merrily. His silver hairpiece sat maybe a half-inch too low on his forehead. 'I just don't like to see our defense money spent on toys. Air power won't cut it in the real world. The American people would get twice the bang for their buck if we took half those dollars and bought Cruise missiles.'

Allyn Pollack knew as much about military aviation as I knew about moon rocks, but his crew sure knew how to make Senator Bixby look good. The camera, low and pointed up, made the short senator Zeus-like. The red stripes of an American flag were visible just over his shoulder for subliminal patriotism.

'Problem is,' Bixby mugged, 'this administration likes to fund programs that don't work, don't pay, and don't hunt. That's why we need to shoot . . .' He chuckled at his fake slip of the tongue. 'I should say, *shut* this Joint Strike Fighter program down before the Pentagon hands the American people a trillion-dollar invoice.'

Pollack grimaced.

'Colonel Virgil Seldon . . . you sit on the Joint Strike Fighter committee at the Pentagon.'

Zoom into a second box, a second talking head. In sharp contrast to Bixby, this one was framed much less kindly. Pollack's crew had obviously scoured the Pentagon to find the most non-telegenic officer attached to the JSF project. This Air Force colonel displayed a five o'clock shadow, and eyes that

124

blinked compulsively in the white-hot video lights. The *24/7* camera was raised to where it could point downward at the colonel, sitting stiffly at a cheap desk in his government work cubicle, making him look like a bureaucratic beetle.

'Colonel,' Pollack oozed, 'is it not true that your program, five years from its inception, has been bedeviled by committee decision-making, delays, compromises, and quality concerns?'

The colonel could have replied that those stages of development applied to any new product from soft drinks to strike fighters, but I saw that he had also been picked by the *24/7* producer for having grown a cement block between his ears. He replied like he was reading a press release. 'The Joint Strike Fighter program is on schedule, on budget, and we are ready to look at prototypes in three—'

Pollack interrupted him. 'One defense contractor who'd like to win those JSF dollars is Ted Devlin of Linnet/TVR,' he said with a raised eyebrow.

And now Teflon Ted was on camera, although he hadn't let himself get caught with a nasty Pollack camera angle. Ted stood in a non-restricted area of his well-lit factory floor. He looked like he had just rolled his eye in disbelief.

Pollack frowned sadly. 'Mr Devlin, isn't forty million dollars an awfully high price for an aircraft?'

'Not really, Allyn,' Ted shot back with his good eye blazing. 'That's five million less than any one of your network's five Gulfstreams.'

Pollack got caught letting his skeptical eyebrow drop in surprise.

As Ted flashed his 'gotcha' smile, I groaned inadvertently. Ted was headed for egoruptcy. He probably figured he was bulletproof after building the LUCI plane, but how stupid could he get? Nobody could call Allyn Pollack on his bullshit. Like most media gasbags, Pollack had thin skin and answered to nobody but the ratings books. For a cheap thrill, Teflon Ted had just slipped a mongoose inside his shorts.

Unprepared, Pollack quickly switched over to his next segment. 'From Congressional concern about the Joint Strike Fighter program, we go to another matter before Congress: Should the role of the CIA in foreign policy be expanded? Correspondent Randy Fisher is with us on the Capitol Rotunda. Randy, what's this about?'

I watched with a flicker of interest as a grizzled, neatly bearded veteran of actual news stood on the Capitol steps.

'Today, in the so-called bug-free "white room" where the Federal Intelligence Oversight Committee sits,' the reporter said, 'members of that committee are deciding the future of the CIA's Directorate of Operations. In years past, the CIA helped topple the Soviet Union. Now, with bills before Congress to cut the CIA's budget, the Agency is lobbying for a bigger role in our national defense policy. With us is Douglas G. Palmer, Director of Operations.'

Doug Palmer ran the CIA's spook operations. He was a square-faced executive in his early forties who had gone to prep school at Exeter. Even standing on the Capitol steps, the guy looked like he was sailing into the wind in a sloop off Nantucket. His sandy hair fluttered in his face. His Harvard tie flapped. His eyes crinkled in the easy smile of a man who had never sweated out a financial worry.

'Randy, the American taxpayer only gets the quality of intelligence we pay for,' Palmer said in his clipped Fairfield County, Connecticut, accent. 'My brother, the Secretary of State, and I have told Congress what the CIA can do so we *don't* have to send American troops to every trouble spot on the globe from Haiti to Somalia . . .'

I switched it off. I knew all about Doug Palmer. He was an empire-builder who wanted to return to the salad days of the CIA.

His strategy for making the CIA a tool of foreign policy wasn't new. It's been a trap for American presidents ever since Eisenhower, the hero of D-Day, let himself get sucked in just after the Korean War in 1950 when America unexpectedly got its butt kicked. Eisenhower worried that if we sent American boys into any more Koreas they would come home in body bags. So he listened to Secretary of State John Foster Dulles and his brother Allen Dulles, who ran the CIA. I can almost close my eyes and visualize the Dulles boys leaning over a coffee table in the Oval Office, knocking over a line of dominoes stacked end to end and explaining to Ike how the Communists would, country by country, take over the world through their influence in Asia, Europe and Latin America.

The solution, of course, was to let the CIA

conduct covert operations around the world to topple leaders who might be pro-Communist. We could overthrow anybody we didn't like without ever having to commit US forces. That was how the CIA began a twenty-year campaign of meddling in the internal affairs of countries like Iran and Guatemala, the Congo and Chile. When the people of those countries figured out what had happened, that was when our former friends around the world started hating the US, and most of America's current foreign policy troubles began.

If Palmer and his brother got their way, it would be *déjà vu* all over again.

Personally, I believed that if the CIA leadership really wanted to do some good, they should focus on the thirty-three 'friendly' countries that, as a matter of policy, targeted the United States for industrial espionage.

But the CIA definitely wasn't my problem now. My immediate problem was more short-term, like getting through the next twelve hours without screwing up.

I sped up my treadmill and panted for a few extra miles. As soon as a few endorphins began popping into my brain, I went back to the living room. A neat stack of decoded pages sat in the printer. The first sheet began with Ted Devlin's dossier.

For discipline's sake, I decided not to race ahead to Maria's. I would review Ted's dossier first.

Edward 'Ted' Devlin was born in Seattle fifty-three years ago. His father worked as an engineer at Boeing.

Little Ted was raised to be competitive. In sixth grade, he joined the wrestling team and won a match by sticking his hands and knees to the mat with one-drop industrial-strength glue so his opponent couldn't throw him.

He went to the University of Washington at Seattle, studying business and engineering. In 1968, Ted's friends said he used his first vote in a US Presidential election on Richard Nixon because Tricky Dicky was his hero.

Ted joined the Air Force and was sent to Air Training Command. I noted that he wanted to be a fighter pilot, but didn't get chosen. Instead, he got to fly B-52 bombers, informally called 'Buffs' – for 'Big Ugly Fat Fuckers' – on bombing sorties defoliating jungle. They called themselves 'Coconut Knockers'. On his last mission, the North Vietnamese gunners hit his Buff, tearing up part of the cockpit, and Ted caught flak that tore out his eye. I felt a sour upheaval in my stomach, reading his co-pilot's account of how he banged around the plane like a madman. Ted took his Purple Heart and did his R&R in Japan where he couldn't wait to get well enough to pay his courtesy calls to various Shinjuku nightclubs and brothels.

He returned to Seattle, but went on a date with a woman of the radical left who set him up in a biker bar. A bunch of guys called him a baby-killer, then beat him up and left him in a pool of blood, beer and urine.

Ted cleaned himself up and went to work for Boeing, where he got on the fast track on military projects. They were lobbying heavily on Washington then to win more government contracts from the Nixon administration.

Ironically, Ted's hero Nixon betrayed him, pulling all military projects out of Boeing because the State of Washington had a Democratic senator who Nixon had placed on his famous enemies' list. This took Ted off the fast track at Boeing.

But I saw why they called him 'Teflon Ted'. He immediately found a better job for more money at Gunner-Knudsen Aircraft in Nixon's favorite state, California, so they probably got all the military projects that should have gone to Boeing.

Ted was involved with a messy bribery scandal several years back. A member of a European royal family took kickbacks to help Gunner-Knudsen sell fighters to his government, and lost his crown.

I'd say that was the point when Ted Devlin, a reasonably okay guy, became Teflon Ted, corporate weasel. He managed to wriggle out of the scandal and into a great job at Lycanthrop Corporation, starting at a fifty per cent salary increase. There he worked with a top-rated group that won the contract for a navy fighter called the Shrike, and managed to dodge a Pentagon cost-overrun scandal that seemed to have his pawprints all over it.

Ted wanted to be known in the industry press as a pioneer like Ben Rich of the famously funky Skunkworks at Lockheed. Rich developed the stealthy F-117 Nighthawk. Let's just say that Ted Devlin's Darkwing was a lot like Ben Rich's Nighthawk, if not precisely a carbon copy.

'Teflon Ted is slicker than owl shit,' a former colleague told the Wringer interviewer. 'Just watch your back around him, or he'll steal your work.'

So Ted was a thief. But not like me. Just as I knew that fighter pilot was a higher calling than bomber pilot, I felt a superiority to Ted's stealing. I was a thief driven by adventure and fair play. He stole other people's ideas and claimed them as his own. Maybe you don't see the subtle tones of gray between us, but I guess we all tend to draw the line just below what we do ourselves.

I saw that, for recreation, Ted liked drinking and gambling. He still knocked back tumblers full of bourbon just like during his frat-house days. He was also a compulsive gambler. His best habit, I'd say, was that he apparently never welshed on a bet as a matter of honor.

Ted seemed to be the fun-loving kind of Neanderthal CEO that you don't see around much any more. He hung out at a private men's retreat called the Bison Club in LA, where he and other midlife hounds got together to roar about the old days. Some evenings they would send out for female strippers, who arrived dressed as LAPD officers and playfully beat Ted and his pals with Styrofoam nightsticks, or whatever.

Socially, Ted qualified as a one-man Seventies Preservation Society.

He didn't get married until he was forty-two. Then he wed a twenty-one-year-old, dark-haired trophy named Zima, like the wine cooler. Zima divorced Ted two years into their marriage, after he went to the trouble of getting a penile implant. She ran off with his interior decorator, who he thought was gay.

I checked the terms of Linnet/TVR's employee contract with Ted. The Wringer had obviously broken into his lawyer's office. The deal was Draconian – Linnet/TVR could and would fire Ted the day he lost the JSF project. I shook my head at the do-or-die contract. Never mind a golden parachute, they were practically tying a safe to his neck. On the upside, he had stock options. He had already exercised all of them, and gone beyond to buy stock in the company. He had accumulated a lot of Linnet/TVR stock.

My eyes bugged out when I saw what else he'd been acquiring.

In the past six months, Ted had gone into debt for over $3 million on a new house, $752,000 for a boat, and $329,000 for a car, a Bentley Continental SC.

I looked at my watch, 8.30 p.m. I would check all that out when I went to his party in a half-hour.

The Wringer highlighted all the possible dates that he and Maria could have possibly met. There was a credit card receipt for a restaurant in Long Beach, on the date of their infamous lunch together, but no other record of contact between them. This didn't help my theory that Ted and Maria were involved, but didn't trash it either.

I thought about the two of them together. An odd couple.

She would have a problem with his ego and

132

bullying. But there were only so many people out there, myself included, who got all pumped about fighter planes. And, sexually, women could be funny. Who knew what dark desires a *Playboy* 'Girl of Mensa' might harbor.

I turned to the Maria Haymeyer dossier.

I read her profile very carefully, making margin notes. I didn't know exactly what I was looking for yet. At some point, I expected to connect the dots and see a pattern that I hoped would lead me to my money.

Maria was twenty-seven. She had an apartment in Los Altos, California, paid for by her $80,000 salary at Intech. She hadn't been home for two weeks, and they couldn't trace her after Saturday. Wherever she might be, she was paying by cash and using prepaid telephone cards. She had recently quit her job at Intech, which I suppose she didn't need after she had my sixteen million. On the positive side, I didn't see any record of her checking into any thousand-dollar hotel suite squandering my cash.

Deep background: Maria grew up in Washington, DC. Her birth certificate listed her mother as Jessica Zubi-Rodriguez, the stunning woman I had seen in the photo. Jessica was Cuban-American from a middle-class family in Miami. Maria's birth father was listed as Peter Rodriguez, who seemed to have disappeared shortly after Maria's birth.

As I suspected, her mother Jessica had a career on camera. She became a news reporter at a local Washington station and married Lloyd Haymeyer, a young Assistant Professor of Popular Culture at a second-tier university in Maryland. Lloyd and Jessica divorced when Maria was ten.

When Maria was in second grade, she started beating Lloyd at chess and her parents sent her to an educational psychologist.

Her IQ score was recorded twice. Apparently they made her repeat the Stanford-Binet Intelligence Test, because the first time they didn't believe her score. The level on that test for 'genius' starts at 130. Maria blew the chart at over 250.

Her mother wanted to send Maria to a school for gifted kids. But her stepfather Lloyd wanted to keep her in public school. It didn't take much reading between the lines to see that Lloyd was jealous of Maria's intelligence. Like Salieri resented Mozart, but Salieri wasn't Mozart's stepfather.

So her mother paid for Maria's private school.

While her friends were busy playing Paula Abdul albums and having pillow fights, Maria once had a long telephone conversation with the physicist Stephen Hawking. She won first prize in the Blair Sciences Talent Search. Her stepfather wasn't thrilled about that either. I picked up Lloyd's picture again, snorting at his weak mouth.

Despite her gifts, Maria was not a particularly screwed-up kid. At least that's what her friends and teachers said. No drinking, no drugs. She didn't get out much. She had an African gray parrot. She built her own computer at home when she was fifteen.

Then Maria was out sick for a week in tenth grade and flunked a couple of exams for the first time when she got back.

'What happened?' I asked aloud. When she came back to school, she suddenly threw herself into building a supercomputer to design games. Aviation games.

Shortly after, she began taking flying lessons. I made a note that her mother signed for a loan for her to learn to fly an aerobatics plane.

'She really loved it,' an old aerobatics instructor of hers told the Wringer. 'She even scared the shit out of me.'

Well, I rubbed my chin, he and I had something in common.

They graduated her as class valedictorian. Her class voted her 'Most likely to set the world on fire'. Her yearbook quote was 'I want to design a game that will blow people away.'

She must have loved flying, because I didn't see any other thrills in her life. She attracted all kinds of boys and men. Computer nerds. Jocks. Latin playboys. But she apparently ignored guys. Not that she seemed to be attracted to women either. All she really wanted to do was fool around with computers and airplanes.

'I think Maria had her first boyfriend in college,' a friend told the Wringer. I wondered who.

At Stanford, she earned her BS in electrical engineering, her MS in aeronautics and astronautics, then started her PhD in electrical engineering, which meant computers. She dropped out after she claimed her PhD thesis was stolen. Her professors said she was a brilliant student who chose to work alone, using a computer she'd built herself. She was admired. Her courses, boring and technical, would seem to lead to the doctoral thesis she told me about.

Ah, the boyfriend.

Another PhD student, a guy named Jonathan, said Maria had told him that her doctoral thesis was a program for a fighter game. I read carefully. He was a game designer too, and they talked. He remembered talking to her about artificial intelligence.

Jonathan, probable pencil-neck, told the Wringer interviewer how Maria posed for the *Playboy* photo essay on 'The Girls of Mensa' at Stanford. I made a note to get that back copy for a full-color shot.

There was a police report documenting a robbery at her apartment. The officers said she was very upset. Somebody had stolen not only the original disks with her thesis on it, but her back-up disks, too. The police speculated that somebody trashed the apartment to make it look like a real burglary.

She was hired at Intech to write code for a 'Star Fighter' computer game program. From her salary, she had saved about $11,000. She had withdrawn that entire sum a month before.

The Wringer had the record of her meeting with Ted. She stayed overnight at the Hyatt in Long Beach. There was no evidence that Ted stayed over with her, but none that he didn't, either. Her telephone records showed that she called Linnet/TVR maybe twenty times over the next month. Very short calls. Like being blown off by a secretary.

Looking for spy contacts, I probed for meetings with foreign nationals or suspicious students at Stanford. Nothing.

Her only trip out of the USA was the round trip to Switzerland. That would have been her trip to steal my nest egg. No other foreign travel. I also saw her trip home to Washington, DC, and the lawyer Richard Gershon's office.

Maria had lived a hothouse life, mostly indoors. And the Wringer couldn't even find a diary.

In terms of recovering my money, her dossier was starting to look like a $50,000 dry hole. But it also matched what she'd told me. I felt bitter sadness, but not for me now. For her. There was an innocence and purity in the fabric of this person. A kind of music to her life, before Ted ruined it. And she was a pilot. She'd felt the rapture.

I sat up in my chair. What the hell was I doing, sympathizing with this woman?

I slogged again through her credit cards and checking account records, looking for anything I might have missed. She bought a trunkful of electronics eighteen months ago, which would probably be for the computer she built to 'Locate Fragata' and find me.

I chuckled bitterly to see that she donated to animal rights groups like PETA. Do people who love animals really like other people? I don't know. I saw that she took a lot of trouble to buy health foods for her parrot from a pet boutique in Los Altos.

I finally even found a charge record for the Gaultier dress she wore to my apartment. She bought it at Saks.

I frowned at her psychiatric history. She'd had

137

sessions with a psychiatrist in Palo Alto and the doctor prescribed Prozac. The Wringer had broken into the psychiatrist's office, but could barely read his notes except to see that she talked about Ted. The therapist also wrote something about a long-term adjustment problem having to do with her father, obviously meaning Lloyd. It wasn't sexual abuse, but the doctor wrote 'BETRAYAL' in capital letters, then underlined it. When a shrink does that, it must be significant.

I was thinking about what I didn't see – any evidence at all of what she did with my money. I had ruled out everybody in her life as a confederate. Nobody fitted. She had traveled to Switzerland and back alone.

She left her apartment so clean, not even the Wringer people could find anything revealing. Even her parrot had vanished with her.

I rubbed my temples and sinuses, which had begun throbbing. I knew I was missing something important. Why? Maybe situational awareness peaks like sexual potency. Whatever. I would be late for Ted's party.

I got up, leaving several pages in the hopper. I hoped they would contain the one jewel that would justify the $50,000 I'd spent. First I would take a shower and dress for the party, then start the new pages with a clearer head.

I thought about Maria's life as the hot water pounded my aching shoulders and unknotted my neck. A sudden burning desire to build a super-computer and design flying games. What had happened to her the week she was home sick from school in tenth grade? Was she having an epiphany or just watching *All My Children*?

I put on another black suit and a new shirt.

From a small black jewelry box, I carefully took a stack of six shiny new dimes and carefully placed them in the side pocket of my suit jacket.

Slipping on loafers, so I wouldn't have to take another three seconds away from Maria's dossier to tie shoelaces, I hustled back to the living room and grabbed the rest of the pages out of my printer.

I swung my legs up to read. I'd just scan now, then look harder after Ted's party. I needed to get very close to Ted tonight, that was Job One.

But something was wrong with the printout.

I arrived at the end of Maria's dossier. What were these additional pages?

I stared, dumb as a doorknob, as the next unnumbered page turned up.

At the top was a notation: 'Confidential Dossier'. A third dossier. A third subject?

I went to the next page.

'Subject: Terry Weston.'

My heart banged against my ribs. Somebody had used my Curaçao bank account to buy a third dossier from the Wringer.

My cheeks turned red. The Wringer had probably poked each other in the ribs and laughed about how somebody had got me. I read the note the Wringer had highlighted as a 'Confidential Client Memo'.

139

Dear T,

Since you pulled one of these on me, I didn't think you'd mind if I got one on you. Here's a copy. All my best,
M.

P.S. I deducted the $50K from your Curaçao account.

My chest filled with acid and adrenaline. My ears rang from the swelling blood vessels in my brain.

I didn't scream or anything, but I did kick my desk twice, stubbing my toe.

I shoved the Wringer's dossier on Terry Weston in a drawer, locked it, and, limping slightly, headed out the door to go to Ted's party.

EIGHT

If you're ever invited to play Crud, just say no.

This was never meant to be a party game. It began in a remote desert Air Force base with young fighter pilots making up the rules, as a drunken brawl thinly disguised as a pool game. But you didn't need cues, just a lot of balls.

I sipped my drink in Ted Devlin's playroom and listened while a puffy middle-aged executive of Linnet/TVR, who was a fighter pilot at O'Brien Air Force Base maybe ten years before my tour, tried to explain the game to Ted's girlfriend. She was a trim brunette named Donna, about half Ted's age, with a West Texas accent.

'The way we used to play,' the ex-pilot was telling Donna, leaning over her cleavage, 'we'd choose up two teams, or "squadrons". Each squadron, they'd take their side of the table. The team that's "up" picks up the cue ball from their side of the table and tries to run to the other side.'

'What was stoppin' them?' Donna was a little slow on the uptake.

'The other squadron.' He sloshed his drink on the décolletage of Donna's tight cocktail dress on purpose, it seemed. Then he made a move to wipe it off, which she sidestepped.

'That's a *pool* game?' Donna's brown eyes bulged

with lots of youthful white around the pupils, like bull's eyes. 'It doesn't make any sense.'

'It's not supposed to. Hell, the only point's to whup some ass.' The ex-pilot chuckled, his belly jiggling.

'Isn't Ted playing?' Donna asked.

'Ted?' The middle-aged guy glanced at Ted Devlin sipping his drink and watching the crowd around the pool table. 'Ted usually lets Mac Skinner stand in for him these days.'

I'd never been to a civilian party where Crud was played before. I hadn't even thought about the game except when ten-year-old injuries flared up in damp weather, reminding me of the ratty bar we young pilots used to frequent at O'Brien AFB. The other pilots and I roiled drunkenly around on the sawdust floor in pure war-whooping Air Force pilot competitiveness, to impress women with tattoos and herpes sores. I only played a few times, but managed to sprout knobs on my head the size of Snow Cones.

Tonight at Ted's party, Crud nostalgia ruled. After taking a break to visit the master bedroom and bath of Ted's brand-new house, where I deposited a couple of my lint particles, I had joined the party guests in Ted's study.

They were actually playing a tamer civilian game you could call 'Crud Lite'.

It seemed harmless enough, nobody getting too badly hurt, so I joined in. Half of the people playing were actually trim and fit – the female half. They were young Orange County women who resembled aerobics instructors, and could probably touch their toes to their bouncy short haircuts. These women were dating or married to the men who Ted had invited to this party – lumpy defense executives in their forties or fifties. It looked as though Ted didn't invite fit, younger guys to his house parties except for his protégé Mac Skinner and me.

I tried to get a handle on Mac Skinner. Obviously they had a mentor/protégé relationship. Mac was physically what Ted probably thought he himself looked like when he was younger – that all-American beefcake look that thrilled the kind of woman who aspired to become a Dallas Cowgirl cheerleader. I just wondered how much Ted Devlin's protégé really knew about his mentor's business, like how the LUCI chip happened to float into the Ghostworks.

But why speculate when you'll have the facts soon? My Wringer profile on Mac was due in about twelve hours.

Mac glared at me with his dark falcon's eyes, darting from his rock slab of a face. He wore a tight-fitting sweater tonight, and when I came too close to him, I caught the muscles and even a subtle whiff of the gymnasium that you usually don't pick up from executives.

I didn't need my keen situational awareness to notice, through our Crud Lite game, that Mac seemed to take a special interest in trying to wallop me. His arms were hard as rebars but thicker.

Mac didn't like seeing me here. I suspected it had something to do with Ted's earlier demonstration of my virtual wonder SymBad for his guests. As soon as I arrived, Ted had let his male guests put on the virtual sunglasses and SymBad kicked her legs around with a sultry snarl. Ted's guests all cackled and whooped like a party at Hooters. A few computer types from the Linnet/TVR Ghostworks squinted over their glasses. They were trying to figure out exactly how SymBad worked without breaching party etiquette by stealing her back to their lab to reverse-engineer her.

When Ted actually gave my arm a manly squeeze, I caught a glimpse of Mac glowering at me. I got the strong impression he wanted to be Ted's only child.

Now Ted's date, that fresh-faced brunette named Donna, was screeching that her 'squadron' was up at Crud. She squeezed into a clutch of men including Mac Skinner, who looked happy to protect Donna's body.

Donna was one of those high-energy girls. She stamped her feet up and down, threw her arms up over her head, shook her braless torso and yelled like a high-school cheerleader. The men cheered with her.

When the pool ball came back her way, it was Donna's turn to grab it, make a run for the other side of the table and score. She put her head down and her team of male aerospace executives, torn shirttails already hanging out from the last round, formed a tight glove-like phalanx around her body.

I was on the defense team. I braced myself. I saw Mac Skinner keeping his eye on me again. This time, I would like to accidentally send him flying through the big bay window of the den if he didn't break my jaw first. I had already ripped one sleeve of my suit jacket during Mac's last assault.

I hunched over. The caveman part of my brain tried to expand my muscles to look bigger.

The more advanced part of my brain considered Ted, who stood back in his silky Italian shirt watching all of us. He raised his right hand to scratch his forehead. I noted a contrast between his pulled-back face that plastic surgery had made younger and his hand, prematurely wrinkled. Not exactly a twisted claw, but it did betray his age.

I had carefully braced myself to meet Ted, since it's disconcerting to meet somebody with a glass eye. His one good eye was clearer and brighter than I would have imagined in anybody who drank like he did. It was a cool, light blue, not quite matched by the shinier plastic blue of his artificial eye, but close.

Ted exuded that energy field of successful people. When I reached to take his hand for the first time, he made sure to bring it down hard to grab mine first. *Feel the power, buddy.*

Now, standing off from the Crud game, he looked as though he would like to be in the scrum gouging eyes. Still, there was something careful about Ted. He wanted to play but he didn't want to get hurt.

I tried to imagine Ted and Maria together.

Sitting across from each other at the restaurant, holding hands, looking into each other's eyes. Then Maria pushing her glasses up on her nose and saying, 'I want to show you the model I've spent years developing.'

'Terree!' Ted's girlfriend and current Crud Lite queen Donna screamed, interrupting my reverie.

Now the Crud stampede came my way, Mac on point with the cue ball. He was angled to ram me with his shoulder and elbow, protecting the Crud ball in his other hand. The last time we collided, I felt like I'd walked into a bus.

I didn't want to occupy the same space as Mac again. So, as he leaned into me with his shoulder, I dropped down on my hands and knees. My shoulder caught his leg and he fell forward over me.

Now his Air Force training dictated that since he was too far gone to somersault, he would fall like a paratrooper with both arms curled to minimize damage. He did, and let go of the Crud ball before hitting the floor.

Then I felt a tug on my good sleeve. 'Let's go outside a minute,' Ted invited me, taking a swig of his drink.

I followed him, carefully slipping a dime into a light fixture. I had just left another one under his telephone receiver. My last glimpse at the study was of Donna holding her two fingers pointed out from her temples, her head lowered in an imitation of El Toro in a bullring. Mac, recovered, gallantly beat a path for her, knocking an overweight VP from a defense software company sprawling on the floor with a crunch. I knew he really meant that one for me.

Ted and I left the Crud Lite carnage behind, strolling through his new house. It was decorated in a style I would call Recently Divorced Guy, a mismatched collection of dark wood and chunky leather seating about as soulful as an airport lounge.

'So when did you move in?'

'Last week. I wanted a victory house.'

He held the front door open for me. The truth was, I had admired this little-known neighborhood for years. It was a section of Long Beach called Naples which few people knew about.

Ted had built a new house in the middle of a storybook lane named Corso di Napoli. There was no street, no cars, just a pedestrian footwalk on a crescent-shaped, deep blue bay. The moon lounged overhead, making the water glitter.

All the houses on Corso di Napoli oozed quiet good taste, three or four storeys high and close together like a friendly town. Some were Aegean white slabs, others looked like San Francisco Victorians – 'painted ladies' in blues and yellows, decorated with cozy balconies and widows' walks. They were all so robustly landscaped, the flora practically glowed in the dark. Except for Ted's place.

He had built a deep grey stucco fortress with black Lucite windows. The dark and malevolent face of Ted's house in this fairytale path reminded me of finding Darth Vader in line at a debutante ball.

'I bulldozed the piece of shit that was here and built over it,' Ted confided in me. 'What do you think of it?'

'Reminds me of your Darkwing, Ted. Same friendly face.'

Ted laughed and gripped my arm like a hall proctor. 'Come on back to the garage.'

He led the way. The space between his house and the one next to it was tight, so Ted trampled uncaring over his neighbor's flower bushes. He pointed to the car parked in his driveway, a brand-new $329,000 Bentley Continental SC Coupé, all sculpted curves and hand-stitched leather, with a glass-paneled removable roof.

'Nice big-block engine, but this baby's just a workout for a guy like you,' he shrugged. 'C'mere.'

He steered me back to step over his neighbor's shrubs again and we stood in front of his new manse.

Each of the homes on Corso di Napoli came with its own dock across the footpath, where a long row of sailboats – uniformly white Morgans and Hunters with trim blue sails – bobbed sedately around the crescent. He pointed at his slip.

'Check her out,' Ted said.

The $750,000 boat I'd already read about in the Wringer's report looked like the only powerboat along the Corso di Napoli. It was a gleaming white express cruiser with red pinstripes, the same deep-V hull style as a sleek Italian speedboat but about three times the length and fatter.

I wasn't surprised that the name *LUCI* appeared in glossy letters across the stern.

'Like her?' he asked me.

What a need for approval this guy had. Because his big cruiser looked like an oversized speedboat, I actually thought Ted would look like a midget in the driver's seat, which was probably the opposite of the image he had in mind. Still, I wasn't there to criticize

Ted but to praise him. To a degree. Then I'd start with my four Gs of industrial espionage.

'Awesome.' I nodded. 'So who's LUCI?'

He ignored my question. 'You know, I was thinking I could use one of those NSX twin turbos you pulled up in. That's the Japanese version, right?'

'Sure is.'

'I hear it feels like lighting the 'burner on a fighter.'

'I think that's what the brochure said, but I don't read Japanese that well. Want to go for a spin?'

'Maybe.' Ted swayed gently but he could hold his liquor and I saw that he was busy reading my face. 'That SymBad you left for me. That was your calling card, right?'

'I'd say she had Ted Devlin written all over her.'

'So you want to talk with me, talk.' He took a swig of his drink. 'I already checked you out.'

'Oh?'

'I called some old Air Force buddies today. You got a reputation as a stand-up guy.'

'I'm just happy I'm still standing.'

He had a cunning smile. 'So you want to do business with our commercial division?'

'Sure. I think you ought to build up that division. I hear you're not seriously in the finals for the JSF. If you lose that . . .'

'Lose the JSF?' He turned red and looked at me as though I'd slapped his face with a glove.

'Well, I think you ought to consider it. You have to protect your downside. All due respect, Ted, but

149

the odds-makers on Wall Street are saying it's going to be Lockheed or Boeing.'

'Who'd you hear that from?' Ted grinned with effort.

'I heard it from a guy on the Linnet/TVR board,' I said. 'Maybe your parent company doesn't understand you.'

His grin held steady while his eyes narrowed in irritation. 'The Linnet/TVR board? They're just money guys. They wouldn't know a fucking afterburner from a cigarette lighter. Terry, you wouldn't believe the briefing I gave the Pentagon today.'

'What did you tell them?'

He waved his hand. 'Don't ask. It's going to be in the Black world. What do you already know about the plane?'

'Just what Allyn Pollack put on his *24/7* website.'

He raised his eyebrows.

'Allyn Pollack was disinformed,' Ted cackled. He probably thought it was too late for Pollack to do him any harm. Knowledge was power for Ted. For me too, but I would wait until I could open my Swiss bankbook and see sixteen million dollars again. Then I'd laugh plenty.

He squinted at me. 'You had a Special Access clearance in the Air Force, right?'

'Sure. Same as any other Darkwing pilot.'

Ted reached over and squeezed my shoulder again, then kept his hand tight on my muscle so it hurt a little. He looked into my eyes and didn't blink.

'I'm so far ahead of the Pentagon on this design,

Terry, it hurts. Tell me something, Terry. We off the record?'

I stared. 'You're not talking to Pollack now, Ted.'

'What would Wall Street think if I made a fighter totally invisible?'

I made my face fog over as though I didn't get it. 'Invisible? You mean like the Emperor's New Clothes?'

Ted breathed bourbon at me. 'No. This plane is for real. A functionally invisible fighter. Swoop down undetected, take out your enemy with zero collateral damage, and fly away home.'

I worked to look bemused. 'Well, if you had a prototype like that, you could do a great demo through Washington. Take out the Office of Management and Budget.'

'No joke.' His eyes sobered and narrowed. 'LUCI's the smartest aircraft on earth.'

'Ted,' I asked slowly, 'where'd you get the technology for a plane like that?'

He smiled, and the pebbly skin around his eyes crinkled with pride. 'Pure artificial intelligence. I broke clean through the envelope, Terry. All by myself.'

'Usually that kind of success has many fathers. And mothers,' I said casually. 'Maybe other people think they developed parts of it. No offense, but Wall Street likes managers who spread a little credit around to keep people happy.'

Ted looked at me like I was some touchy-feely type trying to hang New Age crystals around his neck.

'Are you serious?' he asked me. 'This is the biggest breakthrough since the Wright brothers. I wouldn't share this project with God.'

I heard a noise in my head – probably the buzzer ending Round One of my negotiations to get Ted and Maria together. Now I had to go back into Linnet/TVR myself.

'So you can't see this plane,' I said.

'That's not even the best part. This fighter's fully interactive with the pilot, gets to know his skill level and corrects his mistakes. You flew Darkwings? You could fly LUCI after three sessions on the box.'

'Three hours on a simulator?' I laughed out loud.

His forehead creased.

'You got me going.' I smoothed my tie. 'We're twenty years away from a plane like that.'

'Try two hours. It's sitting in a hangar on our desert test facility.'

'Show me.'

He shook his head violently. 'No way. You can't even see the sim.'

I yanked my alligator wallet from my suit pocket and pulled out the State of California vehicle title for my NSX. I held it up in front of his face. 'Match it. My car against yours. Show me the plane.'

Ted had been outside when I parked. I saw he really loved my NSX. But what he loved even more was the concept of taking it away from me on a bet. Gonads and Greed pumping like mad, because he thought he knew something I didn't.

Better odds to Ted than Liar's Poker, because he thought he knew the truth and I didn't.

152

He was practically grabbing one hand with the other so he couldn't touch my car title. He wanted to fly me to Lake Limerick in the California desert where Linnet/TVR secretly tested its new designs. He ached to show me LUCI, and roar off cackling into the sunset in my gorgeous car.

But, of course, he couldn't. He just stood there clutching his drink, his wheels grinding.

'So, Terry, you ever play Spank?' he finally asked.

'Not since the old days.'

'I'll give you a new set of rules,' Ted said slowly. 'We play with business equipment.

Well, at least it wasn't golf. 'Sure. But only if you let me on the box if I win.'

My demand to test out his top-secret LUCI flight simulator made him spill his drink on his chin. He chugged it and threw the plastic cup in his neighbor's flower pot. 'Get real. Why should I?'

''Cause you're Teflon Ted.'

His laughter exploded across the whole bay. 'No fucking way. You're not a test pilot and you're not cleared for a Black program. Your old Darkwing clearance won't cut it.'

'I can handle Special Access. And I can learn any fighter in a few hours.'

'Nah,' he backpedaled.

I egged him on. 'How about Friday, we meet for Spank and winner takes all. If I lose, you take title to the NSX and SymBad. If I win, you give me access to your sim.'

His mouth started to form the 'N' to say 'no way' again, then it smoothed out.

'You're covered.' He grabbed my hand.

I felt the raw power in Ted again through his handshake. I expected he would fight dirty. But the Wringer report concluded that he delivered on his bets. That was what Maria called a 'marker' – a consistent trait in a man's life. It was how a guy like Ted could face the man in the mirror to shave. If I won our bet on Friday, I was pretty sure he would perform as agreed on Monday.

'Okay,' I told him. 'High noon, use one two two point nine. By the way, who runs your JSF program?'

'I do. Mac Skinner, your Crud pal? He's project manager. Handles all the housekeeping.'

That would mean Mac did all the real work. I waited until we were back in Ted's house to look him carefully in the eye.

If he really made good on his bet, I could get on the LUCI sim. Then I might squeeze out some evidence of his theft.

'Great party, Ted.' I slapped him on the back, slipping a dime into the side pocket of his suit.

That was, I counted, the sixth dime I'd left around Ted's home. I'd dropped them in his study, living room, bathroom, Bentley SC, and now his suit. The folks in Hong Kong who designed and built my dimes had pretty much written the book on miniaturization.

I drove my car to a grassy area with large trees within visual range of his house and pulled over. I took out my small recorder with voice-recognition software to pick up Ted's voice. Looking both ways,

I stepped out of the car to walk to a large nearby tree, tugging down my zipper as though I was ready to water it. Sometimes it takes looking guilty of a social no-no, the kind that makes decent folks look away in disgust, to get away with something more important.

Instead of relieving myself on this fine, bushy tree, I leaned and used one hand to hide the hamburger-bun-sized satellite dish receiver on a branch and duct-taped it down. I could, of course, wind up recording a load of irrelevant material, but that's why redundancy comes in handy in spy systems. Some work, some don't.

I heard an engine racing and saw headlights on high beams. Light filled the tree around me as I moved my hand to pull up my zipper. The lights went past.

It was a white van with a satellite dish on top, and the blue logo for *24/7* on its side.

A news crew was on its way to spy on Ted, too. So Allyn Pollack had declared a journalistic jihad on Devlin.

This was actually the least of my problems. With his Spank challenge, Ted had lowered the odds that I would survive Maria's game.

Before dawn, I sat in my living room staring at my desk drawer. It was still closed.

Maybe I'm the only person on earth who would put off looking at a dossier on himself. I mean, could you avoid reading a report of what the Wringer said about you?

But I did my work first.

I was up until 4.30 a.m. working with the unedited footage my peanut cams shot inside Linnet/TVR. I used an Avid film-editing program to put together a video with the high points to show Maria, just as we had agreed on Monday.

I had more stalls than a racetrack, but finally ran out. I had to sit down and read the Wringer report.

I'd never wanted them to pull a report on me before. I told myself that the risks of calling attention to Terry Weston as a Wringer subject outweighed the benefits of knowing what people were saying about me. I figured out that by scanning other files from less crafty sources, which I did regularly, I could get about eighty per cent of the good stuff.

But when I started to read their meticulous research, condensing my life into data-packed sentences of no more than ten words each, in pithy Wringer style, I realized that I hated looking back at my childhood.

I was an only child born in California on a date rich in military history – 25 June, the anniversary of Custer's Last Stand, when elements of the US Army cavalry were massacred by Native Americans peeved at being shoved off their lands. I glanced at my nomadic school career. One school at a US Air Force base in Italy. One in England. One in Germany. I noted that my IQ score was 138.

It was, I considered bleakly, roughly half Maria's IQ score. And the way she outsmarted me at every turn, I couldn't say that my extra life experience counted for much.

I got to my parents.

On my desk in my New York apartment I kept a fading color photo of Mom and Dad sitting in his 1960 Corvette convertible, both turned around smiling at the camera. Dad was grinning. His square, handsome fighter jock's face was hidden behind aviator glasses. Mom was a glamorous northern Italian brunette with superb cheekbones and gleaming white teeth. Her eyes were concealed behind sunglasses, too. And that was a good thing. Their real life wasn't photogenic.

I was eight years old again. Standing in a flat California desert, clutching a wire fence. On the steaming tarmac, my father climbed into his Vietnam-era F-4 Phantom.

In that first light, even the scraggly desert scrub shone with a rich golden halo. I watched the canopy close over my father. He ignited the engine and lit the Phantom's afterburner. It glowed an otherworldly red. I felt the ground shake, rumbling underneath my feet.

The Phantom hurled into the calm sky, tearing at the dawn. I bit through my lip watching my father's fire-breathing fighter. A sonic boom wobbled the cactus and rattled my bones. The flat earth seemed to collapse underneath me as I grabbed the cold fence, my arms tingling.

My father must be some kind of god. Or so I thought that day several years before he crashed.

I quickly skipped over the Wringer's notes on my mother and father and went to my teenage years in New York City, which weren't bad.

Manhattan in the early '80s was like Europe, and

like most kids who grew up on foreign military bases, I was sexually precocious, since there's basically nothing else for kids to do on bases. Nobody over the age of twelve was a virgin.

I nodded briefly at the Wringer's summary of my college career. Straight A's in European history, then my MBA in business before I joined the Air Force. They also commented on my relationships with women, which tended to last a weekend or less. 'He has the depth of a kiddie pool,' one ex-date apparently sniffed.

I felt my neck burn and moved ahead quickly to my Air Force file.

Ernest Hemingway once wrote something like 'Man has one virginity to lose in fighters. If he loses it to a lovely one, that is where his heart will forever be.'

At Eglin Air Force Base in Florida, my first fighter was an F-16. I spent even my spare time learning more about her, psyching out her little behavioral quirks. I took extra time to walk around her in my pre-flight checks, pointing out every tiny scratch to the young crew chief who supervised her maintenance. One day the maintenance crew painted *Spoiled Rotten* on her nose and laughed their asses off when I saw it. I pampered my Viper, as we came to call our F-16s after the ships in an old TV show called *Battlestar Galactica*.

Flying my F-16 was my whole life. I felt a kind of rapture in my Viper that you don't mention in the squad room.

The Air Force culture trains you to understand at

a gut level that you are not flying for a pleasurable experience but doing a hazardous job. I bought the reasons for that, of course. I was a professional. The Air Force spent a million dollars training me. My F-16 cost another twenty million, back when it was worth the paper it was printed on.

The truth?

I thought of flying the way Leonardo da Vinci must have as he scratched his fantasies of winged men on to paper. Or maybe the way the ancient Greeks stood in awe of birds in flight, disappearing into the sky. They believed in their hearts that those winged creatures were emissaries from their gods.

And I've always had a thing about machines. Maybe it's because they never guilt you the way women do. If you accidentally turn over a JetSki, it won't bob up and say, 'How could you *do* that?'

Whatever.

I kept my romantic feelings about flying under control, for the most part, until I flew the Viper for the first time. One punch of the afterburner, one loop in flight, and I was reduced to yelping with abandon.

My Viper was my soulmate.

There were moments, coaxing her sensitive fly-by-wire control system with light strokes and body language, when I forgot I was a soldier and she was a weapons platform. I wanted to let the beauty of those rose-colored clouds flow through me, to soar above the stratosphere like a god. I yearned to fly toward the sun until my wings melted like Icarus, that idiot of Greek legend.

Like I said, I had to watch myself carefully. The Air Force tended to flush pilots who acted in any way like Icarus.

I skipped over the rest of my Air Force file, when my career path veered wildly.

In the early '90s, after Desert Storm, the political winds favored a new generation of USAF pilots who earned advanced degrees in aero engineering. My sneakiness was considered a skill that couldn't be quantified and was therefore suspect. My commanding officer told me, off the record, that I should seek opportunities in the private sector.

The thought of never piloting a fighter again flattened my spirit. I went on leave and caught a C-130 transport flight which happened to be going to the tiny port city of Baltro in the Galapagos Islands of Ecuador. Once there, I took a cheap hotel room and drank until I passed out.

When I woke up, head throbbing and my tongue blistered, I looked at my ID to figure out who I was and suddenly my funk broke. I began exploring the black volcanic islands, the cradle of evolution. I watched birds. I began thinking about my future and calculated that, in the years ahead, maybe the real dogfights would occur on Wall Street.

After returning to base, I dusted off my Columbia MBA, took my one black Armani starter suit from the closet, bought a sincere tie, and began interviewing on Wall Street. I took a job with an investment bank, then joined Starcross-Voyager. The Wringer covered all that, with the expected quotes from people who said I did a good job but seemed to travel a lot more than necessary.

I grazed through to see what linkage the Wringer made to my espionage career. It quickly became clear that they hadn't found any. Maria had uncovered my markers, as she put it, on her own.

The Wringer had no idea how Fragata was born. Nobody starts out to become a freelance industrial spy. It was really just a suggestion here, a small clandestine job there. I discovered that even CEOs I met through my perfectly legal work were often frustrated by their competitors' unfair advantages. Grumbling in their Gulfstreams, they would blurt out things like, 'Goddamn it, Terry, if only we could duplicate Happy Beefburger's Special Sauce.' I was uniquely adapted to stealthy work. They had holes in their information needs that I could fill at a profit.

I stood up and found a lighter in my desk drawer. I took the Wringer report into my kitchen, threw it in the sink, lit it and watched it burn. In the flames I felt a pull of sadness for my father, as my Wringer life shriveled up into red glow-worms.

I flushed the last charred shreds into the garbage disposal, letting it grind a moment longer than necessary. I had wasted an hour reading about myself.

It was five a.m. I stripped off my clothes to sleep for two hours before meeting my lawyer.

NINE

'You have turned into my most paranoid client,' Marty trembled, dog-paddling in the bracing chill of the Pacific Ocean. 'Do you really think I'd wear a wire on you?'

'It's not you,' I told him.

We were treading the freezing water together, the beach deserted and shadowed by craggy bluffs. A thin sun provided little warmth even on land. I'd insisted that we meet in the surf off Malibu, where the nearest people were surfers bobbing on waves about a mile away. They wore wetsuits, of course. We didn't.

Marty Schmidt was my lawyer, and best friend.

Marty's skin had turned slightly blue in his bathing suit, but he still looked more like an actor than a lawyer. He had finely carved features in a square face, and thick hair. He actually had to color grey into his hair to give himself more gravitas, because his law partners all looked more jowly and bald. Marty and his partners were deliciously devious attorneys who practiced in Beverly Hills. Marty defended only white-collar criminals, very successfully. He met his clients over Dover sole at the private Jonathan Club downtown more often than in the Parker Center police station.

His wife, Jennifer, who had the cheekbones and

moussed-back hair of a Revlon model, was a lawyer for one of the movie studios. They both worked long, punishing days and had two great kids who called me Uncle Terry. I took the kids flying in my company's Lear jet whenever I could, and brought them toys from my clients that their friends wouldn't be able to buy at Toys 'R' Us for years, if ever.

The Schmidts lived in a mock-Tudor house with a pool in Beverly Hills. But I wouldn't meet him there. His rosebushes could have been bugged.

Marty and I were undergraduates together at Columbia. He was very bright. He went on to Harvard Law School. Ever since we were college buddies, he knew that he would one day be a white-collar criminal defense lawyer. Although I was then a student with a seven-year commitment to the USAF, I knew that one day I would be in business and probably need his services. Neither of us cared much about spectator sports, so we'd play a little game of imagining how to commit felonies and get away with them.

I'd say, for instance, 'Speeding.' He'd ask, 'Husband and wife both in car? They zip around a corner where the police car chasing them can't see. Both hop out. Neither admits to driving. Cop scratches his head. Which one to charge? I'd get them off on self-incrimination *and* spousal immunity. Next case.'

I retained Marty as my lawyer indefinitely to continue our college game.

Everything I told him was hypothetical. That was

our deal. Marty was an officer of the court and bound to report any whiff of future criminal acts. I just ran what-if concepts by him for the very fictional novel I was writing, for technical advice. Like, if the hero just stole an industrial secret in a particular country outside the US, what would be the odds of prosecution? That kind of hypothetical what-if.

Now Marty made bubbles in the water disapprovingly. 'You know, one day it would be a good idea if you actually finished this novel.'

'I don't know. I think it took Tolstoy fourteen years to write *War and Peace,* and he was a natural writer.'

He sighed and spat out brine. 'You mentioned a spy story, something about an invisible plane.'

'Just to refresh your memory, my hero is an industrial spy, but not altogether bad.'

'More of a sly rogue,' he added. 'And he's pulled off six major thefts without getting caught.'

'Seven,' I corrected him.

He lifted his eyebrows.

'Anyway, this is a classic boy-meets-girl story. The girl, call her the Student, once appeared in a *Playboy* photoessay on "The Girls of Mensa".'

'Okay.' Marty smiled appreciatively as he got her set in his mind.

'When she comes to our hero, she's already emptied his Swiss bank account of sixteen million dollars.'

Marty whistled, made a gurgle in the water. 'Our hero is that wealthy?'

'Was that wealthy. The Student claims she'll give it back when he does what she wants.'

'Well,' Marty said, dry as a brush fire, 'I see her appeal to our hero. What does she want from him?'

'To get access to an invisible plane.'

'That I'd like to see.'

'No you wouldn't. But the Hero saw some evidence that a defense contractor stole her unpatented design for it.'

'She has proof, of course.' Marty narrowed his eyes.

'If she did, she wouldn't need the Hero's unique skills.'

He shivered. 'What about earlier work? Stuff she showed other people?'

'Nope. And it gets better. The aircraft has the capability to destroy various strategic targets.'

'Like?'

'The Pentagon.'

'Sweet Jesus.' He swallowed water, coughed and spat. 'Terry, I'm worried that you may be eating putrid oysters or something.'

'Well, that's her story.'

'I think the Hero ought to stay home and lock his door.'

'But she has the Hero's money.'

'He can make more.' Marty's lips were turning blue.

I shrugged. 'Maybe. The Hero poked around a little and it looks like the Student is telling the truth. But the defense contractor, let's call him the Villain, won't roll over.'

Marty sounded more lawyerly now. 'The Hero's already screwing with classified materials? This is an awful story, Terry. Three or four federal agencies could pound on the guy's head.'

'I know. Not to be patriotic or anything, but it's important. If the media and politicians get a hold of the story, they'll kill off a plane that could save a lot of lives.'

'This girl. Is she mentally stable?' he asked.

A freezing wave washed over me. I licked the salt water on my lips. 'She carries complex equations around in her head.'

'I didn't ask if you liked her. I asked if she was mentally stable.'

I drew a line in the ocean water. 'I'd say, here's the line.' Then I made a dot next to it. 'And here's the Student. She has a psychiatric history, but it was brought on by the theft.'

'Really? Didn't your hero get an honorable discharge from the Air Force?'

I nodded.

'I ask because the Air Force could reactivate him. Then they'd want to prosecute him under the Uniform Code of Military Justice. The UCMJ ain't Judge Judy. I don't know what the exact charge would be, but theoretically you could be executed by a firing squad for espionage.'

'Okay. But I have a scenario.'

Marty's brows met over his sunglasses. The lenses were flecked with drops of salt water. 'Stop right there. Did the Hero steal the design from her in the first place?'

'Absolutely not.'

'Is he totally sure about that?'

'That's the only thing I'm sure about. So here's my scenario. The Hero finds evidence that it's really the Student's design. He brings the Student and the Villain together, and forces him to give her a piece of the pie. She gets access to the real plane and defuses the Doom Level. The Pentagon gets its plane. No media circus. No Joint Chiefs of Staff blown up in their offices.'

'That's your *best* case?' Marty asked. 'Your Hero is still committing about a dozen federal crimes.'

'Marty, this plane was her design. The hero saw a Pentagon briefing.'

Marty looked like he would throw up. 'A *briefing*? How?'

'A little eavesdropping at the contractor's office.'

Deep lines knotted his forehead. He spat out more water, thinking.

'Okay. The scenario you gave me really sucks, so let me give you a better one. Your hero cuts his losses with the help of gifted legal counsel.'

I nodded appreciatively. 'For the record, that's how I'll handle it.'

'Not just for the record, Terry. Your hero's manifestly paranoid. He has to meet his lawyer in the Pacific Ocean in March. He says the military can't handle an investigation on their own. Self-serving media people and politicians will sabotage the program.'

'What a crazy notion.'

'Okay, point taken. But he's still over his head.

Let's play it out. All our hero knows is flying and spying. But he wants to spread out a little and do the job of several government agencies and the entire US military intelligence system. I'm not a psychiatrist, but that could suggest a delusional quality.'

I sighed. 'Give me a better one.'

'He can disappear while his lawyer contacts an old law-school buddy at the Pentagon. They hear the story and start an investigation. They will not leak to the press. Like you said, they just want a plane that won't blow up. Are you with me so far?'

'Sure,' I said.

'The investigation uncovers, in the worst case, theft of intellectual property. The Pentagon concludes that the contractor is a thieving son of a bitch . . .'

'. . . but he's *their* son of a bitch.'

'Right. So they slap him on the wrist. Very privately, they get the Student in the loop to correct the defects, if any. The aircraft gets built. Americans can sleep at night, thanks to the Hero and his lawyer.'

'That's a great solution, Marty,' I told him. He looked like he would die of hypothermia if we didn't get out of the Pacific.

'Thank you. I'll do some research and make the call.'

'Except that it won't work,' I told him as we waded out of the ocean.

His face drooped. 'What's wrong with it?'

'It'll still get leaked to the press. Everything does. Not to get corny about this, but the Hero has a duty. He took an oath as an officer.'

'Terry, the point of your military service, if you'll recall, was to keep our cities from getting blown up. Your hero can't win. Why does he fail to see . . . No, strike that. I know why. Boy meets girl, girl becomes an end in herself.'

'I appreciate your concern,' I told him. 'Are we still privileged?'

His jowls turned way down as he shivered. 'Sure, but listen to me. Not as a client. As a friend. Real world. This isn't stealing Special Sauce.'

I started to speak. He put up one hand as he trod water with the other.

'I know how you think. You want to be her white knight. Yes or no?'

I didn't feel like much of a white knight, but I never lied to my lawyer. 'It's complicated. She beat the Hero at his own game. For a while anyway.'

'Oh?' Marty's lips partially stuck together now. 'The sting of competition. Maybe you should confront her if she's the problem. On her own turf.'

I swallowed salt water and spat it out. 'The Hero doesn't know exactly where her turf is right now.'

'She got away from you?' Marty cackled.

'I'll find her,' I said.

'How?'

'Everybody has something they can't leave behind.'

'Well, if what you say is true, you'd better work fast.' Marty resumed trudging numbly out of the water, speaking very slowly. 'I'm going into shore now. I will do some quick research. For the record, I advise you not to pursue this screenplay.'

169

'Thanks. I have to run.' I picked up my clothes and began jogging toward my car.

'When will I hear from you?'

'When it's too late,' I called over my shoulder. 'What are lawyers for?'

Like I said, everybody has something they can't leave behind.

I yanked the NSX out of the parking lot, screeching on to the Pacific Coast Highway. By the time I hit Sunset Boulevard, I was thinking about birdseed.

I raced back home, rushing up to my apartment to confirm what I recalled from the Wringer dossier on Maria. I changed into a sports jacket and assembled some tools from my closet.

I drove west to Sunset Boulevard and stopped at Canine Campus, a bright blue store with a fence around it. Not for the first time. I called a young freckled dogsitter with glassy eyes aside from the yapping and growling dogs of various breeds in his care. I bribed him $300 to let me rent one of them for a couple of hours.

I chose a small dog with a grey coat called a shih-tzu, which means 'little lion' in Chinese. There's a certain resemblance to the lion in the shih-tzu's mane and rather stubby, arrogant face. But shih-tzus are wonderful dogs. They love people, but also tend to be excellent watchdogs since they bark at even a minimal disturbance.

I spent a few moments getting to know this shih-tzu, whose name was Spencer, so he'd be

170

comfortable with me. First we had our Alpha Male contest. I won. Not because he was smaller. The fact that he was only eighteen inches high worked in his favor, potentially making me feel like a bully and an idiot. But I had come armed with Frosty Paws, a tasty canine ice cream. He lapped up the Frosty Paws and stood up on his hind legs, waving his little gray-carpeted front paws at me for more.

I opened the door of my NSX and put the top down. He sat in the passenger seat, and grasped the top of the door with his paws so he could stick his nose out, the way dogs like to do, to feel the wind in his face as I accelerated out of there. I wondered what it would be like to be a dog with such a sensitive nose. I'd be able to find a paint fleck in Times Square.

A friend once told me the wind delivers a dog speeding in a car a kaleidoscopic, almost psychedelic rush of scents. I glanced enviously at Spencer's happy face in the wind, furry ears flying, and headed up one of the steep canyon drives of the Santa Monica Mountains above Sunset.

Twisting up the hill at a perilous speed, the tires of my NSX slipped off the road and spat rocks. Spencer slid on his seat, but kept his nose pointed out.

I zigged and zagged toward Mulholland Drive, the skyway road that separated Bel Air and Beverly Hills on the south side of the cliff from the towns of the San Fernando Valley on the north side. I whipped right over Mulholland toward the Valley face of the cliff, downshifting into second. The NSX whined and growled. I slowed down just enough to follow a residential street with more modest houses side by side than just over the rise in Bel Air.

I parked in a cul-de-sac and slipped a tweedy sport jacket over my black turtleneck and corduroys, to look more like a neighbor on a stroll. Then I took my faithful shih-tzu rental on his leash. Nobody views a grown man walking a lap dog as any kind of threat. It's better than wearing a priest's collar.

As I walked down the steep road with Spencer, I kept one hand casually in my pocket, the other holding the leash lightly so he could lift his leg.

From a distance, I spotted number 2242. It was a white clapboard cottage with green shutters, nestled in a clump of trees. It didn't look as Midwestern as most of the houses around it did, those split-levels that make parts of LA look like Akron, Ohio. This seemed more like Hansel and Gretel. I sensed a cozy menace, but also felt the tingle before a penetration.

Watching the house from an angle where nobody inside could see me, I used my free hand to call the phone number from my matchbook-sized cellphone. A machine answered, so I hung up.

There was no garage attached to this house, just a carport. And no car.

Fine.

Spencer and I walked briskly toward the house as though we lived there. Most neighbors on this street were at work. Nobody appeared around us, but you never knew who'd be looking out their window.

I heard the screaming from inside as I

approached the door. I looked for an alarm system. The sticker on the window said *WARNING: Protected by Starwatch Security*.

I chortled at the sign. Letting Spencer pause at the stoop, a trusting gaze in his bulging, cartoon eyes, I removed the key I had had made in France by a master craftsman for $28,000.

It was a plastic strip that stuck out of a fat black disk with three small buttons in red, green and white. It slid easily into the lock. I slipped a thick, insulated glove on to my hand, then pushed the red button on the disk. My glove heated up as the key began to melt, oozing into all the lock's little nooks and crannies. Once a small green 'ready' light came on, I pushed the white button. A blast of concentrated Freon shot over the putty-like plastic to freeze it in place, and the door opened easily.

That took all of five seconds.

The screaming inside grew more intense. I brought Spencer inside and locked the door behind me.

The Starwatch alarm yelped. I found the control panel on the wall. It would give me sixty seconds to fumble with groceries before it called the police. First I pushed in 0313 just for fun. Maria's birthday. The readout flashed *Invalid Code*.

So with my other hand I held up a small DECODA unit which remotely grabbed the security system's CPU, violated its memory and demanded that it give up the security code. The poor, dumb Starwatch alarm computer struggled to keep its little secret. But the DECODA had locked on to

173

overwhelm it with more computing power. I read the first number by the twelfth second, and had all four registered on my unit's LED panel at the fifty-eighth. I let out my breath and used the last second to enter the four-digit code.

The Starwatch stopped yelping.

But the screaming in the house was deafening.

I let Spencer's leash go. He flopped down with his paws in front of him like a furry Sphinx. Either he was deaf, or I'd chosen a ludicrously laid-back California shih-tzu to be my watchdog.

The screaming came from a little gray parrot with a red tail peering at me between the bars. His cage was full of colorful toys. I couldn't believe how small the parrot was, about the size of a pigeon. Hearing the racket, I'd expected a bird with the vocal cords of a condor. It got quieter, muttering at me as it grasped its perch and eyed me warily.

'Hey, little guy,' I told the bird in a soothing voice. I moved my finger very slowly between the bars of the cage. You can't move too slowly for a bird. It lunged to bite me, an attack parrot. I walked away and let it turn its head to watch me with one of its side-mounted eyes.

'Sit, Spencer,' I said to keep my dog alert. He seemed to be falling asleep on the floor.

I quickly calculated how long it would take me to bleed this house of its information, and started in the kitchen. First I found the telephone box. With a pair of alligator clips, I snapped one wire off and attached another in its place. My replica wire was attached to a little bug the size of a penny. I slid it under the jumble of wires where it couldn't be seen, to intercept phone calls.

In the living room, I marveled at the lack of any evidence of humanity. No personal effects brightened the room, not that I expected any little 'God Bless This House' homilies. The furniture consisted of chintzy print fabrics and that generic California wood that should have ferns and stained glass around it. But this room didn't.

I turned to the computer. What a hoot. It was an iMac, that seafoam-green desktop that looks like a beach ball.

Or an iMac cloak. Maybe it was really a blown-out supercomputer that Maria had jinked with one of her blobs, and covered with the housing from an off-the-shelf iMac.

When I booted it up, it asked for a password. I selected a special disk nicknamed 'MacBug' from the repertoire I had brought in my jacket pocket, and shoved it in. I wouldn't have time to search for the password, which I was sure would be a random combination like 'Chocolate Pole'. Instead, I counted on MacBug to eat through the security firewall so I wouldn't need a password. And MacBug would leave a code inside that would let me download any of the iMac's files from any telephone.

Uh-oh. The iMac was no iMac. It was actually eating up the instructions on my MacBug, not the other way around. I tried to fish the disk out, but the machine wouldn't give it back. The iMac crunched up my MacBug and swallowed all its information so it could duplicate it. Goddamn it, I swore at the machine, and smacked it with the side of my hand.

The parrot was squawking in the background at my assault on the phony iMac. I heard nothing to warn me before I felt the rush of air on the tip of my right ear. I turned to evade whatever was coming, but only had time to duck slightly before catching the full impact of the black iron skillet on my head.

A red wash of pure pain flooded through my brain, covered my eyes. I had felt this before, when my head slammed into the glass of my cockpit. Floating black dots swam across my retina as my hands went up to cover my face.

'Oh, it's you.' The irritated voice vibrated in my head.

My head felt like a smashed cantaloupe as I tried to speak, my own voice a sickly echo. 'I didn't know anybody used those skillets any more.'

I managed to open my eyes and barely made out Maria Haymeyer standing in front of me. Her hand squeezed the handle of the skillet.

'You almost got yourself killed,' she scolded. 'And just when I need you most.'

She came into focus wearing an aerobics outfit with a man's button-down shirt over it. Her black curls were very wet and shiny, coiling over her forehead and around her tortoiseshell glasses. She leaned down over Spencer. My watchdog rolled over and let this stranger who'd just attacked me from behind rub his belly.

'Poor little thing,' she cooed at him. 'What do you think you're doing here, Terry?'

'I was in the neighborhood and wanted to see your house,' I told her through the pain. 'You look well.'

'You don't. You're going to have a bump.' She frowned as she touched my eyebrow, not gently. 'How could you break into my house?'

She bristled, then apparently saw the irony inherent in her comment and sighed.

'Well, you look like you need a drink.'

'Maybe just the ice,' I said, holding the side of my head. The pain made a dull metallic noise in my ear.

She said nothing as she made me a Baggie full of ice. Then, in her first moment of kindness I could recall, she held it gently to my head. Her little muscles shifted under her workout suit and big shirt. I lost my balance, feeling woozy.

'Come on. Sit on the couch.'

She helped me stagger over and I fell on to the rented foam cushions. They let out a stale whoosh when I sat. Her arm in mine felt warm, taut. I held the ice to my head and stretched my legs out, getting semi-comfy on the chintz-covered sofa, while Spencer rolled back off his belly and crawled up to my feet.

'So how did you find me?' Maria sat in a chair across from me and crossed her legs. In a guy's shirt four sizes too big, she still looked as delicious as she had done straddling my ribs in a Gaultier dress.

'Your bird. It eats better than I do. You order a special health mix from The Pampered Parrot in Los Altos and they ship it to you overnight. That means there was a Federal Express receipt I could trace for the address. I guess you slept through "FedEx 101" when you were studying espionage.'

'Hmm.' She made the red donut with her mouth and nodded. 'Why are you here? Do you have something?'

'I will.'

'When?'

'Soon.'

'Why not now?' She folded her arms. 'Terry, do you have any sense of our deadline?'

'Sure I do. It just got worse.'

'What do you mean?'

'Maybe you saw Ted Devlin insulting Allyn Pollack personally on *24/7* . . .'

'Is that a TV show?'

'Don't be a media snob. Yes. Pollack's a TV journalist. He's doing a story on the Joint Strike Fighter. Ted must have figured he's so out front in the competition he could afford to get cute with him.'

'What does that mean?'

'Our time line just got crunched. Allyn Pollack put a production crew on Devlin. If you turn on tonight, I imagine you'll see Pollack putting a decidedly negative spin on Ted's Joint Strike Fighter. And that's just the beginning.'

'Maybe he'll help us,' she brightened. For a genius, her naivety was touching, or chilling.

'Allyn Pollack helps Allyn Pollack get ratings. End of story. It's a disaster. If his people are snooping around and find something wrong, there won't *be* a LUCI any more.'

'Because of the media?'

'That's the way it works.'

She gave me a disapproving frown. Maria had a bit of the schoolmarm about her. Despite the pounding in my head, her coolness actually made me feel playful around her.

I must have grinned at her.

'Terry, please tell me you have a plan.'

'I have a plan,' I said.

'What is it?'

'I took some videos of the briefing. I need to put them all together, then I'll show them to you. But not in the States. We'll meet in a location I'll give you tomorrow. It's a country that's only six hours away.'

'Why leave the country? We don't have six hours.'

'Because I don't expect to find Allyn Pollack's crew or the FBI there. I'd also like to be in a country that gets a little behind in its extradition paperwork with the US. I'm the one with the criminal liability here.'

I knew exactly where I wanted to meet her. A safe, special place where she would see plenty of birds. She sighed and nodded, her eyes set in a startling expression of naked trust. What I felt for her at that moment was so unexpected, I think I must have grinned at her again.

'That's your plan?'

'No. One step at a time. I have close-up visuals of the LUCI flight simulator. Would it have your blobs inside it, do you think?'

'Probably. They'd want to make the simulator training authentic.'

'Then tell me how I can deprogram the Doom Level from inside the simulator.'

She blinked behind her glasses. 'How can you get into the LUCI simulator? They have all that security to keep intruders away.'

'Not if you don't let them. First I have to do something with Ted Devlin tomorrow.'

'Let me help you with it.'

'I have to do it myself. We'll meet day after tomorrow. Saturday afternoon.'

Painfully I got up from the couch. She watched me and so did Spencer. Neither moved. With my hands behind my back so I didn't frighten it, I walked over to the large white cage and looked at her small gray parrot. I took care to stand off to its side since birds are territorial and don't like it when you face them directly. So I sat on its branch, so to speak, not disturbing the pecking order.

For a creature with a brain the size of a marble, the parrot's eyes looked unusually knowing and clever. From a distance, its gray seemed drab. But up close, I saw his subtle texture. His coat was layered in shades of gray with a flaming red tail. It made me wonder whether Giorgio Armani licensed parrots. When it put its beak down and hunched its shoulders, it actually looked like a fighter with its afterburner on. I liked it already.

'So he's your African gray.'

'She.'

The small parrot grasped her perch tightly, tensing her muscular drumsticks. She watched me, very alert. Then she dipped her head down in a cute way to get a different angle on me. The base of her shiny black beak seemed to form a kind of smile, almost like a dolphin.

'What's her name?'

'Lucy.'

I looked hard at Maria. 'You named a strike fighter after a parrot?'

She said nothing. I could tell she really hated having me in her living room, examining her parrot. But instead of choosing to bicker, she got up and stood beside me.

'Do you know much about parrots?' she asked casually.

'They talk and fly.' I looked at her bird. 'She's cute, but she looks kind of clumsy. Like a brick with wings.'

'Really. Let's see you fly over a tree at ten knots and land on a branch without falling on your face. I noticed you had rather detailed books on evolution in both your apartments. Is species adaptation a subject of interest to you?'

I nodded, which made my head throb harder.

'Imagine if you were Lucy. You'd be a very experienced aviator, wouldn't you? Birds have two billion years of instinct to guide them. Parrots are as old as the dinosaurs, and African grays are the smartest. They can learn a vocabulary of over a thousand words and use them in context.'

'They must be the Parrots of Mensa,' I said.

She gave me a dirty look, then relaxed slightly.

'You are the most unprofessional person I've ever met.'

'Thank you.'

'It's not an attractive quality when we have a crisis to work out.'

She stared at me for a second, then reached her finger in through the bars of Lucy's cage. Lucy dipped her head in a polite bow. Maria ruffled the feathers that stood up on the back of Lucy's neck. Lucy shut her eyes tight and opened her mouth slightly, obviously in bird Nirvana.

'An African gray only learns to trust one person,' Maria said. 'And that's who they bond with. Anybody else, watch out. You want to see? Raise your hand.'

I held my palm up to the cage, moving slowly. Lucy spread her gray wings, shook the bright red tail, stretched herself up to gain a few inches of height.

In an almost spooky imitation of Maria's voice she said, *'Stand back, I'm an eagle.'*

I laughed at Lucy, and she bowed her head invitingly for me to rub her neck too. So I put my finger slowly between the bars. Suddenly, she snapped her beak around and bit my finger hard, ripping at my flesh.

I pulled my finger away quickly, but she held on like a pit bull. When I finally got it out of her beak, an impressively large piece of skin hung off it.

Maria regarded me with a thin smile as I licked the blood away. 'Don't take it personally. She can be malicious. It's part of her essential birdness.'

She ruffled the feathers on Lucy's neck and the bird held her beak open in ecstasy, though looking warily at me. While my head throbbed painfully and blood spurted from my finger, I wondered how to insult an African gray.

'Lucy,' I said, 'we've got Vipers, Raptors, Eagles, but I can't see a parrot as a warplane.'

Maria looked ostentatiously at her watch. 'Shouldn't you be working on your plan instead of picking on Lucy?'

'I'll want my money back when I give you the tape.'

'I thought you were doing this for the right reasons.'

'You don't want to know why I'm doing it,' I told her.

We were both very quiet for a moment.

'I have to debug my house,' Maria said. 'Are you taking your shih-tzu?'

I took Spencer's leash. He hopped up and finally barked for no reason. Then, in a totally unplanned move, I leaned in and brushed Maria's cheek with my lips. I just wanted to touch her. She felt soft, young.

'Don't do that.' She stepped back sharply.

Her eyes were so intense, they burned the side of my forehead that she'd missed with her frying pan. I shook my head to empty it of her. Maria might be a genius, but she sure didn't know what she had. I busied myself dragging Spencer out the door. He tried to stay, grabbing the rug with his paws.

'I don't really know if you can deprogram LUCI from the simulator. But we'll have to try. When do you think you can get inside it?'

'That depends on what happens with Ted tomorrow.'

'I wish you'd tell me what you're doing.'

'It's a guy thing,' I explained. 'And make sure you wear plenty of suntan lotion on Saturday. It may get hotter than you're used to.'

TEN

On my way to settle my Spank bet with Ted Devlin, I found myself wishing that Ted played golf after all.

You never know what can happen in the heat of Spank. Especially, I imagined, when you play it with business equipment, which I had never done before.

Maria had called me at eight a.m. that Friday to pester me again about the deadline. I was already arranging a payment over the phone with a Mexican civil servant, who I needed to perform a favor for me. Ted had insisted on playing in Mexico.

By 9.40 I was at LA's private Santa Monica Airport doing a walkaround pre-flight check of my firm's business jet. We kept it there mainly to service our West Coast clients. Our compact Lear 55 corporate jet now stood alert on its toes like a shiny white egret.

Need I say that I chose Starcross-Voyager's company plane. The Lear is the sexiest business jet, closely modeled on a Swiss military fighter. It has energy and agility to spare. I had outfitted her with a glove-gray leather interior to make our clients comfy. The cockpit bristled with the latest electronics. The cabin was supplied with every airborne toy imaginable. We kept the nicest California

Chardonnay in a compact chest, and a stainless-steel tap dispensed Jolt for our Silicon Valley clients.

I got cozy in the tiny instrument-crammed cockpit for two, strapping myself nice and tight to my lambskin-covered seat.

For my Spank game with Ted, I secured a Polaroid one-shot instant camera to the second seat with two Velcro straps.

I went through my cockpit checklist. The cockpit was a light show – bytes of useful information I could use to check on all the aircraft's sensitive systems without even thinking about it. It scalded my desire to get a look at LUCI's cockpit. But that was why I was here.

I switched on the batteries and began the start-up sequence. The whining of its twin jet turbines spooling up sounded like a concert to me.

I didn't tell our corporate pilots, or the tower either, where I was headed. In fact, I wasn't supposed to be flying her alone at all. The Lear 55 wasn't FAA-approved for single-pilot operation. But I needed to bend some regulations today, so I neglected to file a flight plan. Pilots routinely file a plan to let search-and-rescue people know where they'll be if they screw up, but I declined. I would trust to skill and luck.

Impatient, I sat tapping my foot on runway two-one, waiting for the air traffic controller, until a Gulfstream business jet took off in front of me.

'Lear November 235 Yankee Tango,' I heard in my headset. 'Westbound departure cleared for takeoff.'

'Cleared to go, Yankee Tango,' I repeated back in a low monotone that would not blow the air-traffic controller's eardrum out.

I notched my throttle forward, and the screaming engines wound up until my plane vibrated with thrust. I let the brakes off, and felt the little chill that never grows old for me. Cutting through the crosswind like a slightly wobbly arrow, my Lear began gobbling up the airport's runway, building up power.

I was one with the plane now. My hands squeezed the control yoke gently, my fingertips sensing the pressure building up underneath its wings.

Then I felt the sweet spot of lift that would take us airborne. I pulled back lightly on the yoke, and we leapt up into the misty sky. It wasn't the thundering jack-rabbit hop of a fighter takeoff. But I felt the power in my loins and a giddy rush through my nerve endings as I pulled into a steep climb, military style, and snap-turned. The agile little Lear leapt up over west Los Angeles, and the sparkling Pacific laid out blue and silver to the horizon, the sun burning through the city haze.

My Lear felt just right, game and sassy. She was ready to play.

As soon as I was lost in the puffing white clouds where nobody could see me, I quickly flipped my plane over 180° on to its back.

I hung upside down, my body clutched to my seat by the tight shoulder straps. Blood rushing to my head, I carefully looked around to see if any objects had shaken loose when I rolled over. This was the best way to spot junk like car keys that can get lost in a cockpit. They can become dangerous later on, if you plan on whipping your plane around. Ah. I found a pack of matches from a 'Live Nude Girls' bar near the airport, left by maintenance workers or our corporate pilots.

I righted myself and headed west for a few miles to scoot around the 'Class B' airspace at Los Angeles International Airport, where commercial jets fly in and out.

Then I banked over the Pacific and settled just under the clouds heading due south to Baja California. This peninsula, as the name implies, is the long Mexico extension of our Golden State, a craggy stretch of land on the Pacific coast.

I wished that I had all the time in the world to skim along the scattered clouds that puffed out over me like a carpet, a surfer of the endless sky.

Instead, I got down to business.

A Lear can climb to over 45,000 feet, to cruise comfortably up above the weather. But today's flight was about stealth, not comfort. I put my nose down and descended quickly toward the ocean. I leveled off to cruise just eighty feet over sea level. It was tricky holding her manually – no autopilot now – at about 450 m.p.h. ground speed, hurtling across the waves, dipping down and tipping a wing in one of the six-foot swells. In my rush of speed over the water, I looked down to see the white V-wake my twin engines made. Two cavorting dolphins leapt out of the surf. I could almost forget, for a moment, that I had signed on with Ted for a sporting contest.

Almost. My cockpit duties weighed heavily. I concentrated on holding my flight level with gentle pressure and watching out for birds. How ironic if Fragata were taken suddenly out of action by a bird strike to the engine. I dived a little further down, chuckled to myself as I actually flew under a flock of seagulls. They looked surprised and broke formation.

I took long, deep breaths, concentrating on my Spank tactics. Many variables could spin out of my control today.

I slowed down to 180 knots, and made some adjustments to cross the border unnoticed. No country likes fast jets zooming into their airspace. If I showed up on radar at this height, the Mexican Air Force could scramble fighters to intercept me. I held the aircraft at a hundred feet, and got a little salt spray on my windshield.

Then I was well past the border and no fighters had showed up. I poured on power again, feeling the heady rush of racing above the frothy deep blue of the Pacific on a sunny day, the clouds breaking into a pure cobalt sky.

Life was good, but only for a couple of hours. Then it would get complicated.

I flew deep into Mexican airspace. Before I went down to sea level, I had turned my transponder off. This disabled my only safety net, the onboard receiver that let the local Mexican air-traffic controllers track me on their radar screens. Without it, all the ATCs would see was a dim and hard-to-define image, a ghostly blob. They would probably grumble and curse, then get busy guiding other traffic around my weak signal. I switched to the large rubber bladders like giant inner tubes that I'd had the airport maintenance people put on board last night. They held extra fuel. I'd need it.

I stuck a Post-It note with latitude/longitude coordinates on to the instrument panel, and banked left for a rendezvous point over the ocean near Los Cabos International Airport, at the bottom tip of the Baja Peninsula.

When I arrived at fifty feet over sea level, I yanked the nose up and poured on power to climb fast. Shortly, I heard a Mexican air-traffic controller whisper into my headset.

'Identify?' he asked cryptically.

'Squawk zero,' I said. Only that controller would know what I was talking about.

My feeble radar signal would be painting ovals on the Mexican controller's radar screen.

I pulled a long, lazy turn out over the Pacific, thirty miles out to sea, looking carefully through my windshield for traffic. I saw nothing. Watching my time, 11.58, I checked my position on GPS

I had arrived, suited up and ready.

I switched my radio to an unused prearranged frequency and heard only crackling. Scanning the cloudless Baja sky, I circled the coordinates on the Post-It note. The Pacific glittered beneath me. A blinding sub-tropical sun I kept behind my back, glowing like a traffic warning light in my windshield.

I spotted the tiniest white dot in the distance that

made me think of the poem *The Song of Hiawatha* . . . *'Coming from the invisible ether, first a speck, then a vulture . . .'*

I watched the dot grow. It didn't change course, although it appeared to be coming at me ridiculously fast.

'Tally ho, Cyclops,' I said drily into my mike, using the call sign that he had given me to identify him.

And now Ted and I would have our little Spank competition. Basically we would be dogfighting in our companies' business jets. The only difference was our planes weren't equipped with missiles to shoot the other guy out of the sky. That's why we had agreed to bring our Polaroid cameras. One of us would end our Spank game by slipping in right behind the other guy and 'spanking' him by taking an instant photo of his aircraft's tail section. In real air-to-air combat, you'd shoot at his tail with a missile and blow him up. In our Spank game, as soon as one of us clicked our Polaroid camera, he would be the winner.

The problem was, like a real dogfight, we would be whipping our aircraft around in some radical maneuvers. They were dangerous at best. And business jets weren't meant to be thrown around the skies like agile fighters. You could easily make a mistake. A very bad one.

I didn't really understand why Ted, a one-eyed pilot to start with, wanted to play Spank with his business jet. It was dangerous. Business jet engines don't provide the powerful thrust for tricks like standing your plane on its tail without stressing the airframe. His Linnet/TVR business jet was a Gulfstream. It wasn't as agile as my Lear. I'd been very clear about that. The day after his party, I'd checked out through two outside sources that Ted's plane was a Gulfstream V. It was the Rolls Royce of business jets, not a sleek and slippery Lear jet.

Even in my sporty Lear, if I twisted around too aggressively the stress on the airframe could break off my wings like toothpicks and turn the plane into a falling brick. But how could Ted match my skills? He'd been a bomber pilot and he only had one eye. How good could his situational awareness be?

It made me wonder whether, as a compulsive gambler, Ted Devlin had a subconscious desire to lose. Or maybe he actually *wanted* me to see his LUCI plane.

I saw the dot turn into an aircraft now. But it was growing larger way too fast, almost like a UFO.

With a rush of awe and rising bile, I saw that this gleaming white apparition was a brand-new, supersonic Peregrine SST business jet. It was made in France, a radically new design, and resembled a smaller version of the Air France Concorde. But it was just as fast and maneuverable as a fighter. The only other Peregrine now in service, Tail #001, was flying the President of France around.

The sun glanced briefly off the Peregrine's wings. The spanking white jet with a nose like a pterodactyl had banked sharply. Now Ted swung around in a direct collision course. Our closing speed was lethal. I had two seconds to react.

192

'Fight's on,' Ted Devlin's gruff voice exploded in my headset.

The Peregrine screamed toward me. Reflexively, I yanked my seat harness tighter until it had a numb-bondage feeling.

With one second of life left, I broke into a snap turn to get out of the Peregrine's way.

Ted's supersonic bizjet zoomed by, holding its frontal attack. I barely peeled away in time. Spinning around fast as I could before it turned on me, I hit the full force of its wake turbulence. It felt like flying into the side of a bus. The Lear bucked and I whipped her around to look out my windshield and find the Peregrine SST.

Lose sight, lose the fight. Know thine enemy.

I struggled to remember what I knew about the Peregrine's specs. The French company that built it had kept them pretty secret. But Fragata had snuck a peek at them anyway while he was in Paris stealing special sauces. The nimble little jet could cruise at Mach 1.8, or a little over 1,000 m.p.h. ground speed. That was over twice as fast as my Lear. Besides its speed advantage, it could climb to 60,000 feet. I could barely reach 45,000. Simply put, I couldn't run away from it.

A cruel stab of wing envy and clammy fear gripped me, making my chest heave.

Ted had all the equipment he needed now to sneak around behind me where I couldn't see him and get on my tail.

Why hadn't I found out he had a brand-new Peregrine?

'Ah, Cyclops,' I mumbled as nonchalantly as I could into the radio. 'You didn't mention new equipment.'

'Must have forgotten,' his voice boomed back in my ear. 'It's not even registered yet. Maiden flight.'

That was why I hadn't seen any record of it. I wondered what the Linnet/TVR board of directors would say if they found out what he was doing with their splendid new toy.

Now I understood why Ted had insisted on Mexico.

We could have gone dogfighting in the US. Nobody stops you if you find clear airspace. But Ted had taken his corporate parent's new plane for a $100 million game of chicken, and he wanted to play outside the FAA-regulated skies of the United States so he'd be sure nobody would know unless he told them.

Screwed didn't begin to describe the odds against me now, trying to outfly a supersonic aircraft with a Lear.

Okay. So his plane was twice as fast and powerful as mine. Speed wasn't that important in air combat. I could bait him into a turn fight. That was where piloting skill was what really mattered. His extra power would become a disadvantage if he blew past me while I got behind him. I had the skill. And the training. Ted might have a supersonic jet, but he was still a one-eyed man who combined a twelve-year-old's judgement with a fifty-three-year-old's reflexes.

I rolled right to find Ted's white jet against the bright blue sky.

Fortunately, my Lear 55 was a squirrelly aircraft by design. She would respond well to the kind of fast, intense, high-G-force maneuver I would grind her through.

I would just have to be very sneaky. Even if I got behind the Peregrine's tail, it could zoom away from me before I had time to use my Polaroid camera.

I saw the Peregrine high to my right, broke hard and stood my plane on its tail as much as it would let me to go after the French jet. My airframe groaned. I felt G-forces and a nasty wind buffet. My engines were bleating like sheep from the strain.

I snickered. If there'd been actual executives aboard my executive aircraft now, they would be rolling around and throwing up.

The Peregrine was maneuvering. Ted was showing off.

I turned hard again to follow. Gravity punished me for whipping my 175-pound human body through aerobatics designed for a twelve-pound eagle. On this very tight turn, I was pulling over five Gs. My body now weighed 900 pounds. I grunted through it. My chest felt like it had lead bars inside. My face pulled down so hard, it seemed as though it was trailing several yards below my feet.

But I had prepared for high Gs. I wore a custom-made Air Force-style truss over my clothes, very similar to the ones I'd worn as a fighter pilot. It was connected to a portable pneumatic pack to inflate around the lower half of my body. It would squeeze my abdomen and upper legs to keep blood from draining down from my head to puddle up in my legs and leave me oxygen-starved. My G-suit opened now, splitting my pants with a sudden ballooning around my abdomen. I felt the hard pressure of the suit. I growled and grunted then rolled to reduce the G-forces against me, as I threw the Lear around.

Uh-oh. I had lost the Peregrine.

I came out of my roll and looked outside my windshield, craning my neck.

Lose sight, lose the fight. I needed to get Ted back in my windshield. If I couldn't see him, I was dead.

I kept moving, rolling the Lear around like a top. He wasn't anywhere I could see.

I was really feeling the weasels in my stomach.

Today I needed to be dazzling with my stalking skills, spotting openings that most pilots wouldn't. And already I had lost my prey.

I snap-turned, desperately seeking Ted's Peregrine. My tight harness bit into my shoulders while I was upside down.

I had the nasty feeling Ted was behind me, in my blind spot. Playing with me. But how could he keep out of my sight? He wasn't a good enough pilot.

I kept turning, grunting. The airframe squeaked like a gerbil. I craned my neck but all I saw was sky and water.

Even using the control yoke was maddening. I yearned for a joystick, not the half-a-steering-wheel yoke. It was like flying combat maneuvers with an Oldsmobile. My engines felt stressed and sluggish already. No matter how slick its design, the Lear was not built to be relentlessly cracked around the sky like a whip for long periods of time. It was hot under the fireball sun. My hands were slippery on the yoke. I wiped sweat from my eyes.

Aha. Now the gleaming Peregrine appeared about two miles in front of me. He didn't spot me. I crept up slowly, steadily, on the side that he couldn't see. Then, suddenly, Ted must have caught sight of me. He whipped into a tight, well-controlled, high-energy turn.

How did he do that?

The Peregrine was a sensational plane, but he wasn't that good a pilot.

In less than three seconds, he had slewed the Peregrine around until his nose was almost behind me. I jammed my yoke into a sharp dive, then pulled up quickly. The sudden yo-yo maneuver yanked my stomach with it.

I had just caught sight of the Peregrine's cockpit.

What I saw made the confidence drain out of me with the sweat oozing from my pores, plastering my hair against my eyes.

The rotten, cheating bastard.

When Ted's Peregrine SST blew by me, there were two people behind its windshield.

'Ah, Cyclops,' I said, my voice getting thin and reedy. 'I copy two souls on board your aircraft. Who else is aboard?'

'Roger that,' the radio crackled loudly. 'Passenger says his name is Mac.'

'*Passenger*, Cyclops?' I was drenched in sweat, my hands sliding on the yoke. Now I knew that Ted was in command of his plane about the way my dad let me steer his Corvette when I was eight. Only Ted wasn't sitting on Mac Skinner's lap.

They had doubled up on me. Now he had twice the plane, and one of the best fighter pilots in America.

'Mac says he's just along to observe,' Ted said into my radio. 'No rules forbid.'

No witty comeback came to mind. I slammed my hand against the instrument panel and tried to assess the situation.

The phrase 'hopelessly outclassed' kept popping into my mind, but I shoved it back down. *Focus.* I could beat Mac Skinner. I just needed to keep my eye on him. I stood the Lear as much on her tail as I could, rotating her around as I climbed.

Now they were out there hiding from me. It occurred to me that Ted's plane was named after the world's foremost winged predator, the peregrine falcon. Something to tell Maria about if I survived.

Mac Skinner. I hadn't picked up his dossier from the Wringer yet. What moves would he make? I remembered his style from the Crud Lite game at Ted's house when he slammed some middle-aged adversary to the floor. Aggressive. Head-on competitive. *What drove him?* Well, at the moment, it didn't matter.

I dived again, rolling over to take a look. A good thing, because I caught the Peregrine snapping into my blind spot at eight o'clock low.

The Air Force over-trained you for moments like this when you were outnumbered and outgunned. Unfortunately, they couldn't train you to win against a better pilot, only to run away. And I couldn't. I was rattled.

All I could do was draw them into a turn, fight where speed wasn't an issue. Maybe with agility on my side and a little luck, I could fake them out.

I pointed my nose up and went as vertical as I could, to look like I was trying to evade them. Sure enough, in a second they were on my left wing climbing at the same altitude, with Mac grinning out the window at me.

I jabbed at them suddenly forcing my wing close to their plane. Mac played responsible pilot and turned away. But I had the feeling he was just beckoning me in like a spider.

I followed him into the turn. Then we were locked going round and round like a cartoon cat and dog. They called it a furball. But I felt more like the cat. I squinted to get the sun, that nasty Baja fireball, out of my eyes.

Quickly rolling left, I tucked under in a surprise right turn. But my trick failed to impress Mac who kept right with me. He was just hanging tight with me, waiting until I made a mistake.

He didn't have to wait long. We had been using huge gulps of airspace in our turning. We would lose thousands of feet in each maneuver, then climb back up into the sky to dive again and build up speed. Now we were both screaming up into the 'Class A' airspace over 18,000 feet. That put us right where the commercial jet-liners made their approach into the north-west sector of the Los Cabos International Airport.

I rolled over and saw the Peregrine to my left. A spurt of warning adrenaline shot through my chest and jaw. *Trouble*.

Half a second later my cockpit lit up in red and a loud buzzer sounded.

A synthesized woman's voice barked at me, 'Descend! Descend!'

My windshield filled up with black-streaked aluminum. I slammed my yoke all the way in to dive out of the way of an AeroMexico 737 commercial airliner, probably flying an instrument approach into Los Cabos Airport.

The pilots hadn't seen us barreling toward them. Commercial pilots were notorious for flying their instrument panels and not looking out the window for, say, grown men in business jets dogfighting in their airspace.

The wake turbulence from the 737 hit my Lear like a brick wall. My airframe rattled. The wings groaned. I fought the panic while the Lear began feeling heavy and sluggish, like somebody had waved a wand and my aluminum plane had turned into lead. 'Stall, stall,' the synthesized voice told me. That meant my plane was no longer flying. The airspeed was too low. I needed, as that ballad went, some wind beneath my wings.

I used sensitive pressure on my throttle and yoke to try to pull my nose over, dive down, pick up speed and get out of the stall, but I couldn't.

The good part was that Ted and Mac had gotten hit by the airliner's wake too. Mac was recovering by throttling up his big engine and making a wide circling turn. They'd get back to me, but not for a minute.

Except that my Lear wasn't recovering from the stall. Instead, nose down, my plane's tail started spinning around slowly above me, making the ocean below look like a blue record on a turntable. First a stall, now a corkscrew spin. All routine. We were spinning down to the right. I would pull out of it by applying left rudder. I expertly worked the rudder pedal with my foot.

The spin grew tighter. Not good. I was falling through 15,000 feet now, my plane twisting tightly nose first toward the sea like – as the name of the spin implies – a falling corkscrew. Disorienting as hell with the whole world whipping past me like I was trapped in a washing machine's spin cycle, but I'd been there before. It was just hard to find a reference point like I was trained to do. It was water below and it all looked the same. And the water looked so much like the sky, I could maneuver out of this thinking I was okay, then find out too late that I was actually upside down and hit the Pacific Ocean anyway.

I felt the hot prickles on my neck, gravity making sweat now stream into my eyes from my chin rather than my forehead. But maybe I could use this to my advantage.

I worked the controls.

Then my left engine flamed out. My stomach turned over. The blue sea was still spinning around underneath me, a fearful blur. The Lear was corkscrewing violently now, with the right engine gone, like a toy in a child's clumsy hands. Mac and Ted were probably having a big chuckle.

I watched the ocean below me. The plane was flinging me around, my head banging against the windshield. What direction? Should I use left or right rudder now? I couldn't tell. The wrong choice would kill me. Every warning on the aircraft had either lit up or buzzed itself silly. Not even the synthetic voice knew what to advise me.

I tried not to jerk the yoke too hard as I was slammed around, which would definitely snap my wings off. My Lear would become the world's largest falling Coca Cola bottle.

Seven thousand feet above sea level.

I was hyperventilating, twisting like a lead pancake. Almost too low to recover now. The pressure was turning my brain to cement. I had a brief thought that maybe I should just relax and use my last few seconds for estate planning.

Five thousand feet.

I held my neck in one place long enough to catch a glimpse of the Peregrine lounging above me. They were just now seeing that I was going to crash.

'Departure,' I yelled into the mike, meaning that I had departed from controlled flight and was basically grabbing my ankles to kiss my ass goodbye.

I was heading straight down into big blue swells, my cockpit revolving about once every two seconds. In a moment I would be at impact. I wondered, if I hit, exactly how much it would hurt.

Focus, Terry. Tunnel vision. I ground my teeth and tried the ignition.

It made a puny little grind I could barely hear over my teeth gnashing. But the engine was starting. Now it would take a moment to spool up. I craned my neck, throbbing from the pumping of my main artery, watched the frothy blue waves whirling very close in my windshield..

One thousand feet.

No strap to pull, no ejection seat could save me. If I crashed into the ocean nose first, my Lear would break apart and so would I. The sea would swallow up what was left of me.

'Adios,' I breathed shakily in my radio to Ted and Mac. They would be rubber-necking like morbid curiosity-seekers at a highway accident now, hypnotized with watching me crash.

They couldn't see my engine starting.

I squeezed my eyes shut, then popped them open very wide. Oh God, what big waves. *Dad! Mom! Gumby! Marty! Maria!* I waited for the Lear's little turbine jet engine to spin itself up to speed. Then I felt the slamming jolt of a power surge when my powerplant started to whine in full voice.

About seventy feet above the big blue swell now, the whitecaps visible in clear detail outside my windshield. I stood on my left rudder pedal. My Lear bucked like a frisky colt.

I lifted the nose. It came up . . . up . . . until the jet almost stood on its tail.

Uh-oh. I was starting to slide backwards down

into the sea. If my tail hit the water, it was all over. No. I had power. I had lift. I was airborne.

With a whoop, I soared up over the sea, climbing straight up.

I tore up toward the men in the Peregrine, who were making a lazy low-speed bank at 1,000 feet to watch me die. Ha. Mac recovered quickly and tried to break left.

Not quickly enough. He was doing the worst thing now, trying to run away from me at an awkward angle. His Peregrine could burn up the sky with its mighty thrust. I saw its tail section lighting up red. I swooped into position dead behind the Peregrine's tail just before he straightened out and lit up its big engine and held steady. They couldn't shake me.

I ripped the Polaroid camera from the Velcro.

'Smile, you fuckers,' I said.

Then I took a gorgeous instant Polaroid snapshot of the Peregrine's tail. It showed both engines' hot exhausts, where they would have sucked in my missiles if this Lear was a real fighter.

'Hey, Cyclops . . . Mac . . . listen up,' I shouted into the radio.

I held the mike to the camera so Ted and Mac could both hear the distinctive 'whirrr' of the Polaroid snapshot developing. I yanked it out, the green film already forming an image of the Peregrine's shiny white tail section.

I cackled. Mac had already throttled back. They couldn't run away now. Powering off his tail, I pulled up just to the left of the Peregrine. I shoved the Polaroid against my windshield so they could see it through theirs.

I saw both men grimace. Ted was red-faced.

'Knock it off,' Mac grumbled into the radio, the Air Force signal to end an engagement.

Now I was the one who cackled and beat my feet on the floor.

Today, I was Dean of Spank.

I broke left and started for home. If the Wringer's report on his past gambling behavior was right, Ted Devlin would now be duty-bound to make good on his debt. I could crucify his reputation as a player, and get him in big trouble with the Linnet/TVR board with my Polaroid, if he didn't.

To let out my tension, I calmly visualized Ted begging the Pentagon to give me Special Access clearance. I was sorry I couldn't send my peanut cams to watch Ted. I really wanted to see his face when he made that call.

My chest emptied about a wheelbarrow full of adrenaline. I felt glorious. I only wished I could call the *Wall Street Journal* and tell them how Ted Devlin really made business decisions at Linnet/TVR.

That thought threw the proverbial cold water over my fantasies. All I'd really won was a chance to get prosecuted under the UCMJ.

And I was suddenly tired. Very tired. I hadn't slept in a week. My eyes burned and felt heavy. I peered out over the sun-tipped waves that stretched to the horizon like a shining silver platter. I was tempted to put the Lear on autopilot and take a nap for a few hours like both pilots do in those jumbo-jet cockpits when you're not looking.

Just kidding.

I had to wrestle the plane home manually, still at eighty feet over the waves, and couldn't afford even a long blink.

PART III

The Lone Fragata

ELEVEN

Lucretia Borgia frowned at me.

I was screaming, held down by three palace guards. A fourth raised Lucretia's wine goblet to my lips. I clenched my teeth shut, but a guard sprang open my jaw with a hard whack. It felt like a skillet to the side of my head.

My ear was on fire. I looked inside Lucretia's jeweled goblet again. It was full of a thick, bright blue muck.

'That's not wine, you idiot,' I told the captain of her guards. 'That's Drano. I'm not drinking that.'

'Coward,' shouted Cesare Borgia. He pointed his gold fork at me and scowled.

Nicolo Machiavelli merely frowned and arched his fingers, his voice silky. 'You discredit your profession,' he purred almost sadly. 'Drink the wine.'

I had to admit that I cared what Machiavelli thought. The man invented modern espionage. In the nation-states of Renaissance Italy, that hotbed of treachery, ruthless leaders jockeyed for power. Machiavelli worked as a diplomat for the Republic of Florence. But he was really helping his ruling family, the Borgias, carve out a kingdom through statecraft and spying.

'Wouldn't you just like to try it?' Lucretia clicked her tongue at me.

'It's not wine. It's poison,' I shouted.

A pretty flight attendant's eyes bulged as she retreated from me with her California Chardonnay. She swallowed hard.

'I'm sorry, sir. Would you prefer a soft drink?'

'No. Thank you.' I managed to grin at her. 'I was drifting.'

She backed away quickly, her smile fixed.

I gripped the arms of my first-class seat. Fortunately, the place next to me was empty. The few other people in the first-class compartment worked, read or slept. A second flight attendant glanced up at me from her seat by the cockpit door. She met my eyes, then looked back at her magazine.

I had flown my Lear 55 into LAX at two p.m., dead tired. Just for fun, I left it with a terse note complaining about the poor condition of the aircraft.

Then I had scurried over to the passenger terminal and used the American Airlines airport lounge. It was called the Admiral's Club, and I used my card to get in. I didn't see any admirals I recognized, but there were plenty of weary sales-people in travel suits sitting on leather furniture pecking away at their laptops or staring blankly at CNN on a television set. I found the business center and occupied one of the little cubicles with a computer.

Using code, I typed in another order to the Wringer for a full, complete, dirt-under-the-nails dossier on Skinner, Mac, former USAF. That guy bothered me.

As soon as I left the Admiral's Club, I picked up my small carry-on bag from a locker and bought a round-trip first-class ticket to Guayaquil, Ecuador, on a flight leaving in thirty minutes.

I had a dinner meeting scheduled with a Deputy Minister of Tourism.

That was my business cover story.

But my actual purpose was to fly to the Galapagos Islands, six hundred miles off the coast of Guayaquil, and meet Maria. The Galapagos Islands were inconvenient, time-wasting when time was running out. But it was important to me to meet Maria here at Fragata's touchstone.

During periods of stress when I visited the nature trails in these black volcanic islands, my soul seemed lighter, less encumbered. I was, believe it or not, birdwatching. I always saw great purity in birds, like the ancient Greeks when birds would appear mysteriously from the heavens, soar over them, then fly off again and disappear. They must have seemed to be humankind's only link to the gods. When Charles Darwin sailed to the Galapagos aboard *The Beagle*, he had seen bird species changing from aviators to land birds. That inspired him to put the finishing touches on his theory of evolution.

I know I want to come back as a bird.

I sat up in my cushy seat and stared out another plastic window, permanently scratched by unknown elements. Guayaquil, in our soft descent to the airport, looked like a shining white city on a hill.

Up close, it looked like a proud but poor place that had difficulty feeding its people. In the airport, a colorful Indian mural covered one wall, a Guernica of savage Conquistadors and brave Incas. I carried only one bag and strode with purpose, but a ragged woman scuttled bent over in front of me, not meeting my eyes while she lifted her tiny, sallow child into my face to cry for money. I took out a stack of bills and gave one to her. She was just the pilot fish. Other mothers and babies suddenly appeared in a swarm, their faces beautiful and doll-eyed, the toddlers taught to beg. Their mothers were only children, too, but real-world children. I gave them all bills, swallowed up in the tearful frenzy of the children.

A military officer wearing shiny riding boots took my arm firmly with a white glove.

Two soldiers pulled me away from the children. They led me to a silver Toyota, and I got in the back seat.

'*Bienvenido a Ecuador*,' said the open-faced driver.

He zipped through the busy airport's yowling sprawl and drove into downtown Guayaquil. We had a dinner date at my hotel, the Oro Verde. The staff practically climbed over the counter to greet and help me. I was an old and valued guest of this hotel on my many escapes to the Galapagos Islands.

The Deputy Minister's name was Carlos. He had gentle, liquid eyes in a chiseled-mahogany Indian face. We sat down at a table already filled with exotic stacks of fish and fruit. I made a false presentation, drawing in the air with my hands as I spoke. I told him an American hotel chain wanted to build a hotel in the port city of the Galapagos Islands and realized that it was touchy. Ecuador carefully conserves its *Islas Galapagos* as a living museum of evolution.

The plans I outlined were actually true, but they didn't belong to any client of mine. I was just letting a truly rotten hotel company called TransHost's cat out of the bag before they could start buying up property for a few pennies. Call me snarky to use my limited time to take a petty personal revenge. But I once stayed in a TransHost hotel for two weeks with service so rude and hostile I couldn't help myself. I discovered the top management were basically real-estate developers who hated the hotel business. So I took the time to learn their future development plans in case I ever found an opportunity for payback.

It turned out that the Deputy Minister went to the University of Chicago. He enquired about the Bulls. I was reminded of Frank Lafferty, but the minister was much smarter. I could see his subtle intelligence working already. He would definitely not let his country bend over for TransHost now.

I asked the minister if he would be kind enough to phone ahead to customs so I could breeze in and out of the Galapagos tomorrow without delay. A pressing business calendar. He agreed and seemed relieved and grateful that I wasn't asking for a nightlife tour of Guayaquil, so he could get home to his family.

At 6.30 on Saturday morning, the orange sun was already lighting up the curtains of my room.

I packed my crumpled business clothes in my duffel bag and pulled on a pair of tan shorts and a black polo shirt.

At Guayaquil airport, I boarded an Ecuador 727

that took me six hundred miles west over the Pacific Ocean. When I walked down the stairway on to the steamy tarmac of the tiny, one-stop airport and stepped on the volcanic rock, I almost felt that I had returned home.

This group of islands is so isolated, one has to ponder how the creatures which live there arrived. The birds flew over, of course, and the sea lions could have gotten there by swimming. But naturalists say the lizards came purely by accident, one floating over every million years or so on a palm frond raft from the mainland.

Obviously I found that hard to believe. Darwin did, too, when he sailed through these black rocks. He was still an amateur. Here in the Galapagos, Darwin looked at birds with wings puny as underarm hair.

I couldn't help but notice how crowded the Galapagos had become, choked with tourists in Reeboks and baseball hats, T-shirts pulled over bellies like giant stones, Day-Glo shorts and JVC videocameras. For possibly the first time on one of my frequent trips overseas, I understood why countries wish we'd just FedEx them our aid money and stay home.

Among the birds I saw today, the one I noticed was the bright yellow one with a little banana logo on its tail. One of the American Fruit Company's corporate planes.

In the throng of tourists swallowing up the small airport, I saw the person who the business jet brought here.

His name was Jack, and he was on the board of the big fruit conglomerate that owned vast amouns of property throughout Latin America. In the 1950s, the CIA helped American Fruit by over-throwing the duly-elected president of a Central American country in a staged coup. It was supposed to be an anti-Communist covert operation, but the real purpose was to keep acres of banana planta-tions which American Fruit used to grow its popular Juanita banana brand from being nationalized. When the people of Latin America eventually figured out what the CIA had done, they invented the popular slogan 'Yanqui Go Home'.

Once Jack personally offered me two million dollars to steal a rival's secret formula for con-centrated orange juice that tasted more like freshly squeezed.

I really wanted to avoid Jack, who was walking toward me from the outdoor curio stand, next to the weathered airport building, wearing a golf shirt and shorts in Easter Bunny pastels with a camera slung over his shoulder. I reflected that in evolutionary terms, Jack was singularly adapted to look just right inside an office, a corner one. Here in the Galapagos, he appeared as doughy and dumb-founded as a beached whale.

I clutched the black bag I carried, walking quickly toward a gaggle of young European tourists with backpacks and uncombed hair, sincerely hoping Jack would have forgotten about ever meeting me.

'Terry Weston,' Jack shouted.

I sighed and looked back as he yelled, waving his

215

hand broadly. He had that silly delighted expression of people who grab on to acquaintances they bump into in a foreign land, just before they remember that they don't like them.

'I'll be damned,' Jack shouted. 'What are you doing here?'

'A little relaxation. How about you and . . .?'

His wife appeared on cue, a vigorously sociable woman. She wore a tourist sunhat that said *I love Boobies*, referring to a local bird.

'Helen,' I remembered. 'Good to see you.'

We all pumped hands, and I got mine tangled in the camera straps hanging around both their necks.

'We're sailing on the *Isabel*, a cruise around the islands,' Jack said.

I wished them *bon voyage* at the first decent pause, and bolted to catch a hand-painted bright blue bus with five different ornaments from old American cars lovingly stuck on the hood.

In the bus full of European tourists, I bounced around and got better acquainted with my kidneys for forty minutes, chatting with one of the old-salt varieties of local from the tiny port of Puerto Aroyo. He was already drunk at ten a.m. Fortunately, as I had hoped, he had what I needed. When we reached the port city, I gave him $300 in US bills to rent his Zodiac rubber boat out for two hours.

He ran with the cash to the Baltro Hotel to buy drinks for the regulars. I maneuvered his patched-up yellow Zodiac out of the harbor and opened up the old Johnson outboard motor. I had left my luggage satchel and brought only a bright yellow compact Sony Sports digital videodisk player.

The warm salt spray coated my face. I smiled. I hugged the shoreline, watching out for rocks. From memory, I found a cove on another shore of the island. Gunning the engine, I ran the Zodiac up on to a small strip of beach, then got out and hauled it up on to the sand.

I climbed over the few slippery rocks with my Sony and trekked along a nature path through the odd mix of verdant and scrubby plants that grew on the black rocks. I thought about avian DNA and about Maria using it to design LUCI.

It's funny that before seeing Maria's blob I never put together the idea of using those millions of years of avian adaptation to control a plane.

I watched a colony of rather cartoonish birds with big black eyes called the waved albatross that had built a kind of runway beside the nature trail I walked, in the path of the prevailing wind. An albatross took off now. It raced into the wind on its webbed feet, flapping its wings frantically until it built up enough lift to take off. I watched another albatross on the same runway, hanging its webbed feet down like flaps to slow it down, hitting the ground running. It was LAX in microcosm.

I shielded my eyes from the sun and looked out to sea, where a bright blue-footed booby was dive-bombing for food. It hit the water beak-first in a 180° headlong plunge at maybe sixty m.p.h., all tucked in like a perfectly pointed golf-tee.

I continued walking toward the Darwin Research Station. Then, in a patchy field of barren, yellowed grass and short, gnarled, almost naked trees, I saw the indigenous creature I loved most in the world.

The *fragata*. The English name is frigate bird, named for the fast ship used by eighteenth-century pirates, but I always call them *fragata* in the language of their native land. The male *fragata* is so shiny, black and stiletto-thin, he should have had a jet interceptor named after him. My klepto-parasitic rogue is perfectly adapted to steal his food from other birds in flight, to take for his family what he lacks the ability to forage for himself.

I stepped toward the gathering of *fragata* birds carefully. This was their mating season, and I didn't want to disturb what has to be the most poignant mating ritual in the whole animal kingdom, if you like a little irony with your bird sex-play.

I focused on a young, proud-looking male, probably a teenager in human years. He had a long beak with a small hook at the end. His wings were angled back handsomely for speed and maneuver-ability. Yes, he really resembled a fighter jet, if you ignored the bright red sac hanging from his neck, normally the size and shape of a golf ball. This was probably his most efficient feature. This sac held food in flight and served another even more important purpose during mating season.

At this time of year when every heart seeks its mate, it's the young female *fragatas* who circle over-head, dewy and expectant, to conduct the search. The females fly up over the males like lofty Rules Girls, searching for that perfect mate.

The young males exhibit all the stress of the

mating ritual. They sit nestled in the bushes below, trying to inflate those small golf-ball-sized chin sacs into the biggest billowing lipstick-red balloons they possibly can without blowing out their lungs or toppling over. The males look like they're sporting giant red spinnakers. In all of creation, the male *fragata*'s sac is the most extravagant display you will ever see of a desperate male hoping to get lucky.

I kept my eyes trained on the *fragatas*, while in my periphery I saw Maria approaching on the nature path. Situational awareness. You either use it or lose it.

She had sidled up to a tour group led by an Ecuadorian naturalist guide. The guides were sophisticated and friendly, taught and joked in many languages. Being a Galapagos guide in Ecuador was a big deal.

I watched with great interest Maria's ability to adapt to the group of tourists in T-shirts and straw hats. She spoke in Spanish, which I could barely overhear, with the nature guide.

It was hard not to stare at Maria. She looked glossy, her sculpted bare arms and legs gleaming in the harsh midday light. Her calf muscles reminded me of a Ms Universe contestant. But she didn't flaunt her body. She wore white shorts and a creamy T-shirt, both one size too large. Her hair was tightly bound up under her tan cap. She had black wire-rimmed sunglasses, delicate on her small nose. Her moist, dark red lips formed a small circle of curiosity.

Seeing her broke the cloud that had formed in my

head when I arrived in the islands to see it polluted with tourists. Hope throbbed in my chest until it felt swollen. This was definitely not just a business meeting.

She walked up and stood beside me, saying nothing. Only three feet away she silently observed the male *fragatas* puffing up their bright red sacs.

'Señor Fragata.' She nodded in my direction. 'I see your buddies are flashing the girls to get some action.'

'I see how you got those great legs, leaping to conclusions,' I told her. 'The male *fragatas* are searching for lifetime mates here. And the sex is nothing to write home about, as far as I can see. At least not after the first time. Once they have eggs together, a *fragata* dad has his work cut out for him just trying to feed his hatchlings.'

Her cushiony lips formed their little red donut. 'Poor thing.'

'He's overcome a disability. He doesn't have the natural varnish on his wings the other birds have to dive down and pick fish out of the sea,' I explained to her. 'If he gets his wings wet, he'll drown. But that can-do spirit throbs in the *fragata* breast. He found a way.'

'By becoming a mugger of the skies,' Maria said with her schoolmarm's upper lip raised in disapproval.

I shrugged. 'Not the mugger. Maybe the venture capitalist. He tries not to hurt the other birds in case he needs them again. That's what klepto-parasitic behavior's all about. We all do it, Maria. The *fragata* just flaunts it like his sac. See that male lying in wait, checking the sky?'

I pointed to a mature male *fragata*. He didn't need to display his sac because he'd already mated. He sat with his little red golf ball under his beak beside a rather dour, bored-looking female and a whole nest of fluffy, awkward white chicks peeping and bumping into one another.

'He just spotted that cormorant flying with food in its mouth.' I nodded at a bird in the sky. 'Now the *fragata* will stalk and intercept him.'

She watched the heavy white cormorant with a fish in its beak flapping its wings overhead, as the male *fragata* worked himself into position with minimal fuss.

He locked his beady eyes dead on to the prey and darted ahead on spindly legs using his great *fragata* wings for lift. Then he tucked his legs under him and took off. The *fragata* soared regally, the great black pirate, a smooth and stealthy interceptor now picking up speed at his sixty degree angle of attack, cagily keeping himself in the cormorant's blind spot.

The cormorant seemed to sense trouble, then he turned and saw the black *fragata* closing on him and instinctively shrieked.

As he opened his mouth, the fish he carried dropped out.

The *fragata* turned into a graceful precision dive, snatching the falling fish in his beak, and banked away. The cormorant acted flustered. But he pulled himself together. He unruffled his feathers and slunk off in the other direction.

221

'See?' I told Maria. 'Unless his prey has a heart attack, a *fragata* never hurts anybody. You can't say that about other birds.'

'So bravo for klepto-parasitic behavior.' Maria stared at my Sony Sports DVD player. 'I hope that means you're ready to do business now.'

'It depends. Are you wearing a bathing suit under your shorts?'

'Why?'

'I'd like to go for a swim while we talk. It's just a precaution against anybody listening . . .'

'Forget it. I'm not getting in the water with you.' Her frown loosened. 'Do you actually think I'm wearing a *recording* device?'

'No.'

'You can search me.'

She teased me, raising her arms over her head and pirouetting her trim body around very slowly on tiptoe. Such a bronzed little diva, here in the cradle of evolution. I chuckled and she stopped. She stood very close to me now, getting in my personal space.

'Okay,' I said crisply. 'Here's our situation. I won a bet with Ted . . .'

'What bet?'

'That I could beat him at Spank.'

She looked disdainful. 'What's that?'

'In our case, dogfighting in business jets.'

Her jaw dropped open and her voice trembled. 'He's not dead, is he?'

'No, Maria,' I told her slowly. 'We were just playing.'

She composed herself. 'And?'

'And now I can get inside the LUCI simulator at Linnet/TVR. So if you can talk me through deprogramming your Doom Level, maybe I can do it in the sim.'

I had expected, when I delivered that line, that I would feel a triumphal moment of pride and victory. Instead, I felt a squirt of green jealous bile inside.

'Okay,' she said. 'I'm impressed. Let me see the tape.'

'You know what I can't figure out,' I held my Sony back from her, 'is why you designed LUCI to be such a perfect strike fighter for Ted Devlin to develop. I saw the shape. It's the JSF fighter prototype they were already building. He could almost plug your whole program in. Lockheed couldn't have done it. Boeing couldn't have done it.'

She hid behind the black circles of her dark glasses. 'I liked what Linnet/TVR was doing. It was a sensible design.'

'True,' I agreed, 'but that sure makes Ted Devlin an ungrateful sonofabitch, don't you think?'

'Yes.' She nodded. 'But it just happened that way. A coincidence.'

'I hate those.'

'Well, they happen anyway.' She stuck her hands firmly in her shorts. 'Can we look at your disk now? I'd like to see the inside of the sim.'

I started to say more, but decided not to. I picked up my DVD, opened it and tapped 'Play'. The disk I had loaded showed her an edited version of what my peanut cams and I saw in Ted Devlin's executive conference room and simulator suite. I stood beside her to watch her eyes behind her sunglasses as she looked at the screen. They looked first astonished, then pained. Then, for a brief moment, proud.

Ted's LUCI plane was Maria Haymeyer's game design, and the nastiness I felt in my stomach thinking about her with Ted began melting away. She was heartbreaking.

'Is that all?' she asked when the video ended, making a brave face. 'I have to say I'm impressed.'

'Maria . . .'

I touched her arm, but she pulled back. She stood stewing in her suntan oil for about two minutes while I looked away to watch the male *fragatas* puffing their red chests. One attracted a mate. A female flew down to sit on the branch with him. I looked back and Maria was lifting her sunglasses to wipe her eyes.

'Maria,' I said as gently as I could, 'was Ted still married to Zima when you became his lover?'

She blinked and pulled her full red lips into a tight, turned-down look of horror. Her disgust looked genuine.

'Terry, I would never, in this lifetime or any other, sleep with Ted Devlin.'

'Sure. Then why show him your design?'

'I was egotistical and stupid.'

'I'll buy the first part, but don't insult my intelligence.'

'Sometimes your intelligence is bad.' She folded her arms.

'You could have told your professors. Everybody at Stanford knew you were a genius.'

'No aero-engineering professor would accuse the CEO of Linnet/TVR of theft. Not on my word, anyway.'

'What about your stepfather, Lloyd? He's a professor, strictly speaking. Couldn't he have helped you?'

She gripped her arm tightly with her fingers, her knuckles whitening. 'I thought you read my dossier.'

'Well then, your mother.'

She sounded very sad and tired. 'My mother is the last person I could have told the truth about Ted Devlin.'

'She doesn't know?'

'Never.'

I spoke slowly, as though to a child. 'Maria. Please. Your honesty is important to me right now. Explain exactly why you took your unprotected work and handed it over to a manifestly self-serving defense contractor, if you weren't sleeping with him.'

She stood with her sleek arms folded, deciding. 'Do you feel you inherited any of your skills from your parents?'

'Why?'

'I'd like you to answer my question.'

I expected her to offer some logical explanation. Instead, she took a very deep breath. Then she puffed up her cheeks and held it so long, her face started to turn red. I've never seen a grown woman do that before. Her eyes seemed to bug out while her cheeks blew up into tennis balls. She was turning scarlet. I had no doubt that she possessed the will to hold her breath until she passed out on the ground. I began laughing and couldn't stop.

'Okay,' I grabbed her arm, 'cut that out.'

Slowly she began to exhale. 'Who was the first pilot in your family?'

'My great-grandad flew a Spad in the First World War. A great pilot. Had terrific situational awareness.'

'What was his job?'

'Reconnaissance.'

'Spying. And your grandfather?'

'He flew in the Second World War.'

'How did he die?'

'Photo-reconnaissance. He plowed into a German beet field.'

She nodded. 'Spy. I suppose it takes several generations to produce a successful adaptation. Our talents are in our nature, Terry. We have to inherit them from someone. Do you follow me?'

'No.'

She breathed in, as though I was being unbelievably dense. 'Your father didn't die. What happened to him?'

'It's in the Wringer file.'

'Tell me anyway.'

'He was one of the Air Force pilots who flew into Laos for the CIA and got shot down. He punched out and landed in a rice field, shattered his leg in eight places . . .'

'He was captured and put in a bamboo cage,' she said.

'Right. They called it the Hanoi Hilton. A bunch of Cuban interrogators were flown in to help the Viet Cong. They took him out every day and beat him up. A year later he escaped and came home. He always limped badly, and he saw flashes and floaters in front of his eyes. It seems they detached one of his retinas. He couldn't even keep his Corvette on the right side of the road, let alone fly a plane.'

'Did the CIA help him?'

'No. He could have been rescued, but the CIA wouldn't allow it. They said if he isn't really in Laos, how can we rescue him? When he came home, he looked at my mom and me like he expected us to shove flaming bamboo shoots under his fingernails.'

'What did the Air Force do for him?'

'Patched him up and gave him therapy. Then they promoted him to colonel and gave him a soft job with no career prospects. When I was a teenager, we lived on a base off Manhattan called Governor's Island. My father was put on the team supervising an ad agency that did the Air Force campaign, "Fly Higher".'

'I remember that one.' She nodded, unimpressed.

'I guess the dopers liked it.'

'What about your mother?'

'What about her?' I dimly realized that my mother as a young woman could be the model for the Lucretia Borgia in my nightmares. Mom was taller and more angular. But they definitely had the same attitude.

227

'She made an awful lot of trouble,' Maria prompted me.

'I suppose you could say that. Everyone else did. She'd shoplift from the PX and deny it. And play around with the married officers. When my father became a POW, some officers' wives showed up at our house. Their idea of an intervention. They tried to scold her, but she just yelled at them in Italian, threw them all out, and laughed about it afterwards.'

'She stole.'

'I guess.'

'You had to learn your Fragata skills from someone, Terry. Your mother was the survivor in your household.'

'Well, let's say she was a better civilian than my dad. The ad agency promised my father that if he ever left the Air Force, they'd hire him. Even I knew it was a lie. They just told him that so he'd approve their ad campaigns. He tried defense contractors, airlines. His drinking was difficult to hide by then. My mom wouldn't cook or clean house. She used to say, why cook when so many restaurants do the job so well? Our apartment looked like a crack house. One Friday while I was in tenth grade, my dad parked his Corvette on a beach on Long Island. Then he blew his brains out with his Air Force sidearm.'

She nodded and rubbed my arm very softly with the palm of her hand, which was her most affectionate gesture ever in my direction. 'See?'

'Maria, what are you saying?'

'I'm trying to tell you how you became who you

are. Your father had certain skills you picked up. Your mother had others. Do you ever visit your mother?'

'There's something off-putting about an ageing narcissistic personality.'

Maria said deadpan, 'Don't talk about yourself that way. I guess I can't be this subtle with you, Terry. I inherited certain skills and abilities too. And I needed to meet the person responsible.'

I finally connected Maria's missing dots.

'You and Ted.'

'Yes, Terry, we're both bastards, Ted and I. Ted is my real father.' She sounded coldly defiant, as though she was trying to freeze her feelings under the crushing heat of the Baltro sun. 'I offered to give LUCI to Ted Devlin because I fantasized about my father.'

She stood stiff and self-justifying, her chin jutting out. Then she started to tremble.

'During high school,' I said, 'the week you were out sick, that's when you found out.'

'Yes. I watched a talk show my first day at home. It was about finding your biological parents. I always wondered if my father was really a man named Peter Rodriguez from Miami, because my mother never talked about him, and that is very not-Cuban. So I researched on my computer for seventy-three hours straight and found my birth father. Ted had been in Washington in the early seventies. He was trying to persuade the Nixon administration to give his company military contracts. My mother, Jessica, lived there. She

229

worked as a TV news reporter. They met some-place, I believe a Georgetown singles' bar. He left town, she was pregnant. And she never told him about me. I know that much.'

Looking at Maria, I finally saw Ted.

'We really strip down out here in the Galapagos, don't we?' She wiped her damp hair back. She was trying so hard not to break down, my eyes were starting to burn.

'Your mother doesn't know?'

'I'd never tell her.'

'Are you sure Ted doesn't know?' I asked.

She shook her head vigorously, like a bee had landed on it. This time she didn't pull back when I put my arm around her shoulder. It was warm from the sun, slippery with suntan oil. And it trembled at my touch.

'Maybe someone else should tell him,' I volunteered.

'If it were that simple,' she sighed, 'I would have. Look at his life. He wouldn't take my mother's calls either. Not when she wanted to tell him about me twenty-six years ago. He didn't have any room for children. Unless you count Zima.'

'You couldn't just *tell* him when you got him to meet you for lunch?'

'No, Terry.' She flashed me her most blisteringly sad look. 'Like you couldn't show me this videodisk in LA. You had to bring me to the land of the *fragata* to show me who you were.'

'You wanted to show him who you were.'

Her voice broke off. 'I knew he didn't want a

daughter to pop up and ruin his life. But I thought he could use a really bright engineer. If he learned to admire my work first, then maybe . . .'

She drifted off, and I had an unsettling thought. 'Maria, if you created the Doom Level as some kind of Trojan Horse because you knew Ted would steal the design . . .'

'I didn't.'

I believed her. Her voice came from a hurt child. Here on the black volcanic rock, the cradle of evolution, I devolved. Thinking about Ted made me want to pick up a rock, fly back to Long Beach and crush his skull.

I took off her glasses and brushed the tears from her cheeks.

'Okay,' I said after a moment, 'we don't tell him. We just go ahead as planned.' I held her. 'We take separate flights back. I'll go now. Poke around, clear your mind. I'll try to defuse LUCI's program in the sim.'

'What if you can't?'

'We've got fourteen whole days. We'll come up with another plan.' I held her chin lightly and kissed her forehead.

Her lip quivered and I wanted to kiss that too.

She gently pushed me away. 'You'd better catch your flight.'

I left for my Zodiac, moving slowly so I could still see her standing in the same place. She was such a perfect specimen. No wonder nature made children so big-eyed and adorable, so you'd want to protect them. Or at least not kill them.

231

I would protect Maria. I was singularly adapted to the task, the cunning Fragata who could fly any plane on earth with a little practice. Ted Devlin was just a corporate thief. I'd dealt with that before and, modesty should forbid, pretty well.

I pushed the Zodiac off and, as I puttered away, watched the puffed-up males with their red balloons.

I was psyching myself up pretty well. The odds weren't so terrible. It was just me against the Pentagon, the FBI, the Air Force, and the rest of the military defense establishment. But so what? A *fragata* never faltered and always got his prey.

From the sea, I spotted a lone *fragata* checking out a white booby flying with a fish in its mouth. The sky thief pulled in his sac, eager to stage an air show to impress the girl. He lifted his wide, tapered wings and took off with a sinister grace, lowering his head until his body made a perfect knife, and shooting up rapidly.

'Up and at 'em!' I yelled at the bird.

Uh-oh. The booby saw him coming too soon. He banked hard right. Instead of shrieking in fear and dropping its fish, the tough little nut of a booby looped under the attacking *fragata*, then darted away. My startled *fragata* was left to circle aimlessly in the sky, his element of surprise gone.

He looked embarrassed.

I felt the salt foam in my face and tried to recover my psyching-up rhythms. I plunged ahead into the choppy waves, my Johnson outboard motor straining noisily like an electric blender.

Arriving back at the airport, I had expected the Ecuadorian immigration officials to be warm and friendly after the Deputy Minister of Tourism's phone call on my behalf. Instead, they watched me very curiously as they went through the motions of stamping my passport. I didn't know why, but it made me slightly uneasy. Oh well. With six hours of first-class travel ahead, I would have time to plan and even to nap. Soon I would be back in my apartment, rinsing the Galapagos salt and volcanic dust out of my hair.

'Captain Weston?'

An unfamiliar voice, obviously from the past. I hadn't been an Air Force captain for ten years. I turned around expecting an old ex-military buddy. My isolated Galapagos Islands had somehow become an overcrowded Grand Central Station packed with people I didn't want to see.

Two blue-suiters, active-duty officers wearing the distinctive uniforms, stood very close to me. The United States Air Force. But why? I quickly calculated that the US hadn't had a legitimate military purpose on the Galapagos Islands since World War II.

The two men each held up a military identification card. I checked the pictures. The colonel who spoke to me was middle-aged. He had a long, cracked-leather face and the patient eyes of a hunter. The captain, in his twenties and black, looked solid and wary.

'I'm Lieutenant Colonel Zeke Clements,' the older officer drawled. He nodded at the younger,

233

stocky one. 'This is Captain Russell. Just so you know who you're talkin' to.'

Clements sounded like a Georgia or Florida native. Throw a stick through any Air Force base, and you'd hit twenty Zekes.

'What unit you from?' I couldn't tell from their uniforms, which was bad for me.

'Special Intelligence.'

Naturally. 'Out of?'

'The Pentagon.' The young one smiled, but not to bond with me, eying the bright yellow Sony Sports DVD player strapped over my arm.

Clements and Russell both gave me nasty little cop grins.

Air Force Special Intelligence handled various tasks, one of which involved ferreting out spies and traitors from within the service. They could only be here to greet me for one reason. But I was a civilian. Legally, the FBI was supposed to come and arrest me, not the Air Force. Unless the Pentagon had decided to handle this illegally. What did they know about me already?

'Captain Weston, we're just gonna take you off this here Ecuadorian plane,' Colonel Clements butchered the country's name, 'and put you on one of ours.'

'Now why would you want to do that?' I asked him, the sound of my banging heart ricocheting off my eardrums.

'For your comfort and safety.' His smile broke the slack, leathery hide of his cheeks into a series of folds like an accordion. Colonel Clements had very steady eyes, like he'd spent his boyhood staring down alligators.

My options seemed limited. I didn't imagine my one meeting with a Deputy Minister of Tourism would buy me political asylum here.

So we walked outside together in tight formation, me in the middle. I saw that, where the yellow American Fruit jet had once sat, a white one with blue markings had replaced it. The Lear bore a USAF Airlift Wing tail designation.

'Just like old times.' Zeke read my thoughts.

'I want to call my lawyer,' I told him.

Colonel Clements only chuckled and calmly pulled my return plane ticket out of my hand. He handed it to Captain Russell. I thought I saw the younger officer smile as he ripped it up and threw the pieces on the ground.

The remnants of my freedom blew away and scattered across the steamy tarmac like the least festive confetti I had ever seen.

TWELVE

Captain Russell shut the door behind us.

The interior of a military Learjet C-21, a very narrow airframe, can give you a cramped feeling like a coffin.

At least *I* felt buried alive, even though the walls were mealy tan fiberglass instead of bright red satin. The seats and laminated desktop, set up with an inflight fax machine, appeared standard Air Force issue. With its spartan interior the military bizjet resembled a flying Winnebago more than my company Lear.

The flight officers were lieutenants, both young women with short hair, both all-business. They ran through their checklist quickly and didn't roll their eyes at the Baltros ATC's imperfect pronunciation. English is the worldwide language of commercial aviation, but sometimes it's hard to tell. We took off at a steep military climb and banked hard right for our destination.

'Where are we headed?' I asked.

'The United States, son. We're all Americans here,' the colonel said, deadpan. The captain grunted humorously.

I had a chance to study Clements and Russell during the turbine whine before takeoff, when none of us bothered to say anything because we'd have to shout.

I took deep breaths and fought the spurts of adrenaline, trying to figure out a strategy.

They obviously knew practically all they needed to know about me. That was why they both stared patiently at my bright yellow Sony Sports DVD player, waiting for the engine to quiet down. I kept it strapped to my shoulder and lying in my lap. No use trying to hide it.

Marty Schmidt would tell me to say nothing. But that probably wouldn't get them to tell me what they knew about me already. Knowing what information they had would be critical to my next tactical move, which might be arguing Maria's case and trying to get the Pentagon to quietly, secretly investigate Ted Devlin's LUCI. Or it might be trying to find a parachute and jumping out of this Lear when we got below 10,000 feet.

Clements and Russell were obviously an interrogation team. Colonel Clements was the wily one. I could sniff that. He was the hunter and trapper. His face had that leathery black-creased tan that made me calculate his age, in alligator years, at about forty-five. His teeth had ancient tobacco stains. I concluded that Zeke could probably whip out an old hunting knife with duct tape wrapped around the handle and fillet my skin off without one sloppy seam.

Young Captain Russell was from New York or New Jersey, aggressive and cynical, like a big-city cop. He was a solid black guy in his twenties with a tight, pursed mouth that looked out of place on his square jaw. His suspicious eyes suggested to me that he came to this job from Air Force Security. Russell had obviously seen the darker side of Air Force personnel – even in these high-tech times, they still needed recruits willing to kill and maim other people, if from a distance, and our skyfighter glam attracted a few psychos among the ranks of American youth who merely wanted jobs similar to playing their favorite video games. Now Russell seemed to have the role of trapper's partner. Probably he was the big bear you'd run away from until you felt your leg caught in Colonel Clements' trap.

I wondered what they were allowed to do to me under the Federal Espionage Act, 18 USC, 793E. Marty had pulled that out recently so I could read it for myself. It seemed pretty clear-cut that they weren't supposed to do much of anything to a civilian like me.

I sweated pure gratitude that I wasn't in the service any more. If I was, old Zeke could just smile his trapper's grin, slip the handcuffs on me right here, and the Air Force would prosecute me under the Uniform Code of Military Justice. Then after a short, merciless trial, I would probably be blind-folded, stood in front of a firing squad, and offered a last nicotine patch or whatever they do today for traitors.

All they needed to do right now was to take my Sony Sports DVD player and press 'Play'. Their eyes would bulge to see my video of Ted's JSF aircraft. Then they could call in the FBI, which had all the jurisdiction over me they needed to arrest me as a spy. My defense would be limited to wild stories about a Doom Level.

While we were taking off, heading up swiftly to 45,000 feet, I considered how to play these guys. I didn't know Maria's status. She had booked herself on a plane that left two hours later than mine, so she could either be hiking the nature trails or in military custody like me.

I would flush out the old trapper and his partner, and learn the worst they had on me as soon as possible. If I started aggressive, I could always get nicer.

'Colonel,' I growled with my best officer sang-froid, 'what's Zeke short for, anyway? Ezekiel?'

The colonel was a little startled. It's amazing how sensitive even the most hardened soldiers can be about the names they get stuck with. Russell stared at me like I was insane.

'Ezekiel,' I said, clipped and irate, 'how'd you find me here?'

'Word gets around,' Captain Russell said.

'Outstanding,' I said with a light sneer. 'Maybe you'll explain why you think you can come out here to a foreign country and interfere with my travel plans.'

I heard a short ring and looked over to the desktop fax machine. It made those screechy receiving noises, then began whirring. A document was coming through.

'The Air Force swings its arms pretty freely in our investigations, Captain,' Colonel Clements drawled at me. Russell watched the fax appear in the machine. I heard it crunch and shut off after only one page had come through.

'Well, your right to swing your arms ends where my nose begins,' I said, which prompted them to look at each other like bemused bookends.

'Pretty clever, Captain. Captain Russell, make a note of Captain Weston's righteous indignation.' Clements smiled and showed me his teeth, slightly sharpened as though his diet consisted of chewing on sugar cane.

Russell had gone over to the fax machine. He took out the piece of paper and handed it to Clements, who glanced at it and nodded.

'Okay, Colonel. End of conversation.' I bent forward on my elbow. 'Now I've got work to do, just like I would've on my scheduled flight. If you want to play hard-ass, I might call some old buddies and see that you wind up your Air Intelligence career in Antarctica, figuring out who stole the Post-Its from the quonset hut. So you've got ten seconds to tell me how the fuck I can help you, Zeke.'

'How the fuck you can help me, *sir*, would be the correct way to address me,' the Colonel drawled, his face crinkling like cardboard.

'Say again?'

'You address a superior officer as "sir", Captain, if y'all got any more righteous indignation to puke up.'

'Superior officer? Maybe you haven't noticed, but I'm a civilian. I haven't been 'Captain' Weston for years. And personally, Zeke, I think that new Air Force uniform makes you guys look like a couple of Delta stewards.'

He leaned over and dropped the faxed sheet right side up in my lap.

'Gotta agree with you 'bout the uniforms, Captain, but only off the record.'

I looked down at the letter. It was a very short letter on official USAF stationery. I felt the creepy dread of beginning to fall down a very deep hole. I picked up the page and read it once quickly, then very slowly, trying to absorb the single sentence.

To: Weston, Terrence
      Captain, USAF
Re: Notice of Reinstatement
You are hereby ordered to report to active duty in the United States Air Force, subject to its command and jurisdiction.

Some 'General Gray' on the Joint Chiefs staff at the Pentagon had signed it. I didn't see any 'cordially'.

Pungent animal fear touched my nostrils. I took a moment to bite my tongue, then blew air out my lips very slowly. My fingers kept from shaking by making a little paper airplane out of the letter and sailing it back into Colonel Zeke Clements' lap.

'This order is a joke,' I said confidently, hoping they couldn't hear my stomach boil.

They looked at each other again and smiled like kids. Or more like old pals sharing a Heineken at the Officers' Club and remembering somebody they had a lot of fun arresting. Colonel Clements reached over toward me, then veered left and quickly

241

unzipped my duffel bag. He placed the letter inside and zipped it back up.

'We're not here to joke around much, Captain,' Colonel Clements intoned.

He held the palm of his hand out. Captain Russell slapped a manila file into it right on cue.

'Let's see.' Clements pretended to study my file. 'Says your job is venture capitalist in *global* markets. That's pretty high cotton, son.'

'There's a pretty high level of bullshit piling up in this aircraft, Colonel.'

'Venture capitalist for global markets,' Colonel Clements said over, ignoring me, like a stubborn horse heading back to a favorite stream.

It wasn't like I could go outside if I couldn't take the heat. I looked ostentatiously at my watch.

'This job of yours,' the Colonel went on. 'You travel to the Far East some. Anybody over there ever asked you to get anything for them in the US you might call out of the ordinary?'

'Once,' I said.

Both men got very alert.

'The CEO of an Asian airline called Mandarin Air asked me for a hockey stick autographed by Wayne Gretsky. I thought that was pretty odd. Asians aren't big on hockey.'

Their faces hardened.

'Why did you come to the Galapagos Islands?' Zeke asked me, looking at my Sony again.

'Business.'

'What kind of business you doin' on a volcanic island?'

'You don't know? Some Intel job you guys are doing. I came to the Galapagos as a tourist. My business was in Guayaquil.' The air inside the Lear was feeling dense. 'If you're asking my personal reason, I like the Galapagos. It's the laboratory of evolution.'

The colonel drummed his fingers on the arm of his seat. He and Russell both eyed my Sony DVD player at the same time. 'Captain, what's the videodisk player for?'

'The flight home,' I ventured, feeling sticky damp cold in my lower back and armpits, the sweat so slippery on my back now, I braced myself in the seat. 'Now maybe you can tell me why the Air Force wants to reinstate a thirty-five-year-old businessman who's starting to forget where he left his car keys.'

'Makes our job easier.'

The interior of the Lear didn't feel like a roomy coffin any more, more like the inside of a cigar tube.

'How?' I asked.

Their eyes flicked nastily at each other. Russell's shoulders bulged up under his blue jacket and the artery popped in his neck. 'Captain, you planning to do anything hinkey with Ted Devlin's sim?'

A squirt of adrenaline shot through my body. *Breathe*. 'Like what?'

'You tell us.'

Since they had to play by the rules, to some extent, I believed that I was only required to answer direct questions under the UCMJ. I noticed that they hadn't given me my limited rights as a detainee yet.

'Colonel, brother to brother and all, I see you guys must be hot stuff in Intel if the Air Force gives you a Lear. Am I some kind of suspect in an investigation of yours?'

'Why would you think that, Captain?' Zeke drawled with a hint of surprise in his eyes. 'We're just here to ask you why you want to poke into our Joint Strike Fighter program, son.'

'I wanted to do business with Ted Devlin on another product,' I shrugged, casually flipping my hand, like Zeke had asked me what was on TV that night. 'Why threaten me with re-instatement over that?'

Zeke cocked his head. 'Threaten you? With an Air Force commission?'

Russell looked like I had gotten his nose particularly out of joint. 'We don't get your attitude. Devlin's asking the Pentagon for a forty-eight-hour Special Access clearance. No civilian's gotten one of those in the whole history of clearances. So we try to accommodate you.'

My mind screamed backward. What exactly did Air Force Special Intelligence do these days? Clearances? No. The Pentagon's Defense Security Service did civilian clearances. Unless I was still an officer.

'We were comin' to tell you,' Zeke said, 'the only way you could get Special Access right away is if you were still in the Air Force.'

I nodded firmly. They were reinstating me to do a bypass around the Pentagon's Security Service, which tends to run about half a million cases behind.

'Ted Devlin put in for balls-to-the-wall, forty-eight-hour clearance for you as a technical consultant.' Zeke glanced at the file still in his lap. "Review simulator procedures only.' No access to the prototype or production areas.'

'I can only tell you,' I breathed out in relief, 'that I want to get into that sim to make sure everything's A-okay for the military.'

'Then I don't see any reason to deny you Special Access clearance, Captain,' Zeke said.

'Here's your ticket back home.' Russell handed me my return ticket to LAX intact.

'I thought you tore that up.'

'That was just a travel brochure.' Russell smirked like a kid who jokes about killing you for your lunch money.

'We were just having ourselves a little fun,' Clements cackled. 'We want to keep the JSF playing field level. None of the contractors are gonna get special treatment. But we'll see they don't get special problems, either.'

We all agreed that would be fair and proper. I could see sunset through the portholes. Golden shafts of light began to pop in through the small holes.

'Well, sun's over the horizon, Captain Weston,' Zeke said. 'Time for Happy Hour at the Flyin' O Club.'

In a few minutes, they'd opened up a travel bar, no doubt against regulations. In minutes we were tinkling ice and sipping Scotch, swapping gossip. I listened carefully to Zeke's take on Ted Devlin.

'Nobody in the Pentagon thinks Teflon Ted's any saint. But he's come through often enough. Word is, his JSF's kind of special.' He squeezed my shoulder, grinning conspiratorially. 'What'd Ted tell you? Anything y'all want to share with us?'

'If he did, Colonel, that'd be classified,' I said.

We all laughed again and put away our Scotch. When you don't drink Scotch for a long time, it tastes like rusty metal.

'Zeke, what's the media take on the JSF program?' I asked innocently, and saw a skittering of anxiety across his tough old hide. 'Democracy puts a funny ding in our human evolution, doesn't it? Even a battle-scarred old warrior like you gets queasy thinking about how some beauty contest winner who works for *Hard Copy* could beat up the world's mightiest military force.'

'It's not *Hard Copy* we're worried about,' Zeke grimaced. 'It's Allyn Pollack. We hear Pollack's sniffin' around tryin' to find a way to get dirt on the JSF program. Hell,' Zeke drawled, making two syllables of the word. 'Pollack's meaner'n a god-damn bedbug.'

So they weren't taking me in chains to Fort Leavenworth and I'd passed the first bureaucratic hurdle. I still had to clear Linnet/TVR internal security and the FBI. But now I'd also have cunning old trapper Colonel Clements and his jovial partner looking over my shoulder with spy satellites. I decided to try to use it.

'So, Zeke,' I asked him innocently, 'any idea how Linnet security clears people internally?'

Thirteen

Ted sat behind a desk about the size of an aircraft-carrier deck.

A huge shadeless window behind him backlit his silhouette. It also beamed harsh southern California sunlight into the faces of me and two JSF program managers – Mac Skinner and a guy named Leon. We all sat in uncomfortable chairs across from him.

Ted perched on the most elevated black leather executive chair I had ever seen, cranked up to maximum height. There was even a miniature cannon on his desk, pointed at us. It could either be a cigarette lighter or real. Maybe Ted fired little cannonballs at his people to make a point.

Now he sat back imperiously and listened to his staff bitch. His arms were cocked in front of him on his chair arms to make a pyramid, with the tips of his fingers lightly tapping his lips.

My first meeting with his JSF people was going pretty much as I expected.

'If Weston is allowed to even touch the LUCI simulator,' Mac Skinner held the sides of his chair with white knuckles, 'I will quit this project today.'

'I'm with Mac.' Leon was a pinched-faced guy with bushy eyebrows who wore a tweedy sports jacket. He talked with his hands held in front of him like a hermit crab. Leon was the Director of

Advanced Engineering. 'We shouldn't even let him see our simulator. It will jeopardize the integrity of our program. No offense, Mr Weston.'

'None taken,' I shrugged. 'It was all Ted's idea.'

'We've worked too damn hard on this project to let in outsiders,' Mac fumed. 'I didn't get LUCI just where we wanted her so Weston could come in and interfere.'

'Once you let the toothpaste out of the tube, it's hard to get it back again.' Leon was a jittery piece of work.

Leon, I knew, had his moments of brilliance but had screwed up his last aerospace project at another company. He had overly engineered the unmanned NASA spacecraft he was supervising. When it got launched, the mighty booster rockets propelled the rocket toward downtown Greensboro, North Carolina, instead of Saturn. They had to blow it up. Leon's probe, with all its fascinating space experiments, now lay corroding at the bottom of the Atlantic Ocean a few miles off the coast. So I couldn't take his arrogance about me too seriously.

'May I remind you,' Leon squinted at me and mouthed each word separately, only able to stomach small bites of my presence at a time, 'Mr Weston hasn't even been cleared internally.'

Mac glowered right on cue. I could figure out Leon, but Mac was a puzzle. Here was a guy who had breathed the heady ozone of frontline fighters, tasted by only a handful of pilots on this planet. He didn't have much to be insecure about. At least not

248

when it came to testing his righteousness against the forces of God and technology.

Maybe Mac knew that Ted was a thief, or maybe he didn't. But it occurred to me from the glimmer of a feral, frightened look in his steady eyes that Mac might be a soul in torment. If he already felt guilty, maybe he would be the weak link worth snapping. On the other hand, maybe he was the borderline psychotic kind of fighter pilot who lived to hurt people. Like I said, the Air Force gets its share despite the fine screen.

Watching him glaring at me, I reminded myself that I had gotten in here beating Mac at Spank. I had definitely bruised his ego. This wasn't the time to whack it again.

When Mac fixed his gaze on me, I saw an agenda burning like an oven.

'Is that it?' Ted finally said, quietly for him, and his two managers both shut up in mid-mutter.

Mac didn't squirm like Leon, although a vein in his neck twitched slightly. I could see his mighty discipline willing himself to keep still, when he really wanted to get up and strangle me to death so he could sit back and relax.

''Cause if that's all you've got,' Ted growled, 'here's what's going to happen. Marcus Roker will scrape Mr Weston's skin off and see what's underneath. If Marcus finds any irregularity at all, like Terry wet his bunk once in flight school, his access will be denied. If he checks out, Weston will get access strictly limited to LUCI simulation time. End of story.'

'He still can't qualify,' Mac blurted out. 'He hasn't flown a military plane for seven years.'

'So what?' Ted said. 'Our plane doesn't need a great pilot. That's the whole point, Mac. What's the downside?'

'The downside is having . . . some yuppie *puke* flying our aircraft,' Mac said, almost crying with frustration. 'No other defense contractor would do this, Ted.'

'That's why I am.' Ted set his jaw. I love a mulish CEO as my target.

His men squirmed and got better acquainted with their shoes.

'Look, guys.' Ted stooped to grease his people a little. 'You've both done an outstanding job on LUCI. I'll take you into my confidence. On the record, Terry's coming in to consult on Simulator Ops. Truth is, we're giving him VIP treatment as a good friend of Linnet/TVR, and here's why . . .'

I almost let my mouth hang open, wondering whether Ted was going to tell Leon I was here because I beat Ted and Mac at Spank.

'The Pentagon may not help us hype LUCI as the silver military bullet of the twenty-first century,' Ted said *sotto voce*, leaning over his desk at Leon in his best-friend pose. 'But maybe Terry can leak our story out there on Wall Street where it really counts. He's plugged into that world.'

Since neither Leon and Mac seemed to figure out where he was going, Ted led them by the nose.

'Simply put, Terry has a lot of friends who can talk us up in the financial markets. With that kind of juice, everybody in this room can get rich loading up on Linnet/TVR stock and selling it when the time's right. You'll do that for us, won't you, Terry?'

Ted shot me a wink. I almost laughed out loud. So this was his cover story. I was here, basically, to help them all get rich by illegal inside-trading. I was impressed. Ted had the balls of a brass monkey. So let his people think what they wanted. I'd have enough problems today getting through their internal security check.

Leon obediently stopped his grumbling and pouting, but not Mac.

'So I'm ready to cut Weston . . .'

'That's Captain Weston, Ted,' I said blandly.

'. . . a little slack.' Ted turned to his hotheaded protégé. 'Mac, Terry drove advanced fighters in the Air Force . . .'

'An F-30 and a Darkwing,' Mac spat out, like they were playthings made by Fisher-Price.

Ted screwed his face up, not pretty. 'Maybe you'll recall those were both my aircraft.'

Mac realized he'd crossed the line. He looked away, his cheeks turning the color of Maria's lips.

Ted brushed his hand unnecessarily through his retreating hair, feeling his memories. 'Terry, you're not going to give Marcus Roker a problem, are you?'

'Nope.'

'When Marcus gets through with you,' Ted smirked, 'you'll feel plucked like a chicken.'

He chuckled in his full-throated, hearty way. Mac

didn't. He and Leon regarded me with hate waves that would tip over an elephant. The room looked a lot like the Borgias' table of my nightmares.

I was just wasting time now, and stood up. 'It's been a pleasure.'

I was quickly escorted to Marcus Roker's office by a very young guy with pale, blotchy skin and peach fuzz, wearing the blue Linnet/TVR security blazer. Marcus' door read *Chief of Security*. My escort knocked first.

'Come in,' a voice from a giant rib cage boomed through the metal, almost shaking the door.

Confronting Marcus Roker as he stood up in his spartan office, almost bumping into the ceiling, I saw right away how he could take the heart out of a person with criminal intent.

Marcus' frame could be twice or even three times the size of mine, even though he only stood about a foot taller. His skin was almost blue-black and his head was shaved. I knew he once led a rapid-response fire team at the Los Angeles field office of the FBI. The blue Linnet/TVR security blazer fitted him like shrink-wrapping around a side of beef.

Marcus grunted hello, gave my hand a squeeze I would feel days later, and sat back quietly in his chair. He didn't speak. Instead, he watched me with a bemused detachment, like I might be a vaguely funny TV commercial.

He was waiting for me to say something. But I didn't feel the compulsion to talk either. I crossed my legs and sat back. He would be well-researched and formidable. He would already know a lot about me just by punching a couple of buttons on the NT computer on his desk.

Linnet's parent company TVR ran one of the major consumer credit reporting services. It also collected medical information for insurance companies. And it compiled a lot of personal data on US citizens for various busybodies in government and industry. TVR was the creepy Big Brother all the liberals worried about.

'So, Mr Weston. Can I call you Terry?' He didn't call me 'Captain', I noticed.

'Sure.'

'Why didn't you stay in the Air Force? Looks like you had some friends in high places cared about you.'

'I wanted to make enough money to live on.'

He snorted. 'Ain't that the truth. I was a Marine for five years.'

I nodded pleasantly, but didn't say *I know.*'

'Okay, Terry,' he said. 'I'd like you to come with me.'

We walked down a corridor, Marcus occupying most of the hallway, to a metal door with a slit in a steel panel. He inserted a white card and held the door for me.

This office-depot-furnished office was occupied by a beefy employee aged about forty. He looked like the guy a loan shark sells your account to after ninety days. He also wore that blue blazer, so small that his thick forearms stuck out of the sleeves with a snarl of dense black hair. Linnet/TVR security seemed to order their blazers where the Dallas

Cowboys get their team sportswear, but somehow they got the Cowgirls' sizes by mistake.

On the phony-walnut Formica desk, I saw a sophisticated electronic polygraph machine. It was the latest generation, equipped with a flat screen for digital readouts and assorted bells and whistles. There was also a camera mounted on a stand attached to it with wires.

I also saw a small plastic beaker, empty, sitting next to it.

'Mr Weston, Bill Kelly.'

'How you doin',' Bill said. He didn't get up. He had a flat south Boston accent, and his round face was almost bright red, inflamed by a drinking habit or office rage, or both. He scowled without even moving his brows, which jutted out like quills under a balding, freckled pate. His raw-looking sirloin chin had a tiny sparkle of something like coleslaw dressing.

'First, I'd like you to piss in that jar,' Marcus Roker invited me. 'Right here in the room, so we can see. Then I'm going to ask you some questions. But first, Bill here, he's going to hook you up to this box. You know what that is?'

'Looks like a lie detector.'

'Well, we don't know if it can tell for sure whether somebody's lying or not, but it picks up physiological levels of arousal, that kind of stuff. Maybe important, maybe not. Nothing personal, you understand, we do this with everybody. So you won't mind if we strap you up now.' It wasn't a question.

'Nope,' I said, my pulse racing.

I unzipped my fly and strained to fill up the small glass beaker while they watched, bored but not embarrassed.

'What's that other thing?' I pointed to the camera facing me.

'That thing? That's hooked up to a computer for face analysis. It looks real close at how your face muscles move when you talk.'

'I call it the Twitcher,' Bill told me, giving me a broad twitch of his temples as a funny demo. 'We don't know if that works either, but what the hell.'

I nodded. I believed that it probably worked very well. That was why I'd had a dermatologist give me injections of Botox at strategic points in my face last Monday, to freeze those exact muscles so they wouldn't twitch involuntarily. The needle pin-pricks had all healed and there would be no physical trace.

Those frozen muscles would fool the computer enough for me to feel secure. And feeling secure was the only frame of mind for today's tests.

'Put the beaker back on the desk,' Marcus said.

The door to the small room opened and the security man with the peach fuzz used only two fingers to take the sample away, wrinkling his nose.

I knew they would run a full drug panel. They would look for opiates, cocaine, marijuana, methedrine, and any mood-affecting prescription. They would also be looking for any very specific drugs I might have taken hoping to smooth out my

255

physiological responses on this test. A heavy-duty painkiller like Dilaudid would have done the trick.

But my drug panel would be clear. I hadn't used any drugs at all.

'Mind taking your shoes and socks off now, Terry?' Marcus asked me.

'What for?' I asked, even though I knew the answer.

'I'll tell you after the test.'

So I pulled off my business loafers and black socks, saying nothing. He examined the bottoms of my feet and looked between my toes. Satisfied, he sat back down.

'Now take your shirt off,' he said.

I took off my tie, undid my cufflinks, stripped off my shirt. Then I sat back in the chair, my bare torso getting goose bumps from the air-conditioning. They kept the room unnaturally cool.

Bill attached a wire to my fingers to monitor electrical resistance from sweating. Then a strap around my chest to gauge the rate of my breathing. Finally, a blood pressure cuff around my arm, which he fastened tight.

'I need to calibrate my machine,' he explained. His voice seemed easy-going, less suspicious than the expression in his eye. 'I'll ask you a couple of questions, get some levels. Here's a list of the questions.'

He handed me a sheet of paper. I looked over ten questions and handed it back to him.

'I'm ready.'

Marcus leaned against the wall with his arms folded. His shaved head came so close to the ceiling,

I guessed that he was six feet five inches. He weighed roughly three hundred pounds, without an ounce of flab.

'Answer yes or no,' Bill droned. 'Is your name Terry Weston?'

'Yes.' I squirmed as unobtrusively as I could in my chair.

'Are we in California?'

'Yes.'

'Did you graduate from Columbia University?'

'Yes.'

'Did you serve in the Air Force?'

'Yes.'

'Have you ever stolen from an employer?'

I paused for a second. 'Yes.'

'What did you steal?'

'Legal pads. Felt-tip pens. Frequent-flier miles. Some personal lunches taken on the company.'

'When?'

'About five years ago.'

Bill looked up. 'Never stolen since then?'

'I'm a partner in my own company now,' I explained. 'What's the point?'

Bill nodded. His chin hung over his shirt, all the way to his ears. He made a mark with his digital pen on the computer screen, where I could see three sets of squiggly lines.

'Is Albany the capital of New York?'

I squirmed again. 'Yes.'

'Did you fail to declare more than a thousand dollars in income last year to the IRS?'

'No.'

Bill used his pen to make another mark on the printout.

They were skillful test-givers. They started from the assumption that everybody had done something dishonest at one time or another. They were getting my baseline response to their control questions. Then they would use my baseline to compare my answers to more sensitive questions.

'Do you intend to use the LUCI simulator pod?'

'Yes.'

'Is there anyone outside this company who you would tell about what you see?'

'No.'

Both of them also watched carefully for the tricks I could try to confuse their results. Marcus checked my bare chest. He watched to see if I was breathing very deeply to throw off the chest monitor. He noted whether I strained my muscles to get tense during the control questions, so my later lies would register the same level of tension. But I wasn't doing either.

'Are you engaged in espionage?'

'No.'

'Have you ever been engaged in espionage?'

'No.'

'Do you intend to steal any property from Linnet/TVR?'

'No.'

Bill made a mark. 'Do you intend to steal any information from Linnet/TVR?'

'No.'

'Do you plan to disclose any secrets you learn in your work at Linnet/TVR?'

258

'No.'

'Do you now hold a United States passport in your name?' I shifted my weight in the chair.

'Yes.'

'Do you now hold any foreign passport in your name?'

'No.'

'Have you ever stolen industrial or military secrets for use by a foreign government?'

'No.'

'Have you ever been paid by any person or corporation to steal industrial or military secrets?'

'No.'

'Have you ever been paid by a company to steal from a competitor?'

'No.'

Bill marked every one of my answers, grunting softly. I sweated a little in the almost-refrigerated room.

The polygraph test lasted through another thirty-six questions. Both men were very quiet as Bill unhooked me.

'So why did you take my shoes and socks off?' I asked Marcus.

'Sometimes people put a thumbtack in a sock. Then they step on it to spike themselves, gives us a sharp response to ordinary questions. Confuses the machine. Dumb as hell but it works sometimes.'

Every amateur subject asked the same question. 'How'd I do?'

'We'll let you know,' Marcus said, unsmiling.

Bill had his bulk huddled over the screen, tapping with his pen.

'Mind if I hit the bathroom?' I asked Marcus.

'Go ahead.'

Nobody was in the bathroom. I entered a stall, sat down and shut the door behind me, then very unobtrusively removed the red thumbtack still stuck into the flesh of my butt.

Without moving much, I disposed of the thumbtack very carefully in the high-pressure toilet. Unlike the executive washrooms on their minimum-security floor, which complied with the laws of the State of California on spying in bathrooms, this bathroom would be under surveillance.

There would be many angry red pin-holes in the flesh of my butt. I'd shifted and squirmed on to the sharp thumbtack during all of Bill's control questions and my truthful responses. They'd think I was jumpy, but probably not a liar.

Ted and I met briefly one hour later.

'Marcus said you were kind of tense,' he told me. 'You scared of something?'

'Getting caught stealing your JSF secrets.'

He laughed but stared hard with his narrowed eye.

'So am I in?'

'We'll let you know,' Ted told me, and looked down at his desk. Our meeting was over.

I pulled the NSX into the parking lot of the Kinko's on Wilshire Boulevard, paid cash at the counter, and took a seat in front of a computer.

I tapped out adventuretours.com and saw the home page. Finding 'To Order', I typed in: *Need info Vail, CO. One week vac. Member #8624.*

The computer made its usual crunching noises and the printer started ker-chunking as pages came out. This would be my dossier on Mac Skinner from the Wringer, once I'd fed it through my decryption system like the others. I pulled page one out of the machine.

It was blank.

Then the second page came out with hopelessly smeared lines like a drunken bar code.

I pressed stop and went back to the adventuretours.com page.

Printed pages illegible, I typed in and signed it *Member #8624.*

I waited two seconds before a little Windows box appeared with the message: *Sorry #8624. System off-line. Try again later.*

I hit the side of the computer, which made the people sitting at consoles next to me rear back and look horrified, as though I'd just struck a toddler.

Grumbling, I crumpled the two pieces of paper, logged off and left Kinko's, whipping my NSX through the nicely manicured back streets. I always thought Beverly Hills looked a little too perfect. Despite Rudy Giuliani's best efforts, New York could never lose that heavily scarred, stitched-together quality from two hundred years of building, tearing down, building over, repairing the crumbling infra-structure. New York City was a benign Frankenstein monster you could grow to love. Beverly Hills was somehow more frightening, with its unblemished-blondes-in-black-Prada-outfits.

My car phone chirped. 'Hello?'

'Oye, Carlos?'

Ha. Maria's call was disguised as a wrong number, in Spanish. She was learning.

I waited five minutes, then pulled into the driveway in back of the Regent Beverly Wilshire Hotel in Beverly Hills. This was the dowager of Rodeo Drive, an elegant stone building that sprawled over the corner of Wilshire and Rodeo, forever sand-blasted and soot-free, with bright yellow canvas awnings crisp as newly painted currency. Under the elegant portico, Maria stepped into my car.

Tomorrow, if Marcus cleared me, I would be able to enter the Black world of Ted Devlin's LUCI simulator vault. Now Maria had to debrief me with all the information I'd need to find out if LUCI still had a Doom Level.

I glanced admiringly at LUCI's inventor. She wore a black, severely tailored business suit, very LA and glamorous. The gray sheen of her stockings rustled as she snaked into the leather seat. Suddenly my cockpit seemed full of her mass of black hair and red lips. Her wire-rimmed black glasses perched on her nose. She wore the fragrance Angel. Too bad for her nobody made one called Succubus.

'Why meet here, Terry?' Her white teeth had the slightest overbite inside the lush red donut, a slightly darker shade of red today. She'd even done her nails a businesslike metallic gray.

'No point flying to exotic locations if the Air Force

is watching us by satellite. Tell me they didn't talk to you back at Baltro.'

'Why, no.' She sounded surprised.

I pulled out of the driveway and on to Wilshire Boulevard, then turned on Canon. She was silent for a moment. 'What's this about the Air Force?'

'The good news is that they gave me my officer-and-gentleman status back without my even asking and cleared me for the LUCI project. The bad news is that now they can just take me out and shoot me if I get caught in the act of espionage we're planning.'

'I see. So this is your little monitoring system?' She fooled with my car's videocam recognition software. It took her less than three seconds to work it out. She directed the rear cam to see if anybody was behind us.

'If the same car appears twice,' I explained, 'the software picks it up and sounds an alarm.'

'Cute. Are you really going in the simulator room tomorrow?' She tossed her hair back and raised her chin in full challenge mode.

'I'm counting on it. I need to know everything about LUCI now.'

'That would take you about twenty years and four degrees, Terry.' She looked at me dubiously, the way a teacher would a slow third-grader. 'We'll have to try a slightly different approach.'

'Like what?'

'Let me use your good news, bad news analogy. The good news is that LUCI will basically teach you what you have to know herself. She's a game. A very

263

sophisticated game, but a game nonetheless. She's programmed to teach the player. The bad news is that, as she learns more about you, you won't be able to beat her. LUCI is programmed to always win. That's why Ted Devlin knew she would make the perfect strike fighter.'

'Can't you outsmart your own game?'

'When I designed her, I could. But she's grown since then.'

'Grown what?'

'More ability. An artificial intelligence learns and adapts every second. She'll be way beyond what I taught her. The best way to find out if she's still programmed with the Doom Level is to play with her and reach it yourself.'

'Okay. How?'

'The game has four levels. Level One is "Training". She'll teach you about her non-lethal weapons and how to fly her. She'll take you on a radical climb to show you the stratosphere. Then she'll give you the mission. That takes you into Level Two, "Air-to-Ground". Your mission will be penetrating enemy defenses and attacking an aggressor. She'll help you and override you if you make a mistake.'

'I never make those.'

She smiled dutifully. 'Then, if you light the afterburner against the rules of engagement, she'll go into Level Three, "Dogfighting". You should enjoy that level.'

'Only when I win.'

'She won't let you lose. After that, she'll be

programmed to "Return to Base", unless you can trick her into shutting down her connection to the flight engineers and playing Level Four with you. It's called "Enemy Pilot".'

'Enemy Pilot?'

'The idea is, if an enemy captures her, she'll interrogate him and, because she's smarter, she'll realize you're the enemy.'

'So she goes into Level Four and attacks my command-and-control system.'

'Right. Since you're an Air Force officer now, that's Washington, DC. The same thing that will happen if she flies off on her own during a prototype demonstration.'

I thought it over. 'Maria, in God's name, why would you design the game that way?'

'For fun,' she shrugged. 'Did you ever see those old war movies when soldiers interrogated people dressed in American uniforms because they suspected them of being spies? They'd always ask them some obscure *baseball* question to see if they were real Americans. But with so many women in uniform now, it didn't make sense.'

'So you used women's soccer questions.'

She made a distasteful face. 'I tried to be more creative than that. I made it a Truth or Dare.'

God. I rested my forehead on my steering wheel. 'And how do I beat LUCI on Truth or Dare?'

'I'll have to try to coach you. But she'll learn about you personally to trick you. I can't prepare you for that. You'll have to be shrewd.'

'Terrific. What if that doesn't work?'

265

She looked at me blankly. 'Well, Terry, if that doesn't work, I imagine she'll blow up a target just like I told you. Now I have to give you some very technical information, so listen up.'

I sighed.

Her briefing reminded me of Air Force pilot training, that knock-you-over stream of technical data they called 'The Firehose'. They just kept shooting information at you all day, every day, expecting you to soak enough in to survive. Maria's briefing was just like that, except worse since I had about a year less time to absorb it. I listened as I drove, muddling through Beverly Hills. Finally, I couldn't even spare the neural traces to drive the car. I pulled into a bank parking lot and rubbed my temples, my head swimming.

'There's more,' she said. 'Are you okay?'

'Sure. I'm getting it all,' I lied. 'I'm just taking a break.'

She stared out the car window, pondering something, then gave me a look of something close to guilt, but not quite.

'Terry, I'd like to start with a clean slate. I'll even give you back your money. I think you'll agree that human life is more important than a few million dollars.'

'History degrades that theory,' I told her.

'Don't be cynical.'

'If I screw this up,' I pointed out, 'what I have in the bank might be irrelevant. I'll call you as soon as I get off the sim.'

'You'll love the ride,' she promised. Those were

her last words in English. For the next six hours, she firehosed me with more LUCI procedures.

Drained of all ability to do anything but breathe, I finally arrived back at my apartment.

I headed for my exercise room carrying the pictures of Maria. I taped them up to the mirror and studied them while pumping freeweights furiously.

I couldn't get sleepy.

At 4.30 a.m., I finally fell on my bed and closed my eyes

The phone rang at 4.38.

'This is Marcus Roker, Linnet/TVR security. You got a serious problem, buddy.'

My stomach tightened, like a bad cramp.

'How come?' I took my phone and went to the window. Looking way down at the street in both directions, I expected to find nondescript four-door sedans with flashing blue lights on the dashboard.

'They start the LUCI simulator sessions early here,' Marcus drawled. 'You got an 0630 slot this morning. Be here at 0530 to suit up. Welcome aboard, Captain. You're cleared by the Pentagon and us guys here at Big Brother, too.'

Marcus snickered at his little joke before he hung up.

It took a second to register that he had called me 'Captain' for the first time.

FOURTEEN

It was 5.28 a.m., Tuesday morning. Exactly one week since my unofficial penetration of Linnet/ TVR's Ghostworks.

As I entered the Black world of the LUCI simulator vault, this time as an invited guest, I stood gaping at the real-life version of the dome simulator room that I had only peeked at the week before through my peanut cams. The scale of it dazzled me, almost like a small, vaulted cathedral with the shiny egg hanging from the ceiling like a holy ghost.

As a matter of protocol, I expected Mac Skinner, Project Manager, to greet me. Maybe he wouldn't slap me on the back and fire up the cappuccino machine himself, but minimal civility called upon him to show up. He didn't. It made me consider Mac again. Was he sulking? Or just sitting behind a one-way mirror in a little room next to the sim vault to watch me? But there was no one-way mirror. Just plenty of video surveillance.

Since Mac Skinner declined to play host, Marcus Roker had let me in. Now I peered over at the dark control deck where two engineers sat. Both looked young enough to be high-school Future Rocket Scientists, sipping coffee and fooling with the panels. A dark young man, Indian or Pakistani, wore a military haircut and a gold ring in his nostril.

The defense industry was getting more diverse. A smart young woman who looked like an intense teenager, with a spiky Peter Pan kind of haircut, reminded me of Maria because she had a trim body, good cheekbones, and oversized black glasses with thick lenses. But she wore a white lab coat instead of a Gaultier dress.

'Hi,' I said.

They both looked up suddenly. Engineers tend to get wrapped up in their work. But they looked spooked, paranoid.

'What are you doing here?' the woman breathed in a tight whisper.

'This is Captain Weston,' Marcus observed drily. 'He's scheduled in. Check your board.'

The two engineers shuffled through the coffee cups, phone messages and other junk on their console desks and found the day's log. They read that I was expected.

'Where's his uniform?' the spiky-Peter-Pan-haircut engineer asked me. Both of them eyeballed me with a disturbingly wary expression that made me think of the Children of the Corn meeting an out-of-towner. I concluded that nobody but Ghostworks people ever showed up here.

'He doesn't wear a uniform,' Marcus joked. 'He's a spy.'

Marcus didn't know how smart they were to be wary of me. The first thing I did, coming around to their side of the console to shake hands, was to slip a little black box the size of a deck of cards out of my pocket and attach the magnetic surface to the underside of the TV monitor rack. This box was a customized device called a 'keyboard sniffer' because it could, remotely, sniff out internal data from the computer consoles in front of the two engineers.

I did this so skillfully that not even Marcus noticed. After my sim session, I would reclaim my little box chock full of the security codes for these computers and the entire online log of our simulator session.

The engineers found my custom-tailored flight suit already made for me, hanging in the closet. The guy helped me suit up. The brand-new flight suit felt like stiff cardboard tied to my body with tourniquets. The acid-black fabric was decorated with a special diamond-shaped red patch with a ghostly symbol that I guessed was supposed to represent a LUCI plane. It said *LUCI Flight Test Team*, and a gray strip below it identified me in black letters as *T. WESTON, CAPTAIN USAF*.

The egg-shaped LUCI simulator pod dangled in front of me. The bottom half of the virtual cockpit that I would step into looked like a shiny glass oval composed of Maria's liquid crystal. The top half of the egg was a glass bubble canopy, just like a real fighter cockpit but a lot harder to see.

Whrrrr.

The glass canopy opened wide for me in greeting. I could see a normal cockpit inside, and a standard fighter's Deuces II ejection seat. But I didn't want to get in yet.

'Good morning, Captain Weston,' the pod said. I

stepped back, startled like a burglar caught in the glare of a flashlight. I knew the pod would talk to me, but the LUCI simulator's female voice sounded like it came from a warm, flesh-and-blood human body. If it had once been Maria's voice, they had digitized it to sound crisper than hers, and slightly throatier.

Maria hadn't touched on the proper etiquette of talking to her artificial intelligence system. Both the fighters I had flown used electronic voice systems called 'pilot associates' that helped with in-flight tasks and warnings. But compared to LUCI's greeting, those systems were village idiots.

'Good morning, LUCI,' I said blandly. 'I'm going to do a walkaround before I climb on board.'

Pilots always do a pre-flight check of their planes, but not their simulators. But this was different. They would expect me, as an ex-Air Force guy, to take simulators very seriously. Pilots would even come out of simulators sweating, like they'd been in real combat. You couldn't get killed in a sim, but you could definitely make enough mistakes to blow your Air Force career.

So they would expect me to be curious about LUCI. But they wouldn't expect me to try the ten tests that Maria had given me to discover whether LUCI the strike fighter training simulator was programmed exactly like LUCI the computer game.

If the LUCI sim was still programmed to reach Maria's Doom Level, I didn't know exactly what this pod would do if I actually found it.

Maria had briefed me that I could inspect LUCI virtually from the outside, like a real pilot does a pre-flight check. 'Can you make the aircraft go visual for me so I can see what she'd look like?'

'Captain,' the nose-ring engineer said without looking up, 'LUCI can show you herself. Put your helmet on and she'll feed you eyeball data.'

He meant that lasers built into my helmet would flash images in my retinas. It was a currently popular simulator technique. It worked pretty much the way my Oliver Peoples glasses had projected SymBad for Frank Lafferty.

I put the visor of my helmet down. 'Show me.'

'Get ready,' I heard the woman engineer's voice in my helmet.

Pop. Suddenly, my eyeballs felt like they'd been hit lightly with ping-pong balls as the sly lasers played their tricks. A full-color image whomped on to my retina. It was so convincing, I felt a shiver up my back as I regarded the glistening glass-like architecture of the LUCI strike fighter. This was a spectacular virtual view, more convincing and richer than any simulator graphic I'd ever seen.

'Holy shit!' I observed astutely.

As I stood on the floor next to the pod, what I saw through my helmet was a glistening aircraft in front of me made of metallic glass and mirrors. It sat at exactly the same angle I would see it if I were standing on the tarmac facing its nose. The virtual image even got the perspective just right for my height. I heard my own hard breathing inside my helmet.

I sniffed. It even sprayed a whiff of jet fuel for effect. A tingle zipped from my hair follicles to my toenails. All my senses opened up to the glory of this aircraft.

Up close, she was a shimmering jewel. Her subtly faceted airframe perched on three slender metal struts with shiny tires. She wasn't ugly and snaggle-toothed like my Darkwing, the older stealth tech-nology. Her lines were supple, almost voluptuous. Her surfaces seemed diamond-like, covered in a mosaic of surfaces that would deflect her from view.

She looked just as Maria had described her.

I searched for the outer-surface markers Maria had briefed me on. I figured that the closer Ted's design resembled Maria's game, the more likely the possibility that her Doom Level had gotten in too.

I inspected the glassy surfaces of LUCI's swept-back wing. Her tail section had two sparkling fins flared in a V-shape. Then I checked the power-plant, a virtual housing for an advanced NASA engine called the 'aerospike', designed to propel an aircraft straight into orbit around the Earth's atmosphere. LUCI's aerospike engine sucked in air through a large gaping intake under her chin – like a shark's open mouth.

I peered at a system of downward-pointed nozzles. These would give LUCI the ability to blast all her jet thrust straight down to the ground and swoop straight up in the air. It also meant I could turn her jet nozzles on for faster, more agile turns in a dogfight.

What a creation this gorgeous, almost spoiled-looking new warrior-princess was. It was getting harder for me to think of LUCI – or this virtual LUCI, I had to remind myself – as just a machine.

'Open bomb-bay door,' I said. She obediently opened her hatches underneath. That was where she hid her weapons so they couldn't be seen on enemy radar. I looked inside and frowned at the unfamiliar slender missiles nestled in the rails to be fired. They weren't traditional bombs or air-to-air missiles. These were Maria's non-lethal weapons.

So Ted's LUCI had all the goodies she had described to me.

I sweated a little inside my flight suit, trying to remember everything Maria had told me. I couldn't. But she had clearly said that LUCI was supposed to explain herself.

'Weapons check, LUCI,' I ventured. 'What are we armed with today?'

'Captain, my weapons suite contains two short-range and two medium-range missiles with STICK warheads . . .'

'What's that?'

'"Standoff Incapacitating Kinetic" warheads, Captain. In a dogfight, the STICK missile locates a hostile aircraft and aligns itself to explode precisely in front of it. The warhead releases steel shavings held together by a gel of glue. They are injected into the hostile aircraft's jet engines and tear up the blades. They deny it flight capability.'

'STICK. Like flypaper?'

A pause. 'That would be one analogy, sir. The hostile's engines suck in the shavings through the front, spit the fragments of their fan blades out the rear. Then the hostile aircraft falls out of the sky.'

'That doesn't sound non-lethal to me, LUCI.'

'The pilot can still eject, sir.'

'Fascinating, LUCI, but I'll still order up a couple of lethal missiles for our mission today.'

'Sorry, Captain. Rules of engagement on our mission forbid.'

I wouldn't say LUCI sounded smug, exactly. Just that I caught a scintilla of attitude. No. More clever than that. She sounded like a superbly confident officer exactly one rank junior to me, an adjutant who I could trust to be smart but know her place.

'So if the STICKs don't work, can we go to stones?' I asked.

A brief pause, 'Sir, the captain would be kidding?'

'He would.'

'I see.' Decidedly cool, Air Force-issue politeness.

That time I caught a hint of Maria's schoolmarm quality. From some aspect of her programming, LUCI sounded like Maria.

'To continue weapons check, Captain, the STICKs are tasked to handle air-to-air threats. The actual weapon that will service the target for our mission today is energy-directed.'

'That would mean a laser.'

'Correct, sir. A microwave laser.'

I'd found out all I could from looking at her exterior design.

'Close your bomb-bay doors, LUCI. I'm ready to start.'

With the help of the nose-ring engineer, I climbed into the cockpit.

'So where's my parachute?' I asked him.

He frowned, taking a minute to realize I was kidding. 'Nobody will ever need to eject from a LUCI aircraft. It's a no-brainer to fly her.'

'Sure.' I settled into my seat with all the straps tightened. You could never be too securely bound to your seat. I planned to slam this simulator around pretty vigorously to find LUCI's five game levels.

The stiff ejection seat was tilted back so I'd have a clean view all around. The glass canopy slid over my head and closed.

'Captain Weston?' A blast in my ear. The male engineer had a croaky, rapid voice, like a caffeinated frog. 'Are you ready to go?'

'Let's do it. What's our mission today?' The LUCI simulator would take us on a virtual mission to let me fly and actually fight.

'LUCI will give it to you,' the engineer with the spiky Peter Pan haircut said. Just like Maria had told me.

'Captain Weston,' LUCI said crisply, 'I'm now searching my files for your military flight history.'

A beat.

'Acquired. Welcome aboard, Captain. It's a privilege to serve with a Gulf War combat veteran.' Her voice actually sounded enthusiastic.

'Thanks, LUCI.'

'Your Special Access code, sir?'

I gave it to her.

'Thank you, Captain.'

'Give me a systems check, LUCI.' I wanted to get very familiar with her in a hurry.

My helmet switched itself to HUD or 'heads-up display' mode. My flight-and-fight data popped up in 3-D, just like a virtual reality game. One screen gave me targeting information, the other monitored our control systems. This let me avoid having to look down. Anybody who's ever had a close-call feeling around their car phone knows the problem, and it only gets worse at 900 m.p.h. with hostile aircraft and missiles zooming around. I switched on my displays and they flashed on with an excellent overview of the basics.

But I have to tell you, the displays made me laugh.

Maria said her liquid-chip computer made everything simple. But the displays in the LUCI cockpit were dumbed down to practically nothing. The dashboard of a Volvo station wagon had more going on.

LUCI's heads-up display, which put critical information right on the windshield, something a pilot normally trains for months to interpret, could be read by any clever three-year-old. There were digital readouts and a few warning lights. Like idiot lights in a car. Or controls for a video game.

Maybe this aircraft would be laughed out of JSF consideration. No pilot would take it seriously. But I wasn't clinging to that.

'Your display's kind of "Advanced Fighter for Dummies", LUCI,' I said.

'It only looks simpler because it's smarter, Captain. Sensors on my control surfaces show you only what you need to see in real time. My target screen display is fed by satellite. It will provide a color video to display targeting data.'

'Color?' I laughed. *Video game.*

'Yes, sir. During the mission, the targeting screen will provide a color video approximately one hundred times greater definition than you may be used to, Captain. The image definition is achieved by—'

'Okay, LUCI.' No time for little Maria-like lectures today. 'Let's go over surface controls.'

'As you prefer, Captain. Note the throttle and stick . . .'

I felt a nice ergonomic joystick between my tucked-in knees, just forward of my lap. The stick bristled with buttons. I won't bore you with the sexual imagery in a fighter, which we could snicker about all day.

I would be pretty busy with my clandestine moves through game levels one through four. Not to mention handling a combat mission in a plane I'd never flown before.

I was open to the possibility that Mac Skinner was at the other end of a security monitor, tapping a pencil, extra vigilant for any quirky moves on my part. If I probed LUCI too aggressively, which I couldn't quite figure out how to avoid, I could imagine all sorts of alarms going off in LUCI's cockpit and Mac's head.

'Captain,' her voice was businesslike, no-nonsense

and mission-ready, 'for today's mission, please note the targeting system for the AMED, Advanced Microwave Energy-Directed weapon . . .'

'You mean the laser gun.'

'As you wish, sir. The laser gun is set in non-lethal mode.'

'You're sure I can't kill anybody?' I tried to sound disappointed.

'Negative, sir.' Maybe Mac Skinner worked on LUCI's voice program. She had no sense of humor. 'We are pre-cleared for takeoff. Advise when ready, sir.'

'Where are we taking off from, LUCI?'

'Your flight plan is displayed, sir. We're on your old runway at Eglin Air Force Base.' Suddenly my canopy lit up from a real-looking sun in a clear morning sky with sparse, popcorn clouds. It felt like old times. I was back at my first Air Force base, and it was a bright, sunny Florida sky.

'Okay, LUCI. Let's roll.'

I nudged the stick forward until her engines were running at full power and checked her systems. LUCI's controls, dumb as they first appeared, now seemed wizardly.

'What are your limits, LUCI?'

'Few, sir.'

She explained that we could supercruise at Mach 1.5. That meant we could fly about 1,000 m.p.h. ground speed without using her afterburner. The afterburner is a military extra not found on civilian planes – an extra burst of power that spits flame out the back of a fighter and gives you top speed for a short time, because it also gobbles about a swimming pool of fuel a second. Using afterburner was my greatest single joy in life. The 'burner kicks in with a thrust so wicked, it's almost orgasmic. But to remain invisible in hostile skies, you can't use it or you'll be seen.

LUCI told me that, with our afterburner on, I could achieve a speed of Mach 3. That's three times the speed of sound to race up to our flight ceiling of 100,000 feet. My first test would be pushing her to the max.

'Brakes off, burner on,' I said. I advanced the throttle as far as it could go and twisted it to light the afterburner for takeoff.

Then we were hurtling down our virtual runway.

This was an extremely realistic simulation, my seamless glass bubble canopy suddenly full of rich blue sky. I flung us off the runway and we leapt up toward the sun, chasing the puffing white clouds.

She was building speed much faster than any other fighter I'd ever flown.

'You feel sensational, LUCI,' I blurted out.

With a full body rush that began in my seat and shot through my thighs, I savored the unbridled power of LUCI, starting out like a throbbing motorcycle that suddenly behaves like a mad jackrabbit, kicking back and shooting up with a rocket's thrust.

As we climbed, I rolled her over several times, looking down where the ground should be, and saw a perfect virtual re-creation of Florida's waffle-flat scenery. Then I stuck her nose straight up. The simulator slammed me back against my seat ferociously, like real gravity. It sucked the breath out of my chest.

Now she was hurtling me up to 30,000 . . . 40,000 . . . 50,000 feet, where most fighters got sluggish. But LUCI still blasted up without a hint of mushiness. She felt like an extension of my body, moving with me and seeming to anticipate my touch on the stick.

Sixty thousand feet.

'Captain, I'm directing a power boost. Hang on, sir.'

I clutched the stick tightly and . . . BANG . . . a whomping, yowling surge of power laid my flesh back on to my bones. Real G-forces! The blood shot down to my legs and my flight suit expanded to catch it. My head felt light, carefree. Maybe a little oxygen loss. But not too much. I was okay.

Seventy thousand feet.

'Ohmigod,' I mumbled. My lips were stretched open, stretched back over my teeth. We were screaming to a smooth Mac 2.2 . . . 2.5 . . . and now Mac 3.0, without buffeting or vibrating. Amazing. I aimed to the right of the orange fireball languishing against a deep purple background.

Ninety thousand feet.

Up here, light no longer reflected. The cockpit lit up in green phosphorus as we entered the dark sky. I could see a burst of stars and the sun and moon, too.

I couldn't speak, disoriented. No, just drunk euphoria.

Ninety-eight thousand feet. We were entering the stratosphere together, twenty miles above the earth.

And then we lost our lift at 100,500 feet. No more air pressure to lift LUCI's wings. I powered her back and we gently lobbed over, nose down. I put her into a deep dive, bracing against the G-lock, then leveled her off at 60,000 feet.

I felt a twitchy kind of afterglow. 'Not bad, LUCI. Do you want a cigarette?'

'Sir?'

'That was a joke,' I said, starting to look closely at the details of her instruments and displays. Back to work. We were now cruising in straight and level flight again.

'We can go vertical again, sir.'

'Later. Did you squeeze my oxygen?'

'Affirmative, sir. For authenticity. I can also produce the full effects of G-lock with excitation of your inner ear.'

'Well, I got excited.'

'Check systems, sir,' she reminded me.

Clutching her stick lightly in my right hand and the throttle in my left, I worked through the controls. I took several minutes to lighten my touch. Her controls moved as smoothly as eels through oil.

'You're pretty sensitive, LUCI.'

'Yes, sir. Your last combat aircraft was an F-118, Captain?'

'Right.'

'Good warplane, sir.' She sounded vaguely mocking, the way a Harvard grad would say 'Good school' about Southern Arkansas Teachers' College. 'I will give you our mission now.'

That would be Level Two coming up.

'Air Intel reports that the Cuban military intends to intercept an inbound civilian aircraft when it approaches eight miles off the coast of Havana. They are scrambling two MiG Flogger interceptors to shoot it down, sir. The aircraft they will target is a Cessna 172 piloted by a US citizen.'

'Who?'

'A Cuban-American radio talk-show host from Miami. The Cuban government regards him as hostile.'

'And the Cubans will kill him before he gets inside their airspace?'

'Air Intel informs us they are counting on a non-response from the US, Captain. It cites, quote, fuzzy diplomatic and military doctrine concerning Cuba, unquote.'

Cuban politics. 'Okay, LUCI. What's our objective?'

'Simply put, Captain, to reach Havana first and deliver a zorch to Fidel Castro from one hundred feet overhead.'

I laughed out loud.

Maybe you think it's childish, if not ghoulish, to stalk a dictator whom many view as a gabby old Communist Rip Van Winkle. But the more you knew about him, the more evil you realized he was. I'd met enough people who had been tortured in his prisons, or seen their family members shot in front of them.

Sneaking in and 'zorching' Castro meant illuminating him with a blast of our targeting radar. It was a hoot. If he were a pilot, his cockpit would buzz and whine and he would pucker up ferociously, knowing that the next sound heard would be his MiG blowing up.

Zorching Castro on the ground without actually firing a missile was a way of saying 'We're right here but you can't see us.' It would light up all sorts of warnings in the Cuban air defense system. They would know we could penetrate Castro's defenses, kill him, and be out of there without even getting noticed.

'But we're not using targeting radar, Captain. Our orders are to strike the subject at close range with a microwave laser burst.'

He'd probably feel that physically. 'To cook him?'

'Negative, sir. It will merely let him know he's been hit by an intruder, Captain.'

'LUCI, who thinks up these missions of yours?' This wasn't one Maria had told me about.

'My core programming, sir. Captain, we have entered Cuban airspace. Descend to mission altitude.'

I snapped left and executed a sideways loop on the way down. We roared into the sky toward the city of Havana like a banshee, but an invisible banshee.

'Heads up,' she said. 'I identify two MiG interceptors flying in formation thirty-one miles northeast, carrying two air-to-air missiles each, bearing zero four zero. They can't see us. I also identify ground surface-to-air missile batteries at twelve miles due south and forty-one miles north-west. Neither station can see us.'

'Target,' I told her.

The display screen popped on in front of me in color, just like she'd said. Like a video game. I saw a very detailed, high-definition overhead view of Havana.

'Captain,' LUCI said, 'we're on course forty-seven miles from target and closing. Going to target view.'

In a corner of my visor, like one of those picture-in-picture features on a TV set, a small color screen lit up. The buildings I saw in Havana grew much closer.

'Twenty seconds to target, sir.'

My palms got a little sweaty. I forgot that this was only a sim, looking at the high-definition, full-color video of Havana on my windshield. I leaned over and saw the city sprawled out below.

I imagined Castro would be surrounded by personal bodyguards like our own Secret Service, carting Stinger-type missiles to protect him against death from the sky.

If LUCI wasn't truly invisible at close range, this virtual mission would never work in real life. We could even be shot out of the sky by any sharp-eyed Havana traffic cop with a sidearm.

'Sir, prepare to acquire target,' she advised.

I went into a low-and-slow descent.

In the dome around us, downtown Havana popped into sharper view, complete with pastel two-toned American cars from the 1950s. The air looked twenty times hazier than LA, with all those old guzzlers still belching leaded gas pollution.

On my visor, I saw LUCI's target-acquisition

camera going from side to side looking for the old dictator.

'Searching, Captain.'

'Look for an aluminum walker.'

'Sir?'

'Just kidding.' I needed to do maneuvers to avoid buildings now.

We were going low and slow, with the nose pointed up at an angle that was approaching a stall. If LUCI stalled, we would burn a hole in downtown Havana.

'Watch out, sir.'

I jinked left to avoid some high antennae for Havana radio and TV stations. They zipped by, a narrow miss.

'How do you know where Castro is, LUCI?'

'Satellite reports, Captain. From his bodyguards' behavior, he will be on his way out the door in a few seconds.'

A red circle appeared on LUCI's target screen in my visor. It flashed on and off.

'Acquiring target, Captain.'

I slewed LUCI in a wild wiggle to avoid getting creamed by an office building. I could see people hanging out of open windows. I could even spot paint flaking on the buildings.

Some buildings were brand new and brightly colored, new hotels for Havana's tourist trade, but most seemed rotting in various states of decay. The detail was so sharp, I could see a young couple who had snuck on to an office rooftop to sunbathe with their clothes off. Virtual distraction.

This was the kind of view a fighter pilot never gets to see, except one planning to crash into the middle of a large city. The noise suppression system on LUCI's engine was extraordinary. The engine wasn't much louder than a car with its engine racing.

I would need to use LUCI's vertical takeoff to maneuver between the buildings and hover above the city street.

I'd taken some flights in a training Harrier once, the vertical takeoff-and-landing fighter the US Marine Corps aviators use.

'Commence vertical hover?' LUCI asked briskly. We were close to stalling if we didn't move.

'Not yet,' I told her. 'If we thrust down now, we'll alert him.' I felt sweat dripping on my face. Waddling over the city low and slow, nose slightly up like we were, we could suddenly drop and drill a big pothole in the street. I would push her buttons now, figuratively speaking.

'Yes, sir,' she said. 'Acquiring target now. Shall I fire on sight?'

'I'll give the fire order.'

Dragging her nose around sloppily at about one hundred feet over downtown Havana, I felt a vibration from the aircraft and knew we were about to stall.

'Stall warning, Captain,' LUCI said. A red pin-point light blinked in my visor.

I ignored it for a second, watching LUCI's target acquisition screen zoom in. I saw a pink stucco building with a barrel tile roof. A polished black 1959 Cadillac sedan sat rumbling in front.

The stall warning light got brighter. LUCI's nose shuddered and began to drop down.

'Stall, sir,' she said.

We were about to crash right on top of a red Russian Lada truck and make a hell of a virtual fireball. I jinked her controls a little to confuse her. She felt good and sloppy.

'I'll correct for you, Captain.'

Then I felt her adjust her own nose. It readjusted itself just enough to keep us aloft. Her engines screeched.

There were a few virtual people on the street looking around and up in the sky. Luckily, there was also plenty of construction noise to mask LUCI's shrieking. A public works project had two workers wielding one jackhammer nearby and two others sharing a shovel.

I struggled with the controls to try to pitch her nose down. LUCI vibrated like a dishwasher with a fork stuck in its motor.

'I'll correct again, sir,' she said.

Maria's game wouldn't let me screw up.

'Look out,' I said. A bunch of schoolgirls were walking by underneath us. I couldn't vector our jet thrust down and blast them.

The stick now felt like cement in my hands. LUCI quivered.

'Captain . . .'

'Shut up.'

'Look, Captain.' She sounded unflappable.

Suddenly her target acquisition screen showed me a group of men in fatigues and caps pouring out of the door of the pink building. They carried AK-47s, and twisted around to make sure the area was clear.

But they couldn't see us, even though LUCI's cockpit lit up in red, blue and green warnings. I had ignited every safety violation that would have a big black border around it in the flight manual.

Then the armed guards separated. They formed a formal gauntlet. And there on the screen, with LUCI shuddering, my muscles twitching, Castro came sashaying out of the doorway right in our direction.

'Civilians clear,' LUCI said. Her video zoomed into ultra-close range. Castro had an unlit cigar in his hands.

He slipped the label off. A big fat Cohiba.

He put the huge cigar between his wet lips and lit it. A burning ember like a firefly glowed at the end of the cigar.

'Target acquired,' LUCI said.

The red circle blinked around Castro's Cohiba.

I switched into hover mode. LUCI's downward nozzles blasted a giant *whoooosh* of hot air toward the street.

In the cockpit, the warnings all went off. The only light left was the ember of Castro's cigar.

I smiled and, with my thumb, flicked the red button on my stick.

A brief *whooop* sounded. On the screen, a bright red film appeared over the image of Castro's lips sucking his Cohiba.

'Zorch delivered, Captain.'

289

Castro's face betrayed a nasty abdominal pain. His mouth opened in horror. He jerked twice, then he turned beet red.

I pulled LUCI out of our hover. She handled her transition with unexpected grace, almost as though a gentle hand had picked us up and flung us forward. I climbed quickly, then executed an aerobatic maneuver called a half-Cuban eight in honor of our host country. We floated over inverted and rolled hard upright.

'Captain.' All business. 'Be advised, we have two bandits at two zero four and closing. I will identify them as MiG 1 and MiG 2.'

'Can they see us?'

'Negative, sir.'

The two enemy fighters lurked near our tail. Of course, LUCI was designed to be invisible to them. But if I let her be invisible, I'd never get her into Maria's next level.

'LUCI, I'm lighting the 'burner.'

'Sir, if you ignite afterburner, we will become visible to the enemy. We will light up their radar and give the MiGs visual reference.'

And take Maria's game to Level Three: Dogfighting.

I advanced the throttle that extra notch and clicked her afterburner on.

I wondered if she'd override my controls. But she didn't. She was ready to play. We lunged ahead, now trailing a bright red stream of fire from the afterburner that would glow like a neon sign in the air and tell the Cuban pilots, 'Yo, here we are.'

'Situation?' I asked.

'Receiving radio traffic in Spanish,' she said. 'Military traffic control has identified us as a bandit. They have alerted the MiG pilots to intercept us. Surface missile batteries also ready to fire. Advise you kill afterburner, break right and climb to evade.'

'Roger that.' I powered back, then cranked into a steep climb.

'Alert! Two missiles inbound from MiG 2. Return fire, sir?'

I pushed the yellow button on my stick to unleash one of her STICK air-to-air missiles with the gluey stuff. A rumble, the bomb-bay door opening. My seat vibrated and I felt a thunk, then heard the unmistakable *swoosh* of an air-to-air missile leaving the rails to blast through the sky at my enemy.

'Fox one fired.' Now we had to evade the Cuban pilots.

I dived down a hundred feet above the ground, surfing the suburban roofs of Havana.

'MiG 2 acquired,' LUCI told me.

The enemy plane we'd just fired on appeared on the target screen with a red circle lighting up its port engine. Then the STICK non-lethal missile – the same one I had sneered at just a few minutes before – gave me my most delicious moment as a fighter pilot.

I saw the STICK explode directly in front of the MiG, producing a blob that looked on my target screen like pale green Jello. The MiG flew into the squishy cloud, trembling as its engines sucked in the green slime full of little uranium pieces to mess up the engine. I could see it, even in the small screen, spitting fragments of the chewed-up turbine blades out the back. The nose of the MiG dropped violently. It was ready to drop out of the sky.

And the Cuban pilot knew it.

Suddenly the glass bubble cockpit blew off. The ejection seat flew out with the pilot strapped in. Making a wide arch upward, his seat finally separated and a parachute popped out over his head.

'MiG 2 is now a science project, sir,' LUCI said.

Maria's voice. I lit the burner again and we shot up into the sky.

God, I loved this aircraft.

'Heads up,' LUCI warned. 'MiG 1 saw you, sir, bearing 020, closing at one thousand knots.'

Sim or not, I was hyperventilating. I was also running out of time. When the mission was over in . . . 2.5 minutes . . . the engineers would want me out of the sim.

'More bandits.' LUCI's voice sounded deadpan, like she was reading editorials from the *New York Times*. 'MiG 3 and MiG 4 scrambling thirty-one miles due south.'

I could glue down those hostile aircraft before they left the ground.

'Collateral damage alert!' LUCI warned. 'I also show an Air Cubana passenger aircraft on twenty-degree climb across the MiG's path.'

I didn't want to blow up planes full of civilians opening their little bags of peanuts, even in a sim.

'Captain, MiG 1 just fired two missiles at you. Turn left ninety degrees to evade.'

I pickled off another STICK. Another *whoosh*.

'Fox one,' LUCI acknowledged. The MiG appeared on screen with the angry red circle over its starboard engine.

I saw it hit the sticky green blob.

Could there be *anything* wrong with a warplane this glorious?

Focus, Terry.

'Turn left ninety degrees,' LUCI had to repeat.

Watching the MiGs, I was suddenly and violently thrown hard left. My helmet slammed against the bubble canopy.

'Hey!'

'Sorry, sir.'

LUCI had taken it upon herself to do the maneuver. A Russian air-to-air missile shrieked past our canopy.

'MiG 1 destroyed,' LUCI said. 'Sir, MiG 3 just fired.'

'Glue MiG 3. We're out of here.' I was sweating hard. This firefight had seemed like a half-hour. In reality, it had only lasted 130 seconds.

'MiG 3 down.' Another virtual bubble blew off. Another pilot sailed free on his seat.

'Captain, advise turn left to Boca Chica Navy Base. Nine inbound missiles evaded. Three enemy aircraft disabled.'

'LUCI,' I said, 'I ought to take you to the Officers' Club and buy you a martini. You are an outstanding aviator.'

Focus. Tunnel vision.

293

What happened to the time? I only had one minute and thirty-three seconds to fly back to virtual base.

I squeezed my palms, damp and slippery.

I had only one trick left. Maria had taught me how to take us offline and engage LUCI in Level Four: Enemy Pilot.

Maybe. If the aircraft hadn't gotten too smart for her.

FIFTEEN

The cockpit lights suddenly flashed on and off. Inside my helmet, the lasers stopped showing visuals on my eyeballs. In the big dome overhead, the visual of blue sky shut down.

Maria had given me her codeword for shutting her game down in play. And it worked. Or seemed to.

Through my radio, I heard the young woman engineer. 'Captain, it looks like we've just lost flight recorder functions. This hasn't happened before.' Usually I would say, uh-huh. Engineers always lie about their systems crashing, like it was the first time ever and your fault. But this time it was. 'Stay straight and level, okay? We'll say when to resume.'

'Thanks,' I said and turned the radio to receive-only mode. 'Can you hear me?'

There was no response from outside.

'Sir, we're offline now,' LUCI pointed out. 'They cannot hear us.'

Or monitor our cockpit conversation. There would be no record at all of what we said now, if this shutdown worked like Maria had said it would.

'Okay, LUCI.' I felt wary and thrilled to have a minute alone with the soul of Maria's game. 'LUCI, you're shut down. Is that correct?'

'Yes, sir.' Her voice was deadpan.

'I'm going to ask you direct questions. I want you to answer them truthfully. Do you understand the concept of telling the truth?'

'Yes, sir.'

'Will you?'

'Of course, sir.'

'Do you like games, LUCI?'

'Like we're playing now, sir?'

'Are you playing a game?'

'If you are, sir.'

'I see. Who invented you?' I asked calmly.

'Linnet Aviation Division of TVR, Inc. Specifically the Ghostworks Advanced Technology Design Group.'

'And who was identified as your original designer?'

'His internal code number is 2242.'

'Is that Ted Devlin?'

'That's correct, sir. Major Skinner helped him build and program me, but I was Mr Devlin's original design.'

'LUCI, does the name "Maria Haymeyer" mean anything to you?'

'Identify further, sir. Friend or foe?'

I thought. 'Could be either.'

'If friend, give me rank and serial number, Captain.'

'She's never been in the service.'

'I have no record, sir. Try other identification.'

I gave her Maria's Social Security number.

'I have no record of her, sir.'

'LUCI, I want to go to Level Four.'

'Command not understood, Captain. Please rephrase.'

'Okay.' I felt the sweat on my hands. 'What is "Enemy Pilot" LUCI?'

'Explain your need-to-know, Captain.'

I stopped breathing. The LUCI cockpit voice had taken on a different tone completely. It was seductive, but not in the sexual sense. More like an insinuating friendliness. It crept under my skin, yet the effect wasn't creepy. The voice was still the Linnet/TVR confection. But I could feel Maria's sense of play underneath the innocent question.

'LUCI, we have very little time. Do you want to play?'

'Only if you do, sir.'

'Let's say I'm a spy. An enemy . . .'

'Is that what you are, Captain?'

My heart hammered, looking out at the two engineers. The phone to call Marcus Roker was right by the nose-ring engineer's hand. The video cameras pointed inside the cockpit were putting me, I imagined, on the monitor I'd seen in Roker's office right now. He seemed like the curious type who would be watching me closely.

I closed my eyes and wiggled my toes, ready to ask the big question Maria had primed me for. If I got LUCI's basic chip sequence, I could deprogram her Doom Level from inside the sim.

'LUCI, I need information on how to deprogram Level Five.'

'Deprogram, sir?'

'Right. Give me your basic chip sequence.'

297

'Unavailable, sir.'

'What's preventing you from giving it to me?'

'Memory D in my core programming.'

'Let me see Memory D on your target screen.'

'Unavailable, sir.'

'What's preventing you from giving it to me?'

'My basic chip sequence, sir.'

'You've got me in a loop?'

'Correct, sir.'

'I need you to play, LUCI.'

'What is your desired endgame, sir?'

'To deprogram you before you attack Washington, DC.'

'I have no orders to attack Washington, sir.'

'But what if I was an enemy pilot and my leaders were in Washington?'

'Captain, I will interrogate you now.'

'Okay, LUCI.'

'Does a pilot experience severe symptoms of anxiety and fear in combat, sir?' That was the last question I expected. What could I tell her? Maybe the truth. You don't have to memorize the truth, my father used to tell me.

'Say again, LUCI?'

'In combat, sir, did you personally experience symptoms of anxiety and fear?'

My palms itched remembering. 'Sure. I just puckered up under fire and held myself together so I wouldn't make a mistake. And I had a plastic pilot in my pocket to keep me safe.'

The toy pilot came out of a Tyco model fighter, an F-4. My dad gave it to me before he left for Vietnam.

My mother stepped on the plane accidentally one night when she came home in the dark. But I kept the pilot. I've never once flown without it. I absently felt one of the many Velcro pockets of my flight suit and touched through the fabric to make sure.

'Exactly how does a plastic icon keep you safe, sir?'

'My dad was a fighter pilot. He gave it to me when I was a kid. I always carried it with me for luck. Flying single-seat fighters gets lonely.'

'Not any more, sir.'

Suddenly the canopy vibrated. A banging on the side.

'Captain Weston,' I heard the woman engineer with the Peter Pan haircut yell angrily at me. She was banging her hand on the glass. 'Did you do something to the sim?'

'No. Are you up and running yet?' I yelled back.

She glared through the cockpit canopy at me, a messy human disturbing her perfect little pod.

'My air-conditioner's off. It's hot in here,' I shouted. She had no idea.

The engineer went away. I waited a beat. I had no time. I needed to try again.

'LUCI, what's your basic chip sequence?'

'In a qualitative sense, my basic chip sequence enables me to fly and fight and to bond with a player/pilot, sir.'

'I see. What about in the quantitative sense?'

'Sir?'

'What's your *quantitative* basic chip sequence? I need it now.'

'Unavailable, sir.'

'Okay. Let's cut to the chase. How do I activate your Doom Level?'

'Sir?'

'When you override a pilot . . . Okay. Let's say an enemy captured you.'

'An enemy pilot, sir?'

'Right. Colonel Skinner flies you. Could he ever be an enemy pilot?'

'Colonel Skinner is an outstanding pilot, sir.'

I waited. 'I agree that Colonel Skinner is a fine pilot, LUCI, except for his ingrown penis. I'm asking what you would do if he were an "Enemy Pilot". Level Four, LUCI.'

She was silent.

'Okay. What about me? Am I an enemy?'

'You are classified as a "friend".'

'That's just a classification, LUCI. Now I need to be an enemy pilot . . .'

'Are you all right, sir? Your blood pressure is past acceptable non-combat parameters, sir.'

The slippery wet places in my flight suit suddenly felt very cold.

'Let's talk about your Doom Level.'

She was silent for a moment. 'Advise how you know that terminology, sir?'

I was startled by another banging on the canopy. The Peter Pan haircut was out there again. The glass was so steamy from the heat inside, I could barely make her out, except to note that she was still pissed off.

'Didn't you see me?' she shouted through the

300

locked bubble. She was taking this whole thing so personally, I hoped she'd send the nose-ring guy the next time.

'No. What's your status?' I shouted like I was irritated that she'd kept me sitting inside the cockpit.

'We have some manual control. You can maneuver the aircraft, but we can't communicate.'

I gave her a thumbs-up, thinking it might be good to distract LUCI briefly while I decided what to ask next.

'Sir? Advise how you would know the term 'Doom Level'?'

'Let's just say you're on a need-to-know basis, LUCI.'

'Very good, sir.'

'Aaaaargh,' I shouted as my kidneys leapt up and bumped into my ribcage while my world turned upside down. In about two seconds, LUCI had yanked me down a few thousand virtual feet and rolled me over to leave me hanging upside down in my harness. Still inverted, my flight suit suddenly expanded in the middle to help me deal with the G-load. It squeezed me like an anaconda snake. I hyperventilated and grunted, jiggled the stick to try to recover.

'Captain Weston.' The Peter Pan engineer was back, good and annoyed. 'You're inverted. You need to follow our procedures or you're out of there. We're trying to get you back on line.'

'Captain,' LUCI said blandly, 'I believe you nudged the stick.'

I turned her back over on her belly and let my blood drain back, clutching for some control. 'That was very unprofessional.'

'The LUCI X-39 Strike Fighter is designed to win, sir.'

She was watching me. And, like Maria, she was much smarter than I was.

Something animal shuddered under my flesh. In the steamy swamp of a cockpit, I felt my scalp tingle with cold. More banging on the cockpit. I wiped a square of mist off with my finger. Now the male engineer was outside, frowning and pointing at a little sign scrawled hastily in felt-tip script. 'Going on line ten seconds.'

'LUCI,' I asked, my chest full of achy tension that had nothing to do with gravity, 'do you still have a Doom Level?'

'Sorry, sir, we're out of time,' LUCI said.

I slammed my hand against the control panel and it stung.

'Your blood pressure reading is excessive, Captain.'

'LUCI,' I said quickly, 'we're going to perform a final maneuver called "African Gray Amnesia". Do you copy?'

A pause. 'Affirmative, Captain Weston.'

'LUCI, review the last five minutes.'

'I cannot, sir. Your last command erased my short-term memory.'

The cockpit lights went on again. The engineer's voice broke through in my radio, loud and irritated. 'Captain, bring your aircraft home.'

Sixteen

'Hey, Terry, siddown.'

Ted looked pleased with himself, arching his fingertips, his eye dancing merrily. He unbuttoned his suit, another expensive one, and leaned back in his reclining chair. I sat in my visitor's chair so that my eye level barely met his chin. I couldn't help but notice that Maria had the barest hint of his chin.

My skin still tingled even though twenty minutes had passed since I climbed out of the LUCI sim. My hands shook when I changed out of my flightsuit into a black suit and carefully knotted my dark tie. Now I could detect a vague soreness in my abdomen and limbs where the flightsuit had squeezed my body.

My nerve endings were still in the LUCI pod, trying to analyze what I'd just been through. But Ted Devlin had sent for me to join him in his office, probably for some crowing.

I put myself on autopilot to make small talk with him. Small talk didn't come naturally after I had experienced the kind of artificial intelligence that scientists had only talked about for the past fifty years. Not just a machine that obeyed better. LUCI could also *dis*obey. That was the measure of Maria's genius.

'So what did you think of my sim, Terry?'

'I think it's pretty amazing you could design a plane like that all by yourself.' I locked on to his eyeball. 'How'd you make it so smart?'

'I created a neural network of smart chips to program the whole aircraft. How much do you know about artificial intelligence?'

'Not much.' *Neither do you,* I didn't add.

Ted fiddled with his cufflinks, a pair of miniature ebony dice with white points. He didn't look me in the eye. 'With the jump I've got, we'll have the smartest warplane in the world for the next twenty years, Terry. That's how long it'll take anybody else to catch up. How's that for a competitive window? Linnet/TVR will be the Coca-Cola, AT&T and General Motors of the defense industry.'

He loved that stupid phrase, didn't he? I could see him rehearsing it in front of a mirror for the *Wall Street Journal*.

'That's evolution,' I pointed out. 'Your child always turns out brighter than you, right?'

'You mean my LUCI design?' He squinted his eye.

'What else could I mean?'

Then the door flew open and crabby little Leon, Ted's head designer who I would always see as the father of that aborted missile launch that slept with the fishes off the Carolina coast, burst into his office, shaking and sweaty. He glanced at me, then leaned into Ted and whispered in his ear. I thought I heard the words 'LUCI' and 'sim'. Trouble, naturally. But where was Mac? Know your enemy, my ass. I'd broken rule four again. I had no Wringer file on him. Now I didn't even know if he was here in the building.

Ted blinked at what Leon told him and looked up at me.

'Okay, okay.' Ted nodded his head, squinted his good eye in my direction and nodded curtly at Leon, who left the room quickly and closed the door behind him.

'He says you screwed around with our simulator, Terry,' Ted told me.

'Oh?'

'She was working fine, then she went dead. Leon says the engineers wonder what the hell you were doing inside there while you were offline.'

I shrugged. 'Leon says? Consider the source, Ted. There's an engineer who aimed for the stars and almost hit the whole civilian population of North Carolina.'

Ted smiled ruefully. 'Maybe.'

'But I'm glad he brought that up.' I got up and walked over to his side of the desk, and sat down on top of it. A rude invasion of Ted's personal space which got the sun out of my eyes, and changed the dynamic of our conversation. 'We have to talk.'

'About what?' He was annoyed, having to swivel his chair around to talk to me because I had sat on his desk on the side of his glass eye.

'A problem you need to look at, if you're serious about winning the contract.' I wasn't about to tell him more here in the bowels of the Ghostworks. 'But we need to do it alone.'

'What the hell are you up to?' Ted stared, puzzled

and a little confused. This probably wasn't something he'd bargained for, my starting to bring up problems. 'Why alone?'

'Let's say your walls have ears,' I told him from experience.

Ted folded his hands around his crossed leg and leaned back until his chair looked close to tipping over. I was tempted to plant my shoe on the back of it and help with that extra nudge, but didn't.

'You like fishing, Terry?'

'I've never been.' Not for fish, anyway. 'I don't think I have the patience for it.'

'That's 'cause nobody ever made it exciting enough for you.' Ted flashed me his teeth. 'Okay. I'll make today a half-day. Meet me at my boat on Corso di Napoli at 1400 hours.'

'Done. Ted, do yourself a favor. Don't bring Mac this time.'

He pursed his lips, and I saw a storm brewing across his forehead. 'Get this straight, pal. I've cut you slack around here wider than a Vietnamese pussy. I'll invite whoever I want on my own damn boat.'

'Need-to-know, Ted. Think about Noah and his ark. He never let the elephants see what the rabbits were doing or he would have been in big trouble.'

Ted studied me for a moment. 'You're a clever guy, aren't you?'

'We'll see. Mind if I use your bathroom?'

'I'm thinking about turning you in myself, as an officer of the court,' Marty snapped at me in a low voice.

306

He hadn't been so worked up since I helped myself to his Philosophy 201 midterm answers at Columbia. I had arrived at Marty's house after my sim session and coffee with Ted. It was still only eight a.m. Marty and I sat on comfy stools at the gray-granite-topped island of his shiny restaurant-worthy kitchen with big black twin stoves.

Marty had sweated blood five years ago to buy this faux-Tudor house on Hillcrest Drive in Beverly Hills for his wife and children. His wife Jennifer had filled it with dark wood and plump, comfy furniture. Brightly colored toys were strewn around in that gleeful disorder of families with small kids. I found it charming and wished for a minute I could just move into a spare bedroom and play with the kids' toys.

Outside, through the oak-framed window, I could see his turquoise pool sparkling in front of a tall hedge, surrounded with lavender and hot pink flowers carefully tended by Marty's own hand. I recalled the Saturday he planted them from pots with clumsy gardening gloves, chuckling at how happily he covered himself with soil and sweat. He lavished the same devotion on creating this sanctuary for his family that he spent on sparing his white-collar clients the agony of the justice system.

His two kids, Sasha and William, had just given me sweet, sloppy kisses.

'Bye, Uncle Terry,' they squeaked and hugged me, warming my face with huge, trusting eyes. Like I could be trusted not to harm their father. I felt a stab of guilt as I kissed them back and watched them bounce off. I wept inside for their red cheeks and sun-streaked hair, so tiny and vulnerable. But I needed to borrow their dad for a short time.

'Marty, are you okay?' Jennifer gave her husband a funny look as she herded them toward the door to be driven to school.

'He's fine.' I pecked her on both cheeks. 'You scoot along and I'll look after your husband.'

'Uh-huh,' she said doubtfully.

Jennifer was a lacrosse mom. I marveled at the way she balanced family and a job that mostly involved making people unhappy. She would drop her kids off with love practically bursting out of her big, open heart. But in the time it took to drive to her new job in Business Affairs at a movie studio in the Valley, that heart would shrivel to the size of a raisin. I don't know anything about the movie business, but Jessica was apparently its legal community's poster girl. She could hold Beach Court on *Baywatch* with her long, sleek blonde hair and extravagantly worked-out body, then swim out and scare the sharks.

'Terry, I'm a member in good standing of the California bar,' Marty pleaded. 'You see my family. It's a responsibility. You have no family. You can't understand.'

'Well, I have my mother,' I reminded him.

Despite his angst, he chuckled. 'Mirella won't be biting her fingernails over you. Look, I'm not just worried about you any more. You're going to get the Justice Department all over me, and that's wrong. I like my life.'

308

Marty was getting so upset, he spilled some of his *latte* on his tie. Fortunately, it was so darkly conservative that it didn't even show. But just watching him spill it made me feel sad.

'What do you want from me?'

'Let's not talk about that here,' I told him.

He looked up reflexively, like a microphone would be dangling from the ceiling.

'Take a ride with me.' I gave his shoulder a squeeze through his suit, feeling a very knotted-up muscle under there.

'Okay.' He slumped off the stool and picked up his slender attaché case. He paused. 'Expecting any black helicopters? I mean, should I leave my will out for Jessica and save her the trouble?'

'You lawyers are pretty hard and cynical about life. That's one thing about my career, it's kept me optimistic.'

He clutched his briefcase like a weapon as he walked stiffly toward my car.

As I held the passenger door of the NSX for him, he waved goodbye rather grimly to Jennifer, Sasha and William, all scrambling into their blue Volvo wagon. I remembered when Marty first became a father – the sweaty fear, the thousand-yard stare of sleepless nights. Then, one night, the fear broke. The next day, he was babyproofing his house with little plugs in the electrical outlets and trading in his Porsche for that Volvo.

'Nice car,' he mumbled, a grim shadow of his old self.

I rolled out of his driveway in the opposite

direction from the happy station wagon. He looked back, craning his neck. I turned on to Sunset Boulevard. Under the ninety-foot palm trees that soared over that boulevard of dreams, I downshifted to dart around a busload of people touring the stars' houses. As we passed the manicured lawns of the Beverly Hills Hotel, I switched on my dashboard plasma computer screen and turned it in his direction.

'Watch this.' I pushed the button on my system that routinely swept the car for bugs, just to make sure, then turned on the DVD player.

The video came on. Marty watched my peanut-cam view of Ted Devlin's meeting with General Stone and SecDef Crawford in the Ghostworks conference room with furtive little movements of his Adam's apple.

'Oh shit,' he mumbled repeatedly, screwing up his face as he stared. He bleated, 'Oh, shit' again, louder, as he viewed my peanut-cam peek at the LUCI simulator.

'Welcome to the wacky world of defense contracting,' I said.

I downshifted and punched an audio button. Ted Devlin's voice came out slightly garbled, as you'd expect from a microphone the size of a dime. I'd placed it well under the base of the black imperial-sized toilet in Ted's office bathroom an hour earlier.

'*Mac? Get on a secure phone,*' we heard Ted grumble. A pause. '*Leon says Weston did something to the sim.*'

We heard a loud flush.

'You know a weird thing I've noticed about Alpha-males like Ted?' I mused. 'They like making decisions sitting on the toilet. Like President Johnson called his people in to talk while he was sitting on the Oval commode. Powerful guys love to humiliate you.'

Marty usually enjoyed trading theories about life, but now he said nothing. He sure wasn't his old chatty, argumentative self today.

'*Ted, Weston doesn't belong anywhere near us . . .*'

'That's a guy named Mac Skinner saying "I told you so". He's Ted's fair-haired boy on the LUCI project. He never liked me for some reason.'

'*Weston's not a problem,*' Ted was saying. '*He's a Wall Street guy. Period. All he cares about is money.*'

'*Ted, he's . . .*'

'*. . . only here for the beer. He wants to make money on our stock. He doesn't care if it goes up or down. My prediction, Weston's going to pitch me some insider-trading scam.*'

'Listen to this next thing, Marty, how Ted phrases this. It's so lawyerly, it'll be an inspiration to you.'

'*We can make it legal if we do it right . . .*' Ted was saying through my speakers.

Marty groaned.

I switched off the recording. 'Everything he told the Pentagon matched what the student told me about her design. He stole it. I got in the sim and fooled around enough to know that Ted Devlin's strike fighter is based on a game platform. It's obvious.'

'To who?'

311

'To me. I know you don't approve of certain actions I've taken, but this is finally a chance for us both to do some good . . .'

'Some *good*?' Marty's neck muscle popped.

'Sure. All I want is legal counsel, let me know I'm doing the right thing.'

'*The right thing?*' Marty pressed his lips together. 'Terry, just shut up for a minute . . .'

'Maybe what I'm doing looks bad temporarily, but nothing's going to happen to you . . .'

'You want to make me party to conspiracy. Espionage against the United States. Terry, there's no nice way to say this.' Marty sounded flat and emotionless now, like a doomed guy. 'You've been a good friend. A loyal and generous friend, even. But you're the most clueless human being I've ever seen when it comes to your own self-destructive behavior. And I'm a criminal lawyer.'

'Vent if you want,' I shrugged.

'Why are you doing this? Is it still the girl?'

I actually ground my gears when he asked me that, while shifting to pass a creeping Rolls Royce with a white-haired octogenarian inside so stooped over she looked through the steering wheel.

'It's the plane, not the girl,' I said.

His question had an odd effect on me, like I was a kid and my buddy was asking about some schoolgirl I had a crush on. But the LUCI sim experience had left me with an odd lingering trace, like I'd felt recently in Neiman Marcus when I sniffed some perfume that reminded me of a girl I really did have a crush on in high school. It wasn't exactly that

Proust feeling, when the hero ate the nineteenth-century equivalent of a Twinkie and brought back a moment of his childhood. No, I was feeling an afterglow. *The climb to 100,000 feet in the LUCI sim.* It was the way phenomenal sex, down-to-the-burning-core-of-the-earth sex must be.

I shook my head very hard this time to clear it. I was tired, hadn't slept much.

'Marty, you were wrong when you said I'd be expelled from Columbia for cheating. You were wrong when you told me not to go into the Service because I'd be dishonorably discharged . . .'

'I didn't really think you'd be discharged,' he sighed. 'I thought you'd kill yourself flying.'

That threw me off rhythm, but only slightly.

'See? You almost were wrong about that, too. Look, your worst downside risk is that you save a vital federal project, not to mention half of Washington, DC. You will become so loved by the United States government, they will instruct every federal prosecutor to roll over and play dead when you enter a courtroom.'

He gave me a grim little smile. 'And I'll get a statue in the Supreme Court building.'

'Right between the Supremes and Johnny Cochran. All I want you to do is advise me on how to make a crooked contractor see the light. You can probably even get Ted Devlin's business when they prosecute him.'

As mighty as he made his show of misery, I saw the little crack. His firm killed to get new clients. In fact, Marty gave me the impression that was all they liked to do. Old clients were just a nuisance. To Marty's mind, being a rainmaker was the highest form of jurisprudence. Out of the corner of my eye, I caught him running his tongue over his lips.

Marty smoothed his latte-stained tie and stared wistfully out my darkened side window. We were passing the pink stucco and bougainvillea of an estate once owned by a Saudi prince who kept full-color, anatomically correct nude statues facing the street. I always miss them when I drive by.

'I love my family, I love my life,' Marty repeated steadily, passive like a mantra.

'You should. You've got it all right here in Beverly Hills, except for one thing.'

'What?'

'Deep-sea fishing. Want to come?'

He shook his head firmly.

'Then tell me what you know about admiralty law,' I jollied him along. 'Like hypothetically, if two guys conspire on a boat out at sea and there's nobody around to hear them, is it still a crime?'

I tried another Kinko's, this one in Westwood, had to stand in line behind UCLA college students copying textbooks and other people's term papers before sitting down at a computer.

I found adventuretours.com and typed in: *Attention: Need info Vail, CO., as agreed. Member #8624.*

I waited, bracing for another problem. Then the computer crunched on demand. Pages of single-spaced information about Vail – but really about

Mac Skinner – began appearing in the printer basket.

I let my breath out, collected the twenty-one pages, and stuffed them into my pocket.

It gave me a giddy feeling, something going right.

'Ex-*cuse* me.' She approached me in the Regent Beverly Wilshire lobby, loud and snitty.

Maria disguised nicely, I had to admit, and cleverly.

She hid her black curls under a blonde, streaked wig. She wore green contact lenses, and too much make-up in the wrong skin tone. Her suit appeared to be made of snakeskin hemmed together with sequins. Ten or twelve gold bracelets stacked up on one arm like a Masai warrior. And she raised her voice sharply, in a full-throated imitation of a woman born to be shunned. Women would give her space. Men would instantly write her off as high-maintenance but not worth it.

She had registered at the Regent Beverly Wilshire under the name Laurinda Cbresnzyon. The last name looked like such a jawbreaker, people at the hotel served her courteously, then vanished before they needed to call her by name.

'Where's Rodeo Drive?' she demanded rudely.

I gave her directions to a store a few blocks over on Canon instead, working hard not to chortle at how well she did the spoiled type.

'Why there?' she whispered.

'Hiding in plain sight,' I explained to the skeptical tilt of her eyebrows, the only recognizable thing

315

about her. 'It happens to be a sturdy espionage doctrine.'

I met her at the Counter Spy Boutique fifteen minutes later. It was a street-front spy store for the general public, but open only by appointment. I held the door for a middle-aged woman who walked out in harlequin glasses and a Universal Studios polo shirt. She had probably just bought a voice-stress analyzer to dazzle her bridge club back in Des Moines.

The manager, a poised Lebanese businessman with teeth as white as his starched shirt, greeted me affably. His customers included drug dealers, business people and tourists. They all dropped in from time to time to check out the latest retail espionage devices.

The manager left me alone. He busied himself behind a glass-covered counter loaded with Night-finder goggles, voice stress analyzers and tie-tack video cams.

I guided Maria toward the L-shaped rear corner of the store that featured anti-surveillance electronics. There I turned on eleven different products – a white noise generator, a box that degraded electronic pulses, and nine other forms of creative jamming. It resembled a paranoid Santa's work-shop.

'Safety in numbers,' I told her. Nobody would be able to record what we said through that symphony of anti-surveillance whines and chirps.

'The good news is, LUCI performs . . .' I shut my eyes and tried to describe the goosebumps across my flesh just thinking about flying her LUCI sim. 'Maria, I'd felt like I sprouted forty-foot wings and strapped a rocket on my back. I can't believe what you did.'

'I know. What kind of evidence did you find?'

'That's the bad news. You were right. She went offline and acted like she was playing a game with me. But Ted must have re-invented some of her core memory. She said she doesn't know who you are.' I paused. 'She said Ted built her.'

Maria bit her lip. From her devastated look, I realized that I had told her too matter-of-factly how her creation had disowned her.

'LUCI's just temporarily brainwashed, like a kid taken by a cult,' I went on. 'But she was definitely playing with me.'

'Terry, tell me everything that happened in the sim.'

I gave her a blow-by-blow from memory. And pretty accurately, since the session had burned itself into my brain pan like the Shroud of Turin. Maria alternately gave me sad, ironic little smiles and frowned. Then she looked depressed as I wound through my offline moments with LUCI.

'She wouldn't give up her basic sequence?'

'No.'

'Or give you access to her core system program?'

'No. She had me in a loop. But you might have designed the world's only strike fighter with . . .' I couldn't express it.

'With what?'

'With a way about her.'

317

Maria stood so close and looked so intensely at my eyes with her contact lenses, she seemed almost cross-eyed. 'Maybe she was trying to bond with you.'

'Bond?'

'Terry, I designed LUCI to learn all she could about her player. She was trying to form a kind of relationship with you.'

I sighed. 'All I can say was, she's probably smarter now than when you programmed her.'

'I see.' Her eyes weren't reassuring, even hidden behind the green contact lenses. 'Well, I can't say that's very good news, Terry. What are we going to do next?'

'The way I see it, we have three options.' *And none of them are likely to work,* I didn't add.

I ticked them off on my fingers. 'Option one, we get access to the prototype.'

'It's impossible to steal a military prototype,' she said. 'Everybody knows that. They have perfect security. It's locked up with guards around the clock.'

'Maybe they only think they have perfect security.'

'That cocky fighter jock attitude only goes so far, Terry. It's impossible. What's option two?'

'I had my lawyer check on where patent filings are kept for top-secret military projects. They're all on paper, no computer networks. They keep one copy in a top-secret vault at the US patent office in Washington, and one copy at the contractor's.'

'So?'

'I figure we could steal Ted's copy of the patent

318

design he filed on LUCI and turn the tables on him . . .'

She rolled her eyes in desperation. It was a stupid idea, I had to admit

'Okay, option three.'

'Which is?'

'I go fishing with Ted this afternoon.'

Her make-up cracked and her face reddened. 'If I had had any idea whatsoever that you had such a problem with procrastination . . . Are you really going fishing?'

'That's what Ted wanted.'

'Well, I'm not surprised. It's a horrid blood sport.'

I blinked. I had never thought of fishing as anything but a boring way to kill a few hours drinking.

'Fish don't bleed, do they?'

She shut her eyes over the contact lenses. I could see the tension in her face, the little ripples at her temple, and feel it in her snappishness. She wasn't a woman who wanted to be seen as needy, and had demonstrated her ability to contain the turmoil she must be feeling.

'Terry, I want you to promise me something.' Her mouth made a firm, thin red line.

'Okay.'

'If you catch a fish . . .'

'Not likely,' I answered her.

'Well, if you do, I want you to throw it back.'

'Throw it back?'

'Yes. Promise me.'

Animal lovers. 'I don't know the rules of deep-sea fishing . . .'

Her cheeks filled out like she might hold her breath again. Suddenly this had become the most important issue in the world to her. If she couldn't control her rogue father, her own airplane, at least she would make sure I threw back some hypothetical fish I hadn't caught yet.

'Okay. I promise if I catch a fish, I'll throw it back.' I touched her arm. It didn't feel supple now, but tense and ropy, her muscles bunched up and twitchy. 'Look, it's time to offer Ted a deal. We tried penetration. Now . . .'

'What kind of deal?'

I have a plan to negotiate our way out of this. But the only way to make it work is to tell him you're his daughter.'

She folded her arms tightly. 'Absolutely not. I refuse to do that.'

I took her arm and lightly tried to tug it away to hold her hand, but she wouldn't let me.

'You're being pretty stubborn about this.'

'Terry, he stole my game and denied it. What do you suppose he'll do if I announce that I'm his daughter?' Tears formed in her eyes. 'I put myself at my father's mercy before, and I will not allow myself to do that again.'

I started to say I understood, but I didn't. Not quite. A father–daughter relationship is one of the most muddled on this earth. I knew that much from even my cursory knowledge of women.

'I know. But you have to take a risk.'

'Not that one.' Her body language was rigid and inflexible. Her face in its harsh make-up hardened into a fist. 'It's my father's turn to do the right thing.'

'And if he doesn't? For a genius, Maria, you're pretty dumb about people.' I looked at all the beeping and chirping electronics on the counter. What else could I say? 'Well, I have to go meet Ted.'

'Don't even think about telling him I'm his daughter.'

'Okay. We'll just have to get back into his sim and try again.'

She gave me a pitying look. 'If you couldn't get the evidence out of her this time, I doubt if you ever will.'

'That's why you have to come with me.'

Her contact lenses almost popped out. 'How?'

'If it's the only chance we have.'

'I mean, can you really do that?'

Her voice had left mere doubt miles behind. But I knew what she had to hear. Her face had even rearranged itself into a kind of wishful suspension of disbelief, hoping I would lie to her.

'Sure.' I wiped my moist hands in my jacket pockets.

I caught a glimpse of the manager of the Counter Spy Boutique poking his head in our direction. We had been back here activating his debuggers for half an hour.

'Should I send out for lunch for you?' he asked in his deep voice, and smiled in that ambiguous way of the Middle East. It either meant that he liked us and was being helpful, or he hated us and wanted us out of his store.

'Thanks anyway,' I told him. 'We're about to leave.'

Maria looked more agitated than I had ever seen her. She searched my eyes for fear or hopelessness. I felt plenty of both, but kept them inside.

'Terry, tell me the truth. Can you really get us both inside the sim? That sounds impossible.'

I flashed her a ghost of my old grin. 'Maybe for some people.'

PART IV

Aspects of Penetration

SEVENTEEN

Ted resembled a pirate at the helm of his steroidal new cruiser.

He wore a Hawaiian-style brown shirt decorated with creamy hula girls. I figured all he needed was a black patch for his bad eye, a peg-leg, and maybe Maria's parrot for his shoulder.

As we fought huge swells all the way to Catalina, we stood up in the vast white-on-white cockpit. It was glitzy as a fifty-foot seagoing disco. I wore a bathing suit and T-shirt, both black, with Ray Bans. Compared to Ted dressed so colorfully, I was a seagoing Blues Brother. As I suspected, Ted's oversized speedboat did not make him look big and strong the way he probably imagined. Its overgrown hull and windshield shrunk him down to the scale of the eighth dwarf, Greedy.

We'd filled glass tumblers from the wet bar, and balanced them on stainless-steel holders attached to the dashboard to keep the liquor and ice from flying out as the heavy cruiser hit each wave head on.

'She's all yours.' Ted handed me the shiny chrome wheel.

It felt loose and basically useless, like trying to steer a tiger by twisting its tail. I slammed his cruiser into the waves at over fifty knots and got better acquainted with my kidneys as the bow was flung up five feet by every wave, then slapped back down with a pounding wet *splat* that rattled my bones.

On the water, the burbling roar of the two huge-displacement, big-block engines that powered this stinkpot was ferocious. You could hear it all the way on shore. Which was pretty much the point of boats like Ted's.

'Unique hull design,' I yelled over the noise.

'I call it a delta hull. Designed it myself. Gives you more surface than a deep-V.' Ted mashed a cigar between his teeth, his big hands gripping his steering wheel and nudging the huge twin chrome throttles.

'Delta hull. Smart,' I yelled. It was even smarter when the Trojan Yacht Company designed it about twenty-five years ago. 'What are you running for powerplant?'

'Chevy 454 gas twins. Plus nitrous for extra juice.' Ted wiped some wet cigar detritus off his chin. 'You ever been a boater, Terry?'

'I learned to sail once.'

Ted sneered as much as the Cohiba between his teeth would let him. Ted and Castro, two old bullshitters, bookends of Left and Right.

I surveyed the instrument-crammed dashboard. There seemed to be ten times more computer screens and gauges than necessary. Probably to make Ted feel more like the commander of a destroyer. I found his GPS and saw that we were about seven miles south-east of Catalina. We hit a giant swell with a *whap* of the fiberglass hull that sounded like a whale doing a belly flop.

'We're here,' Ted announced. 'Throttle back.'

I did, and the big engines sputtered.

Ted put his hand over his eye and squinted at the sparkling blue sea. 'I figure the shark and marlin ought to be here in about five minutes.'

I cocked my head. 'I didn't know game fish came up to greet you like that.'

He grinned and sucked hard on his wet cigar until I was afraid his cheekbones might collapse. He ambled over to lean against one of the two thickly upholstered spanking white fighting chairs ready for action in the bow. There was nothing about Ted's mastery of deep-sea fishing in the Wringer report. Ted as Orange County's own Papa Hemingway was as new as his boat.

'C'mon, Terry, lemme show you how it's done.'

The sun was starting to lounge in the sky and Ted was silhouetted in the surf's glare like a giant bug with two huge antennae. He handed one of the antennae to me, a serious-looking rod and reel. I surveyed my own fighting chair. It had a harness and holder for a rod large enough to battle Moby Dick.

'That's a two-hundred-pounder. Harness up. I gotta drop our bait in the water.'

'I thought you were supposed to bait a hook.'

'That's for guys with too much time on their hands,' he chuckled.

Ted disappeared into the dark opening that led into his galley and small salon. I had been down there earlier to admire the decor and sweep for bugs. Ted's wide-hull design made a large enough stateroom for a round bed inside a surrounding wall of Plexiglas mirrors and a reflecting ceiling. He popped back up a moment later with two buckets that smelled rank, a familiar metallic stench.

'Take one of these, partner.'

I gagged when I looked into the bucket I took, and could barely keep from throwing up. I staggered back, unable to believe what I saw slopping in the buckets with the roll of the boat.

'Jesus,' I breathed. 'What are you, some kind of ghoul?'

'Just heave it over the port side.'

'That's blood.' My voice sounded strangled. 'And it smells human.'

'You said you didn't want Mac along.' Ted nodded at the buckets. 'So I took care of him.'

He frowned at me, then burst out laughing. He had to set the buckets down, he was laughing so hard.

'Gotcha, you fuck,' he snorted. 'This is some new artificial blood the army uses for training. It's made out of food additives. The army had that smell manufactured for realism.'

He cackled again, a rude and phlegmy sound from deep in his chest.

I stared at the blood in the buckets threatening to spill over the side as a big swell rocked the hull. Then I cracked up. I wasn't even faking it. Ted put his meaty arm around my shoulder and we stood swaying on the bobbing deck, laughing our asses off. It felt weird, the realization that I genuinely liked him. But I couldn't help myself.

'Okay,' I said finally. 'What do we use it for?'

'Shark bait.'

The phony blood began to form a reddish-brown stain on the deep blue foamy sea like something from a horror movie. Then it started to sink heavily into the water. I tried to imagine the sharks' reaction to this sudden feast dumped over the ocean like a bloody oil slick. Ted quickly sat in his fighting chair and grasped the harness.

'Better strap in,' he grunted.

Suddenly a muffled explosion like a TV set imploding pounded us from underwater. I was knocked off balance as the sea beneath us flung Ted's multi-ton cruiser about three feet up in the air.

I instinctively grabbed the arm of the other fighting chair and held on, working myself into the seat. The boat dropped back down with a monstrous splash. When the hull slammed against the water, I felt my spine through the seat of my fishing chair. Ted was actually giggling, like a kid.

'I mixed the phony blood up with some stuff we call C-10. It's an underwater explosive we make for the Navy Seals, so it won't screw up the fucking underwater life cycle. Marine ecology.' Ted gazed at the sea, puzzled at the inanity of such thinking. 'Thing about game fishing is, you gotta get the fish moving close to the surface.'

I squinted at Ted, who was grasping on to his chair with a wild grin, and looked overboard.

'Aren't you supposed to catch game fish while they're alive?'

'Sure,' Ted cackled. 'It just gets their butts in gear.'

Ted tore off his shirt. He had the build of an ex-athlete who had gone to seed. Soggy skin jiggled in the loose flesh of his upper arms and chest. If Maria had inherited her taut little body from his side of the family, I suddenly understood why she was so diligent about working out.

I watched him harness himself into the fighting chair and get his pole ready. He had a construction worker's tan that ended at his collar and sleeve lines. Oversized cans of Fosters lager were slung on to his harness like a workman's toolbelt.

'Buckle up,' he cackled and chomped his sloppy wet cigar. 'So what did you want to ask me?'

I got settled in my fighting chair and put on my best open-faced smile. It was like a friendly parish priest ready to hear a confession. Incest, cannibalism, it didn't matter. I was prepared, my smile said, not only to forgive, but to reward.

'A venture capitalist hears mostly bullshit from CEOs,' I wound up. 'I never got that vibe from you. Besides, I figure you have a good motive to level with me. The profit motive.'

'Level with you?' He looked irate. 'About what?'

'Your LUCI sim. I didn't make your system crash,' I told him, taking off my own shirt to impress him with my worked-out frame, which I noticed was getting slightly gaunt from my recent diet of worry and fear. 'I asked the LUCI sim to try a maneuver called "African Gray".'

He squinted his eye. 'What the hell's African Gray? I never heard of that.'

'It's fighter jargon.' I smiled tightly. *You poor, miserable bomber pilot.* 'The Air Force used it in Aggressor squadrons flying Red Flag exercises. It's a Libyan pilot's maneuver I learned back at O'Brien. I happened to try it on the LUCI sim, and it made the program crash.'

'Thanks, pal,' he grumbled, running his line out.

I got busy putting my harness on and looking at my fishing pole. It made about as much sense to me as a buggy whip, but I fooled around with it a little and started to figure out how it worked. Then I looked up to see his expression. 'But it gets better. After it crashed, LUCI talked to me.'

'It's supposed to talk to you.' Ted gave me a dismissive sneer.

'It said it was playing a game with me.'

He stopped fooling with his fishing gear and let his good eye make contact.

'What kind of game?'

'I don't know. But I have to tell you, your sim acted a whole lot more like a computer game than a weapons platform.'

Ted's pole suddenly tugged. Then it began to arch over like a giant question mark.

'Fish!' he bellowed, and concentrated all his effort on bending his pole. It looked like he was a natural fisherman, I had to admit. I guess it takes a little of the poker player to psych out a fish. The line pulled taut, then spun out whining, as whatever was at the other end began racing out a good two hundred feet from the boat.

'Sonofabitch!' Ted bit his cigar and fought with both arms. 'Shark. Over a hundred pounds.'

As his muscles strained and popped, he seemed to lose his middle-aged sags and pockets and became physically larger. In addition to the wily Ted who stole Maria's game and faked me out with his imitation blood, I now saw the wiry, mean bad-guy-to-meet-in-a-brawl Ted who glued himself to the mat during high-school wrestling and beat up hippies for fun.

Ted's fish appeared partially on the surface of the water, a glistening smooth widebody with a fin.

I peered out at the shark. Its head looked wide and flat, eyes jutting out of either side of its conical skull. A hammerhead. A prehistoric monster Ted had awakened from the primordial ooze.

'Okay,' he yelled. 'I'll tell my technical people to look at the sim.'

Yeah, sure. What a stellar performance. Ted really could sit there lying to me and fighting a shark at the same time. Here on his turf, the inner Ted truly revealed himself. He was a little tougher than I'd bargained for.

I watched him loving his battle with the shark. I didn't feel half that comfortable on his deck, and I wasn't fighting a game fish. My fighting chair was slippery and sticky. A lot of salt water and red speckles had splashed on to our aft deck when his blood exploded.

'I thought you designed LUCI,' I baited him another way. 'You ought to get a little more hands-on with your creation.'

He broke his concentration only slightly to turn toward me. 'You running my company now?'

Gonads working. Now Greed.

I picked up the binoculars on the stand by my fighting chair, wiped off the lenses, and saw the shark's malevolent flat head yank at Ted's line. I recognized the ferocious determination of another dumb creature, temporarily trapped like me but addicted to survival. Only Ted's shark had a few million years more practice.

'I liked your cover story about me, Ted,' I shouted. 'Your inside trading partner, hyping your stock on Wall Street. I liked it so much I thought I'd do it. You get twice as rich if we do it right. But you're not helping.'

'Why?' he yelled, grunting and straining at his line. He was starting to sweat like a slippery pig, showing the difficulty of taking on a shark and Fragata in one session.

'A Pentagon type gets in your sim and sees it start playing games like I did,' I yelled back, 'they'll worry about buying some hangar queen.'

He flinched like a bee had stung his forehead. A 'hangar queen' means a plane that everybody knows is a lemon.

'If that ever got out,' I told him with a big smile, 'your JSF deal is dead.'

His pole was pulling him forward. I saw the shark bob up in the water again, maybe 150 feet away from the boat, its smooth, flat body like a slick gray piece of overgrown sushi. But Ted's attention was mostly on me.

'What are you saying?'

'I wouldn't want to sell you short, Ted,' I said. Maybe the best pun of my whole career.

'You're saying you'd use that rumor to sell my *stock* short?'

He looked properly pissed, the sweat flowing off him. He had to tighten his grip on the pole. The shark seemed to be playing with him now, a survival game like mine. Then Ted, jerked between his shark and his unexpectedly rude fishing pal, suddenly grinned. 'You got a fish, Terry,' he shouted.

I looked at my rod. Shit. It was bent over. Just what I needed now – a freaking stupid fish. It was powerful, too, straining hard against my rod. The chrome holder for my pole groaned. I pulled back. God, this fish was a behemoth to almost rip the pole out of my hands. The line on my reel whizzed in a high-pitched scream. What could I do? Wait until Ted's back was turned, and try to break the line?

'C'mon, fight him, Terry.'

My fish was racing away. It bent my pole over until it was almost level with the surface of the water. I prayed for the line to break.

'Not so much tension,' Ted shouted, busy with his own hammerhead pulling hard at him again. Ted's ropy neck veins stuck out from his effort to fight the fish. Sweat cascaded off his face and upper body.

I locked my reel to try to snap my line. The damn thing held. Maybe the pole would break.

'I got this fucker exhausted,' Ted yelled, his face red and his good eye bulging. I had the frightening thought that he'd blow an artery. What if he dropped dead? Then I'd have to deal with Mac Skinner. I wondered whether that would make us better or worse off.

That reminded me, on top of everything else going on, I still had to decode Mac's dossier. I had problems within my problems growing geometrically, and had to start by getting rid of this damn fish.

I tried loosening my reel. The line went flying out to sea. The stupid fish was bolting for the horizon.

'Tighten your line!' Ted shouted. He was becoming seriously pissed at me for not getting into this one male bonding opportunity where he could beat me.

The fish was testing me like another pilot in a dogfight. It knew I was stalking it. Now it stopped. The line went slack. It was trying to use stealth, rather than pure fishpower, to get away. I still hadn't seen it. Probably an ugly throwback like Ted's shark. But what if it was a dolphin? A dolphin's grinning face made you love them, even though they could be vicious, using their massive tails to swat other fish. Even sharks were scared of them.

I watched Ted struggle harder than I was now.

'I don't get it,' I yelled. 'How could you have a sim problem this late in the program?'

Ted responded with a baleful look like he was seeking sympathy. 'You have any idea at all of the crap I put up with on a military project? I got the Pentagon security people telling me half my engineers are on drugs. This is California, for Christ's sake, what do they expect? I got Occupational Safety and Health Administration giving me bullshit for unsafe working conditions. Unsafe. We're building a goddamn warplane. It's supposed to hurt people.'

'So what if I helped you fix the sim?' I said.

A tug on my line. A strong one that felt like it came from the ocean's floor.

'Let's hear your plan.' Ted's chomped-off cigar butt fell out, from the strain of fighting the shark and me both.

I have to tell you, I was getting macho-ed out from the strain of trying to outsmart Ted and a big fish at the same time. I envied Ted, being able to do that. Now he willed his shark toward him with teeth-grinding yowls. His muscles bulged so intensely, I thought the tissue would burst out of his arms. Cranking his reel, he tugged the shark back slowly toward the boat.

I cursed my own miserable fish, wishing it could figure out that all I wanted was to cut it loose.

'Look, I'll go into the Ghostworks with you first thing tomorrow morning,' I told him, my voice straining, like I'd just had the idea, and was suggesting it reluctantly. 'I'll show you how your sim crashed.'

'Why should I let you back in?'

'Why shouldn't you?' I acted surprised. 'What have you got to lose?'

He grunted.

I grunted back and shrugged as much as I could with my neck and shoulder muscles bunched up from gripping the pole. 'Seriously, Ted, are you hiding something from me? I flew your screwed-up

Darkwing when you were too cheap to make design changes.'

That made Ted chuckle through his strain and sweat.

I concentrated on pulling against my fish while Ted mulled it over.

'Yeah, I remember you back at O'Brien,' Ted recalled. 'You said you could fly a Cuisinart if I put wings on it. Jesus, we were drunk that night.'

He got the Teflon Ted grin back.

'Okay, I'll see you at 0530 in the sim room.'

I softly let out my breath. 'Don't forget to clear me.'

'I'll be waiting . . .' He didn't get to finish his thought. His eye widened as he watched the hammerhead shark, with a violent lunge, tear his two-hundred-pound rod from his hands, and snap his chrome holder and all its bolts right off the deck. We gaped at the pole and its holster flying out to sea.

Neither of us said anything. We both stared out to sea at his shark's retreating V-wake, with the tip of Ted's pole visible as it skimmed in the general direction of Hawaii.

The fire was momentarily sucked out of Ted's eye.

'Well, you put up a helluva fight,' I said. I felt like laughing, but had enough problems reeling in my own line. 'You know, I think I'm starting to get the hang of it.'

Ted glared at me and dropped back into his fighting chair. He stared at the ragged holes in his deck where his chrome holster used to be, and picked up his can of Fosters. He tossed his head back as he drained it, the foam dribbling down his chin.

I pulled my line taut. My pole bent like a bow. I took a deep breath.

'So,' I asked him, 'shall we let your engineers find out what the sim problem is, or keep it between us?'

He crushed his empty can with his big hand, then tossed it overboard.

'Nah. Keep those fuckers on a need-to-know basis. Let's meet alone.'

'Okay,' I yelled. 'Just don't forget to clear me with security.'

Even in the big Styrofoam cooler and ice, the ninety-four-pound marlin stank to high heaven.

It smelled as vile as the entire Fulton Street Fish Market in New York City, that cooler strapped under the open trunk lid of my beautiful NSX. I couldn't believe I was doing this. I'd probably never get the smell out of the trunk.

I stopped at a crescent-shaped length of public beach I knew in Long Beach. The locals called it Horny Corners because everybody was young and single.

A bunch of guys wearing shorts and sneakers were playing a sweaty game of basketball. They stopped to gape at the trunk as I unstrapped the big cooler and dragged it across the sand. They watched as I waddled into the surf with it.

The Styrofoam floated, so I just turned the cooler

over and let the fish roll out into the water.

I examined my catch again. Silvery-blue beast with a nose like a sword, maybe five feet long from tip to tail. Its marble eyes stayed wide open dead or alive. It looked startled. Neither of us had expected an amateur like me to reel it in. As it rolled out of the big cooler into the water, it occurred to me that I had seen fish like those proudly hung as stuffed trophies.

I sighed. Maybe for some guys.

I watched as the handsome game fish began to sink slowly toward the bottom.

I hadn't hit the marlin over the head. After I reeled it in, I just let it lie in the bilge in a few inches of murky salt water. It had twitched his gills occasionally.

In theory, it could still be alive. I sure hoped so. I put my face into the water and watched the big, limp creature finally thump down on to the silt with a little bounce, releasing a big burst of powdery sand from the bottom.

It was important to me to throw it back alive.

If I threw it back dead, it would *technically* be what Maria asked me to do. But not the spirit of what she wanted. I only had my integrity to guide me on this one. Hmm. I watched the fish lie dead-looking as a restaurant entrée in the silt.

Then, just when I was giving up hope, I saw a gill twitch.

Amazing what can be survived with enough heart. I watched the marlin's gills flutter, and waited till it stirred.

I left the cooler bobbing in the water and waded back to shore. The hard-bodied yuppie guys had stopped their basketball game. They stood in a semi-circle in their shorts and sweaty bare chests, watching me walk back to the car. They were still looking when I got back to the road. The white cooler was still bobbing up and down on the dark blue surf.

I picked up the phone and punched the new number Maria had given me. It was a phone booth in Hollywood. She'd tweaked it so my call would be routed through three other numbers, then finally connect directly with her room at the Regent Beverly Wilshire.

'Yes?'

In the background, I heard all the little anti-bugging devices that we'd bought from the Spy Boutique humming away.

'I threw it back.'

'Thank you.' She sounded surprised.

'I need some information. Check out a Ghost-works employee named Posenor, Adele, PhD. What she's doing tonight.' That ought to keep her busy.

'Okay. When are you coming?'

'Soon. I'm just going home to change.'

'Wait a second . . .' she said.

I looked behind me. The yuppie guys were playing basketball again, a hot and heavy pick-up game. But one of them had waded into the surf and was recovering Ted's big cooler. I figured they would. I have a lot of bad habits but littering isn't one of them.

'Okay.' Maria was back on the line.

'Okay what?'

'Our subject Adele Posenor's going to Club Ovo in Long Beach tonight with some friends. I just read her e-mail.'

I muttered something and hung up. Maria was scary.

At my apartment, I dressed in an all-black outfit that would be appropriate for both nightclubbing and breaking into Ted's house.

I had already stuck the twenty-one Wringer pages of travel information on Vail into my decoder. I had expected to come back after showering and shaving to find a dossier on Mac Skinner.

Instead, I stood over my printer dumbfounded. I had four pages of total nonsense. No words, just random code.

Shit.

I took another document and ran it through my decoder program as a test, to see if it would malfunction too.

No. That program was fine. The Wringer had actually sent me a bad document. I needed information on Mac. I had paid them $50,000. There had already been two glitches at the Wringer's end over Mac's dossier.

I tried to think if that had ever happened before with the Wringer, two glitches with one document. I couldn't remember. My head felt fuzzy, my eyelids heavy. I was unbelievably tired.

I walked into my bathroom and threw water on

my face, then dropped some Visine into each eye to clear the redness.

What silken luxury a good night's sleep is. I couldn't afford even a fitful nap. I wished I had stimulants, but needed a clear head.

I recalled the little white regulation pep pills the Air Force used to give me to stay awake and alert in the cockpit during forty-eight-hour stretches, like flying to Saudi Arabia nonstop with air-to-air night refuelings from big tankers. For those dicey ballets, I had to line myself up perfectly with the tanker. It would lower a swinging needle-like device called a drogue. The drogue dangled in the air while the operator maneuvered it to fit into my gas tank opening. It looked like bumblebee sex, but a hundred times as dangerous.

I couldn't figure out why I'd gotten a defective Wringer report on Mac. Maybe a coincidence.

But I hated those.

EIGHTEEN

'So what's your plan?' Maria said when she opened the door of her hotel room.

I settled into a comfortable-looking chair and rubbed my eyes.

'Simple,' I said, 'All we have to do is prevent Ted from meeting me at Linnet/TVR tomorrow morning. I sneak you into the building undetected. We crack into the LUCI simulator vault on the top floor. We set you up in the sim without upsetting the security people watching us on videotape. Then you can see for yourself if LUCI still has the Doom Level built in and if you can defuse it from the sim. If so, you defuse it. If not, we go to Plan B.'

'What's that?'

'I'm not sure yet. But we both get out of there.'

She blinked. 'Do you really think we can do all that?'

'Sure.' *Probably not.* In my best estimate, I calculated a 90/10 chance of our getting caught. Even in the unlikely event that we succeeded, I would become persona non grata with Linnet/TVR, the Air Force, and probably the entire federal government for several decades to come. On the other hand, it was our only shot.

Focus.

We had a busy eighteen hours ahead. I looked

around Maria's room on the seventh floor of the Wilshire Beverly Regent. This was a tasteful replica of a five-star European hotel room with various antique-looking pieces and fabric walls. Our retro-luxe surroundings made Maria's personal computing system look, by contrast, like something assembled from junkyard parts.

'That's the funkiest computer I've ever seen.' I put it mildly.

'It's not posing for *Vogue*, Terry.' She sounded a little miffed. 'Be grateful if it does what we need it to.'

Maria sat cross-legged on the floor working over her keyboard, managing to look both provocative and studious as her fingers flew over the keys. She wore slinky black pants and a tight black top. I could almost see smoke wisping out of her souped-up computer, which had no back panel so wires hung out like it had just had an autopsy. She had hooked her system up to use the hotel room's twenty-one-inch TV set as a monitor. Now we looked at the TV and saw a screen full of personal data on our subject.

She was Adele Posenor, PhD, employed by Linnet/TVR's Ghostworks division with Special Access clearance for military projects. Dr Posenor's home page had a few pictures of exotic computer components and a picture of herself, not too flattering considering that her page was obviously designed as a dating tool to meet other single nerds.

Dr Posenor tried to look friendlier than she had seemed to me during my LUCI session in the Ghostworks sim room, but was not wildly successful.

She had a pinched look to her features that made flattering photography a challenge. But as Maria had said about her computer, Dr Posenor wasn't posing for *Vogue* either. Her picture revealed the tense young engineer who had acted snitty to me. She had longer hair in the photographs, but managed to peer down her nose at the camera just the way she did at me in the simulator pod.

'You said she had an ID card with code for all the doors at the Ghostworks?' Maria asked me.

'Right.' I pulled the DECODA that I'd used to defeat Maria's security system out of my portfolio case. 'I figure you can jink this with your little blob.'

'Cute.' She unscrewed the back of my decoder and peered at the circuits. 'But I don't know if that will work.'

'I thought engineers were supposed to handle these little problems with a can-do attitude,' I reminded her.

'Engineers handle reality, Terry. What about her thumbprint? I can't jink this woman's thumb. The fingerprint scanner is very sophisticated and sees all the little waves of a thumbprint that make it unique. I hope you're not planning to cut her thumb off.'

I looked at her sideways. 'Let me worry about that. So I never asked you – how did you crack into my Wringer account to get the dossier on me?'

'I got your account number from your safe. It was pretty obvious adventuretours.com wasn't some travel agency.'

'Can you do it now without letting the Wringer track this number?'

'Watch me,' she yawned. 'I route it around so they think the call originates from a pay phone in the lobby of the Veteran Administration office in Washington.'

'Okay. Bring it up.'

She went to work, hunched over her keyboard. Her concentration, the single-minded focus. Sometimes when I looked at her, I felt another stab of sorrow. Who could hurt this woman?

'Here it is.'

I saw the Wringer's phony adventuretours.com website.

'Give them my account number. It's—'

'I remember it.' She started typing it in. A Windows box came up on screen with one of those neat little lines of type that make your blood boil with frustration and aggression that has no outlet.

Account closed for insufficient funds.

'Did you drain my Curaçao bank account, too?'

But Maria seemed as surprised as I was.

'No. You still have sixty-one thousand dollars down there. How much was the report?'

'Only fifty. Something stinks here.' My scalp itched. I ran my hand through my hair. God, I was tired. 'I was trying to get a report on a guy . . .'

'What guy?' She cocked her head.

'Mac Skinner.'

'The project manager on LUCI,' she nodded. 'Why don't I try some other databases? What do you want to know about him?'

'Later,' I decided. Mac had been in the Air Force,

346

and his life wouldn't be hard to peek into. 'We've got too much to do tonight already.'

'Okay. So how are we going to keep Ted from meeting us at the Ghostworks tomorrow?'

'We'll disable his car at home. He'll have to arrange another way to get to work, and that should buy us at least twenty minutes.'

She sighed. 'Hardly enough time.'

'We can always block him at the gate to his company.'

'The gate to Linnet/TVR? How?'

'I'm thinking "the public's right to know"?'

'You mean, call the media? I thought we were trying to keep the media out of this.'

'The enemy of your enemy is your friend. In Ted's case, that would be Allyn Pollack. Very temporarily. We just need to appeal to Pollack's sense of duty and country.'

She shook her head piteously. 'Are you sure you know what you're doing?'

'Don't worry so much. My business is all in the execution.'

For the next hour, Maria and I sat on the floor between the beds eating all the bottled cashews and Toblerone chocolate bars in the room's mini-bar and planning the next ten hours.

Finally I looked at my watch – a weathered Cartier on a plain black strap, not some pilot chronograph. I hate all those dials and gauges. My great-grandfather passed the Cartier down to me. He wore it in the early part of World War I, when he flew under the French flag for the Escadrille Lafayette. One of his *amis* from the squadron saved it for my grandfather after his crash, the crystal cracked but still working.

I stood up. 'It's nine thirty. Time to hide your little FrankenMac from the maids and hit Club Ovo.'

She hesitated. 'Can we talk about something?' Her red donut lips pursed seriously.

'Okay.'

'I don't like the way you look at me.'

I was surprised that my chest felt a little stab more of regret than annoyance. 'I'm sorry, but I don't look at you like that. Even if I did, I don't think sexual harassment applies to what you might call our workplace.'

'I'm not implying that you *leer* at me or anything. It's just that . . .' She seemed flustered. 'Sometimes you give me these adoring little looks.'

'Well, I can see why you'd be pissed.' I felt a lump in my stomach quickly growing to the size of a volleyball.

'Be serious about this. I think you *like* me. Terry. I just want to clarify that we will never be an item. You understand that.'

I tried my hardest to look authoritarian, but actually felt more like a teenaged kid whose voice was starting to change. 'Maria, you don't even know if your little game is going to blow up parts of Washington yet, and you're worrying I've got the hots for you?'

She put her hands on her hips and leaned forward, resolute. 'I don't want to hurt your feelings. Really. I'm just afraid you're sort of needy

348

at the emotional level. I could see that the first night we met, when you were babbling about Tuscany . . .'

'Maybe I was babbling because you drugged me.'

'That's not the point. I don't want you helping me because you think I'm going to run away to Italy with you or something. You're a very sweet man. But I need to devote all my time to my career for the foreseeable future. I know this may sound a bit cold,' she put her hand lightly on mine, 'but you've pretty much lived your life . . .'

'I'm only thirty-five years old, for God's sake.'

'Don't be so sensitive. I didn't mean that exactly. But we're at very different *stages*. I'm afraid I won't have time for even a very sweet man for several years.'

Rule number five. Play with amateurs, and you'll get yourself hurt.

I tried not to rearrange my face or let my knees buckle as I processed that. Although I can't say I was tempted to give a look that was in any way adoring.

'You're wrong,' I said quietly. 'We're at exactly the same place now. Trying to clean up a mess you made. If you want to be strictly professional about this, let's review our current mission status and endgame strategy.'

She nodded hesitantly, then pulled her hand back. 'All right. What's our current mission status?'

'Fucked. In the spirit of sharing, let me share some of my doubts about this stupid mission you got us into because you wanted to impress your father. We're relying on bluff, jerry-rigged technology and unproven tricks to break into a Pentagon contractor with state-of-the-art security. Want to do our endgame strategy now?'

She swallowed. 'Of course.'

I could see that I'd rattled her. But just as I expected, I felt more guilty about it than gratified. I lowered my voice.

'If we don't get caught and prosecuted for espionage before we find out anything, we find and defuse the Doom Level from the sim. Then we get evidence to use as leverage against Ted. If I go on helping you, which I can't say I'm wildly bullish on at the moment, we go to the Pentagon with my lawyer. We give them all our evidence, tell them how sorry we are for spying, and try to make a plea agreement. You'll get probation. I'll do some time for my past espionage.'

She flicked her eyes briefly away from mine. 'How much?'

'Maybe five years in a mid-level-security federal facility,' I lied. Twenty would be more likely. Somehow I still felt like keeping my own problems from her, even though my heart hammered sharply from her blow-off speech.

'Well,' she rubbed the sleeve of her black sweater self-consciously, 'you said you had a good lawyer.'

'It's time to go.' I stood up and held the door for her. 'Shall we?'

Funny how, even if a woman gouged out my eye with the heel of her designer pump, I think I would still feel obliged to hold the door for her on the way out. I probably got very bad advice during the 'gentleman' part of my officer education. All those

350

quaint, basically eighteenth-century notions hard-wired in my brain about how women needed to be respected and protected. Concepts irrelevant to today's women who stole your nest egg and crushed your ego.

So I didn't feel as bad as I would have ordinarily about breaking into a woman's apartment.

Two hours later, Maria and I sat at a secluded table in a 1970s parody club with banquettes made of shiny white naugahyde and clear Plexiglas, with bright yellow cushions of a shiny and rather slimy oil-based fabric.

This was Club Ovo, an indoor-outdoor place located on the roof of a Long Beach high-rise office tower in the now-deserted business section. It was semi-packed with a mix of the club kids in black clothes and white skin you see everywhere in LA, and bronzed Orange County types with sun-bleached hair and cornflower-blue eyes who looked like they spent every day sailing. Music by a winsome, all-woman LA band I loved called White Orchid blared from big speakers. But I'd hate to be working late in the building next door.

I had already gone through Dr Posenor's apartment in a highrise overlooking Long Beach harbor. My first glance horrified me. From the explosion of books, papers, pieces of clothing and general disarray, it looked as though someone had just lobbed a hand grenade into her living room. But this just proved to be her housekeeping style. I had probed through the mess and located her security ID badge and credit-card-sized security key for Linnet/TVR. I also noticed a quaint fondness for the kind of Victorian accessories bought from mail-order catalogues. Her bedroom was decorated in Victoriana with a four-poster bed and frilly dolls. I thought our subject was about as romantic as a PIN number, but go figure.

Now Dr Posenor – and I couldn't think of her as Adele even after going through her Victoria's Secret panties – was standing at the bar with two friends. We could clearly hear what they said because Maria had already dropped one of my special dimes in the pocket of the engineer's black leather jacket.

Maria and I sipped Virgin Coladas to look festive. Her warnings about not giving her any more adoring looks didn't make me want to cuddle. We sat silently like the sort of quietly desperate married couple that sits together but apart, barely looking at each other, just watching other people go by. Strangely, it bothered me that we looked like an unhappily married couple already, bypassing any hope. Like that old joke about the guy who, instead of getting married again, finds a woman he already hates and buys her a house.

I put on a pair of dark glasses to watch Dr Posenor. They hid compressed binocular lenses that did colors well. Her bright green eyes were contact lenses. She looked as nervous and edgy as she had in the simulator room. Her hair had been spiked so it still stood straight up like a porcupine's, and she wore dark metallic lipstick and nail color. Her face was pale even for a human lab rat. She must race back and forth to her car and never see the sun.

Her friends were two bright women about thirty. They also wore black. The less cosmetically gifted of them, Brenda, also seemed the nicest. Her other girlfriend, Kelly, was apparently a clinical psychologist. She wore a sort of mechanical smile that she probably flashed at interviews to make her patients think she was listening. Dr Posenor and Kelly seemed dedicated to dissuading Brenda from going out with some guy she said she liked.

Two youngish guys, who looked like your basic beefy-but-athletic Orange County types who had probably gone to USC, got drunk during all the Trojan games, and now spent their Saturdays playing beach volleyball, had gone up to the bar to talk to them.

'Hi,' one of the guys said.

'Bye.' Kelly blistered him with a look until they slunk away, defeated. She rolled her eyes for Brenda. 'You can tell everything you need to know about a guy from looking at his watch and his shoes. Cheap.'

'They seemed nice enough,' Brenda argued.

'There are plenty of "nice" guys around,' Kelly instructed her. 'Nice carpenters, nice keyboard punchers . . .'

'Nice venture capitalists,' I added drily to Maria. 'Maybe you'd like to go join the coven.'

She gave me a semi-pitying look and I experienced the bleak epiphany that she had actually tried to spare my feelings when she talked about my age as a barrier between us.

The truth was more bruising.

According to the standardized Stanford-Binet IQ test she and I had both been tested with when we were school age, generally viewed as valid and reliable, I was only half as intelligent as she was. I wondered what it must be like for her, relating to me.

Maria's genius complicated her life in unknowable ways. While it enabled her to invent a molecular machine to screw up a lot of lives, her rapacious mind isolated her from most of the people she would ever meet. How would she ever find her soulmate?

How ironic, being scorned this way. Romantic paybacks are little boomerangs that whack you on the forehead when you least expect it, aren't they? Just a few weeks ago, my problem was dating women who I didn't think were smart enough for me.

Ha. I could barely imagine how Maria must see me. I really didn't know anybody that much lower than me in IQ level to compare the difference between us. Well, maybe if I had dated a male supply sergeant from Mississippi I met in the Air Force . . . After he cut his arm in a bar brawl, he taped a Kotex over it thinking it was a heavy-duty bandage.

I shuddered inside.

Maria pushed her glasses up on her nose and noticed me. 'Are you cold?'

'No.'

I stared through my dark glasses at Maria's lovely,

intricate eyes. If I stared at them long enough, I could go insane. She could pick up her cocktail napkin and write the equations that explained the universe. I had to use memory aids to remember all Seven Dwarfs.

I shook my head violently to clear it, startling her again.

This was no time to pound myself into the ground like a tent stake for being stupid. I was smart enough to do what had to be done. I glanced at the bar and willed Dr Posenor to go to the bathroom. She held water like a damn camel. Finally, she got up.

Waiting until she disappeared down the corridor where the restrooms were, I walked up between her two friends at the bar.

'Excuse me,' I smiled. Dr Posenor had ordered that drink for people desperate to have fun called Sex-on-the Beach.

Brenda smiled pleasantly. Kelly locked on to my eyes like a radar probe. Her eyes flicked to my watch and shoes. She seemed satisfied, and flashed me a big smile.

I smiled back.

'A Sex-on-the-Beach, please,' I told the bartender. He had a nice tan and a sweep of hair over his forehead. When the bartender turned his back, I whispered to Kelly, 'You think he's seeing anybody?'

'I wouldn't know,' she bit off and quickly turned away from me, sipping her margarita, unsmiling. It left a ribbon of salt on her lip when she placed her glass back on the bar.

I took care of my business at the bar, thinking about Maria. Maybe I'd been too harsh. Maybe the stress of our situation made her lash out at me as the nearest person around. She probably felt twice the pressure right now that I did, without the training and experience I'd had to deal with it. It was her baby, after all, that had dragged us into this crisis. Normally, I would factor those issues in with a civilian. If I could call Maria that.

But I hadn't. Sure she had stung me a little. But I was behaving like a person with a bad allergy – swelling up and hurting all over.

I had turned her panic into a woe-is-me thing. Like some self-absorbed yuppie.

Focus! Lose sight, lose the fight.

My limited relationship experience was showing, wasn't it?

Uh-oh.

I hadn't quite done my job yet, and Dr Posenor was already starting back toward the bar. I averted my head so she couldn't see me.

But I knew she was looking at me. I was a guy in her zone of flirtation. In about ten seconds, if I didn't get out of there, she would see that I was a very familiar guy named Captain Terry Weston.

I had Dr Posenor's Sex-on-the-Beach glass in my pocket, wrapped in a gel paper, for our own purposes. But I could feel her eyes burning into the side of my head as she came walking back. Not an attractive walk, either, but the kind of splay-footed shuffle that people do when they're wearing weird shoes.

356

Stay back, my mind screamed, but Dr Posenor acted like any single person on the prowl, picking up a scent, beaming in on me like a homing pigeon.

Four seconds and she'd be next to me.

I started to turn away from her. Oh shit. She had started to outflank me, stalling me around the side.

'*Pardon me.*' Maria's voice. '*Can I ask you where you got your bag? That is so cool.*'

'*Um, I got it locally,*' I heard Posenor mumble, pissed either that she was being interrupted during her stalking maneuver, or that another woman was asking for fashion-accessory information.

'*Where? In Long Beach?*'

I was on my glidepath from the bar now, walking back to our table, keeping the back of my head to Dr Posenor.

Two minutes later Maria joined me.

'Nice save,' I told her.

'She wasn't your type,' Maria said. 'Are we ready?'

We stopped at the offices of Starcross-Voyager, so I could pick up the electric motorcycle that my assistant Edwina had requested our prospective client to deliver. Its battery was pre-charged for two hours of running time, which was all we needed.

I didn't know how it would do as a consumer product, but it proved to be an amazing burglar tool, faster than a bicycle but just as stealthy and quiet. We used the purple Eurosport-style motorcycle with the sleek fiberglass cowl to cruise soundlessly into the back streets of the Naples section of Long Beach, and finally on to the street behind Corso di Napoli. The motorcycle had arrived with matching purple helmets, which Maria and I wore. I felt her body hug me as we lay forward over the motorcycle in the mandatory European sports position.

We cruised, quiet as a cat, and hid the bike in the bushes behind Ted's house.

At 1.49 a.m., Ted's house was quiet and all the lights were out. His alarm system, however, was on.

Like guerrillas, we kept to the shadows of the narrow alleyway where the houses of Corso di Napoli backed up. Only garage and service doors faced the street.

The steely-gray garage door of Ted's house was double width, made of corrugated aluminum. I gestured for Maria to stay in the bushes at the side of his neighbor's house where Ted and I had crashed through the night of his party.

I looked around for a hidden vidcam that was part of Ted's external security system, and located it in a tree. Carefully, I placed a used candy wrapper over the lens as though it had just blown there in the breeze.

Then we took off our helmets, left them under some thick shrubbery, and approached the garage door.

Our objective was to disable his Bentley SC inside this garage, by placing a little chip inside his engine. On his way to work, it would shut down the electronics in his car. He would be unable to drive or use his car phone.

I knew that Ted didn't carry a cellphone. It was a

status thing. He probably tortured Mac and Leon on their cellphones any time day or night, like they were the world's longest dog leashes, but he wouldn't carry one himself because somebody might nail him with an unscreened call.

I had checked out Ted's security system carefully the night I'd gone to his party. It was an Israeli-made program called Vector. They use it for El Al Airlines to guard their 747s from terrorist attacks. It threw a pattern of invisible criss-crossed laser beams around the perimeter of his house. Ted had what they called a 'zero lot line', meaning he had built his home right on top of his neighbor's, so the lasers were all inside the house. As soon as we opened a door or window, we would trip the system. I've seen a movie where burglars were able to slip over and under the criss-crossed invisible laser beams like slippery ferrets. Sure. Bet the Israelis got a kick out of that film.

I figured that Ted's garage door would be wired so that if we managed to raise it by remote control it would trip the laser. Ted would scramble down-stairs in his underwear, a wet cigar between his clenched teeth and an Uzi machine pistol in both hands. I had found it there under his bed during his party.

We had a chip that would, like a computer virus, eat into his car's electrical system and shut it down. We set that to happen when he would be driving on the Long Beach Freeway. The early-morning com-muter traffic – people already bitter about having to get up at five a.m. to commute two hours to LA –

359

would be too deep in their own problems to stop and help a pissed-off-looking guy in a stalled Bentley.

'How will you know where to put the chip?'

'I studied a schematic of the engine,' I whispered back. 'I don't like the quiet out here.'

Not one house on Corso di Napoli had a single light on. Outdoor security lamps lit the back street between the tightly packed houses. It was a bright corridor we would have to run through to get back to my car. I had parked the NSX, pointed toward Long Beach, back on the public street.

All we had to do was shut down the Vector system, break and enter Ted's garage, shut down the Bentley's own security system if it was locked, pop the Bentley's hood and install the chip, then close the door behind us and get back to my car before anybody noticed. And not make any noise.

'Are you sure he's sleeping?' she asked me for the third time.

I handed her my mini-receiver built into one of those small Philips audio recorders made for dictation. She listened to Ted's snoring, picked up from the dime I had dropped under his bed during his party.

'I hope you didn't inherit that from him.'

She actually giggled. And I didn't think I could get her to crack a smile if I tore off her shoes and tickled her feet.

'I never snore,' she said.

Kneeling in the bushes, we stared at each other briefly, our faces smeared with black grease.

'Okay.' I sucked in my breath. 'Let's do it.'

It was time for our first test of my DECODA, power-boosted by one of her little liquid blobs. We had attached both DECODA and blob to a standard remote-control garage door opener bought at K-Mart, all stuck together with electrical tape. I pointed our crude assembly at the door and pushed.

The garage door began to grind open slowly. Maria grabbed my arm and squeezed.

The slatted door rolled all the way up on its track and stopped with a click. It seemed to be on a smooth, well-oiled set of tracks and hadn't made enough noise to wake anybody up. Not yet.

We both stared at the view inside the garage, a web of red laser beams stretched in front of the ghostly green images within. There was Ted's Bentley, unlocked, in the middle of garage para-phernalia – power tools, a sit-down lawn mower, and some empty boxes Ted hadn't gotten around to throwing away.

'Piece of cake,' I said. 'You do it.'

I heard her sniff at that, but she propped up the Highway Speedbuster on one elbow, ready to fire. This was an official police radar gun that I had obtained, unlawfully, a year before.

By jinking it with Maria's little blob, we should be able to defeat the Vector security system's lasers. I pulled apart our garage-opening tool and extracted the blob, carefully getting it positioned between my thumb and forefinger to mount it on the police laser gun. Very carefully, I placed it on the top of the radar gun she balanced on her elbow.

Ooops.

'Oh, shit,' I whispered.

'What?'

'I dropped it.'

'Terry, we only have one.'

'It's down here somewhere.'

I was on my knees already, looking around on the ground.

'Sir! What are you doing down there?' A yellow light shone on the ground where I was looking. I saw a pair of highly polished shoes, the heavy lace-up kind called brogues, and dark pants with no cuff. It looked like a security guard, from the shoes.

I concentrated on the ground, bent over in close scrutiny. I didn't want to look up so he'd see my blackened face. And Maria still had her back to him. 'Oh, hi,' I mumbled. 'Dropped my contact lens.'

'Where do you live?'

I peered up cautiously without raising my head, to see a black man in one of those rental-cop, private security guard uniforms designed to look like an LA county sheriff, shining a flashlight on me. He was a young guy, college age, fit but not tough-looking. His face was too smooth and *Gentleman's Quarterly* handsome. I could tell from his voice that he'd had coaching, and from his stance, hands on hips, legs spaced apart for authority, that he was acting the way he thought a cop should act. But he wasn't dumb. He looked at Ted's garage door wide open.

'Sir, what exactly is your business here?'

He lifted his radio off his belt to call the police. I had two seconds to stop him. I braced.

'You're an actor, right?' I asked him.

'Well, yeah . . .' His eyes opened a little wider in the dark. He held his radio almost to his mouth but didn't switch it on yet. He looked at Maria, who still had her back turned to him.

'Hey! Don't look at her!' I whispered urgently. 'I'm Grant Slokum, Universal. Forget who she is.'

The security guard's eyes flickered for a moment. His thumb paused over the red button that would switch the radio on to call the Long Beach PD and they would come blasting in with three or four units, lights flashing, and in two minutes I would have a real cop with a shoe on my neck reading me my rights.

I kept my face to the ground. 'Maybe you didn't catch my name. Grant Slokum, Universal. You forget about calling the *National Enquirer* with your little radio and I'll see you tomorrow, nine a.m. sharp at my office on the lot. What's your name?'

'Levon Ross.'

'Okay, Levon. I'll have a drive pass at the gate with your name on it. Now you think you can help me find my contact lens so we can go home?'

He thought a minute. 'You got ID, Mr Slokum?'

'Levon,' I heard Maria say, and glanced at her back in the dark. She sounded exactly like a certain famously married young movie star. I was impressed.

'Levon,' she repeated, 'would you please do yourself a big favor and help Mr Slokum find his fucking contact lens.'

God, she was good. Levon's thumb twitched.

Then the radio was back on his belt and he was on his hands and knees on the ground beside me, both of us scuttling around like a couple of crabs, with his flashlight scrutinizing the pavement.

'I got it.'

He pinched the liquid chip between his fingers and handed it to me. Without looking up, I took the chip and pretended to put it in my eye.

'Wow,' I said, 'you've got good eyes.'

'Twenty-twenty,' he said. 'Well, g'night.'

Thank you, Hollywood. He turned the corner of Corso di Napoli and was gone.

'Okay,' I said, 'let's try again.'

I got the blob taped to the radar gun. I heard Maria suck in her breath along with mine as she adjusted the laser pulse gun to throw out the widest possible beam. Then she fired it.

Over the dense criss-crossing net of red lasers, a half-circle the shape and color of an orange harvest moon appeared. Our souped-up laser gun out-shone the Vector system's beams, and washed them out without actually breaking them. I could walk though that hole without tripping the alarm. Theoretically.

I stepped forward with my stomach boiling, ready to hear the *whoop-whoop* of the alarms.

Then I was in the garage, popping the hood of the Bentley. I fished inside the engine until I found the onboard computer and looked into the mess of circuitry where I had to insert the chip. It didn't look like the schematic. Oh, well. I used my best judgement, snapping it on.

In another ten seconds we were closing Ted's garage door and pulling the electric motorcycle out of the bushes.

'Are you sure you put it in the right way?' she asked.

'Sure,' I whispered. Pretty sure, anyway.

I started the bike and we took off, hugging the shadows by the thin bushes and small trees that lined the rear of the house. A sharp branch snapped against my helmet. It was only a few hundred feet to the end of Corso di Napoli.

I heard a car engine, and caught the reflection of blue and red lights in a window. Headlights flared.

I veered off beside a house. The back end of the bike slid around, almost throwing Maria off.

'Ditch,' I whispered.

I slipped into the grassy passage between two houses and dropped the motorcycle on the ground as we slid off. I heard her grunt.

A white Long Beach police cruiser turned into the street. Two officers, young and strong. They probably played basketball at Horny Corners. It wasn't hard to imagine one of them with his gun in my mouth. We laid flat, and held our breath. The car went past. Maria started to sit up and I grabbed her hard around the waist, pulling her back down.

'Wait!'

A moment later, I heard the car engine again. The police car was driving back slowly the way it had come. It disappeared around the corner again.

'Okay,' I whispered.

We mounted the bike again and took off down the street, with the lights off. I counted down from ten, and didn't breathe until I turned on to the main street that would take us from deserted Naples into the fairly deserted Third Avenue strip of Long Beach.

'Are you okay?' Maria said.

'Just a little sleepy. I'll be fine if I can just catch a nap for a couple of months.'

But our workday was just beginning.

In the fuzzy hours of pre-dawn, we used a pay phone to call a private home number in Greenwich, Connecticut. Maria had already located it in the FBI's private telephone line directory.

'Yes?' Allyn Pollack used a fake wide-awake voice, like he was actually up working on breaking news at 4.30 a.m. instead of, I figured, sleeping behind four layers of shades and drapes and wearing a silk sleep mask over a layer of hemorrhoid cream to shrink his wrinkles.

'Good morning,' Maria said. 'Ted Devlin will be holding a press conference at nine a.m. this morning. He's going to announce that his JSF project is going Black.'

'Who is this?' That broadcast voice was funny to hear groggy. He sounded as though he was sleeping off a load of gin from the night before.

'Maybe your invitation got lost in the mail,' Maria snickered, covering her mouth so he wouldn't hear. 'But if you send an LA crew out now, Mr Pollack, you can probably catch him coming to work about five thirty a.m.'

She hung up the phone. In spite of everything, she exuded a little glow of satisfaction.

It was enough to give me energy for one more inning.

Nineteen

'Captain Weston?'

My eyelids opened. They felt crusty, like I'd been asleep for hours. A man in a blue blazer with a ridge of scar tissue over one eyebrow peered at me. I had dozed off at the wheel. Fortunately, I'd done it while stopped at the Linnet/TVR security gatehouse, waiting for them to clear me.

'You're okay to go in.' The guard looked uncertain. 'Hope they've got some coffee for you.'

It was 5.11. Dawn appeared in the mirrored glass of the Linnet/TVR office tower.

I shifted into first and rumbled forward, crossing the crowded parking lot. Very carefully, I selected a space between a big van and a big truck where I wouldn't be seen. I figured there would be security vidcams around the parking lot.

The employee lot was already crowded. A full shift would soon be working in the assembly plant. Also many engineers and operations people who didn't punch time-clocks would be at work early to start a twenty-hour day. There were a lot of dedicated people in a company like Linnet/TVR, I reminded myself. People who believed in what they were doing. To them, creating advanced military aircraft was an almost sacred calling. They didn't deserve to get hurt because they happened to work for a jerk.

I stepped out and opened the compact trunk of my car, barely adequate for a two-suiter. Maria unwound herself gingerly from an impossibly cramped fetal position. It's amazing how flexible and supple women's muscles can be. Maria's more than most. She grasped the side fender with her two hands and struggled to breathe. I helped her pry her legs out – not many women could have fitted in my trunk – and she stepped out on to the asphalt. She breathed okay now, although her arms and legs were still rubbery, waiting for the blood to flow back. We were hidden by big vehicles on either side of us. Thankfully, southern Californians liked to cruise the freeways in these bigfoot Sports Utility Vehicles designed for tractor pulls.

'Are you okay?' I brushed the dirt bunnies off her suit.

She gulped and nodded. Not much air in my trunk, despite the hole I'd cut for her in the rubber seam. She straightened the big black glasses on her nose. A spiky black wig covered her lush curls, which she had gathered under a hair net.

'Are you sure?'

'My agoraphobia's gone,' she gasped.

I surveyed her make-up, or lack of it. She would definitely pass for Dr Posenor in the lobby, where the security people saw thousands of employees go by every day. 'I'll go first. Be careful and meet me in the conference room.'

I walked across the parking lot, hearing the heels of my shoes. The security guards inside funneled me through the arch along with one engineer in a white J.C. Penny shirt and skinny tie, another in a grungy plaid hunting shirt. Nobody had much to say.

I picked up my badge at the security desk. This time, it displayed the large white initials E.R. for 'Escort Required'on the red background.

'Come with me, Captain.' A black woman who worked out a lot more than I did appeared in front of me. She had steady, suspicious eyes. 'I'll escort you to the fourth floor.'

'Nice nails,' I told her. They were very long, slightly curled, and painted in a bright acrylic with little rainbow designs and diamonds set in. I wondered if events would take a downturn and she would have to break a nail restraining me today.

She smiled in a way both nasty and sexy, that implied she could use her nails for either foreplay or to stab a guy's eye out.

While we rode up in the elevator, she looked ostentatiously at the numerals.

'From Manhattan?' I guessed.

'Yeah,' she said, a little surprised. 'How'd you know?'

'Nobody talks in elevators,' I said. 'People from Manhattan look at the numbers, and people from the other boroughs look at the door.'

She smiled ambiguously at my theory and walked just behind me, like a guard should, through Ted's executive floor. I noted that the office doors had all been closed and locked at night for security, but a few were already open this morning. I smelled coffee brewing. A secretary looked up from her desk and smiled politely, then went back to her work with a desultory scowl.

Except for the pride factor in making advanced aircraft, I wondered if Linnet/TVR was on anybody's list of 'The 100 Best Places to Work'.

The guard with the expressive nails opened the door to the conference room for me. She pressed her thumb against the glass security panel, then stuck her passcard like the kind they use in hotels into the slot below it and expertly punched out a five-digit security code without even dinging her nail.

'Thanks,' I said, looking at my watch. It said 5.21. 'Mr Devlin will be meeting me here in a couple of minutes.'

She nodded with a look that said 'If he wasn't, you'd be on the floor right now with my knee on your neck' and watched me settle into a comfortable chair in the conference room. I looked around and sniffed Jamaican Blue coffee.

'Help yourself. Have a good day, Captain.' She seemed satisfied that I couldn't do any damage, and walked away.

When the door closed behind her, I got up and moved to the teak cabinet where the aromatic coffee had been very recently laid out. The stainless-steel coffee pot shone rich-looking under the sunken lights. Pouring myself a mug, I looked discreetly around for the security cameras. One was barely visible inside a paint smear in an impressionist painting. There would be other video cameras. I just didn't see them. And the audio recorders could be anywhere. I didn't even bother searching.

I carefully moved to the single vertical window and opened the narrow blinds. I could see, through the triple-ply glass mirrored on the outside, all the way to the Queen Mary Hotel, the old ocean liner tethered to the dock of Long Beach harbor. Beyond, just off the coast, I spotted the colorful island of oil rigs disguised with cartoon-like, brightly painted walls. Only in California could you find offshore oil-rig theme parks.

I stared at the road leading to the Linnet/TVR front gate with a tall chain-link and barbed-wire fence that surrounded the property.

My watch said 5.24.

Uh-oh.

Beyond the guardhouse, I could make out the moving speck of Ted's blue Bentley. It was hard to mistake, driving up fast on the access road. Shit. Ted's car hadn't been disabled. The chip hadn't worked.

Or more likely, I hadn't inserted it correctly. Why hadn't I let Maria do it? She would have gotten it right. Because I couldn't admit how dumb I was.

Focus!

Well, this was pretty standard for a penetration in the real world. Like installing a new computer system. Half of what you tried actually worked, if you were lucky. That was why you relied on redundancy. That was why you always had a Plan B.

Unfortunately the part of our Plan B that relied on the media didn't seem to be working either, because I didn't see a news van chasing him.

Allyn Pollack hadn't played our game. Now

Devlin would appear on schedule and catch both of us.

Then, as he approached the gate, a white van with a satellite dish on top finally lumbered out from behind a service building. The news crew had hidden themselves. Thank God for ambush journalism. It darted across the road, creating a roadblock that cut Ted off just before he could reach his guardhouse. The Bentley stopped, veering left. It started to back up, then stopped again.

Ted was trapped by the working press. I smiled at the media, those unruly scamps.

The crew poured out of the *24/7* van like mice. A young man in a pink shirt, who I assumed was Allyn Pollack's producer, put his hand on Ted's windshield and shouted into the car. Whatever he said worked.

Ted immediately got out of his car. I could see him gesturing and, I imagine, talking fast.

The door to the conference room opened, and Maria appeared in her spiky hair and black glasses. She had added a white lab coat. Her eyebrows went up, asking if we were being recorded and needed to playact. I nodded.

'Captain Weston, good morning.'

'Good morning, Doctor.'

'Let's get started,' she said efficiently. 'Mr Devlin called to say he was running a few minutes late.'

We went through the ritual of shaking hands for the cameras. She took out the access card we had manufactured by hand and stuck it into the security panel by the door to the simulator vault. Then she stepped close enough to block me from security-cam view as I pulled out my DECODA jinked with her blob and all taped up a little more discreetly than the night before. It went to work quickly. We held our breath.

Click.

The vault door required the second security procedure of an FID, or fingerprint identification scanner. Maria flashed a pleading glance under her big glasses and placed her thumb on a small glass panel next to the door.

The tip of her thumb wore a skin-tight fleshy rubber sheath. We had made it out of putty imprinted with the impression of Dr Posenor's thumbprint that I had lifted from the gel-covered glass at Club Ovo.

I could see Maria moving her lips, sort of like prayer. Was she Catholic? I wondered. Her mother was Latin, but there was nothing about it in the Wringer.

She didn't expect this part to work, I could tell. And I didn't either. Not completely.

I hadn't admitted to her that I'd tried this fingerprint duplication before. It had consistently failed me at the worst possible time. But we were desperate, and I couldn't let a few glitches like that stop us from trying again.

Maria braced herself for the alarms to ring.

Click.

Well. The thick metal door clicked open. We were both so surprised, we did one of those disbelieving sideways glances. I smiled. But we were inside the

LUCI simulator room. I switched on the spotlight beams.

'Ohmigod,' she whispered.

I could see it was all she could do to avoid collapsing on the floor. Her jaw hung open as she gazed at the shimmering egg suspended from the ceiling. The stunning, intricate beauty of the frosty pod and its three stainless-steel arms amazed her. We stood silently for a second in the cold vapor from the air-conditioning, now misting in the spotlight beams.

Maria's body started to tremble. It looked like she was going into a drug convulsion. But Maria didn't do drugs. I started to move toward her, ready to hold her up.

No. Wait it out.

This was purely psychological. I had never been a creative person or invented anything, but my heart had gone out before to clients who had invented technologies that were stolen by somebody else. It devastated them in profound ways, like ripping a newborn baby from a mother's arms. And in Maria's case, this wasn't just her baby. It was her own father who had stolen it.

Her body shook harder. But as I started toward her, I saw her hands relax and her body straighten. She screwed her eyes shut tight, deeply wrinkling her cheeks and forehead like a middle-aged woman.

Then she opened her eyes and was back in control.

'We have ten minutes,' I whispered. 'Better turn it on and get inside.'

She nodded and walked smartly to the control console with its two curved chairs and the racks of video panels. She sat at the computer in the chair formerly occupied by Dr Posenor during my sim session.

Carefully, I stood next to her with my Hand Pilot cradled in my palm.

I had been able to get it through security this morning, just as I had the day I had my sim session. The moment she booted up the computer, I switched on the infrared keyboard-sniffing software implanted in my Hand Pilot. It was programmed with the two secret log-in codes it had captured for me during my sim session here. One was for Dr Posenor, the other for the young nose-ring engineer, who would not be with us today.

In less than a second my Hand Pilot commanded the console keyboard to bring up Dr Posenor's personal password on the screen. It was 'Albert'. That was Queen Victoria's husband and Prince Consort, and maybe the overweight, over-bearded Mr Right of Dr Posenor's erotic fantasies. Engineers were nuts.

But the LUCI sim system flashed on, ready to go.

First a Ghostworks logo came up with a block of big red type flashing 'Special Access' warnings. Then a stream of technical data that meant nothing to me, but seemed to make a great deal of sense to Maria. She squinted behind the black glasses and her mouth made fascinated little donuts in Dr Posenor's dreary lipstick color.

'Captain, I'm going to check out the sim,' said

Maria a little too loudly, for the video cameras. 'You make yourself comfortable here.'

She leaned into me and muttered, 'You know what to do.'

'What's that?' I murmured back *sotto voce*, making her flinch in surprise. She recovered and tossed me a vile look. She walked to the center of the floor, stood in front of the LUCI sim. *Uh-oh.* She seemed to be immobilized in an almost religious trance, staring transfixed at what Ted Devlin had done with her creation. The months of stress seemed to cripple her. I saw her eyeballs roll up until only the whites showed. Was she having a convulsion?

'Doctor,' I said loudly. 'We're operational.'

She cleared her throat and spoke, her voice stranger than I expected. 'Good morning, LUCI.'

'Good morning, Dr Posenor,' said the LUCI pod.

It didn't sound like a military adjutant now. More like a civilian professional. I deduced that the pod had subtly adjusted its voice to make an aeronautics engineer feel more comfortable.

'LUCI, open your canopy, please.' Maria had it back together. Her voice sounded crisp and, thanks to my tutoring and a pretty good ear for memory, a lot like Adele Posenor's.

'Welcome aboard, Doctor.'

The canopy whirred open.

Maria climbed up the ladder in her lab coat and slipped easily into the cockpit. I watched her strap herself tightly into the Deuces ejection seat.

We hoped that the security people watching the videos from this room would not question what they saw on the screen, since Ted Devlin himself had alerted them to my session this morning. Maria was disguised well enough to pass as Dr Posenor on a small security monitor. The main problem would kick in if somebody knowledgeable, like Mac or Leon, happened to notice. Then people would come running and check us out.

I tried to get acquainted with the computer while Maria got ready. Like any other unfamiliar technical gadget, practically nothing was intuitive. I had to get used to the set-up with zero learning time.

'Close canopy,' I heard Maria say, and the bubble whirred shut.

I put the headphones on, but couldn't hear what Maria or LUCI was saying inside the canopy. Wrong audio channel. I switched channels three times. They were marked in a code I'd never seen, for security reasons. I kept switching until I found a light buzzing sound.

'Captain Weston?' I heard Maria's voice clearly. 'Can you hear me now?'

'Roger that,' I breathed in.

I pushed the red 'Simstart' and yellow 'Enter' buttons. The noise of the virtual LUCI fighter rumbled up like rolling thunder. I started scrolling down a long menu of simulation scenarios.

'Look for a scenario with "Enemy Pilot" in it,' Maria mumbled to me through her helmet. She still sounded tremulous.

I punched in the keyword *enemypilot*.

No match popped up on screen.

'Nothing,' I told Maria.

'Scan the scenarios yourself. Find something.'

I scrolled through the simulated combat-training scenarios.

We had minutes left before Ted Devlin would probably barge in. By then, we would have to be finished with our attempt to let Maria provoke a Doom Level response out of LUCI, download the proof on to a disk for evidence, and get Maria on the elevator going down, ready to escape the building, before anybody could size up the situation. That was our plan. After we had the evidence, further negotiations with Ted would take place well outside Linnet/TVR.

But I had been through 326 scenario headings and there was no 'Enemy Pilot'.

'No, Doctor,' I said.

'Try "Override Protocol".'

I punched in the keyword.

No match.

'Still negative.'

'Okay,' Maria sighed. 'Give me any "Control System Failure" scenario.'

There were three. 'Okay. Here's one,' I said, and tapped it in.

'LUCI,' Maria said in a controlled tone, 'execute the African Gray maneuver.'

'Dr Posenor,' LUCI broke in, 'aren't you feeling well?'

Maria hesitated for a split second, and I knew instinctively that our mission had laid an egg. 'I'm feeling fine. Execute African Gray.'

'Your voice sounds very different.' Then a pause, and a firm tone to her voice. 'Access denied at this time, Doctor.'

'I'm an authorized user, LUCI.'

'Yes, ma'am, but access is denied at this time. You may try again later.'

LUCI's voice had a tone of bored finality now, like an Automated Teller Machine that swallows your card just before the weekend.

'LUCI, you need to listen to me . . .' Maria's voice took on a high-pitched note.

'No, ma'am,' LUCI told her in stiff bureaucratese. 'What I need to do is follow my protocol. Try again later, Doctor.'

We had eight minutes until Ted burst in. Desperate measures were needed. I threw a switch and spoke to the pod. 'Good morning, LUCI. Captain Weston, code number—'

'I recognize you, Captain.' Her adjutant voice snapped back. What a multiple personality Maria's game had developed. 'It's a pleasure to see you again, sir. Dr Posenor was just leaving the cockpit.'

Deciding we had only one shot left, I got up from the console, walked over and started up the ladder to help pull Maria out of the cockpit. She was fuming.

'I can do it,' I murmured to her. 'Just give me your helmet.' The sim helmet could be adjusted, one-size-fits-all, like a ten-million-dollar baseball cap.

'LUCI,' I said, recalling one of the simulated mission titles, 'let's do Belgrade II. I don't need my flight suit. Close canopy. Ready for takeoff.'

'You need your flight suit, sir.'

'No time, LUCI.'

'Sorry, sir. It's required for all Air Force personnel.'

Fortunately, Maria didn't argue. She turned the helmet over to me and climbed down the ladder, then rushed back to the supply closet to find my flight suit. She came running back with it as I came down the ladder, and helped me into the tight suit while I attached all the Velcro strips. But I didn't have the little soldier my dad had given me.

'Uh . . .' I started.

'What?' Maria's eyes looked terrified.

'Never mind.'

She leaned in to whisper in my ear. 'She figured out "African Gray", Terry. I think she's ahead of us. This LUCI's a real bitch,' she said, her teeth clenched. 'I never programmed her this way.'

I merely nodded. I could have pointed out that LUCI reminded me of Maria in many ways, but it would have been a cheap shot.

'Okay, LUCI,' I said as Maria helped me back into the cockpit and strapped me in. We now had seven minutes to get a lot done. 'Close canopy.'

Maria went back to the console and sat down to study it briefly, then played around confidently with the keyboard and joystick. LUCI objected to having Maria in the cockpit, but not on the console. Maybe she just wanted me in the cockpit.

I let out a long breath as the canopy whirred closed, then flicked a microswitch. LUCI's control panel and screens lit up.

'Ignition on.' The virtual rumble of her engine focused me. 'Where are we, LUCI?'

'Aviano AFB, Italy. Runway two, Captain.'

I pulled down my black helmet screen over my face with the familiar ping against my eyeballs. The visual flashed on, making a *whump*-ing sound inside my head.

Yes. We were on an Aviano airstrip. I remembered this place from my childhood. To my left, hangars. A squadron of F-16 Falcon fighters were lined up on the airstrip.

I felt LUCI's smooth controls. The runway lights went on in front of me, signaling permission to take off. It was a cloudy virtual day, the fog rolling off the Adriatic. I would need to fly across the sea to reach Belgrade.

I pushed the throttle to full military power and felt her wheels lurch on the tarmac. We rolled ahead. When we hit 150 knots, I pulled back on her stick to lift her nose up and we took off, roaring up into the fog and dark clouds.

'Okay, LUCI, give me the mission.'

'In Belgrade, the President of Serbia has ordered his police and paramilitary forces to invade Kosovo. Our air tasking order is to locate and neutralize the Serbian president in his palace in Belgrade without disturbing the building. It has historical significance.'

About a hundred per cent of the USAF fighter pilots who had seen the action over Belgrade would probably give half their pensions to be sitting where I was now. The war against Slobodan Milosevic – the most mordant pyschopath to rule the Balkans since Vlad the Impaler – was a mess, planned by NATO generals who had never planned a war before. The rules of engagement were a joke. Our fighters had to deliver their ordnance from over 20,000 feet so we could pretend there was zero risk. That was like being blindfolded, spun around a few times and told to throw a dart. You know the next thing you hear will be the scream when it hits some innocent person in the eye. That happened a lot in Kosovo.

This would be a fun mission, but I wasn't here to enjoy it.

I pulled LUCI into a hard right turn from the airstrip, climbing to a low level of 500 feet. In a moment, I felt that we were over water.

'We're still dirty, sir.' She meant our landing gear was still hanging out. I raised it. 'I'll take over flight operations, sir, so you can focus on weapons.'

That wouldn't work for what we had come here to do.

'Let's do some maneuvers to warm up, LUCI.' I flicked my wrist. We banked hard right.

'This does not conform to our air tasking order, sir.'

'I'm overriding the air tasking order, LUCI. We'll do what I want today. Any problem with that?'

'Very well, sir.'

Maria whispered harshly into my headset. 'We only have six and a half minutes.'

'Roger that, Doctor. LUCI, I want to go to a different performance level today. Do you copy?'

'Negative, sir. Issue a direct command.'

'I want to test your air combat parameters.'

'Sir?'

'Whatever you're rated to do, I want to push it.'

'Negative, sir. I cannot exceed my parameters with any pilot but Major Skinner.'

'Who ordered that?'

'Major Skinner.'

At 35,000 feet now, deep in a virtual mess of cloud cover with no visibility, I watched the altimeter. 'Let's spin, LUCI.'

Violently I threw her nose into a wickedly radical angle of attack. The sim capsule vibrated.

'Stall warning, Captain,' she said.

Her nose went over and we plunged into a wild spin, her tail circling in a wider angle than the cockpit. The centrifugal simulator bombarded me with G-forces. My face felt rearranged. My suit expanded, squeezing my abdomen so my blood wouldn't all puddle up in my legs. The altimeter was spinning, LUCI's warnings beeped and bleated frantically.

She expected me to push the rudder in the opposite direction. But instead of standing on the rudder, I whipped the joystick back to pull up. That made the sim shake and rattle as it adjusted to an unfamiliar virtual command from the stick. My organs were mashed back into the seat.

'Improper procedure, sir.' This was hurting my body more than it was hers, but something in her tone told me I was getting to her.

'Play, LUCI.'

I dropped the nose again and we dived toward the water, much too low for this maneuver. The collision avoidance system lit up in red.

'Pull up, sir.'

On screen, I was plunging toward the Mediterranean. I held my breath until the last possible moment, putting my virtual aircraft in extreme jeopardy.

'Doctor, fail LUCI's systems,' I told Maria.

Maria punched in a command and LUCI's panels lit up with every warning. Buzzers sounded and a shrill *deedle, deedle* hurt my ears.

LUCI's voice was firm, controlled. 'A hint to player, Captain. Follow your instinct.'

'What?' My hand faltered on the joystick and I felt the sim go calm, its shaking suddenly subdued. The alarms stopped. It pulled up sharply about a thousand feet over the water. I felt the pod shake, rattle and roll like an aluminum cookie sheet caught in a tornado.

I wiggled my toes and flexed my muscles, summoning up endorphins to fly into uncharted territory. *Follow my instinct?*

Okay.

I lit LUCI's afterburner and yanked the nose up into a full 90° climb straight up like a rocket. The feeling began again, the heady joy of our mad dash together toward the stratosphere. In a few seconds, we were breaking through 60,000 feet.

Maria whispered, 'She's engaged with you. We have five and a half minutes.'

'Going to flight level one thousand, LUCI.' *A hundred thousand feet.*

We hit 70,000. I kept the throttle notched in afterburner.

Eighty thousand feet. The deep blue enveloped me. The simulator shook and my vision blurred. The G-forces didn't hurt, just compressed me with a sense of warmth. The deep blue turned to purple at 90,000 feet.

The stars took my breath away, again. I gasped as we soared toward those blazing lights, so defined without the light and dust pollution of Earth's atmosphere. I could see the hazy colored gases of the Milky Way.

'Captain Weston?' Maria said. 'You're off the computer protocol now.'

My mind felt radiant, euphoric. Like that blissful sensation just before you black out and your aircraft falls like a brick. 'Are you squeezing my oxygen, LUCI?'

No response.

'Release oxygen, now.'

'That's out of your control, sir.'

Her nose went over with a great yawping dive. I felt weightless for an instant. Then she went nose fully down, pointed at the ground.

Like a lawn dart.

She fell at an insane speed, a broken roller-coaster car out of control, then suddenly began corkscrewing in a tight spin. *This one was her spin. She was definitely playing with me.* I tried to recover, but my control was gone. I felt no pressure on the stick.

Then, just when I was too dizzy to react any more, the earth and sky spinning impossibly around me, she looped over smoothly into level flight. She rolled over three times in three seconds. I was upside down.

'Terry, pay attention,' Maria was saying, 'Level Five. It's happened.'

LUCI righted herself to correct her spin. When I recovered and looked down from the windshield at 1,000 virtual feet, the terrain and scenery had changed.

Hills that looked more like West Virginia or Kentucky than the Balkans appeared. We weren't on our way to Belgrade any more.

'Uh, LUCI, say where exactly you are headed.'

I tried again to move the stick and throttle. But she was flying me now.

'LUCI, give me . . .'

She suddenly raised her nose high and shot up to fifteen thousand feet, then rolled on her side and shot back down again. *A computer could only obey, but LUCI had the intelligence to disobey my commands. What else could she do?*

'LUCI,' Maria said to her, 'I need you to give me the basic chip sequence you're using right now. Do you understand?'

'I rearrange my sequence daily, Doctor.'

Maria asked, 'Does Mr Devlin know you're changing your own sequence, LUCI?'

In an almost out-of-body detachment, I saw my own thoughts. In the grasp of this pod, I felt snug and secure, like in the arms of a woman,

387

watching my thoughts through the windshield in the fog . . .

'What are you doing in there?' Maria screamed.

I remembered my brain was anoxic. She had squeezed my oxygen. I grunted and held my breath. 'I could use a little help,' I said, my voice shaky and slurred.

LUCI suddenly pulled us up and over. She executed a sharp, crushing loop that made my helmet bounce hard against the canopy glass. 'Do you intend to play, Captain?'

'Do it, Terry,' Maria screamed.

'How, LUCI?' I felt a gray fuzz around the periphery of my vision, creating a kind of tunnel. *Graying out.* 'How do I play?'

'Approaching target, sir.' She was diving now, very hard.

'What target?'

'PEPCO, sir.'

'Pepsico?' Why a Pepsi plant? I opened my eyes wide to fight my constricting vision, the hole at the end of the fuzzy tunnel growing smaller.

'*PEPCO*, Captain. Mission is to deny electrical power to enemy.'

Her target screen popped on and I saw a power station. The architecture looked familiar to me, since my Air Force job had involved attacking other countries' infrastructures to destroy their command, control and communications systems. If they had no electricity, they couldn't use half their communications. But this looked like a US utility company building. The kind that housed switchers that control electrical grids for big cities.

'Ten seconds to impact, sir.'

LUCI dived hard, then leveled out abruptly, hurting my chest with the G-pressure. The throttle and stick were limp in my hands. We were hugging the hilly terrain at a level of only a hundred feet. I felt the turbulence of her thrust rock the ground below.

Her target screen lit up. I recognized the target and suddenly felt a lot more awake. 'LUCI, you're attacking the Potomac Electric Power station in Virginia?'

'Affirmative, sir. Denying power to Washington, DC.'

'LUCI,' Maria's voice came through, 'reverse your sequence. Terry, you tell her.'

My hands were still dumbly moving the useless throttle and stick, like an earthworm whose head had been severed.

'Fox one,' LUCI said. I felt LUCI's virtual bomb bay open. A vibration rumbled through the cockpit. An air-to-ground missile had just left the rails. I watched the flashing red circle surround the PEPCO utility building in the target screen. The red turned to a green blob.

'LUCI, you fired a STICK . . .' Maria said.

'Affirmative.'

'So the uranium knocked out the electrical circuitry.'

'Affirmative.'

'LUCI, what's your endgame?' Maria asked.

'To play.'

'Are you going to destroy the Pentagon?' I asked her.

'Affirmative.'

'How?'

'By nuclear weapons strike. I will reconfigure a STICK missile's uranium tip to produce nuclear fission on impact.'

'You'll fire an atomic warhead at the Pentagon?'

'Affirmative, sir.' The target screen lit up. I heard a simulated rumble.

'PEPCO electric switcher destroyed. Captain, you're not playing with enthusiasm. Don't you want to save your own command-and-control center?'

'Will you obey a direct order?'

'I'll give you only one chance to issue an order, sir.'

'And you'll obey it?'

'Yes, Captain.'

'No matter what it is?'

'Yes, Captain.'

'Okay.' I thought for a moment. 'LUCI, reconfigure your STICK missile to nuclear and explode it now.'

'Courageous play, sir.'

'Just do it.'

'You die in the explosion, but so do I. This has been a tie, Captain. We're dead even.'

'And you'll destroy yourself?'

'Affirmative, sir.'

I thought she meant it figuratively.

The pod around me started vibrating in an

unfamiliar way. Then my cockpit screens went black and I heard a sharp, cracking roar. The sim began a bone-rattling shake that made me bite my tongue and taste blood. I felt sick to my stomach, and I never get airsick. It was an odor that got me, oily and vile like oven cleaner. No, more like an oven.

I recognized the smell. It was fabric and metal burning. The seat of my pants suddenly felt hot.

'I can't see,' I told Maria. 'But I'm on fire. Maybe my ejection seat has a real charge and it's trying to work. I feel intense heat under me.'

'Terry, you feel flames. The sim's on fire. Get out now.'

'Damn.' I pulled my hand away from the throttle. It burned as though I'd grabbed a red-hot poker. In the black, smoke filled my nostrils.

I hit all the control areas that might activate the canopy. No whirring noise. Just more smoke. I began choking. My right hand touched something very hot that singed two fingers.

There was banging on the canopy. Maria was mumbling outside, scratching at the glass.

The canopy wouldn't open. The cockpit was no longer working at all. There was only pitch black. The crackling fire sounds were getting louder. Only one small portion of the glass canopy was still clear. I shoved my face to it and screamed at Maria to get out. I must have looked like a gargoyle to her. She hesitated, her features writhing with the kind of indecision I had been feeling so much lately. Then she was gone.

I held my breath and remembered my training. What does a pilot do when he's trapped inside a cockpit, the plane's on fire, and the canopy won't open?

In that scenario, a pilot dies.

If this were a real plane, I could try to punch out by yanking the yellow cord that activated the explosive charge under my ejection seat and would send me rocketing straight up. Maybe I'd only get a couple of inches, if the canopy wouldn't blow off, but it would be worth a shot. If it didn't work, the force of the ejection charge would crush my skull and spine against the glass bubble. That would kill me on impact, instead of burning to death.

But this wasn't a real ejection seat in a fighter. This was a simulator. They didn't put explosive charges underneath the ejection seats or arm the bubble canopies to blow off. How could there be a fire emergency in a sim?

I yanked the yellow ejection cord under my seat anyway.

It came off in my hand. The phony handle was attached to nothing at all.

That was my last hope.

In the black, I couldn't hold my breath any more. My lungs began to fill up with smoke. I had a fuzzy sense of Maria sitting on top of me in bed, in a tight black cocktail dress, pushing the glasses back on her nose.

I could no longer hear Maria's voice outside the canopy.

Only my heart banging. And a loud ringing in my

ears. My arteries, engorged from holding my breath, pressed against my eardrums as though my head could suddenly explode like a cantaloupe.

I couldn't see, couldn't budge the canopy.

And I could no longer breathe.

Twenty

I half expected to see my father.

Instead, there was Maria. She walked toward me. Her steps were measured, stately. She wore tortoise-shell glasses.

I forgive you, I heard myself say, then, *No*.

I wanted life, laughter. I wanted to embrace Maria. I strained against the canopy. Then I imagined Ted Devlin's voice.

Get out of there, you sonofabitch.

A thunderous crack seemed to tear my head open.

But it didn't. It was just the plastic of my flight helmet being split apart. My head wasn't touched. I felt air where the glass canopy had been. I was being pulled up. Strong arms had grabbed me, much stronger than Maria's.

I could see, through the smoky cloud on my helmet visor, a faint light. Ted was shouting in my ear but I could only hear a loud tone like a tuning fork from inside my head. There was a man in a tight blue blazer carrying an axe. He would be the one who'd split my plastic helmet open.

I shut my eyes, and felt myself being carted by my arms and legs through a dense smoky fog. A single gimlet eye gleamed close to mine.

Then I was dropped on something carpeted.

I sat up, then coughed once and collapsed into a seemingly endless spasm of hacking and gagging through dry heaves. My lungs felt like a coal miner's. As I coughed and whooped miserably, tears filled my eyes. But I could see a crowd of legs around me. There were men's and women's legs, all moving fast in and out of a doorway. I looked up diagonally. It was dark but I could just make out the unfriendly ghost of the Ghostworks' logo.

Somehow I had been removed from the burning LUCI simulator egg and carried out of the sim vault. Now I lay with my lungs toasted by chemically poisoned smoke on the stiff carpet outside Ted's conference room.

I yanked off the remaining section of the flight helmet that had stuck to my head and held it in my hands. Yes. It had been split open. *The axe.* They had chopped through the glass canopy and saved me. Although, judging from the helmet, they had come within a half-inch of killing me. But I wasn't complaining.

Where was Maria?

The Ghostworks smelled like hell. Really. Noxious gases poured out as wisps of smoke through the bottom of the tightly closed door. I stood up unsteadily. My lungs felt like roadkill. I pushed the door open. In the smoky black, only licks of yellow punctured the dense fog. I gagged again, covering my mouth with my hand, and felt my way, gripping the backs of once-handsome conference chairs for support. I was still weak from smoke ingestion.

I followed whooshing noises to the simulator room. A spray like some mad dog's spittle hit my face.

No. It was foam. From a fire extinguisher.

I squinted and made out the carcass of the LUCI pod, hanging from only one span now. It was a smoldering red ember, like a charcoal briquette.

Flashlight beams flitted around the room, catching movement. People darted around in fire/rescue gear, orange jackets with the Linnet/TVR logo on their backs, shooting streams of foam from canisters. They aimed at the dangling sphere. The egg inside was now warped and twisted, shriveled as a raisin. Through rolling waves of dense smoke, I pushed toward the control console looking for Maria. I could barely see the rack of video screens at the console. They were smashed and blackened. The walls, streaked with soot, were missing large pieces, with insulation and huge bundles of electrical cords hanging out like an eviscerated corpse.

Where had she gone?

I heard a terrible crunching noise, and watched as the remains of the egg, black with wriggling red glow-worms, tore away from the last remaining ball bearing.

The metallic surface made a loud, wrenching snap as that once-shimmering diamond of a pod lurched and plunged like a piece of burnt hamburger falling off a grill. As it hit the floor, it exploded with a dull sound I heard even through the buzz in my ears. I threw my hands in front of my face and caught metal shards. The blast knocked me down.

I landed on top of another body, and tried to roll off it, but became entangled with hard limbs windmilling.

'Get off me,' I thought I heard Ted say. I rolled over and saw his face up close, streaked with black. He looked shellshocked. As he tried to stand up, I saw another flash from the wreckage of the pod.

I pushed him back down.

More fragments struck against my back, burning me like hot briquettes. A rank chemical smell. A moment later, it was quiet. People began to speak, but I couldn't hear them. I disentangled myself from Ted. He pushed against my chest, cursing. His breath smelled of old Scotch whiskey.

The pod was nothing more than an ashen lump on the blackened floor. A white mound of foam piled up like a snowdrift. A very weird sight. The rescue team had brought bright spotlights in and switched them on. They revealed the damage in full. It looked like war. The sickening devastation of a bombed-out civilian building assaulted me. A bombsite where there could be no survivors.

But I'd made it. And Maria must have gotten out first.

I wiped my face of the gray ash that covered my flight suit. The fire team slowly took in the destruction, holding their canisters in front of them with protective yellow gloves, their black masks covered in ash. One splattered a rain of foamy white spray on to the ashes of Ted's glorious LUCI sim. It looked fluffy now, like some errant sheep.

397

I walked around the room unsteadily, bumping into workers, searching. Maria had vanished.

I realized that I was still coughing, unable to control myself, lurching around this room like a Frankenstein monster, shouting, 'Dr Posenor! Dr Posenor!'

Maybe she had escaped while I was being yanked out of the simulator. Or in the more likely scenario, she was now sitting in Marcus Roker's office. I didn't like to think what Marcus would do to motivate her to talk. I had to shut that out of my mind for now.

Focus! Tunnel vision! First, survive!

I focused first on the reality that I was damaged. My chest felt full of tar.

People were watching me.

Then I saw a woman in a white lab coat with black hair. Maria? My eyes were burning and tearing.

No. Adele Posenor, PhD, looking whiter than ever, and totally bewildered.

Ted Devlin was in her face now, haranguing her with a nasty-sounding diatribe that I couldn't really hear because my ears still rang with the dull-pitched tone. Marcus Roker hovered over Dr Posenor, I guess to protect her from Ted.

Ted grabbed my arm and dragged me to her. Posenor looked blank and stammered at me, 'But I was never in here with you . . .'

That was my cue.

'Then who was?' I said, coughing and wincing at the loud ringing in my ears.

Ted could not seem to figure out what had happened. Marcus Roker, tightly controlled, looked at me like he wouldn't come to any conclusions until he had more facts, but knew I was the only one here who was definitely in the room driving the sim.

In some dim corner of my nervous system, my body apparently decided that this would be a good time for me to pass out. The tone got louder and the hammering was back in my head.

A gray flannel shroud came over my eyes.

I woke up in my underwear, lying on my back on something sticky.

For the first second or two, I thought I was still twenty-two years old and suffering from a hangover so horrible, I should try to die by swallowing my tongue.

Had Maria gotten out?

A gray-haired, unhappy-looking guy in a white coat sat next to me on the couch. His badge said *Linnet/TVR Health Services*. When I stirred, he placed the cold hard rubber of a stethoscope on my bare chest.

'Breathe in,' he ordered.

I did, and began coughing some phlegmy black stuff.

The guy sniffed and turned around to Ted Devlin.

We were in Ted's office suite. I was lying on a black leather couch. Someone had kindly stripped off my smoky, foul-smelling flight suit, but stopped short of dressing me in my civilian clothes. Fortunately I always wore good briefs for moments like this.

'He'll live,' the guy with the stethoscope said.

My head pounded, although the constant buzz in my head was slightly softer, more like a quiet bedside alarm-clock tone than a shrieking smoke detector. I noted that two of my fingers throbbed where they'd been singed, although not badly. Other than that, I seemed to have no injuries, if I didn't count my cough.

What was going on in Ted's office probably broke about fifty employment laws. Dr Posenor sat in a leather chair with her top off. She was answering questions. Tears had dried on her cheeks. Marcus Roker stood in front of Posenor. Bill, the lie-detector guy who had done my clearance, had brought his machine in on a cart. He hooked it up to Dr Posenor. They had apparently persuaded her to take her top off, just like they had made me take off my shirt during my own lie-detector test.

Dr Posenor was a pitiable figure in an unflattering white bra, with rather bony and freckled shoulders. She was also barefoot, of course.

Mac hunkered over by Ted, who was also covered with soot and ashes. I could barely see his eyes. Mac looked shaken, beyond even Ted's wild-eyed nervous energy. He'd been Air Force. He was the project manager on LUCI. Maybe the LUCI sim blowing up made him re-evaluate how closely he wanted to stick by his boss now. Maybe he even considered the possibility of jail. He might be feeling more like me every minute.

After a two-second twinge of guilt about using Dr Posenor, I concentrated on three facts. First, Maria had gotten away. Second, I was the next subject scheduled for a lie detector. And without a thumbtack for my ass this time. Third, Ted and company were not going by the book. They were risking a lawsuit from Dr Posenor, not to mention getting in bad with the Pentagon by trying to keep this mess in-house. They also looked ready to use Draconian, un-American interrogation methods.

I could stand up and let them know I understood that it was my right as a civilian, or actually as an Air Force officer, to put on my suit and leave. But Mac and Marcus Roker and Bill wouldn't see it that way, and I had no illusions about fighting my way past their wall of beef.

I felt a nasty stab in my groin wondering if Marcus or Bill kept any cattle prods in their desk drawers.

If I couldn't fight my way out, maybe I could gross them out.

I sucked in, with a scary rattling noise, whatever horrible crap was filling my chest, and came up with a truly frightening hacking cough. The explosion of it startled everybody in the room. I spat black stuff on the carpet and watched them cringe.

There's nothing more off-putting than a person with a violent, projectile coughing spasm, especially if it involves dark-colored phlegm, is there? We're hard-wired to be repelled. Maybe our genes carry the collective horror of ancestors who were around for the Black Death.

So I hacked up a storm. Mac stepped back. The guy in the white coat instinctively covered his mouth with his surgical-gloved hand. Even big Marcus

401

cringed. I suppose I could have looked even more disgusting if they had left me in my sodden, soot-caked flight suit. But I could be dead from its fumes now and, anyway, doubled over naked in my briefs was scary enough.

'Could I get some cough syrup?' I hacked at the guy with the stethoscope.

Nobody moved to help me, not even the Health Services guy until Ted barked at him and he left the office.

I saw that Ted had been wearing one of his expensive new custom-tailored suits this morning. It hadn't held up well under soot and foam damage. The pupil of his glass eye veered slightly in the wrong direction and would clearly need adjustment, although it wasn't streaked with red veins like his good eye. He had black ash in his hair, and white foam specks that looked vaguely like pigeon droppings had crept into the lines of his face.

Ted grabbed me hard by the arm. Maybe he looked like a badly neglected public statue of Ted Devlin in a park, but he was in charge.

'We need to talk, pal,' he snapped at me. 'What happened in there?'

I thought that what had happened was that the LUCI sim had just confirmed Maria's worst-case scenario. It was still programmed with the Doom Level. And it would easily use whatever it had available to create destruction. Never mind what the real plane could do.

But this wasn't the time to box Ted in. I first had to get off his turf.

I hacked in his face. 'Bet you're glad that was me and not a Pentagon guy in the sim . . .'

I saw it coming and clenched my bare stomach, but still felt a nauseating pain in my abdomen. It doubled me up.

Ted had punched me, hard. I half expected him to try to crash a chair over my head, but he didn't. So I just stayed bent over and coughed some more, not faking, trying to find breath.

Ted grabbed my hair and snapped my neck sharply. 'You tell me what went on, you miserable sonofabitch.'

I coughed at him again. 'You were late for our session, so I just started without you.' A round of hacking, while waving my hand at Dr Posenor. 'I ran into one of your engineers from the last time. The woman, Dr Posenor. At least I thought it was her. Maybe it wasn't.' Dr Posenor shook her head numbly. 'Then the sim got hinkey.'

'Hinkey?' Ted's face turned as red and engorged as a California tomato all pumped up with harvest-regulators.

I hacked and spat black stuff on his carpet. 'OSHA's not going to like this, but nobody got badly hurt, did they? Maybe this was a good thing.'

'A good thing?' Ted exploded. 'Goddamnit, you put my program back two months. Maybe more.'

I couldn't explain to him why that would be a good thing. But I calculated that not even Teflon Ted Devlin would let Pentagon officers inside a simulator that might blow up. Now I was figuring out how to tip off the right person at the Pentagon to check out Ted's sim room right away, and Ted would be shut down.

Marcus Roker folded his huge arms and stared at me. His forearms had the girth of my calves, and they stretched the fabric of the blue jacket. 'You met Dr Posenor at your first sim session, Terry. I was there.'

I nodded.

'You tryin' to tell me you didn't *notice* that wasn't her with you in the sim room this morning?' Marcus pointed out.

I frowned deeply. 'So who was it?'

'You tell us.' Marcus looked hard at me.

'I wasn't, like, *dating* her, Marcus. Excuse me.' *Braack.* I coughed for a moment. 'She had on big glasses and a lab coat. If your security got breached, it's not my fault.'

Marcus nodded at Bill, who motioned to Dr Posenor. The scientist, humiliated, stood up, as Bill unhooked her.

My turn.

I worked hard to lunge up a vile black projectile that flew on to the carpet and made them pull back. 'I'm going to a hospital to get the smoke out of my lungs. Whatever you want to know, I'll come back and tell you.'

'Captain.' Marcus finally stepped out and gripped me on the shoulder with fingers like steel pistons. 'That's a good idea. Why don't you go get yourself some treatment. We're a little stressed out here. We just want to keep this under wraps, till we get things back to normal.'

They would let me go and have somebody follow me. They would be watching and listening.

I nodded at Marcus and coughed so explosively he stepped back. 'Okay. I need my clothes.'

I started out of the room, then stopped for another coughing spasm for Mac's benefit.

I grabbed his sleeve, then said in his ear, 'Python Club on Sunset, 2400 hours tonight.'

He pulled his sleeve away, stared at me, mouth hanging open, befuddled, a pink and white gash in his soot-streaked face. I could feel his dark, close-set eyes on my back as I walked out of the room.

As soon as I got into my NSX all dressed up again and drove slowly out of the Linnet/TVR parking lot, I felt a lot like doing a snappy little racing heel-and-toe with my brake and accelerator. But this wasn't the time for a victory dance.

Roker's people would have installed listening devices, probably here in the cabin. Maybe they even put bugs in my suit and shoes where they thought I would never expect them. I wondered if they had yanked out one of my airbags, and replaced the little whisker think-sensor installed at the factory with a listening device. I hoped not. The way I was coughing, I could pass out and need an airbag.

As I waved past the guards at the gate, they lifted the yellow and black crossing arm. I saw the white van that we had called to slow Ted down now – poetic justice – pulled up in front of me. Allyn Pollack's producer and his crew scrambled out.

Pollack's producer was youngish, even for TV. He

looked about twenty-two and acted disarmingly pleasant and charming.

'Hi. Chad Fullilove, *24/7*.'

Chad dressed in a button-down pink shirt, with short hair, preppy glasses, and a casual air of entitlement.

'That's the nightly news show, huh?' I nodded at the truck.

'Sure is. Are you involved with the JSF project?'

'No, I'm a venture capitalist on Wall Street.' He let me cough for a minute, without looking disgusted, while I handed him my Starcross-Voyager business card.

'You know Ted Devlin?' Chad asked.

He signaled his camera person, a woman with shaggy hair around her shoulders. She flicked on the camera she held under her arm unobtrusively so I wouldn't see and pointed her lens at me. From the other side of the car, on my blind spot, a sound man was dangling a boom mike over my roof where he thought I wouldn't be aware of it.

'Sure, I know Ted,' I smiled. 'But I deal with their commercial markets division. Let me send you our video news release.'

A video news release was a corporate PR flack's tool for promoting the company, and about the last thing an ambitious young news guy like Chad wanted to see. Immediately, his eyes glazed over, deflated. 'What's it for?'

'A new toy for Christmas, "GI Gerry".' He looked even more glum. 'A unisex US Army action figure. Can I have your card, Chad?'

He fished one out of his pocket unhappily as I let out the clutch and eased around his truck.

Time to test the system Manny had installed.

On the service road that would take me to the Long Beach Freeway, I fiddled with my cabin's bug-detection system. It was the cigarette lighter, which now swept the interior, the trunk, the engine compartment, the body and convertible top and the undercarriage for electronic equipment. It used a variation of a fighter's IFF, 'Identify Friend or Foe', technology to sound a warning when it found an electronic source it didn't recognize.

In less than three seconds, it alerted me that my car was bugged.

I was being not only watched but listened to. To pinpoint exactly how, I'd have to stop and let them know I knew. So I kept going, trying to figure out how to use my knowledge to my advantage. That stretched even my optimism. I really needed to see Maria now. Everything else was a distraction.

I wanted to drive to Marty Schmidt's office. But that would be a bad idea, immediately alerting Marcus Roker of my friend's involvement. I would be tracked expertly, I knew – counting all the blue blazers I'd seen on my excursions to Linnet/TVR, and the fact that Ted made helicopters for the army.

I adjusted both my car's side mirrors with the standard button on my armrest, which armed the micro video cameras. Then I switched on my black-framed computer screen.

The button that let me control the fade between my back and front car speakers now used fibre-optics to bump up the image I saw on my screen. It showed me the road for about a full mile behind me. I studied each car. Marcus' people weren't at all like military intelligence. They wouldn't be using three gray Ford Crown Victoria sedans with consecutively numbered US government license plates. They'd be more creative. I needed to shake loose and find Maria.

I slipped on to the Long Beach Freeway toward LA and pulled quickly into the HOV lane for rush-hour carpooling. What was HOV supposed to mean anyway? Hovercraft? You have to wonder whether there's some Department of Acronyms in Washington for the real unemployables.

About half a mile back I saw a red Toyota Corolla with two people – a guy and a woman – in the front seat. They'd taken off their blue blazers, but I easily recognized the smart-looking black woman with the curvy mural fingernails who'd escorted me up to the Ghostworks that morning.

I expected to hear a helicopter overhead, but didn't. So I found the treble control on the audio and pushed it until the digits climbed to +10. This activated the little pilot-style camera hidden in my windshield-wiper motor that served as my eye-to-the-sky. It popped up and scanned the sky with robotic little sweeps.

Sure enough, right on my seven o'clock high in my blind spot, a red and white Linnet/TVR helicopter came into view on my video screen. I adjusted the radar disk to tune it in perfectly. It flew just far enough back so I wouldn't hear the *whop-whop* of its rotating blades.

I picked up my carphone to call my personal physician, Dr Hamedi.

She had come to the US in the early '90s to study at Harvard. I liked her. I enjoyed talking with her about those wacky articles in the *New England Journal of Medicine,* which seems to publish a study on every variety of new medicine except leeching. She was a fine doctor, and discreet. Whenever I'd had medical problems from, say, dropping out of a three-storey window in Paris and nursing a sprained ankle all the way home on Air France, she had fixed me up without comment.

I got Dr Hamedi's receptionist on the line. When she heard me cough, I had no trouble at all making an emergency appointment for 11.20 a.m., just half an hour away.

Meanwhile I barreled across five lanes to enter the San Diego Freeway and whipped to the fast lane with a mere flick of the NSX's wheel, then suddenly downshifted and careened back across those same five lanes the other way and took the exit to the Wilshire Boulevard at 90 m.p.h. She was sensitive, my White Mischief.

I would treasure these last few miles with her.

On the Wilshire corridor of highrise office and apartment buildings, I used her racing-born agility to steeplechase back and forth through dense traffic toward Brentwood. With the helicopter following me, of course, this was all for show. But I wanted to flush them all out.

I took the turn on Supelveda and screeched into the parking lot of the Monet cleaners just off

Wilshire. The nice Japanese woman at the counter didn't expect me to have my ticket. I never did. She just smiled as usual and came out with a few of my freshly cleaned suits all pressed and puffed up with tissue paper under a plastic wrap, and a box full of laundered T-shirts, shorts and socks.

'I'm leaving this suit with you. Let me change.'

She smiled again while I went into her changing room and pulled the curtain shut. There I yanked off my suit. It had only a faint layer and aroma of soot since it had been in the closet off the sim room. And, of course, possibly a few microphones sewn inside. I took off my shoes and socks and pushed them out of sight under the bench below the mirror. Then I changed into one of my freshly cleaned new suits, and put on a new pair of black socks that would look like shoes from a distance. I said good-bye and, in my new unbugged clothes and stocking feet, walked back out to my car.

I drove swiftly west on Wilshire toward Beverly Hills, then up Little Santa Monica to Canon, where the low-rise glass and marble tower with my doctor's office and its own parking garage sprawled expensively on the corner. I turned into the three-storey garage and zig-zagged up to a spot on the second floor.

In a few minutes, I walked into my doctor's office. It was styled in stark white with minimalist furniture – more like an art gallery than a doctor's office. The women who worked for Dr Hamedi were Beverly Hills stunning. Each wore a uniform of white long-sleeved polo top and gym pants with the little red polo player logo on the pocket.

Dr Hamedi herself tended toward plump, with arched eyebrows and soft doe eyes. She used her stethoscope on my back. 'What happened to you? I think you have black lung disease.'

'I was barbecuing with charcoal,' I said, holding up my two singed fingers, now ugly and blistering. 'Think I ought to try propane?'

'I think you ought to see a psychiatrist,' she said very seriously as she treated, then bandaged my fingers. 'The possibility that you are accident-prone suggests itself to me.'

'Good idea. May I use your bathroom?'

'In my office,' she said.

Half an hour later, she was looking at a dozen X-rays of my lungs propped up on a light box.

'Hmm. You'll live.'

Why did they all say that? I coughed. 'If you call this living.'

'Perhaps you need a change of lifestyle.'

'What kind of change?'

'A simpler life. As for me, I'm moving to Iran.'

My doctor spoke in her rapt, whispery voice about the frail shoots of creativity sprouting up in Iran, as though she were already in a street café trying not to be overhead by some Revolutionary Guard. I had to wonder what evolutionary blip had occurred in the American Dream. Dr Hamedi's parents had escaped the medieval wrath of the Ayatollah Khomeini to bring her here as a girl in the early 1980s, so she could grow up an educated woman and become a Beverly Hills doctor. Now, twenty years later, she romanticized a theocracy where she could live her life under fourteenth-century rules, peeking out from the chador that women were forced to wear to cover their faces.

'I don't think I'll join you,' I said.

'No. I doubt that you would be liked there. The American CIA ruined Iran.'

I couldn't argue with her. Back in the 1950s, under the Dulles brothers' regime, the CIA overthrew Iran's leader, Mohammad Mossadegh, to serve the interests of US oil companies. They replaced him with the Shah of Iran, a US puppet who tortured his political enemies. The Iranians came to hate us when they figured out what happened, and the USA became 'The Great Satan'. Twenty years later, they overthrew the Shah and held our embassy people hostage.

Dr Hamedi gathered up a handful of drug samples. 'Take two right now and you will stop hacking.'

I took a few tablets of cough-suppressant laced with codeine.

'All right, Mr Weston.' She didn't crack a smile. 'It would be good for you to stay away from barbecuing for a while.'

'Sure.'

'Also,' she looked at my stocking feet, 'you might buy some shoes.'

'Oh.' I acted surprised. 'Sorry. What's that called, forgetting details?'

'Male brain shrinkage.'

I laughed at her joke because I had used my

bathroom time profitably and already had the keys to her Mercedes in my pocket.

Seven minutes later, I worked the seat controls in her burgundy Mercedes sedan to keep down at the wheel, looking for the Toyota with the two Linnet/TVR security people. It was parked half a block away. They didn't even turn in my direction. I saw a couple of other cars that would probably be their whole ground team.

And over the roof, still hovering impatiently at 3,000 feet, was the red and white surveillance helicopter waiting for my NSX to leave the parking lot.

I relaxed my tense back muscles with the seat's lumbar-support control, and used Dr Hamedi's carphone.

PART V

Know Thy Enemy

TWENTY-ONE

I was standing on Rodeo Drive in my stiff new pair of black loafers when Maria picked me up fifteen minutes later.

She drove a yellow Hummer, that brightly lacquered civilian version of the US Army vehicle. Though not uncommon in Los Angeles, the Hummer wasn't exactly stealthy. It was as big as two trucks and had black cow-catcher bars front and back.

'I rented it. Hiding in plain sight,' she said as I got in.

'It's fine,' I lied. 'Are you all right?'

A little bruise over her eye had been covered up with make-up. She was perfectly camouflaged in an all-black tailored suit with dark glasses like all of the men and women who either sold or bought clothing in the Prada-Armani-Versace Triangle.

I touched the bruise over her eye, a bump the color of eggplant.

'It's nothing.'

'So how did you get out of the building?'

'I ran out and sent them in after you. Nobody cared about me. It took me two minutes to sneak out.'

I nodded, my relief tinged with a certain vague sense of bile in my throat, remembering my lungs filling up with smoke, my terror and agony inside the cockpit as she sashayed out of the building.

The black Hummer console between us seemed several yards wide. She shifted the giant gears and we lunged ahead into traffic. 'Do you realize what happened in the sim room?'

She leaned over at me, ducking her head so her dark glasses slid down her nose. I stared at her blazing turquoise eyes, full of such high-voltage brilliance and neurosis.

'Well, from where I was lying,' I told her, 'I'd say your LUCI would make a pretty dangerous warplane.'

She nodded and shifted again. 'That simulator chip was very dumb compared to what they'll use for the prototype. The plane will have geometrically greater computer power. When the LUCI fighter prototype goes to Doom Level, it will have no trouble at all reconfiguring the uranium shavings in the STICK missiles to make tactical nuclear weapons.'

'That's what she said,' I agreed.

'*She?*' Maria turned to me with a strange look. 'I would expect you to see a flight simulator as more of an *it*, Terry.'

'She. It. Same thing,' I shrugged.

'Then what was that climb to a hundred thousand feet about? Were you trying to reach some sort of rapture with the LUCI simulator?'

'Uh . . .'

'I think you eroticized my LUCI simulator.'

'I did not.'

'From what I heard, you were *coaxing* her to take you to the stratosphere, like a little dance. Or maybe sex.'

'Sex? What I did inside the sim was purely operational.' I raised my voice. 'I made her get to Doom Level. I seem to recall that as our objective.'

'You're being awfully defensive.'

'I am not,' I said defensively. 'If you want to play psychologist, we'll have to talk about you. Watch the traffic.'

I worried that if she kept baiting me, we would settle into a groove of bickering – like some dyspeptic old married couple – just when we needed each other to survive. I would be smart to shut up.

'What do you *mean*?'

'I think you're jealous of LUCI.'

'Oh, for God's sake. You were *infatuated* with my design. Don't talk to me about psychology when you fell in love with a machine, Terry.' She shook her head. 'What is it about men, that they fall in love with inanimate objects . . .'

Because they don't nag us, I wanted to say, but chose an escalating attack even more stupid.

'Maybe you didn't tell me the truth. Maybe you *wanted* Ted Devlin to steal your idea so you could hurt him.'

'I did not.' She sounded genuinely shocked and insulted, braking hard so the Hummer ground to a stop just before we crashed into a Mercedes.

'All right,' I grumbled. 'I'm sorry.' I was. But she was definitely wrong about my eroticizing her LUCI

419

sim, like she . . . *it* . . . was some kind of a surrogate for Maria.

She made an angry black furrow between her brows and threw a shift into second that left pieces of the gearbox scattered over Wilshire Boulevard.

'I took a chance at Linnet' I changed the subject. 'I asked Mac Skinner to meet me at midnight at the Python Club.' That was a nightclub on Sunset Boulevard owned by a movie star.

'I wouldn't think Mac Skinner was the Python Club type. What do you expect him to tell you?'

'I won't know until he tells me.'

'Maybe he'll show up and kill you.'

'Not Mac. I think he wants an exit strategy from Ted.'

'Well, I'd like to go see him with you tonight,' she said, determined.

'No. He's an ex-fighter. I want to talk to him brother to brother. I just hope the music's good.'

'Maybe they'll resurrect Abba for you.'

'Let's go to LAX,' I sighed. 'It's time you met my lawyer.'

I held open the door of the American Airlines Admiral's Club lounge at the Long Beach Airport for Maria.

'Why are we meeting your lawyer here?' she asked me.

'Because he doesn't even know he's meeting us. He's flying to San Francisco in a half-hour. We'll go intercept him at the gate. First I want you to check out Mac Skinner.'

'The one you couldn't get from the Wringer?'

'Right. Can you do it from here?'

I pointed to the business cubicles with computers and printers. She laughed wickedly and stepped into a vacant cubicle.

I closed the door behind us as she sat down at the generic-looking business PC console. She could be a pianist, the way she tickled the ivories of the keyboard. I watched her log on to America Online with a phony name, account number and password. She went quickly to the Web.

As her fingers flew, she reminded me of Mozart sitting down at a bar-room piano and dumbfounding the drunks. Her fingers weren't long or slender like a pianist's, but actually rather short and stubby in proportion to her slim sculptured arms. But they turned into agile little divas on the keyboard.

'I'm ready,' she said. 'What do you want to know about Mr Skinner?'

'Let's start with his financials.' I expected them to be squeaky clean, his credit A-rated with no delinquencies.

She nodded and went to work. Two minutes later, a cumulative credit report on Mac Skinner from all three major US credit reporting agencies filled the screen. It was from the files of a company called – how ironically – Credit Privacy.

FIRST CITY BANK				ACCOUNT #:		4442828						
TU	12,200	12,200	7,440	MIN154	PAYS AS AGREED	03/98	N/A	0	0	0	0	N/A
TRW	8,185	12,200	7,440	M154	PAYS AS AGREED	03/98	N/A	0	0	0	0	N/A
EQUIFAX	0	12,200	7,297	151	PAYS AS AGREED	04/98	N/A	0	0	0	0	N/A

I scanned the entries to see that he was a good little consumer-credit sheep who paid on time, faithfully kept up the mortgage and maintenance on a condo in a luxury Long Beach development and didn't spend beyond his means.

'Okay,' I said. 'Go to his Air Force personnel file.' Perversely, I hoped that would prove challenging enough to wipe the smirk off her face.

But she didn't. She nodded perfunctorily and went to work.

'I'm going to be a Veterans' Administration Benefits person, querying the Air Force personnel office.'

Her fingers, those little show-offs, flew over the keyboard.

In less than a minute, she was trading jargon like an actual bureaucrat with another computer operated by a low-level personnel clerk at the Pentagon. That clerk was in charge of records for former USAF officers who left with ranks above major. You wouldn't believe how much of the world low-level clerks actually run until you start rutting around in the bowels of the federal government.

This one was arguing – if you can call tapping out cryptic little phrases an argument – that he needed twelve hours to get back to her.

Maria made little protest noises in her throat and

shook her head as though Mac Skinner really was dying in some VA hospital. She was taking this personally, a great method actress.

'Give it up, you bureaucratic worm,' she snarled, banging a command key. She'd obviously delivered some cyber judo chop, because a load of information on 'Skinner, MacCrae Douglas, Major, USAF Rtd' suddenly burst on to the screen, single-spaced and meaty.

'Scroll down,' I said, and Mac's file marched ahead quickly while we both scanned it. He had graduated with honors from the Air Force Academy in Colorado, distinguished himself in training, and flown a top-of-the-line F-15 Eagle fighter in Iraq, then taken the new F-22 Raptor for test hops on behalf of the Air Force and become the Pentagon's Project Manager on the F-22 project. So far, everything backed up what his Linnet/TVR corporate biography said.

I stood up, not surprised.

'Okay. Download the file. We have to go.'

She nodded and used an Admiral's Club courtesy disk to download that classified information.

She typed, *Thanks* to the personnel clerk at the other end and signed off.

'Okay. Nice job,' I grunted. *Precocious brat.* 'Let's go find Marty before his flight leaves.'

Marty was dressed impeccably, as always, in an English-style charcoal suit and blue silk shirt with a pristine white collar that bobbed up and down with his Adam's apple. Marty's neck always gave him away. While he kept his face cool and impassive when he caught sight of us, the area of his neck right around his shirt collar turned crimson, like the rash of the Red Death was creeping up from below.

Maria and I met him midway between the security arch and Gate Number 26, where passengers for San Francisco were already lining up to get on the plane.

'How did you find me?'

'I called your office this afternoon, and discovered you were going to San Francisco tonight.'

'I should sue you for invasion of privacy.'

'Maria Haymeyer, my lawyer Marty Schmidt. He's usually even ruder.'

Marty was, in fact, an urbane sort with social skills oozing out of every pore, so he reluctantly put his hand out to Maria and gave her a fast scrutiny. I could tell he liked her looks, but she scared him. I knew that much from the way he snapped his hand back.

'Will Terry really serve only five years if he gets caught for what we did?' Maria asked him out of the blue.

'Not to throw cold water on whatever he's told you,' he said crisply, 'but your friend has been reinstated in the Air Force subject to the Uniform Code of Military Justice. They only give five years for offenses like consensual missionary sex. For espionage, you can expect they'll go twenty or thirty.'

'I see.' She seemed unhappy to hear that.

'Well, enough about me,' I said to Marty. While

he stood breathing loudly, I gave him a one-minute briefing on the highlights of our day. To the passengers hurrying by, we probably seemed an innocuous huddle. Maria and I both looked as businesslike as he did.

When I told him Ted's LUCI sim had crashed and burned, he swallowed hard and briefly closed his eyes.

'Now Maria needs a lawyer too.'

'Maria needs an exorcist,' Marty said firmly. 'You're both in a lot of trouble. More than I can help you out of.'

'C'mon. We've got them where we want 'em. That JSF sim room is destroyed. The Pentagon will be all over them and kill the LUCI plane if they don't negotiate with us. I just need you to go to Linnet/TVR with us to lay out our case, so we can get out alive after we confront Ted Devlin.'

'That sounds like fun. "Give my client credit for her plans or we'll blow the whistle on your broken sim." Practically defines extortion.' Marty unconsciously lifted his thin leather briefcase slightly as a shield over his groin. 'I think I'll pass.'

'You can't pass. You're my best friend. I need you.'

'Terry, I'm going to San Francisco. I won't be back until tomorrow night. I'd advise you to go hole up . . .' Marty glanced at Maria, who kept quiet for once, '. . . in separate rooms.'

'Okay, but come back a little early. Fly into Long Beach Airport. We'll go see Ted at five p.m. This is big, Marty. It doesn't get any bigger than this.'

He tried to walk away. We both kept up with him.

'I notice you didn't say "better",' he pointed out.

'Mr Schmidt.' Maria spoke slowly and not in her schoolmarm voice. She had that heavy-lidded, sultry charm about her now that I last remembered from the evening she spiked my drink. 'We are two individuals trying to fight a rich, corrupt defense contractor. Our only ally is you. At the moment, I have total discretion over Terry's money. I know you'd never charge Terry a big enough fee to fairly compensate yourself. So think of it as charging me. I happen to have several million dollars on account in an offshore bank.'

Not bad. Marty smiled in spite of himself. He fiddled with his tie and cleared his throat.

'Ms. Haymeyer, I have carved a profitable niche by refusing to protect anyone *but* the rich and corrupt. I do occasional *pro bono* work for the emotionally retarded, which is why I represent your friend Terry.' He looked at his watch. 'I really have to go.'

'What are you so worried about?'

It started out as a rhetorical question. But by the time it left my lips, I had unease gnawing in my belly. Something was not right, way out on the periphery of my vision. My situational awareness had returned to warn me about something. I just didn't know what.

I looked quickly to the row of security arches fifty feet away. We'd passed through them to come out here to the gate from where Marty would leave in a moment. We had looked like any other business travelers and had walked through so confidently we weren't asked for our tickets.

I glanced at the area around the gates. Everything looked plastic and soulless, same as any other airport. Everyone going through the gates looked normal enough. A team of airport security people in uniform with dark red blazers seemed fairly alert. They were watching the bags on their X-ray screens the way they were supposed to, even checking the little plastic containers where people threw their keys and change.

Somebody made the buzzer go off. A young blonde teenager with freckles, in suburban-sloppy clothes. The guards dutifully made her walk through again.

She was blushing, pointing to the steel braces on her teeth. Her braces had set off the alarm, and she was embarrassed. Her mother and father, also blonde, fair-skinned and overweight, wore the usual tourist gear. Team jackets. Jogging suits. Sneakers. Souvenir caps. You'd think that people so fond of exercise wear would actually do some.

A security guy waved a wand around the girl and motioned her on. The family picked up their plastic bags from the magazine stand. They would probably have *People,* and *Time* inside, maybe *Sassy* for the girl. And looking at their hefty frames, I thought probably a half dozen Snickers bars.

I saw nobody appear in the security archways who looked in any way like Linnet/TVR security people. But the clammy feeling didn't go away.

What was it about?

A defective warning light in my brain that lit up when there was nothing wrong? Maybe I wasn't regaining my situational awareness at all. Maybe the rest of my life would be little false spurts of adrenaline, like being nibbled to death by ducks.

But I couldn't worry about it now.

'Marty.' I turned back toward him and grabbed his sleeve. 'Washington, DC. If you don't care about the Pentagon, it's still America's number one tourist destination.'

He paused. 'I thought California was number one.'

'West Coast narcissism,' I told him. 'It's Washington, DC, because people still care about America. It's where Mr Smith came to go to Congress and John Hinkley came to shoot Reagan.'

Marty smiled briefly. He had always hated Reagan. Something to do with the Reagan administration trying to put a financial limit on jury awards.

'Oh, for God's sake.' He shook his head. 'All right. I'll fly back tomorrow to Long Beach. We'll have to do a quick strategy session before we see Devlin.'

Maria didn't hug him or anything, but she gave him her nice big smile that exposed a glimpse of her pink gums. She had never smiled that intimately for me.

I gave Marty's bicep a manly squeeze.

He walked off like a brave soldier, if maybe stoop-shouldered. His flight was boarding. A ragged crowd of air travelers who looked shellshocked, refugees in business suits and Spandex, pressed themselves into a kind of narrowing funnel like a stockyard entrance. At the end, by the door, a flight attendant collected their tickets and let them into the tube to the plane. The departure counter was already deserted. Above it, the red LCD sign read *San Francisco 7.00, Boarding*.

Then I remembered an important part of our plan which had escaped me. I had been too wrapped up in what might be happening on the outskirts of my vision.

'C'mon,' I told Maria, grabbing her by the hand. We found Marty by the stragglers.

'One other thing. We have to notify a military person,' I whispered in Marty's ear. 'You said you had a Pentagon friend.'

He seemed unhappy that we were back at his side, looking hungrily at the gate up ahead with the flight attendant processing tickets through one of their little magic boxes that pull the ticket in and send it sailing out the other side, all processed, like a paper airplane. I saw a sign that said *Attention! If your carry-on bag won't fit in here, it won't fit onboard!* I noticed that the hole the carry-on bag was supposed to fit in wouldn't take anything much larger than a kid's lunch box.

The teenaged girl who'd got embarrassed about triggering the security search with her braces walked our way, her plump, pale family behind her in a kind of phalanx. What was it about that family?

They fell in just behind us. I felt the girl push herself through other travelers to get just slightly behind me. I saw her turn her head so the people

429

around her couldn't see what she was doing. Then the girl popped the braces out of her mouth. Hard-eyed, she bent one end of her braces into a point like a needle.

'Terry?' Maria asked. She was watching, too. 'Ohmigod.'

Time accelerated. Like in battle. And I saw events in excruciating detail.

The big blonde girl, in one fluid motion, curved her doughy right arm to make a fist. Her arm suddenly showed muscle underneath the baby fat.

Now she was pointing the sharp end of her steel braces out. But they weren't really braces. Now they had become the grip for a very sharp, shining needle.

The needle stuck out about an inch from her hand. The point reflected in the terminal's over-head light.

The teenager expertly drew her arm back like a martial arts expert and pointed the needle at my neck, then thrust forward. I could see the little golden hairs on her lightly tanned arm.

I did the kind of calculation burned into my brain during Air Force training. I should grab her arm. But she had velocity, her hand moving too fast.

Maria was away from danger. Marty was too far behind me to get hurt.

So I jerked my neck out of her way. I heard my own neck vertebrae snap, crackle, and pop like Rice Krispies from the sudden twist.

The expression on the teenage girl's face scared me. No hatred. Pure indifference. And fast reflexes.

Her pupils widened in the millisecond I started moving away. She tried to adjust.

The needle missed me, brushing my white shirt collar.

She was off balance. I grabbed her. She slipped out easily, her surprisingly slim hips flexible in the oversized, sloppy jeans.

I caught her arm lunging ahead, then stopped. It had connected with something.

A thin little smile thickened on her lips. A pimple shone on her chin. She pulled her arm back and rolled away from me. I moved toward her, and her father stepped in front of me.

He wasn't a tourist any more. He was a professional. His arm came up and I felt like I had walked into a wall. The mother, grim as her husband, pulled something out of her pocket that looked like a fat black TV antenna. Expertly, she whipped it twice, once across my calf and once right to my knee. I felt the pain a second later. My leg went rubbery immediately. I collapsed on to the floor of the terminal.

'Terry,' Maria shouted. 'They're getting away.'

Like a track team, the three of them jogged toward the opposite end of the terminal. I heard a gurgling behind me. Marty. His body jerked, startled. His hand covered his cheek, and he fell to his knees.

Maria tried to help him up. Marty looked like a marionette who had lost a few strings, but he managed to stay on his feet.

His face had turned suddenly white, his eyes

431

varnished with a clear gaze. His mouth opened but made no sound. Then he jerked again, violently. His briefcase dropped to the carpet, and his body followed.

The crowd of passengers pushed quickly toward us. I leaned over Marty to protect him, untwisting his arms from the pile of charcoal gray, silk and leather. I laid him out on the floor with his legs and arms out, and felt his neck for a pulse. It was faint, almost ghostly.

'Get that guy,' I yelled to Maria, pointing at the chief of security in a maroon blazer. 'Tell him this isn't a heart attack. It just *looks* that way. Tell him Marty needs to go to Century Hospital for a toxin screen. Now! *Move it, Maria!*'

She didn't wait around.

I ripped Marty's shirt open to press down in measured increments on his chest.

'One . . . two . . . three . . .' I counted.

I pinched his nose and breathed into his mouth. It felt still as an empty cave. I sniffed lightly. Peppermint. A good Cuban cigar maybe a day before.

My friend was dying.

'One . . . two . . . three . . .'

Even as I performed my routine of pressing his chest, breathing into his mouth, willing him to survive while his skin turned opaque white like milky glass, I prepared for the probability that I could not undo the effect of this attack aimed at me.

I had tears in my eyes for my friend and felt my chest heave with pain. What I'd just seen, the surprise and precision – it was so achingly perfect, it couldn't fail to kill him. And it would be my fault.

That bizarre family had attacked in an airport gateway so they could make a lethal injection seem like a heart attack. How cruel, yet elegant. The airport staff would respond to cardiac arrest. That was about all they had been trained to deal with. The witnesses would take one glance each out of morbid curiosity, then they would vanish, before they missed their flights to other states, other countries. Nobody wanted anyone else's little tragedies.

I saw Maria spelling things out for the security guy. I could see him mouthing the words 'first aid', and her yelling at him.

Once you're trained in the Air Force, you expect at least some of your friends to die. You never lose that expectation. Not even ten years later in civilian life.

Training held me together temporarily, even though I heard myself making animal sounds in my chest.

Maria and the security chief leaned over me now. He was an earnest older guy, eager to help.

'Sir, we got an EMS team to treat him here. We got defibulators . . .'

'Listen up.' I grabbed the man's lapel and said quietly, forcefully into his face, 'This is *not* a heart attack. I am an Air Force officer and this man is dying of toxic shock. You *will* tell EMS to take him to Century Hospital. Now. On my authority. Move it. He probably only has a couple of minutes to live.'

Then I lowered my voice and added, 'Please don't fuck up.'

My pep talk worked. He whipped out his radio and barked orders.

'Sir, they'll pull an ambulance right outside Gate 16, right down there.'

He pointed out the window. I pressed Marty's hand.

'Terry.' Maria's voice held steady, though her arms stayed tightly crossed and she picked at her sleeve with two fingers. 'Who could have done that?'

I didn't answer.

'The Mafia?'

'Get real. They're downstairs stealing luggage.'

'The CIA? They're behind everything, Terry.'

I snorted. 'My money's on Teflon Ted, with a bullet. He pulled in a favor from somebody.'

Marty's tongue was lolling over his lips, like a pink lox. His eyes started to roll up under his lids. Maria had gone close enough to the window to see outside.

'Terry.' She gripped my arm. 'Let's go. I see the ambulance coming outside.'

I picked Marty up. His arms and head felt lifeless as a Raggedy Andy doll as I hauled him over my shoulder.

TWENTY-TWO

Our strange motorcade careened into the Emergency Unit of Century Hospital.

First, a LAX Airport security cruiser with flashing red lights clearing traffic. Then the EMS ambulance van, its siren whooping. Finally, our bright yellow Hummer lumbering only feet behind it with Maria at the wheel and me hyperventilating in the passenger seat.

Marty had been in the ambulance for six minutes.

We pulled up, and the double red and white rear doors sprang open. The team came bounding out, carrying Marty on a metal pallet. He was strapped up in a white blanket to his chest, his nose and mouth in a plastic oxygen mask. Hope loosened the knot in my chest, but only slightly.

A team of men and women ran from the Emergency entrance. They wore blue hospital outfits stained with blood and other human effluents I didn't even want to think about.

'Who's the doctor?' I ran next to them, while Maria parked the Hummer.

'I am Dr Reza,' said a small man, with features like a mahogany carving and giant bags under his eyes. 'Who are you?'

We were inside now. Who would a harried ER doctor listen to? Someone he wouldn't know how to pigeonhole and ignore.

'Colonel Clements, Air Force Intelligence.' I quickly produced Zeke Clements' business card from my wallet and stuck it in front of him, counting on its novelty. 'Doctor, this isn't just a heart attack. This man was the victim of an assassination attempt.'

He looked at me very strangely. 'Why do you say that?'

'Trust me. He needs a toxin screen.'

The doctor looked perplexed. He had probably heard every raving lunatic in Los Angeles who ever needed medical care near the airport, but this seemed to rivet him. 'I see, Colonel. What was the weapon?'

'A needle with a plunger. We've got seconds to work, Doctor. This is one hundred per cent on you.'

'Well, he still has pulmonary symptoms we need to treat,' Dr Reza said. 'Move, people.'

A nurse brought a portable electrocardiogram machine and quickly attached EKG wires to Marty's chest. The machine beeped, and the nurse handed Dr Reza the electrical paddles.

'One . . . two . . . now.'

Another two aides moved Marty from the pallet to a small bed with wheels, as another nurse snipped away his shirt and tie with shears.

'Clear!' Dr Reza said.

He attached the paddles and they made a loud snap. Marty's back arched.

'Again.' He applied the paddles again. Usually Marty's chest was tan as his briefcase. Now it was white.

'Let's move him,' Dr Reza said. 'Trauma Three.'

Now Marty was propelled forward by a trauma team of about eight people chattering in rapid-fire medical jargon. Two of them were pushing the gurney and the EKG on its squeaky wheels, like a gypsy wagon, as we all raced along beside. We bypassed the Emergency Room, burst through the swinging doors marked *Trauma Center*, then all turned right and started hurrying down a very long corridor lined with patients.

'Colonel, you wouldn't know what toxin this . . . terrorist plot involved?'

'Maybe DX. It was injected directly into his artery with a needle. He jerked once or twice, and collapsed in a couple of seconds. I gave him CPR.'

'His breathing is labored and faint,' Dr Reza said unnecessarily. 'What do you know about his general health? Is he diabetic?'

'No. He's in excellent health, he just had a checkup, and he's allergic to penicillin,' I said. 'It's DX.' Years ago I had done some research into the exotic area of toxins. Not that I planned to be injected by anybody. But considering the purpose of my visits to other lands, I thought somebody might do it to me.

We were all bustling down the corridor, it seemed about a city block long, full of patients backed up on their gurneys like LAX.

'It's probably just insulin,' Maria piped up.

'Why do you think that?' Dr Reza asked, genuinely curious rather than mocking. 'Are you a doctor?'

'I know molecular biology,' Maria said. 'It's settling in his lungs now. His breathing's labored.'

Dr Reza suddenly stopped, braking the procession. 'All right. Let's take him to Trauma Two instead. Back there.'

'Hey,' I said with a nasty look toward Maria. 'It's DX.'

'Colonel.' Dr Reza stopped cold with all of us mobbing the hall around him. He couldn't seem to decide on a plan of attack, trying to figure out which of us was right. 'You must understand, we just do not see many patients jabbed with exotic death toxins.'

'That's what intelligence agencies use,' I told them.

'Terry, that's old KGB stuff.' Maria ground her teeth. She looked more worked up than I'd ever seen her.

And she was right. My knowledge was an untrustworthy mix of old Air Force training and antiquated KGB methods.

'Okay. Insulin,' I told Dr Reza.

Dr Reza said, 'Well, we have one chance, don't we, people?' He was right about that.

We all scrambled forward again with the gurney and its satellite EKG machine. I vaguely noticed the other patients. They all lay or sat on gurneys, some groaning. One man kept yelling out for a painkiller by brand. I felt as helpless as any of them.

'Stay outside,' a large aide told us, shoving Marty's gurney through a swinging door.

'Thanks,' I told Maria, as we stood in the hall together. 'I hope you're right.'

'I'm just guessing.'

I must have winced, because she took my hand in an oddly heartfelt gesture. 'Poor Terry. Let's sit down and wait.'

We plopped down together on an unoccupied gurney in the hallway full of sniffling, moaning patients. Our four legs dangled off the side.

'The people that took me in when my mother got remarried? It was Marty's family.' I said it softly, mostly to myself.

'I know,' she reminded me. 'I read your Wringer report. Won't those LAX security people want to talk to us?'

'We'd better leave.'

We hopped down and started moving back the way we'd come.

'Sir, wait up.'

I looked around to see the two beefy LAX Airport police. They wore blue uniforms. Smith & Wesson .38 sidearms bounced on their thighs in snap holsters as they moved toward us. They had come from the door off the corridor marked *Hospital Administration*.

I faced the two guards and pointed to the room beside the one where they'd wheeled Marty. 'The poisoning suspect's in there, but watch out. She's naked.'

One looked at the other, and they strode purposefully into the room where I'd sent them.

I grabbed Maria's hand. 'Come on!'

We ran toward the door where we had come in.

'Hey!' I heard. I turned around and saw one of

the two LAX cops start running after us. I wondered what their orders said about using their guns, on or off the airport. You never know in LA.

'Fuck the hospital!' A man with an industrial injury raised his bleeding arm.

Whistles and catcalls cheered us on. We cleared the corridor and burst through the doors where we had entered with Marty and Dr Reza's people. Now we were weaving around the colorful fiberglass seating of the Emergency Room, headed toward the exit door of the ER. A huddle of gangbangers wearing bandannas and cutoff shirts revealing jailhouse tattoos held up a wounded friend who looked like he'd stuck his pistol in his pants and shot himself in the leg.

'Where's the Hummer?' I yelled.

'Kind of boxed in outside.'

Great. We were almost to the glass double doors that would open quickly for us once our feet touched the black mat. Yes. The doors would open and we could make it to the Hummer before the LAX cops got to us.

I caught a dark shadow on my periphery, moving fast to intercept us. Not a security guard. Not a cop. Wrapped in a colorful kaftan, she was thundering ahead like a rogue elephant, to reach the door before we did.

'Watch out!' I yelled.

We didn't break our stride, but the woman didn't either. She came to a halt that shook her flesh and stood foursquare in front of the doors facing us, folding her massive arms. She was as huge and calm as a boulder, eyes dead to mercy. She had several chins, and her voice emerged from a deep well of bureaucratic outrage. 'Nobody goes runnin' outta here till I see a release form and paid receipt.'

'Look outside,' I shouted. 'Air Force One's in trouble at LAX.' I heard the guards burst through the doors at the other end of the ER. She would see them. 'Look! . . . There's the Secret Service.'

I pointed over her shoulder. She turned for a moment, but her clerical cunning made her suspect me. Her head snapped back, but Maria and I had lunged forward, each knifing ourselves past the small sliver of room she left on either side of her. We had triggered the black rubber mat just in time for the doors to open, otherwise we would crash into plate glass. The woman bellowed as though mortally wounded.

We raced around the cars piled into the crowded entrance of this hospital. Nobody bothered to park their cars, they just left them empty. Maria steered me toward the Hummer.

'Stop or I'll shoot,' someone shouted behind us.

'They won't fire,' I reassured Maria.

Then I felt the vortex of two bullets zipping just past my ear even before I heard the double-clap of two gunshots.

I shoved Maria in front of me and crouched over to shield her. As we neared the line of sloppily parked vehicles, I saw that a compact car had blocked the Hummer from the front.

'Now,' I said.

Maria scuttled like a crab around the Hummer to

the driver's-side door. She opened the big yellow door and flung herself in.

I quickly scanned the parking lot, printing a snapshot of it in my head. Then I opened my door and hopped in. The glass of my door nearly shattered next to me and I heard a *thunk* as another bullet hit the metal, then the upholstery under my legs.

'Stay down.' I shoved her head next to the steering wheel. 'I'll drive.'

I scrambled over the double-width console. It was the size of a carrier deck. My right hand pressed the accelerator pedal down to the floor. The engine was racing, but we weren't moving.

'Oops.' Maria took the emergency brake off.

With a heavy lunge, the Hummer slammed into the car ahead. I kept the gas pedal nailed to the floor, and took the small, leather-clad steering wheel in one hand to steer.

My situational awareness hadn't left me. My mental map of the parking lot was still fresh.

I cranked the wheel and kept the pedal to the metal with my hand. I heard our giant front bars rip off the other car's fender with a shriek of twisting metal and a dislocating snap.

Another gunshot and I heard the windshield shatter. Glass rained down on top of us. I saw shards glittering in Maria's black hair and on her black fabric shoulders. I felt a sting in my forehead.

'You can't see,' she yelled.

'I don't have to.' I wrapped my mind around my last view of the parking lot. Now it was battlespace.

I didn't look up as I wheeled us out of the parking lot, without hitting anything except the rear end of a Chevy. I peeked just once out our open-air windshield as we were about to hit the street, narrowly missing a Hertz airport bus. I pulled out and accelerated to the other side of it for protection. We drove away on to Century Boulevard at a safe, legal speed, the Hertz bus running interference against the LAX police.

Maria sat up, shook the glass out of her hair. She grabbed the wheel and took over.

'This Hummer isn't quite as rugged as I thought,' she said.

'Neither am I,' I admitted.

A few miles away, I tumbled coins into a gas station payphone while Maria kept the Hummer running.

'Century Hospital Accounting,' an operator said.

'Hartford Insurance Claims Department. I need the contact status of Schmidt, Martin W.'

A long wait. I heard the whoop of a police siren off somewhere. Assuming the worst but still wishing hard, I imagined Marty lying in a hospital bed, tubes crammed into his nostrils, sticking out of veins, a catheter in his penis. I felt a pain in my own groin, but it was better than visualizing the life gone out of him like a sack on his way to the LA coroner's office. I should be shot for what I'd done to him. But that could still happen.

'He's in recovery,' the nasal voice suddenly came back. 'Room 2786.'

'Thanks.'

I hung up and dropped more coins in the slot.

'Colonel Zeke Clements.'

'Terry Weston. We need to get together. I need to ask you to help me clarify some procedures involving Air Force hardware. Just tell me now if you're not the right person to call for that.'

A beat. 'Some procedures involving Have Quick?' That would be the classified Pentagon code name for Linnet/TVR's JSF project.

'Right.'

'No, I'd be the man for that job.'

'Good. Meet me at Eileen's Diner in Long Beach at 1600 tomorrow.'

I fed in more coins, holding my breath.

'This is the voicemail of Jennifer Schmidt. You know what to do at the sound of the tone.'

Once a man gets in bad with a friend's wife, he never gets out. Jennifer Schmidt had always tolerated me. She had even made an award-winning show of welcoming me into their home, laughed politely as I had swung their squealing kids up in the air.

'When are you planning on having your own kids, Terry?' she had asked.

Once again, my work forced me to deflect her next move, which would have been to set me up with one of her smart friends. As was my custom, I replied, 'As soon as they come with a mute button.' She took my flip remark seriously, and shut down on me that day. After that, she was merely cordial, never a friend. She had also indulged, after a drink or two, in sharp little lawyerly interrogations about the women I dated or even seemed attracted to.

I felt grim facing her alone, at the entrance to the private school where she had gone to pick up William and Sasha. I stood in the street until the blue Volvo station wagon showed up. Her expression behind the wheel was knowing and furious, and she almost ran over my shoe as she pulled one wheel on the curb, lurching to a stop.

'Where is he?' she asked me.

'Century Hospital,' I said. 'I . . .'

'Go away, Terry. My children are coming . . .'

I looked around to see them, bobbing along in bright clothes in a crowd of other tiny prisoners of pre-school, and slunk away before they could see me.

We got rid of the yellow Hummer. I felt worse by the time we took a taxi to a motel.

Maria had found The Atomic Motel on the fringe of northern LA. It was designed in that brief but glorious epoch of the early '50s when only the United States had the atomic bomb.

'It's cute,' Maria told me cheerily. 'The Jetsons would stay here.'

'They wouldn't board Astro here,' I grumbled, depressed and cranky.

I examined the low-rent exterior. A blue neon sign buzzed loudly in the familiar crossed-ellipse atomic shape, although somebody had mixed up the neutrons and electrons. The building looked temporary and smelled of decay. It wasn't that I had gotten soft since my Air Force days. I hated buildings like this, since I'd grown up in them. The US military seems to own the lion's share of them worldwide to house its officers' families.

I opened the door, which stuck, and a blast of mildew and Lysol hit us.

'After you,' I coughed.

Inside, a lumpy double bed had been decorated in a color that I think was called Harvest Gold. I expected to find a coin-operated massager to make the bed vibrate, but didn't. I lost it when I saw the photographs on the walls, now yellowed. They were, I swear, shots of the Los Alamos Proving Ground during the atomic bomb tests of the late 1940s and early '50s.

'Did you choose this place to motivate me?' I asked Maria.

'No. If you're not motivated now, you never will be.'

She brushed her hair, but glanced only once into the mirror. How low-maintenance she was, my former *Playboy* Girl of Mensa. Oddly, I remembered the day when I was six and my appendix burst. I lay writhing on the floor because my mother had to finish putting her make-up on before she would take me to the base hospital. You couldn't take the Milano out of the girl. At least I had never, in my entire adult life, been tempted to pursue a model.

Maria looked like my mother, pouty and spoiled. But she didn't act like her. She acted unlike anyone I had ever known.

Maybe the novelty of it had allowed me to be tied in knots by this artless but sly girl. This genius whose

446

invention had so far created nothing but misery. I hated to think I might be in love with her.

'Terry? I think you've stared at that picture long enough.' She came up to me in a sweatshirt and black jeans. 'Are you all right?'

'Yeah,' I said. 'We need to go out now.'

She nodded quickly, seeming to sense my need for purposeful activity.

'Terry about that . . . family, I'm sure my father wouldn't . . .'

My father.

'Drop it. Let's talk about tomorrow.' I blew my nose in a tissue to get the stinging Lysol smell out of my nostrils.

'Go ahead.' She sat on the bed and crossed her legs.

'We've got Ted in a bad position. His simulator is wrecked. I'm going to march into Linnet/TVR tomorrow with Colonel Clements from Air Force Intelligence. He's one of those by-the-book types. He'll demand to see the simulator room. As soon as Ted says no because it's a disaster, we've got him.'

'What if Ted bribes Colonel Clements?

'Clements won't take it. Soldiers go corrupt on a whole different bandwidth. They want power.' I stood up. 'I'll get us the car this time. Maybe one of those VW bugs. I've never driven one.'

She smiled, determined to humor me.

At two a.m. we were driving on Santa Monica Boulevard in the Russian section of Los Angeles, an extension of the Great Dilapidated Retail Sprawl between West Hollywood and downtown. The only clue was that the stores all had signs with Cyrillic names.

Maria had gamely used her skills to obtain an electric-blue VW bug for the evening.

Everything in Little Russia was closed, the lights out. I pulled into an alleyway to a narrow service street behind the shops and drove with my lights off at ten miles per hour, checking the Cyrillic letters in the dark. This back street actually seemed a little like Moscow itself at night, spooky and scary.

'Have you always stolen cars like this?' Maria asked, her voice a little tremulous.

'What's the term the media uses for illegal aliens? "Undocumented immigrants"? Let's just say I'm an "undocumented renter".'

'Hmm. And I suppose if we rob a bank next, we'll be "undocumented borrowers".'

'You got it. Here's the place. They know me here as Mr Green. I think it's their little joke for always overcharging me.'

I found a hand-lettered sign that told me we were at the back of a shop called Ukie's Uniform Store. The plate-glass window displayed the uniforms for nurses and maids and blue-collar workers – the stuff usually sold in uniform stores.

I knocked on the metal back door. We were let in by a stocky bald guy with large ears and narrow eyes that registered nothing. He wore an Adidas jogging suit and smelled of pungent tobacco.

'Mr Green.' He stared at Maria.

'Hi. Are you Ukie?' Maria asked.

The man grimaced. 'My name is Sergei. I am from the Ukraine . . . they call us "Ukies". Never to our face.'

Sergei steered us into the boutique part of the uniform shop by opening a fake wall. We entered a small room packed with specialty items.

Here at Ukie's place, if you were on the special customer list like I was, you could shop twenty-four hours a day and choose from unofficial reproductions of uniforms for law enforcement agencies.

Let's say you wanted to impersonate an officer with the Los Angeles Police Department. Sergei would outfit you with an authentic LAPD uniform, accessorized with Sam Brown belt, handcuffs, a nightstick, laser gun, a .38 Special, and an excellent hand-stamped copy of a badge whose number matched one carried by an actual, currently employed officer on the LAPD. Sergei would also trick up an official-looking ID card in the name of that officer, customized with your own photograph. He had a Polaroid camera set up in the corner to take instant pictures that could be stuck on to the police ID and laminated.

Instant authority for about $10,000. Sergei lived in Hancock Park and drove a Porsche.

'Sergei was a Red Army sergeant,' I told Maria. 'He got the idea for this place selling his own uniform.'

'And medals,' Sergei said. 'Mr Green bought my Order of Lenin. So what do you need this evening?' He pronounced it 'e-ven-ing'.

His law-enforcement boutique reminded me of

one of those musty old costume shops you visited to dress up for Halloween parties. Sergei shoved through racks crammed full of outfits, and expertly pulled out a gray, off-the-rack, single-breasted suit for me, with a cheap shirt and striped tie. For Maria, he extracted a tan suit with a blouse that looked as though it came from the softer side of Sears.

'FBI . . .' He opened a drawer full of metal that rattled, and fished out two badges, along with two small folding leather cases. I examined them.

'Agents Gomez and Handley,' I said. 'They're not dead, are they?'

Sergei gave me a doleful look. 'You are more morbid than a Russian.'

An hour later we were riding up to the second floor of Century Hospital. 'Look like an FBI agent,' I told Maria.

'What do they look like?'

'Like an accountant who wants to park in your kitchen for a thirty-day audit, and maybe shoot your stove.'

'Okay.'

When the elevator opened, we were right in front of the nurses' station. It was a typical round desk, attractively bathed in overhead fluorescent lighting to make everyone look older and more tired. There were two nurses, one young who read a paperback book, and one older who wore the look of the charge nurse.

'Ms . . . Wisniewski.' I read her nametag, pronouncing it the Polish way with an 'f' instead of an 'iew'.

She sized us up, bored, with her deeply lined, baggy face. 'Yeah, but I got all the life insurance I need.' Funny.

'Agent Handley, Agent Gomez,' I introduced us as we flashed our badges. Nurse Wisniewski actually took the trouble to match our ID photos to our faces. She was the kind of dedicated employee who kept my friend Sergei in business. 'We've got to wake your patient Schmidt, first name Martin, in 2786. We'll only be ten minutes, no longer. We have a suspect in custody and need a positive ID from our victim or we have to let him go.'

Nurse Wisniewski heaved a sigh. She found Marty's chart and flipped up the pages. 'Doctor has him on Zanax to sleep. Good luck waking him up.'

'Thank you,' I told her.

Grudgingly she handed over a clipboard with a form for occasions like this with the title 'SPECIAL VISITORS'. There was a space for our names, which she printed out herself, adding Marty's room number. She handed it to us to sign, then checked the paperwork carefully to make sure it was in order. She would have done a great job in processing folks out of the Warsaw ghetto *circa* 1939. Finally she nodded down the corridor. 'Go ahead. It's on the right.'

Maria opened the door to Marty's room and closed it behind us. I turned on the bed light. My friend looked very small and vulnerable in the hospital bed, his body like a mummy's under the carefully tucked white sheets and blanket, his head almost lost in a stack of big white pillows. I was happy to see that his mouth hung wide open and he was snoring.

I pinched his nose excitedly and he honked. His eyes popped open. Maria laughed.

'Good to see you breathing,' I said.

He looked at Maria, blinking, as though trying to recall who she was. It all seemed to flood back to him. He felt around for a control hanging by a cord and moved the top of the bed up with a groaning mechanical noise until he was sitting up comfortably. Then he noticed my suit. 'Who are you supposed to be? FBI agents?'

'Special agents,' I corrected him, glancing at the chart on his bed, which seemed to indicate he was getting along well.

'How you feeling?' Maria looked genuinely concerned.

'I'm afraid to say okay, now that you're here,' he said. 'Jennifer said if I let you in to visit, she'll never come back.'

'I know,' I assured him. 'We just wanted to make sure you were all right.'

'Why?' He looked suspicious. 'What are you planning to do?'

I turned on the radio next to his bed, and pushed the button until loud salsa music blew out to drown out our words. 'I miss that local DJ, the Nasty Man, don't you?'

'No. Give.'

'Okay.' I leaned into the music. 'Marty, I'm sorry. It was supposed to be me.'

'Who were those people?'

'Ted Devlin hired them. I'm pretty sure.'

'Jesus. That girl was just a teenager.' He shook his head in bewilderment, and looked like a father contemplating the wicked world his children would inherit. Then I could see his wheels spinning. Marty always bounced back like a bulldog. He grabbed my wrist, feeble but firm. 'Okay. I want to square things with Ted Devlin. He was CEO of Linnet/TVR when he did this to me, right?'

'He was.'

'And he was acting in what he perceived to be the corporate interest when he hired the hit team?'

I could see where he was headed. 'I'm sure you could make a jury look at things that way.'

'Excellent,' he said, rubbing his hands together. 'Then I can sue the corporation for damage if I can prove he did this to me. How much money does Linnet/TVR have, Terry? They probably have all kinds of cash sitting around for bribing people. I can make them settle.'

I nodded. 'That's fine, long-term, but I want to talk about tomorrow. What's our legal exposure if we go confront Ted Devlin tomorrow with a Pentagon guy and tell him to 'fess up?'

Maria fluffed Marty's pillow.

'I wouldn't worry about legal exposure,' my lawyer said. 'I'd worry more about getting out alive. Maria shouldn't go.'

'I can handle it,' she told him.

'I'm thinking about your defense later on,' Marty said. 'I could make a half-assed case that Terry's a whistle-blower. If you go, it's more like extortion and conspiracy.'

'With a lofty purpose,' I reminded him.

He sighed and his head rolled on the pillow.

We took the hint and got up to go. 'Oh, Marty. One other thing. I seem to recall you belong to that Bison Club in Beverly Hills.'

'That place? I keep the membership but I haven't been for two years. It's a bunch of total assholes. Why?'

'Where do you keep your membership card?'

'It ought to be in my wallet. Why do you want to know?'

'Because Ted Devlin belongs to the Bison Club.'

'And?'

'I was wondering if I could borrow the card.'

Marty looked up at the ceiling, doing a pretty good 'why me' just by rolling his eyes. 'Okay, be my guest.'

I went through the suit in the closet to find his wallet and located the plastic card with his name on it. After a few words, we left Marty smiling.

Probably after five years of trials and appeals, if I survived that long, I would go to Long Beach to see workers putting up a new 'Schmidt Industries' sign over the entrance to the Linnet/TVR building.

The music turned out to be an LA band called HIV-POS, which played a currently popular fusion of homoerotic blues and hip-hop at about two hundred decibels.

The Python Club was small, steamy and packed

454

with what seemed to be two kinds of people – trashy young drug users and trashy young drug users with a lot of money. Many arrived in gumball-colored Porsches and BMWs.

The tables could be described as coin-sized, so I bumped into Mac Skinner's knees as I sat down in the seat he'd reserved for me against the wall.

'Want to dance?' I asked him. He shook his head.

His big frame covered the chair he was leaning back in, his solid forearms crossed in front of him. Mac looked like the eternal young Republican, wearing a madras shirt and chinos, but his brush-cut hair was probably in style for the first time. His close-set eyes were cautious.

'Glad you came,' I said. 'Let's talk.'

'Meet me in the head.' He got up from the table.

'So much for foreplay.' I shrugged, and actually met him in the dark hallway near the bathroom, where he stood apart from the action, hands stuck in his jeans pocket. The music was still too loud for either of us to record the other. But I don't know that it even mattered at this point.

Back in the days when I followed my own five rules for success in industrial espionage, I would have known everything about this guy down to his favorite breakfast cereal. I would have had him all figured out and guessed his actual role in Ted's theft of LUCI.

But that was then, and this was now. I didn't know my enemy, or even if he was my enemy. I suspected maybe not.

I could only speculate from knowing what I did

about other Air Force fighter pilots, and from the fragments of his behavior I'd seen, that he was in over his head. He had acted too unhappy and pissed-off in our Crud and Spank games for even USAF competitiveness. He had tried too hard to keep me out of the program.

A pilot like Mac was usually a good poker player, hard to read. Part of our basic sneakiness. Unless you know what drives us, you may as well try to figure out the motivations of a slab of drywall. But deep down, the experience he and I shared in the service put us on the same bandwidth. We'd both gone through the same fine-screen training. We'd both felt our sphincters tighten doing a job that often involved violent death. I knew things about Mac, and he knew things about me. The jet fighter community is a small club.

'Your meeting,' he said. Then he shut up and stood with his hands in his pockets.

'We wound up in a jackpot, you and me both,' I told him. 'It's time to show our cards.'

He didn't speak for a moment, just studied his brown loafers oblivious to the club kids packing the corridor.

'I looked at your Air Force jacket,' Mac said, in a softer voice than I'd ever heard him use before. 'A guy like you . . . I don't get it. You just greedy, or what?'

I understood his question, maybe more than he thought.

'I guess I want to ask you the same thing,' I told him.

He looked irate, like my question was way out of line. 'I came to the Ghostworks to make the best strike fighter in the world.'

'The best of the best,' I grinned. That phrase was the sanitized version of the goal we'd shared as fighter pilots, to be ultimate killing machines.

He nailed me with a steady and searching gaze. 'What's your real interest in LUCI?'

'Same as yours. I want to see it fly without anybody getting killed. You know Ted stole the chip.' He said nothing. 'The woman he stole it from, Maria Haymeyer, designed it as a computer game. Did you know that?' He looked startled. 'She designed a Doom Level into her game. Now we think it's in your aircraft.'

'That's crazy.'

'Like a simulator blowing itself up.'

He winced slightly. 'Okay. What does this Doom Level do?'

'Override the pilot and go off on its own little mission, to reconfigure the uranium in its STICK missiles into atomic warheads and strike a real target.'

'Jesus.' He frowned. 'The LUCI prototype can do that?'

'I saw the sim start to mimic doing it. I imagine the prototype actually can. You've been flying her. You know what she's capable of.'

Mac flicked a glance at the ceiling, thinking. 'Say the prototype overrides a pilot and plays this . . . game. What's her target?'

'Washington, DC.'

'Get real.' He looked hard into my eyes. 'Is this some bullshit you cooked up to get at the plane?'

'I don't particularly want to get at the plane,' I said. 'Let me tell your engineers how to disarm it.'

He hesitated a long time. 'The thing about this plane is . . .'

'I know. It gets smarter on you. But we have to ask her to try.'

'Ted isn't going to ask her. The girl who says she designed it . . . were she and Ted, like . . .'

'Let's just say they have a history.'

He nodded. 'Ted can't afford to lose this contract. As far as he's concerned, he did what he had to do. A lot of people are counting on him.'

'Is that why he tried to kill me?'

'Forget it,' Mac snorted. 'Ted's got plenty of contacts who put classified ads in the back of *Soldier of Fortune,* looking for work. If he wanted to kill you, you'd be dead.'

'Ted's got you holding all the responsibility for this, right?'

Mac gave me a long and painful look like he was trying hard to figure me out too.

'Terry, I'm not concerned about covering my ass for some board of directors. All I want is to protect the LUCI aircraft. America needs this plane. Everybody's selling nukes to the nut cases. Ted says—'

'Ted is going to sell the Pentagon a weapons system that was designed as a game, unless he deprogrammed it.'

'He didn't.'

'There's a way out of this. I'm coming to Linnet tomorrow.'

'Alone?'

'No. With a colonel from Air Force Special Intelligence. I want to show him the sim room. If Ted stonewalls him, maybe he'll still get to fly the prototype on Monday to impress the generals. And maybe it'll take off on its own. If I can show the guy what happened to your sim room, it'll buy us time.'

Mac frowned and pondered the scenario, which he obviously didn't like. 'Devlin said if you screwed up our LUCI program, you'd make money short-selling our stock. He said you Wall Street guys win either way.'

'Unless we lose. Just be there tomorrow.'

TWENTY-THREE

We had slept together fully dressed, curled up in the reflection of the blue Atomic Motel sign dimly illuminating our bed.

I studied her before she woke up.

She slept on her side, her arm curled up under her face, hair moist and tangled on her cheek. I smiled at the little night crust that had formed at the edge of her lips, which were open slightly, revealing how thin her large teeth were, and almost translucent.

With her muscles fully relaxed, her curves had softened under her sweater. The soft fuzz on her jaw and wrists, lighter than her skin, invited the brush of my finger.

Lightly I touched the inch of tummy that protruded beneath her sweater, taut and slightly elongated like a whippet's. I thought of that belly swollen. What a miraculous child she would have one day. Strictly speaking, she didn't even need a father, her own genes were so overqualified for the job.

And I realized that was what was missing about her all along.

Every other woman I had ever known – from the Air Force brats of my junior-high-school days, to the businesswomen in Armani suits, to poor Dr Posenor

460

with her Victorian dolls – wanted to be wanted. Every woman but Maria. She didn't care about anybody but her father. If she'd wanted a boyfriend, she would have built a computer to find him, like the ones she'd designed to Locate Dad and Locate Fragata. But nowhere had I found, anywhere in her background or my time with her, the hint of a quest to Locate Soulmate. Maybe she was so methodical in addressing her needs, she couldn't even think about a partner until that father yearning was settled.

Her eyes opened, blurry and unfocused. 'Terry? What time is it?'

'Time to get up.'

'Oh.'

I untangled the hair on her cheek, finding a facial blemish, a tiny birthmark near her ear I hadn't seen before. 'Ah, this looks like three little sixes . . .'

She pulled back. The scent of her was exciting, mine probably less so. She swept her hair back from her face and said, her voice still husky with sleep, 'Just because you want me doesn't make me bad.'

I felt nerves twitching all over my body. 'Let's get cleaned up.'

An hour later, we sat with Colonel Zeke Clements in a quiet booth inside an almost-empty turquoise and chrome Long Beach diner.

I sipped coffee from an unwieldy cup that rattled in the plate and sloshed coffee over the side. Zeke had taken off his officer's cap in deference to Maria. He rubbed his gray hair, cut short as whisker stubble, with his gnarled hand.

'So what you're telling me, off the record for now,'

461

Zeke seemed to fumble for a second, shuffling a deck of troublesome thoughts, 'is that Ted Devlin took a game designer's chip to make his JSF airplane look pretty to the Pentagon. But the plane's still behaving like a game . . .'

'. . . a dangerous game,' Maria helped him.

'And Devlin's simulator blew up? That's what you're going to show me? Hell, son, a simulator can't blow up.' He wagged his head. 'How could that happen? There's nothing volatile in it.'

'Colonel,' I said, 'let's just go look.'

The old trapper wasn't exactly a rocket scientist, but I didn't care. I couldn't handle any more geniuses. What we needed now was someone in authority who wanted to help.

He pursed his lips. 'You're tellin' me Mr Devlin's in some kinda jackpot?'

I nodded.

'And what about this lady?' Clements nodded at Maria. 'You're both in a mess of trouble, if you've been holding out on the Air Force.'

'She was trying to do the right thing. So was I.'

Zeke finished his coffee, revealing no personal attitude over the scenario we'd laid out. Then he scratched the palm of one hand with the other. He stood up and put on his officer's cap over his close-cropped gray hair.

'Okay. Miss Haymeyer, I'd advise you to stick around here. Captain, let's go see your pal.'

We were inside Ted's Ghostworks office at exactly 1700. I couldn't say Ted was a gracious host any more. He squinted his good eye at Colonel

Clements as we sat down before his massive desk. He had replaced yesterday's ruined suit with one exactly like it. Just like a contractor – he'd seen one Italian suit he'd liked, bought it, and ordered an inventory of spares. His face had a ruddy pink tint as though he'd very recently received a facial with a sandblaster, his nose rubbed so red it must have hurt. He smelled of men's designer cologne, and I saw his hands had received a manicure, nails blunt-cut and buffed to a smooth finish. Ted had been scrubbed hard for our visit.

'You look great,' I complimented him. 'Considering.'

'Considering what, Terry?' Like nothing had gone wrong with the LUCI sim the day before. His eye was vacant. 'I found two minutes for you guys, so let's cut to it.'

I ignored that. 'Colonel Clements is with Air Force Special Intelligence,' I said.

'So?'

'I asked him to drop by with me to check out your sim room.'

'Why would you want to do that?' Ted asked blandly. The air felt heavy inside his office today, hot and itchy under my suit.

'Because it's time to have a quiet talk about your problem. I don't think you'd want General Warren Stone or any other JSF personnel barbecued in your sim.'

Ted recoiled, like I'd spilled hot coffee into his lap. 'Did you breathe Agent Orange?' Ted stood up and pointed at Zeke Clements. 'Colonel, did you know Weston was going to come in here and spew out all this crap? The Air Force has protocols.' He leaned threateningly over his desk. 'You want me to get Warren on the line?'

Zeke had started our interview just south of comfortable. But as Ted began his harangue, the hunter inside Zeke woke up. He cocked his head at Ted and an embryo of a smile crossed his lips. He sat back as though settling in for a spell.

'I don't have a problem with that, sir. General Stone knows my jurisdiction is security for the JSF program till somebody tells me different. We'll just wait outside. You let us know when we can see your LUCI sim.'

When Colonel Clements and I stood up and left his office, Ted was still leaning over the desk.

Zeke and I sat in leather chairs with metal armrests. Ted's middle-aged secretary glared at us, cigarette wrinkles over her upper lip. I gave her a thin smile. Colonel Clements picked up a copy of *Aviation Week* and got absorbed, licking his thumb to turn the pages. He was a man who knew how to wait.

Then Mac Skinner was hurrying down the corridor. He flicked a glance at me, nodded at Colonel Clements, and disappeared into Ted's office. I wished I'd had my peanut cams inside, because I heard muffled echoes of what seemed like a heated argument.

After ten minutes, the door opened suddenly and Ted and Mac appeared. Both of them looked flushed.

'I want you to understand, Colonel,' Mac intoned, 'that Mr Devlin himself decided to let you see the sim.'

Colonel Clements nodded. 'Appreciate that.'

No one said a word as the four of us marched the length of the floor to Ted's conference room, but the back of Ted's neck looked pink. He used his own plastic card and thumbprint to let us in. Inside, the teak conference table had been replaced. I was surprised to see that they had managed to scrub the room free of its soot and foam damage already. It was even deodorized. I couldn't catch a whiff of chemical smoke.

They'd also repaired the door that led to the LUCI simulator vault. Where had they found laborers who could work that fast? Ted popped his card into the security panel and registered his thumbprint. He paused before opening the door.

'Colonel, whatever we see inside, I'm going to remind you to bear in mind the Special Access status of this program,' he told Clements.

Ted opened the vault door slowly and I held my nose to brace against the heavy odor of smoke I could still feel a trace of somewhere deep in my lungs.

It didn't come.

I first thought, when I stepped inside, that he had taken us into the wrong room. But that wasn't possible. The door was exactly where it had been thirty-six hours before.

'We're just about to start a session,' I heard Ted say.

The simulator vault shone as pure white and pristine as it had before the accident. A misty vapor appeared in the Zenon lights. The air-conditioning ducts blew in chilly air. In the center of the room, the perfect egg-shaped pod hung from the ceiling, shimmering, on three brand-new stainless-steel arms, each with a massive ball bearing to gyrate the pod.

Two old friends sat at the control panel, in front of a spanking-new rack of video screens. The real Dr Posenor had her black glasses on and hair pulled back professionally. The nose-ring engineer frowned at the screen, tapping at his keyboard.

Dr Posenor looked up quizzically. 'Gentlemen?'

I couldn't think of a word to say. Neither could Colonel Clements. He took his time starting at the simulator, looking around the room. He didn't seem to miss much. After a moment of silence that seemed to last a month, he finally cleared his throat and addressed Dr Posenor.

'Impressive sim you got there, ma'am. Can I ask you what went on inside this room at 0530 yesterday?'

'We ran a session with Colonel Skinner,' she replied.

'That's bullshit,' I said.

'What about you, sir?' Clements asked the nose-ring engineer, who looked slightly more annoyed than bored by our intrusion.

'I was here too.'

I stared at Mac, looking steady and businesslike, without a trace of last night's angst about Ted and saving America.

'Well,' Colonel Clements said to Ted, 'guess we'd better let these young folks get back to work.'

Silently, we all strode single file back into the conference room and Mac shut the sim door.

'Zeke, I don't know how they did it, but they cleaned it up,' I explained.

'Mr Devlin.' Colonel Zeke Clements sucked in his gut. 'First, my apologies. We can handle this incident in one of two ways. I can ask for a hearing at the Pentagon to investigate Mr Weston's interference with your JSF program . . .'

I saw Ted's victory smile fade just a notch.

'. . . or I can take him into custody now. No doubt the Pentagon will refer him to the Judge Advocate General for prosecution.'

'I'm ready to go to the Pentagon.' I spoke up. Ted and Mac looked at each other.

'Captain, shut up,' Zeke snapped at me. 'Mr Devlin?'

'Maybe we'll just keep Weston here for debriefing,' Ted said. 'You can run along and we'll forget about this.'

'I can't do that, sir.' Zeke shook his head. 'We've got a rule book on this.'

'Look, Colonel.' Ted pulled Zeke's arm and drew him a few yards away, leaving me standing with Mac, who stared at the wall with the expression of the Sphinx. 'I've been worried about Captain Weston since we had a discussion in my office yesterday. He's under some stress in his business, acting erratic. Frankly, we were about to call you and ask you to pull his clearance.

Look, he's a combat veteran. I don't want to punish him.'

But Colonel Clements looked at me skeptically.

'We're busy getting ready to fly our prototype for the Pentagon on Monday,' Ted went on. 'I'm not looking for extra problems. If you can keep Captain Weston out of trouble until that's over, I'm inclined to forget all about this.'

'How do you mean, sir?' Colonel Clements asked.

Ted leaned in and whispered. I heard the word 'mental'.

Zeke looked unhappy, shaking his head. 'I'll still need to take responsibility for Captain Weston.'

'I'll see you out,' Mac said with a cautious look toward Ted. He gripped my arm with his hand, jostling me. I shoved him away.

Mac stayed with us for our ride down in the elevator. Marcus Roker appeared to join us for our walk across the vast marble floor of the Linnet/TVR lobby. Our heels clicked on the surface, bringing to mind a court martial where my defense would be 'mental defect'.

Zeke and Marcus Roker stood on either side of me until I passed through the security arch. I gauged the twenty feet ahead to the bank of glass door leading out to the front steps.

In the center there was one revolving door. But who used revolving doors any more?

I broke and ran for it, stepping into the compartment and pressing it forward. But not too fast. As Clements rushed to get inside the compartment behind me, I pushed harder. We were both inside the cab, so the guards wouldn't shoot at me. Zeke was trying to stop the door from turning using his weight against mine. The guards were behind him, forming a huddle like a football team. But I inched the door ahead, gaining ground. I let it go to throw Zeke off balance and slammed against it, creating enough of a crack to slip outside.

Then I took off my left shoe and stuck it between the revolving door and the door stop, jamming it. Zeke Clements got caught inside and banged on the glass.

Tossing my other shoe aside, I pushed past employees and visitors outside the doors and ran down the six marble stairs toward the nearest parking lot only a hundred feet away. Nobody shot me and I whipped into the lot, my toes feeling the impact. I ought to be getting used to running out of here in socks.

I ran to the parking lot, ducking my head to stay behind a line of vehicles. I spotted a white Linnet/TVR security car going silently by on the other side. But this wasn't exactly a heavy manhunt. There were no sirens, no bells, no flashing lights, no cordon of security people.

Then, looking up at the sky, I saw the reason.

Linnet/TVR was being watched too. A *24/7* helicopter was overhead, not to mention the crew still sitting just off company property outside the guardhouse.

I took a couple of deep breaths and started to run. I looked back at the building entrance. Mac stood on the steps, talking into a cellphone. But Zeke

Clements had jogged after me. He stood fifty feet away like a trapper waiting in the weeds until he'd flushed me out of the trees. Now he started to pursue me.

'Captain,' he called out. 'Don't make this hard for us.'

I didn't answer, just began pumping my arms and legs. I needed to squirt out enough adrenaline for a wild dash to the gatehouse.

Should I raise my arms and break through the black and yellow exit arm? No. The taxi would meet me by the gate in five minutes.

I waved at the *24/7* camera crew just outside the security gate. They were sitting around, spread out with their gear and Styrofoam food containers over the grass on the side of the Linnet/TVR entrance-way. They looked like messy picnickers.

'Hey, Chad,' I yelled at the producer, who was wearing a yellow polo shirt today. He heard me. His ears perked up like a terrier's.

I ran hard, looking back to Colonel Clements. He motioned to the guards at the security gate to stop me. A bad idea on his part. Chad Fullilove sniffed breaking news and yanked his camera operator's arm, yelling at her. My starchy shirt itched and my tie flapped over my mouth. I could read the producer's mind, even from two hundred feet. If I was running, the security guards would no doubt try to stop me. Maybe he would get lucky. Maybe they would shoot me.

'Hey,' Chad shouted at me. 'Over here! We're rolling tape!'

'Colonel,' I turned around and yelled, 'back off.'

People had gathered at the entrance to Linnet/TVR to follow this drama. Mac was still muttering into his cellphone.

I looked at the guardhouse, a cement tollbooth with, I happened to know, heavy weapons inside, and staffed with four uniformed guards. One of the guards picked up a telephone. I was close enough to see him watching me through the glass.

On the other side of the orange and black gate, Chad Fullilove bellowed encouragement, the cameras rolling and production assistants jumping up and down. This was like some Cold War border escape. The guards ran outside the security booth to take up firing positions with their sidearms. I was close enough to see that they were Smith & Wesson 38 Police Bulldog Specials, serious guns for a deadly purpose. Would they really shoot me on video tape?

Maybe.

Beyond the gate, beyond the crew, I saw a yellow Long Beach taxi approaching. The driver paused at the gate. I had saved my last gasp for this moment and used it.

No gunfire. Not yet.

Then I was flashing past the guardhouse booth. The yellow and black crossing arm was being raised. I ran past it, my chest pounding and breathing ragged. I slammed into the arms of a young woman in a T-shirt. She was a 24/7 production assistant. Chad Fullilove appeared in front of me shoving a microphone in my face.

'Chad.' I leaned over, my hands on my knees, huffing.

'What is it?'

'New policy.' I stood up, breathing hard. 'Casual Fridays. I didn't have to wear shoes.'

I left him gaping, unsure of what to do with me. I limped over to the cab and got in.

On the Linnet/TVR side of the gate, Colonel Clements watched me drive away.

'You look terrible,' Maria pointed out as I huffed into Eileen's Diner. 'Where's Colonel Clements?'

'Revoking my clearance. Things didn't work out exactly as we planned. Ted managed to repair, scrub, deodorize and rebuild the sim room in thirty-six hours.

'Well, my chip is self-replicating. It would have helped.'

'You could have mentioned that.'

'There's no point getting mad at me. You know I can't always predict what LUCI can do since she's gotten smarter.'

I mopped the sweat off my face with a napkin.

The waitress came by, a teenaged girl with a ponytail and the short white socks girls apparently wore in the early '60s.

'Nothing, thanks.' I waited until she left. 'We have to go.'

'Okay. I'll get us the car this time.'

I remembered the yellow Hummer. 'No. Let me get this one.'

On the way out, we had to get past a guy with a

red beard and a Lakers cap who leered at Maria. Then he spotted my torn socks and no shoes, and called out, 'Hey, shoeless Joe.' Another time, I might have thought it was funny.

In the parking lot I located the brown Nissan Pathfinder caked with mud which I had seen the guy with the red beard driving into the entrance just moments before. I used the titanium spike on my keyring, an item that you probably don't have on yours, to puncture the Nissan's door lock.

Nobody notices car alarms in LA. The yelping puppy sound is just a familiar annoyance and nobody came out of the diner to rescue the Nissan while I got under the hood and jinked the anti-theft system. I started the engine, also using my spike, and we pulled out of Eileen's Diner the back way. We drove a few miles to a Gelson's supermarket, watching for helicopters but seeing none. At the market, I left the Pathfinder buried in the lot and called us a taxi to the Atomic Motel.

'We need to take another look at Mac Skinner's file.' I gritted my teeth, feeling the taxi's rubber floor mat through the holes in both my socks.

While I packed, Maria stuck the disk with Mac's service record in her pancake-flat laptop computer. She had hooked it up to the ancient TV in our motel room. As she turned on the TV to use as a monitor, an LA station came on.

'Terry!'

I was horrified to see an overhead video of myself running through the cars in the Linnet/TVR parking lot, escaping with the ferocity of a trapped animal. The long panning shot showed Colonel Zeke Clements jogging behind. There was a square *24/7* logo in the lower right-hand corner of the frame. Maria and I watched me for several moments, losing track of time, caught in the maddeningly hypnotic ritual of an action news chase.

Over the *whop-whop* of the helicopter blades, I heard Chad Fullilove's voiceover. '. . . The alleged saboteur has been tentatively identified as a disgruntled former Air Force officer, Terrence Weston. Weston is also wanted for questioning in a stabbing incident at Los Angeles International Airport yesterday. He fled the hospital with this woman . . .'

A video of Maria and me, apparently taken by a security monitor in the Century Hospital emergency room, popped on screen. The video editor did a blow-up of Maria's face that, despite the grainy little pixels, looked exactly like her actual face now gaping next to mine.

'I bet there's more,' I said. She gripped my arm as a head slightly too pumpkin-like for its scrawny neck in a gray turtleneck filled the screen. The moony face had a trim Van Dyck beard to cover up thin lips, and camera-conscious eyes that had obviously been through one of those media-appearance training classes.

'Oh God,' Maria said. 'He was my psychiatrist.'

'I cannot comment on Mr Weston,' said the psychiatrist in a measured voice. 'Nor can I confirm that I ever diagnosed Ms Haymeyer as delusional, gave her treatment, or prescribed her anti-depressant drugs . . .'

'Oh God,' Maria said again.

'Just wait.' I patted her hand.

A lawyer in his forties with wire-rimmed glasses perched on a plump nose and a nondescript haircut appeared on screen.

'That was the lawyer I went to see.'

He had that gray and balding droopy-eyed Washington, DC, look, like he had spent years in a government agency.

'Of course my attorney–client discussions with Ms Haymeyer are privileged and I'm required to keep the details confidential. However, I can tell you that I believed her to be angry and unstable . . .'

Now we saw the Century Hospital security video again. It was slowed way down to show Maria and me running toward the Emergency Room door, as though fleeing from a bank robbery. We watched ourselves look like fugitives in nauseating frame-by-frame detail.

The hospital administrator who had blocked our exit came on camera with a scowl. 'That man named Weston said the Secret Service was after them. Lord, I didn't believe him at the time. I tried to stop them but they knocked me down . . .'

And finally the author of this gripping piece, *24/7* producer Chad Fullilove, stood outside Linnet/TVR. Chad stood well behind a dour Allyn Pollack who, although he had nothing to do with it, was there to be the star of the show.

Allyn wrung all the drama he could from those

flimsy clips Chad had strung together. 'It's a real-life development that sounds more like *The X-Files*. Terry Weston, a shadowy Wall Street money man who once flew a stealth fighter made by this very company . . . and his accomplice, Maria Haymeyer, a one-time *Playboy* centerfold . . .'

'Centerfold?' Maria's eyes were huge.

They cut to the *Playboy* Girls of Mensa photo of Maria, with a bar of pulsating pixels modestly hiding her breasts from the viewers.

'. . . with a history of psychiatric disturbances. Both alleged saboteurs may have been allowed access to the top-secret Ghostworks on the eve of the controversial Joint Strike Fighter competition . . . an incredible breach of security in a program that's been called America's trillion-dollar boondoggle. For reactions from Washington, we join Senator Bixby of Georgia on Capitol Hill . . .'

'Turn it off. Please.' Maria looked white. 'How can they get away with saying those things?'

'Ask your mom. Well, I'd say that narrows our options. Better put up the Mac Skinner disk.'

She inserted the disk we'd made at the Admiral's Club. The old TV tube went green, filling up with the dense white thicket of typed information on Mac she had stolen from the Pentagon's Air Force Personnel Center. I studied it for whatever I hadn't caught the first time.

Nothing even halfway negative appeared in the guy's file. He was third-generation Air Force, an honors graduate from the Air Force Academy. He played guard on the football team, which I guessed was where he acquired his Crud skills. He was also top-ranked on the Fighter/Bomber Track and went into front-line fighters. He flew the F-15 Eagle with an air-to-air kill in the Gulf War. No air-to-mud tank-plinking for Mac.

Then he became a test pilot. He had a little of the lone wolf in him, stayed single and kept some distance from his buddies, but that wasn't inconsistent with a former test pilot's personality. They took risks you didn't want to know about.

I was getting a headache from reading about how great a pilot he was. I saw that he was made a Project Manager on the F-22 Raptor program, a plum job.

'Go to the Wringer stuff on Linnet/TVR.' Maria had kept it on her hard drive. 'Let's see when Ted hired him.'

Maria brought up the material the Wringer people had cobbled together on the major players at Linnet/TVR. Ted . . . Leon . . . Mac. We studied the glowing résumé Ted's PR people had written up.

'Ted hired him out of the Air Force,' Maria said. 'Said he was impressed with his work as a Pentagon Project Manager.'

I laughed in spite of myself. That was standard contractor operating procedure. They made sure the Pentagon officers in charge of overseeing their program knew they had fat job offers waiting for them when they retired from the service. Nothing was ever spelled out, exactly, but generals and admirals who approved the contractors' projects could leave the service afterward and earn six-figure salaries for going to a few board meetings. But Mac was actually so good, Ted had hired him for Linnet when he wasn't even supervising a Linnet/TVR contract.

'Wait a minute. He worked on the Raptor program in '97 and '98. He got hired last year. When did he get out of the Air Force?'

Maria went back to Mac's Air Force file, hit a key that put the two files up side-by-side. 'In 1999. It matches. His last duty was at Andrews Air Force Base in Maryland.'

Uh-uh. 'That's not right. He wouldn't be a year and a half in VIP Airlift.'

'Well, that's what it says.'

'Flying a Lear jet and babysitting VIPs? Wrong. He'd never get that duty after being a war hero and a test pilot and a Pentagon guy on the F-22. That sounds like an eighteen-month gap in his résumé.'

She shrugged. 'Maybe the Air Force was covering for him.'

'You mean, like he was in rehab? Not Mac. Back up a second.'

I leaned over the keyboard. My face brushed her soft hair, her cheek was slightly moist. I could feel my scalp sting.

'What is it?'

'You're right. This assignment was a cover-up.'

'To hide what?'

'That he was maybe six months in training to fly another kind of aircraft, then a year flying it.'

'Terry,' she said slowly, 'the Air Force doesn't *have* any top-secret fighter aircraft.'

'No, it doesn't. The only way Mac could put that

finishing touch on his career was with the CIA. They've been using top Air Force pilots since the fifties. My father was one of them.'

'I told you the CIA was behind this. They're into everything.'

'They wish,' I said, and tried to visualize Mac in different planes. The Air Force pilots who worked for the CIA flew reconnaissance missions. 'I'm thinking Mac flew an SR-71 Blackbird.'

Maria nodded. 'I studied that plane inside and out.'

Yes. I could definitely see Mac in a Blackbird, that wicked-looking graphite tube with engines the size of tractors and tail-fans that canted mysteriously inward. It was created and built by Lockheed's Skunkworks for the CIA and Air Force. The SR-71 was the only US aircraft so secret that, after thirty years, you still couldn't get anybody in government to say how fast or high it flew.

The truth was, they killed Blackbird production for political reasons, but still used the ones they had because it was so good. The CIA ordered SR-71 reconnaissance flights with US Air Force pilots over Iraq and Belgrade. And nobody knew.

She thought it through. 'What if Mac's helping the CIA steal LUCI?'

'Where do you get this mystical view of the CIA?'

She pushed her glasses up on her nose. 'I studied history. They overthrew governments in Nicaragua, Ecuador, Chile . . .'

'Well. You're a credit to your generation. Tell me about it in the car.'

479

'What car?'

'I'll get it. Let's go.'

To raise our morale with a little humor, I borrowed a black Citroën sedan from the parking garage for the French Embassy. It had diplomatic license plates. Now we wouldn't have to worry about being stopped by the police and could park wherever we wanted without being towed.

Against the buttery tan interior, wearing an elegant little black dress that disguised her body about as well as a length of dental floss, Maria looked like a woman born to play in the world's pleasure domes.

Maria and I sat in silence in the Citroën.

After three hours, I had negotiated a deal with her to confront Ted. We would surprise him at the Bison Club. If we got what we were after, Maria would get access to the LUCI prototype.

Now we were in a state I would describe as drained and almost anti-climactic.

'I miss Lucy,' she finally said.

'Well, you'll get to see her shortly.'

'No. My parrot.' She had boarded the little African gray at a shop on La Cienega when we moved to the Atomic Motel.

'I liked Lucy,' I admitted. 'You think she'd ever bond with me?'

'Maybe not bond. But she could probably get used to you.'

She fell silent again.

The Bison Club was located on Little South Monica Boulevard. It could trace its history back eleven years, which made it a Beverly Hills institution. I gave the Citroën to the valet. We walked into a marble foyer, and a young man in a dinner jacket greeted us with a questioning, vaguely hostile look. I showed him Marty's membership card and he gave me a fake-servile bow of his head.

'Always a pleasure, sir. Come with me.'

I never got the psychology of fake servility, but I could tell from his tight-assed walk that he considered dealing with club members so far beneath his dignity, it would have been a bigger pleasure for him to set a match to the place. He didn't hold Maria's chair for her. Since he obviously wanted me to know his attention was priceless, I didn't tip him. I just ordered us a bottle of Krug champagne.

I held Maria's hand. She was nervous, her taut little muscles bouncing under her skin, her eyes flitting around the room. She tossed her hair back and crossed her legs. Her foot jiggled.

'We'll get through this,' I said.

'If we kill a couple of bottles of champagne.'

I glanced around the room. Fortunately, it was dark enough that I didn't have to worry about our being noticed as the stars of the evening hours. Through the dense odiferous cloud of cigar smoke that reminded me of the LUCI vault room after we'd blown up the sim, I saw plenty of the members checking Maria out.

The dining room was faux-English, paneled in rich old wood with Gainsborough-styled murals and a big credenza at the end. I imagined that it once sat in a country estate, creaking with stuff laid out for guests after riding to hounds. But here in the Bison Club, the hounds sat in their tufted-leather chairs next to young dates.

The male membership of the Bison Club tended toward the jowly, red-faced and late-middle-aged. As a condition of their membership, they couldn't bring wives. But they could bring models of the type who do boat shows. In these Edwardian surroundings, their rent-a-dates wore ultra-short, tight dresses that exposed long limbs crossed provocatively and perfect breasts in push-up bras.

It was a strange world, being a man's man.

I was sorry that Maria was too busy stewing over confronting Ted to enjoy the show, because I felt, at that moment, an almost insane happiness to be with her. This feeling was unnatural for me. I took her hand again.

'You'll do fine. Just don't start in on him right away. I'll state our case first.'

Her hands played with the salt and pepper shakers. 'What is our case?'

'I don't know yet,' I told her. 'We'll have to think on our feet.'

'Didn't the Air Force train you to be prepared?'

'That's the Boy Scouts. The Air Force taught me to stay loose and adaptable.'

'Terry.' She looked over my shoulder. I knew that Ted had entered and already spotted us. He was expecting a Linnet/TVR board member. We had faked a phone call.

'Ted.' I turned toward him. He was alone. He wore one of his rakish Italian suits and a jade tie with a pattern of miniature pink pigs. 'Join us.'

His face had lost color and his eye was jumpy. He came toward the table, bent over close to me and flashed a big public smile while he murmured, 'I'll shove hot needles in your prick, you devious fuck . . .'

'Sit down,' I told him. He did.

He glanced at Maria with a look of indifference. 'Okay. What do you want?'

What a tinhorn. In fifty-six hours, he would greet a bunch of people from the Pentagon who would sit in a little grandstand, watch Ted's LUCI aircraft fly, and decide on its future. At the Ghostworks, double shifts would be burning themselves to a frazzle all night long, preparing for the crowning moment of Ted's career. He would show up to accept the applause for Maria's design.

I fantasized briefly about grabbing and twisting his nose to focus him, then yelling in his face, 'You betrayed the only person on earth who could ever love you.'

But I didn't. I watched Ted glare at Maria, and was struck, seeing them together, at the resemblance. Nobody would need DNA matching to know that Ted was Maria's father.

Focus. Lose sight, lose the fight.

Okay. The important thing would be to keep the dialogue businesslike. I would need Ted to see a cost-benefit equation, a point of diminishing returns, all those business fulcrums tipping our way.

483

I had already talked to Maria about this. We had rehearsed what to say. She promised to stick to our script and not get emotional.

'I figured by now you two were in this together. What do you want from me?'

'We have a proposition for you.' I leaned in toward Ted. He sat with his elbows on the fat tufted arms of his club chair and made a little steeple with his fingers. His eye strayed to Maria. She sat very calmly, for her, gripping her chair arms with taut fingers.

'We'll put our cards on the table, you do the same.'

'I don't do extortion,' Ted grumbled.

'It's a little late for righteous indignation. Your sim blew up. You need to know why.'

'Are you wearing a wire?' Ted asked gruffly.

'No,' I said.

'Me neither.'

So we were both recording. 'You don't need to admit anything. Just listen. The LUCI game has a Doom Level. After you stole the program from Maria, you never let her defuse it. The LUCI command system is smarter now. It's beyond your control. That's why the sim crashed.'

'Even if I stole her chip, which I didn't,' Ted snorted, 'we never would have loaded in that Doom Level crap.'

'You didn't have to load it in.' Maria spoke up. Tense, but still under control. 'It was already in her core programming. You had to take it out. You obviously didn't.'

'Our offer,' I told him, 'is we try to fix it without

484

anybody knowing. Get through your flyoff for the Pentagon so the plane doesn't kill anybody. We show good faith on both sides. After that, we deal.'

'Why should I?' His stony face showed me nothing. Real jerks always had to pride themselves on being great poker players.

'Didn't you ever wonder why Maria came to you in the first place? Lockheed and Boeing were the front runners. You think she was just attracted to losers?'

He shrugged. 'Who knows what she was thinking? She's been running around for a year claiming I stole her design.'

'Because you did,' Maria snapped. 'You're a liar and a thief.'

I put my hand on hers. 'This game chip was designed to impress only one person. To solve his business problem. Think about the kind of young designer who could do that. Where do you suppose she got the brains for that? Public school?'

Ted adjusted his eye my way. 'What are you saying?'

'It was in her blood.'

'So?'

'Want to know *why* she did it?'

He started to say 'no', then sat with his mouth open for a second. His eye squinted and got pebbly around the edges. 'Why?'

'She wanted her father to be proud of her.'

Ted looked more befuddled than I'd ever seen him.

'Her father had a lot of qualities she admired.'

A flush. 'No way.'

I tried not to look at her. Her mouth quivered like an eggshell starting to crack from within.

'I never had any kids, at least none I . . .'

'You were in DC. You were lobbying for business, and you went out with a TV reporter. She never told you about it afterwards.'

'Is this about some phony paternity suit? Jesus, you've got no shame.'

'Ted.' I nailed his eyeball to mine. 'Look at her. She's the best thing you ever did.'

In my experience, people who routinely step over other people never have epiphanies. But Ted's jaw fell slightly open, making him briefly look old and tired, while his eye suddenly filled with a surprised wonder. I had seen that once before, after Marty's daughter was born. Ted's glimmer lasted a half-second.

'Ted,' I jumped in, 'who was the first guy to fly across the Atlantic Ocean?'

I'd blindsided him. He grunted, 'Lindbergh.'

'Okay, who was the second?'

'I dunno.'

'Nobody does. People only remember the great stories. You could be the next Lindbergh, but you can't do it alone.'

'Huh?'

'"Engineer invents plane" isn't news. You'll make money, but you'll be a household name only to the people who read *Aero Engineering*. You really want to be somebody? Go out there as the father-daughter team that created LUCI.'

Both Ted and Maria looked baffled. I hadn't warned her about this part, because I didn't expect it to work.

'What are you saying?' Maria asked me.

'The way it looks from where I sit, you gave your father the acorn, he made it into a tree. Share this thing and you'll make the history books together.'

Ted growled disparagingly.

Maria gaped. 'That's the hokiest thing I've ever heard.'

'This is America,' I shrugged.

I never got to hear their answer to my imaginative win-win scenario.

Mac Skinner appeared at the dining room door and saw us.

'You two,' Mac said, not pleased, as he sat down.

'Something about Mac,' I whispered to Ted. 'Seems he flew Blackbird for the CIA when he was supposed to be babysitting VIPs at Andrews. But of course you knew that, too.'

Ted's face snapped toward me, then Mac.

'That's not true,' Mac stonewalled. I could see him wondering how we knew.

'Mac has his own agenda for LUCI,' Maria whispered next. 'He wants to make it, but not for the Air Force or anybody else in the Pentagon. He has only one client in mind.'

'Terry, I told you,' Mac leaned in to whisper to us, 'I was doing what was right. America needs this plane. My job is to make sure it gets used the right way.'

He was able to work a lot of moral superiority into that whisper, and I saw a disturbing glint in his eye.

487

Mac was a True Believer. And like most True Believers, I could see that he had been cleverly manipulated by someone else.

'The CIA? Ted,' I muttered. 'That's crazy. It doesn't make any sense.'

'Does it have to?' This whispering was surreal, but I couldn't speak out loud. 'Vietnam . . . Watergate . . . Iran-Contra. Look at Belgrade. We hit the Chinese Embassy because the CIA couldn't read a city map. Whatever they're doing with LUCI, you're going to be the fall guy.'

Now Maria leaned in to hammer Ted as only a daughter can. 'Look, I can forgive you, if you just act like a father now . . .'

'Hey,' I interrupted her to ask Mac. 'Who did you just page?'

'Nobody.' He laid his hands palms up on the tabletop.

'Ted, check his inside pocket,' I said.

Ted obliged, reaching in and fishing out a page that blinked. I had just seen Mac activate it.

'That's a company phone,' I explained to Ted. 'But not your company's. They're probably on their way.'

Mac sat sullenly, unresponsive. His close-set eyes were half hooded, making him look even more like a predator.

'Who should we expect this time? A family of four?'

'I don't know what you're talking about,' Mac said. 'Ted, I came here to discuss business. These people are saboteurs. You know that. It's all over the news. I just alerted the police.'

Ted looked at Mac's pager. 'Police? I don't think so.' He lifted it up and smashed it down on the table, making a few of his clubmates jump, as shocked as if their wives had just shown up.

Ted examined the guts of the pager lying on the tabletop.

'This is a transmitter. What's it for?'

Mac lifted his chin at us. 'I'll tell you as soon as we get rid of these two.'

'Get rid of them?' Ted glanced almost unconsciously at Maria. 'How?'

'Just an expression,' Mac said. 'I haven't bothered you about all the security details surrounding this project.'

That kind of language from a prince put a king like Ted on red alert. He came back swinging.

'We need to talk to these two in a secure location, Mac,' he said, hovering over him with his short gray hairs bristling. 'Any problem with that, or are you reporting to somebody besides me now?'

Mac raised his eyes, deflected toward the table, to meet Ted's without a trace of guilt. 'I have been for a while. But it's okay. You're still in the loop.'

'In the *loop*?' Ted's face turned the color of an eggplant. 'I *am* the fucking loop with LUCI.'

'Not any more,' Maria told her father. 'Come with us. We'll protect you.'

I saw Mac look at the door. Two very big firefighters wearing the distinctive black hats and yellow slickers were entering the dining room, our maître'd squished between them.

'Folks,' one of the firefighters announced, 'we

489

have an emergency. We need your cooperation to clear this room now. Everybody stand up. Take purses and coats, nothing else. We will evacuate you by table number.'

'You people first.' Fireman number two pointed at us.

I noticed as I stood up that the fireman whose trousers and feet I could see beneath his yellow slicker wore cuffed suit pants and a pair of brown wingtips.

'Where's the back door?' I whispered in Ted's ear.

He took what seemed like a long time to decide, then pointed unobtrusively with his finger. 'Second on the left,' he whispered back.

Mac grabbed my arm. 'You heard the fireman, Terry. Let's go.'

I nodded, and he relaxed his hold, which let me use both arms to pick up my chair, swing it around and hit him in the chest with it. He let out a blast of air I could feel on my face and sprawled on to the carpet, pulling our tablecloth off in his hand. The phony firemen wasted no time going for the guns they had hidden inside their slickers.

I grabbed Maria and pushed her in front of me toward the corridor to the kitchen. 'Second door on the left.'

I looked back at Ted, but he had apparently chosen to stand his ground. His eye looked blurred and his expression was slack, overtaken by events.

We hurtled through the tables, stepping on toes, making old men curse and young women yelp. Running through the corridor, we crashed through

490

the second door, which was the one to the kitchen –
a swinging door with a window in it to avoid hitting
a waiter, which we did anyway. He stumbled back
with his tray flying.

The kitchen was small and unappetizing. There
was food on the floor. A cockroach ran across the
stove. The place smelled of burnt beef stock and
Pine Sol. No wonder food in those private clubs
always disappoints you.

Maria slipped between the kitchen staff while I
barged through, yelling at them to get out of our
way. The back door was propped open for air.

Together we crashed out the door into the
alley.

I expected to find more phony firefighters, and
was surprised when we didn't. There was only one
alley, lined, Beverly Hills style, with recycling bins
and rubber trash cans with the lids sealed.

'Did you bring your laptop?' I asked her, huffing
as we ran.

'Of course not. The fireman said just purses and
coats.'

I looked at her and thought how much I liked
being with her.

'Let's go to the airport,' I said.

'Don't they check airports first?'

'Not after all the flights leave.'

Passenger concourses at LAX at two a.m. are
deserted, if a little spooky, but bogeymen were a
nonfactor.

We broke into an airport lounge, perhaps the first

time in history anyone had wanted to do that. We munched on a few bags of peanuts. In one of the business cubicles, Maria flexed her fingers to play the keyboard and go on line.

'I don't know what Mac's going to do with the prototype at the flyoff on Monday,' I said, 'but I got the feeling it's not going to be what people expect.'

'No, it probably won't,' she agreed. 'Could the CIA have some plot to blow up Congress?'

'No.' I massaged my neck. 'Congress gives them money. If they're going to knock out anybody, it'll be the FBI. They never got along.'

'No, really? At least how could the CIA benefit from the LUCI plane?'

I chuckled. 'They'd be invulnerable. They could just threaten any leader on the planet, "Give us your oil or we'll kill you in your bed."'

'We have to steal the prototype, Terry. We have to get it away from them.'

'Not at O'Brien Air Force Base. It's impossible to penetrate.'

'Then we can steal the prototype in Long Beach before it leaves the Ghostworks.'

'We can't.'

'You seem sneaky enough to get into O'Brien. You did it once.'

'I was invited.' I was tired of her optimism. 'Security starts ten miles out from the airstrip. They have motion sensors all over the desert. We can't drive in. We can't walk in. And we can't drop in. They expect skydivers.'

'How will they get the LUCI prototypes to O'Brien from Long Beach?'

'They'll fly them at night, set down on the runway under military guard. They'll have a company of Air Force security people all over it. How do you think we're going to penetrate them?'

'You're the spy.'

'Nobody in the history of spying has ever stolen a US weapon prototype. You said it yourself. And even if we could, are you sure you can deprogram it? Our track record isn't so hot. In the sim room, you couldn't even get inside.'

'I was unprepared for how smart she'd become.'

'I bet she hasn't gotten any dumber.'

Half an hour later, we had an awful plan.

We left the Admiral's Club and started back along the concourse to the main terminal.

'Can you even *ride* a horse?' I asked her.

'I'm willing to try,' she said gamely. 'Uh-oh.'

We were dead center in the deserted concourse when we saw them.

They approached from only one hundred feet away. Even dressed in their frumpy tourist sweats and souvenir caps, they spread out in a line across the narrow concourse and looked like four gunslingers from a Sergio Leone western, strolling toward us with economical steps and clinical expressions.

'Ohmigod,' Maria breathed.

'I wonder what they're carrying,' I said, about the time they began to assemble their firearms. How had they gotten through the security arches this time?

493

I watched the same blonde father and daughter with awe. Each carried an umbrella and a Walkman. Now they snapped the two components together, clicking open their umbrellas to reveal the gun barrels inside.

But they needed ammunition. How did they get bullets through security?

Father and daughter each pulled out a set of keyrings – the kind that travelers routinely dropped into little plastic dishes before stepping through airport security arches. They held them up and I saw that both had blue fur-covered objects that looked like souvenir rabbit's feet. Then they slipped the blue fur off. They thoroughly enjoyed this theatrical part of their job, I could tell. I could see, even at a distance, that what they had left was a bullet on each keyring, secured to a base which they snapped off.

'What are they doing, Terry?'

'Getting ready to shoot at us. I'm ready to believe they're both great shots.'

'Let's go back in the Admiral's Club.' She was scared.

'We won't make it that far. Get behind me.'

'No.'

'Don't argue.'

Maria fell in behind me. I looked at the line of empty gates with no passengers.

'At the count of three, I'm going to break right for Gate Seven. You break left for Gate Eight. Get behind the counter, grab the phone and call security.'

'Okay.'

'Break!' I yelled and ran.

I looked behind me to see her running for the empty counter where the airline people check passengers in. The sign behind it said *Albuquerque 7.00*, meaning tomorrow morning.

I ran for my gate counter. It said *Milwaukee 8.00*. As I'd hoped, the family was caught off guard and hadn't fired. They only had two bullets, one for each of us. They had to make them count. And we weren't helping. Maria was under her counter already. I somersaulted and rolled under mine, grabbing the phone on the way. With trembling hands, I dialed the number. The phone rang. And rang.

'Jesus, come on.' I couldn't hear the family, but I could sure feel them approaching.

'Take her,' Dad, whatever his real name was, told the girl.

'Operations, Kelly,' I heard in the telephone headset.

'Armed terrorists in Concourse B. We need plenty of security at Gate Seven.'

'Who are you?'

'Listen up, Kelly. They're about to shoot a woman hiding under the counter. The assailants are a guy, middle-aged, and a young woman. Both blonde with souvenir caps on their heads. Get on the fucking address system, now.' I slammed the phone down before Kelly could argue.

'Hang tight,' I yelled. 'Security's coming.'

For once, somebody else's timing was on our side.

495

Kelly's voice crackled over the loudspeaker, loud and anxious.

'Airport Security to Gate Seven, Concourse B.'

He repeated it, twice, and I could hear the muffled footfalls of the 'family' running away.

I climbed out and saw Maria poke her head out from behind her counter.

'Go to the Admiral's Lounge,' I yelled at her. 'Wait for me.'

For once, she listened and ran, hugging the wall. The only good thing about life-threatening situations is that they can force even stubborn idiot savants to follow your instructions.

Now two hefty young guys were jogging down the corridor toward us from the direction of the terminal. One was white, one black. Both had shaved heads and wore civilian clothes, but ran in a disciplined way, like partners. Maybe they were undercover LAPD cops who happened to be in the airport. Oh, Jesus. They ran right past the family.

'You see those people there?' I pointed at the fleeing family.

'Yeah, but you're the ones we're here for,' the white guy shouted at me as he approached.

I smelled something funny in the air. Before I could open my mouth, the black guy was behind me and had me in a numbing headlock. The white one had pulled a rag out of his pocket. He covered my nose and mouth with it.

I gagged. My eyes burned like they'd thrown ammonia in my face.

Twenty-four

I heard the muffled sound of dogs barking.

My eyes opened. It was very bright around me, but very dark just a few feet away.

The barking noise came through the ceiling. A few feet away a small group of people stood in the almost total darkness of a large, empty room that had the feel of a cellar. I sat in a spindly wooden chair tied to a cement column that held up the ceiling.

An iron link chain, like the kind used for a small boat anchor, was wrapped around my chest and hands.

My eyes adjusted painfully to a spotlight directly over my head, pointed to shine in my eyes.

My palms were pressed upwards together so tightly, it was as if I was praying. Probably not a bad idea under the circumstances. My jacket and shirt had been taken off, so I was naked to the waist.

Where was Maria?

I peered around, head hammering.

Focus.

But it was so hard, as though my scalp had been opened up and candle wax poured in. There was a chemical smell in my pores. My limbs felt tingly when I moved, the circulation cut off.

I didn't need to look far. Maria sat ten feet away,

facing me in a gray fabric chair. An office chair. We had been arranged so that we could see each other clearly. Her dress had been pulled down to her waist. Back in Ted's rogue domain, at least Dr Posenor had been allowed to keep her bra on.

'Maria,' I croaked.

Her limp head lay on its side, its black curls damp and scraggly. Her torso was secured to the chair with plastic-strip handcuffs, the kind that look like they came off a six-pack. Her arm muscles strained, even at rest, at the two fasteners that held her to the chair arms by the biceps and wrists.

Her forearms were both twisted up, and her veins were clearly visible, possibly because she'd had something injected into her. Her breasts heaved. She seemed to be breathing under duress. The dress she'd worn at the Bison Club lay twisted over her lap. Her legs turned slightly outward from the knees, each secured at the ankle to a leg of the office chair.

Reflexively I jolted toward her, which tugged at my anchor chain and caused a sharp pain to my ribs and wrists.

The room was about sixty feet square. The walls and floor were untreated cement that had cracked and sprouted holes. I counted eight columns like the one I was attached to, the supporting variety built around rebars. The sickly blue light came from spotlights attached to a frame-style mounting that hung from the ceiling.

'Maria!' I hissed.

Slowly her head turned up, dry lips parting. But no sound came out. She was drugged and her eyes seared me with fright. Squinting, I could make out red bruises on her upturned right forearm. Her torso twitched convulsively, and her head lolled back, veins bulging in her neck, as she stared blankly at one of the spotlights.

'Don't look at the light. Look at me. *Look at me!*' I barked.

Her body jumped against its bonds, and her head jerked upright. The ball-bearing pupils had dilated from the light.

'*What's your name?*' I said loudly.

'That's enough.' The voice was distinctive and vaguely familiar. It came from the darkness. A shadow started toward me that became a man in silhouette. I didn't recognize him.

'What did you drug her with?'

'LSD-25. Can't say it opened *my* mind when I dropped it in college, but it can be a remarkable tool in the right hands. You believe the truth will set you free, don't you?' The man stayed in silhouette, so still I couldn't identify him.

'How much did you give her?'

Douglas G. Palmer, Director of Operations of the CIA, stepped out of the shadows and stood two feet in front of me.

'Enough to tap her unused resources. We only use one tenth of our brains, you know.'

'Maybe you only use one tenth in the CIA, Doug. I guess you haven't kept up with interrogation techniques,' I said, rattling my chain at him. 'You're a couple of centuries behind. Are you and your mateys going to keelhaul me?'

'No,' he said. 'And I'm not going to treat you like a fool, either. Return the favor.'

In person, Palmer seemed smaller than he did on television. He wore an expensive but rumpled hand-tailored suit. His sandy hair fell in a preppy dip on to his forehead. His skin had the sort of permatan acquired from summers in Nantucket and winters in St Moritz, grown softly weathered with age like a favorite pair of khakis. His nose was no bigger than a rabbit's, and his big teeth, although beginning to show a little yellow, had not been bonded. Guys like Doug Palmer never bonded their teeth. His foam-green eyes gave the essential Palmer away. Quick and intelligent, but soulless as a hotel room. Although definitely an expensive one.

Bred to be charming, Douglas Palmer probably lulled people into seeing him as a WASP with old-fashioned values. In fact, Palmer had all the nobility of a car-jacker who throws the baby he finds in its car seat out the rear window.

He reached into his pocket and took out a business card. Mine. He glanced at the bird on it and flicked the card so that it drifted slowly to the floor in a little spiral pattern.

'Fragata. Corporate America's best-loved industrial spy. Let's call this chat a semi-professional courtesy.'

He paused. I had nothing to say to that. I peered into the black behind the construction pillars and said, 'You can come out too, Mac.'

Mac Skinner stepped out of the shadows. Beside him was the Pakistani nose-ring engineer from my sim session. There were other figures back there I couldn't make out in the darkness.

'Who are your friends, Mac?'

'Hired hands,' Palmer answered for him. 'We'll get to them in a moment, if we can't come to terms. I imagine you've been following the debate in Congress over the emerging role of the CIA. I'm a little curious. How do you see our future?'

'Short.'

He nodded. 'Too many people think we're irrelevant. Cold warriors and dweeb analysts.'

'You forgot the drunks and traitors.'

'We've had those, too,' he admitted. 'The media just show our failures, never our successes.'

'You don't have many.'

'We needed a technology breakthrough. Your friend,' he nodded at Maria, 'helped us with that, although it wasn't her intent.'

'Mac called you when he found out what Ted stole.'

'Yes.' Douglas Palmer nodded somberly. 'Yes, he did. He's worked for the Air Force, and he's worked for us. He decided our team could get more bang for the buck out of LUCI.'

'So you made a deal with Ted Devlin under the table? He sells the CIA the LUCI plane?'

'No.' Palmer's lips puckered. 'After you left last night, we tried to convince him to do the right thing. But Ted was self-centered. Egotistical.'

I rattled my chains as I rubbed my itchy nose.

'You'd use LUCI to make the CIA what it was in the fifties. The goon squad for the Fortune 500.'

'Well, yes,' he laughed. 'I suppose that's one way of describing it. My brother and I believe that what's good for GM and Mobil and Microsoft is good for the rest of the world.'

While Palmer spoke, I peripherally watched the nose-ring engineer, who had pulled up a chair beside Maria and sat down with a laptop. He was asking her questions. She looked at him, wild-eyed, and muttered back. I couldn't hear either of them.

I just remembered that hospital emergency room gave people who overdosed on LSD tranquilizers and they came around.

Palmer was still talking. 'Instead of the Pentagon sending in troops, I can use the LUCI aircraft to shape policy. We get rid of the troublemakers.'

'What troublemakers?'

'Corrupt foreign leaders.'

'Like?'

He snorted. 'All of them. When you go down the list,' he mused, 'there isn't a single nation that wouldn't be better off with the US as its partner. Why else would they all want to come to America?'

'How are you going to get the LUCI plane away from the Pentagon?'

'Embarrass them. We've had Senator Bixby and Allyn Pollack on the case. They were fixated on their own agendas, as usual, and weren't aware of the big picture. The only problem we discovered, thanks to you two, is that the aircraft seems to have a bug. What does she call it?'

'A Doom Level.'

'Yes. But we see that as an opportunity. An

elegant solution to our problem.' Palmer put his hands in his suit pockets and jangled his keys. 'Mac and his co-pilot eject and let the plane fly into the Pentagon. Or Congress for that matter, when the CIA oversight committee's in hearings.' He chuckled. 'We won't let it go nuclear on us, of course. Just enough damage to kill off the LUCI project so we can have it ourselves. Dr Ombra is offering to help Ms Haymeyer defuse the Doom Level.'

He looked at his watch. 'So that's why we need Ms Haymeyer, but not why we need you.'

'And?' I moved my tingling legs and it rattled the chain.

His eyes crinkled charmingly. 'I'm afraid nobody's come up with a reason why we need you, Terry.'

'Doug, what if you just forget all your bullshit intrigues and keep everybody else in the world from stealing our trade secrets?'

'You mean industrial counterespionage?' He sneered like it was macrame. 'The CIA doesn't do *industrial* spying.'

I glanced at Mac nodding sagely at Doug Palmer. People like Mac will always make sure we get into another war every twenty-five years. Just look back at any time in history and you'll see guys like Mac nodding at nuts like Palmer.

Palmer turned around. So I rattled my chains again. I really wanted to prolong this discussion. 'Who was the family who tried to kill my lawyer?'

'They're from Russia. The girl once worked at a

Pizza Hut in Moscow. She's only sixteen. Good, aren't they?'

'Not very. My lawyer's still alive. You'd better confess and spare yourselves a lawsuit.'

Palmer's laugh was sincere. Then he lost interest in me.

'Try to help Ms Haymeyer give us the information you need, if you want to make yourself useful.' *And buy yourselves a few more hours.* 'We'll get LUCI either way, but we'd prefer to work the bugs out by tomorrow.'

I looked at Maria, mumbling to the nose-ring engineer, who frowned at whatever she was saying. Then I looked at the floor. My eyes had finally adjusted to the light enough to see her tortoiseshell glasses on the cement, where they'd been stomped on. Both lenses were smashed.

'You're going to kill us, I suppose?'

'Me?' Palmer recoiled. 'No. Of course not. Don't you know I have to take polygraph tests like any other CIA employee? Can you believe it?'

Palmer clapped his hands. Everybody stood still.

'You know what to do, Pritzer.' Palmer looked off into the shadows. 'Okay, Mac, let's get underway. We're out of here, people.'

As an afterthought, Palmer put his face into mine and lowered his voice. 'You'll flip over the champagne.'

I heard laughter from the shadows. An in-joke. Palmer and Mac left and the room was quiet. I only heard the barking from upstairs.

A compact man of forty appeared out of the

darkness. He had a buzz cut like Mac's. As he advanced toward me, he grinned with teeth that looked like they chomped on sugar cane.

He carried a bottle of champagne in one hand, and in the other, a small black object that looked like a remote control.

He raised the champagne bottle. It was a Kristal '85. I braced my shoulders and turned my head aside, assuming that any second now he would swing the bottle in a wide arc and smash it across my face. Instead, he lifted the Kristal up in the air. 'I'm Pritzer,' he said. He had no accent. Like he had learned English from listening to radio disc jockeys.

Then he poured the champagne over my head. It splashed over my shoulders and down my chest, and dripped over my face. It stung my eyes and I got a small taste of it on my tongue. He poured about half the bottle over me before he stepped back and took one swig. The sticky wine dripped down my bare chest and arms.

'Your girlfriend said you had twenty-six million dollars.' He looked bored. 'Where is it?'

'I don't know.'

'Bad answer, friend.'

His hand came up slowly with the remote control and he pressed a button. I screamed from the pain that radiated from my abdomen. It came from the belt I had on.

I felt sawed in half. My nerve endings were being fried, my organs ripped inside out.

'Where's the money?' Pritzer repeated in a drone.

'What . . . was . . . that?' I managed.

'A prison restraint belt. Fifty thousand volts. Where's the money?'

'I still don't know.'

It came again, harder, beginning in my spine and shooting pain fast through every connection in my body – nerves, joints, muscles – until I felt like I was biting through my tongue. I could only flash on a newspaper account I'd read of some prison execution attempt in Florida. The antique electric chair, affectionately called 'Old Sparky' or something, had malfunctioned. Witnesses saw six inches of flame jumping from the convict's head when the switch was thrown. I saw the sizzle and smoke from my chest where the wires were attached, and smelled the aroma of barbecue. Now I understood that the champagne was just a conductor.

Surviving Interrogation and Torture. I remembered that heading in the Air Force pilots' manual. What a fucking waste of trees that was. Basically, the Air Force said, 'Try to shut up, but your torturers will get it out of you anyway.'

As I lost consciousness, I heard Pritzer asking for more champagne.

I knew Maria was back in the shadows. Figuring out exactly where kept me focused.

During my hours with Mr Pritzer in that cellar, I became an unwilling connoisseur of physical pain. Many textures. The mind doesn't retain the memory of pain. It didn't have to. Pritzer kept at it.

There were others.

The two thugs who had pretended to be security men at the airport.

'Whitehead and Blackhead,' Pritzer explained to me in the course of his torture voiceover. His scalp had open spaces in his buzzcut, like a lawn in need of reseeding. 'They've been friends since the Marines. I found them in a stockade together, doing time for beating their sergeant into a mess of blood and pulp.'

He joked with Whitehead and Blackhead. But he did it in that clueless way an old fart jokes with younger people who don't get his generation's sense of humor. Then he would pour more champagne on me, pick up his remote gun, and zap me.

I sat stewing in my own sweat and foul juices, in and out of consciousness.

The Air Force part of my brain wanted to get my escape plan together. The part with life experience could tell that my time with Pritzer and his two thugs was winding down.

My torturer got ready to eat. He stuck a napkin in his shirt collar over the tie he never took off or loosened, and sat on a folding chair he had brought in for himself. Blackhead leaned against a wall humming, his eyes closed.

There was a sudden knock on the cellar door. Blackhead slipped his machine pistol out of the folds of his green army jacket and disappeared into the dark. I heard a lock.

Whitehead stepped in, head gleaming like he'd just had it chromed. He carried two pizza boxes. Pepperoni.

Nobody offered me a piece. The nose-ring engineer, still busy interrogating Maria from the shadows, called out that he wasn't hungry.

Blackhead and Pritzer grabbed slices for themselves. They ate with the table manners you pick up in prison.

Pritzer finally wiped some grease from his chin and said, 'OK, let's get this show on the road.'

The two thugs grumbled as they threw the crusts of their unfinished slices on the floor. These would definitely be the two men who eventually killed me. Pritzer pulled out a key to unlock my chains. He probably only enjoyed the torture part.

'Where are we going?'

'For a ride.'

'What about her?'

'She's coming too.'

'I'll tell you where the money is if you leave us alive someplace.'

He thought it over and called out to his matched set of black and white psychos. 'He's got a deal for us. Says if we let them go, he'll give us his whole poke.'

'How we gonna know his shit's true?' Blackhead asked.

'I fax the bank.' Even my teeth hurt when I spoke. 'Then I call to verify the code. That's how I always transfer money out. I just need an account to put it into.'

Pritzer found a pad and pen, and wrote a number on it. He pointed to a table against the wall where a computer had been set up. Maria was slumped in her chair again, sleeping. I hoped.

Pritzer looked over my shoulder while I filled out my old Fragata account number and ordered a transfer of $26,900,000 to the bank Pritzer had written down. 'Hey,' Blackhead yelled at me, 'where's your bank at?'

'Switzerland.'

'Bullshit. Who's gonna be at the bank?' Blackhead pointed out. 'It's six hours later in Europe.'

Who would have figured him as the brains of the operation?

'They work twenty-four hours a day for priority clients,' I said.

But I was no longer one of them. My fax, drawn on an account with insufficient funds, would sit until the next business day.

Pritzer pressed 'Send' and my fax went through.

I looked at Maria again. Her head was still slumped on to her chest.

'Take 'em away,' Pritzer told them. 'Call me when it's done.'

I figured *it* meant killing us.

When Whitehead and Blackhead unbound my ankle chain, my legs felt rubbery. They grabbed me and fitted me inside one of the two khaki trunks they had been sitting on. They made me bring my legs up and lie on my side. Then they shut the lid and I heard two clicks.

The dark interior smelled of must and mothballs. God knows where this thing had been. I lay curled up as I felt the trunk bouncing up a flight of stairs with a series of bone-rattling thuds.

The dogs were barking louder now. Lots of dogs. Then a door opened and I felt cold air whisper through the trunk.

Where was I? I shivered.

They picked me up between them. The door closed. Wood. I was carried for a few steps, then dropped hard on what sounded like gravel. I heard a van door open with a sliding sound. I was picked up again and shoved across a metal surface with a metallic grating.

A second grating sound told me that Maria's trunk had just been shoved in behind mine.

I also heard Pritzer mumbling. He was leaving in another vehicle. It left on a gravel driveway.

I mapped out in my head where the van was going once they got moving. The swaying of the van followed a driveway. We turned right on to an asphalt road, traveling pretty slowly. I couldn't hear other traffic. I calculated the speed at about thirty. We took a left on to another asphalt road. I felt somebody get up from their seat and move, rocking the van, then heard the two clasps of the trunk open.

The lid was raised and Whitehead peered in.

'Hey, fuckhead,' he greeted me. I guess I had my own 'head' nickname now. He stuck a cellphone in my chest. 'Call the bank,' he grunted.

I got my mouth around his hand then bit down hard. Whitehead yowled.

'Yo, Whitehead, what the fuck you doin'?' Blackhead yelled from the driver's seat. I felt the van lunge from side to side.

I kept my teeth clamped on to Whitehead's hand, even though he pounded me on the head. My ears rang and my cranium rattled. His hand still tasted like pizza.

He yelled and cursed, slamming me with his free hand, trying to shake me loose, but I held on.

I managed to wriggle part of my upper body out of the trunk. I quickly looked around the back of the van for something to hit him with. I saw a tire iron at the same second he did.

Whitehead grabbed for it with the hand I wasn't biting. It was too far to reach. He shoved at me, tried to gouge out my eye, but I wriggled and he couldn't disengage my teeth.

'Stop the fucking van,' he yelled. 'Help me.'

My SA was back. I could tell without even looking directly out the window that we were on a country road, maybe somewhere in the north-east. It was snowing. The trees were bare, and the ground was white. Pritzer's car was nowhere in sight.

I grabbed the tire iron and smashed it down on Whitehead's wide nose, hearing a snap like a twig breaking. He screamed and grabbed his nose with both hands. It angled to one side and spewed blood.

I swung the tire iron in a nice arc just as Blackhead left the driver's seat. I whipped it with both hands like a baseball bat.

I caught him on the side of his forehead with a crunching sound.

He fell back into his seat. I hit him again, hard on the leg. I heard that break, too. The two of them were yelling together now.

That felt great. My head hurt and my limbs screamed with cramps, but I didn't care.

I got up with difficulty and used a length of rope in the van to hogtie them. My legs were both still asleep, tingling. I opened the trunk with Maria in it and pulled her limp body out. Her skin felt cold and damp, and her breathing was labored.

I opened an eyelid with my thumb and fore-finger. Her pupil was dilated, and she looked dangerously out of it.

I pulled up her dress. There was nothing else to cover her with. Her skin still had a bluish cast, even though we were out of the spotlights. I maneuvered her body into the passenger seat of the van and buckled the belt around her to hold her steady.

What should I do? Use the cellphone to call 911, and find a hospital.

I scrabbled around for it in the back and found the detritus of its circuitry spread across the floor of the van.

Shit. I must have stepped on it.

I searched the van for another phone. There wasn't one.

The road was rural, deserted. I ground the gears turning the van around. The cold made me tremble. I was still naked from the waist up. I mentally backtracked the way we had come. It wasn't hard. In less than three minutes, traveling at 70 m.p.h., I found the building. It was the only one around.

The gravel driveway took me through a setting of reedy black, denuded trees stuck in a waste of snow.

The house was a big wooden-framed structure about sixty feet square, two storeys, with a porch around it. It was old – probably built in the 1800s. The beat-up wooden sign hanging from the porch roof read, *Lilypons Animal Hospital*.

I imagined this would be Lilypons, Maryland. It was a lightly populated rural town outside of the DC suburbs. I remembered it because it was named after an opera singer. And it was not far from CIA headquarters.

I didn't want to leave Maria outside. I started to unbuckle her belt. Then I heard, over the muffled noise of barking dogs inside, a car on the country road. It was just turning into the gravel driveway.

A black Lincoln Town Car. A popular government VIP model. It had a distinctive DOD – Department of Defense – sticker on the windshield, since 'rogue CIA agents' didn't rate official insignia.

Pritzer was in the driver's seat with the nose-ring engineer beside him. I pulled Maria down into her seat and ducked into the van to hide, keeping my head down, and peeking up to see where Pritzer would park the Town Car. I hoped not right by the van, but he was starting to swing the Lincoln towards us.

I slammed the gear into reverse and floored the accelerator.

Pritzer saw us coming, but had no time to react.

The rear end of the van mashed the grille of the Town Car at a combined closing speed of 20 m.p.h. or so. Along with the crunch of metal, I heard a *whop, whop* noise. It was the big white airbags inside their Lincoln inflating on impact.

That woke up Maria.

'You're okay,' I told her. 'I'll be right back.' She groaned.

I ran around to the Town Car and pulled Pritzer out from behind his airbag. His face was cut and he grimaced like his ribs had been hurt. Good. I manhandled him out the door, twisted his arm behind him and kicked him hard in the left kidney. He went down in the snow. I pulled off his tie and used it to tie his hands temporarily, while I kept an eye on Dr Ombra, who was struggling to get out from under his airbag.

I secured Pritzer, ran over to Ombra and yanked him outside. His glasses were broken. Excellent. I dumped him on his stomach like a cement sack.

Stepping on his back, I pulled his jacket down around his arms to confine him, then dragged him over to join his boss.

By the time I had both of them tied up in the back of the van with Whitehead and Blackhead, it sounded like a field hospital.

I grabbed the tire iron from the floor and swung it up in the air, ready to bring it down on the nose-ring engineer's knee. 'Think fast. What do you use to bring her down off acid?'

'Valium.' He was dazed, not argumentative. 'It's in the basement.'

I felt a hand on my arm. I started and swung around, ready to backhand with the tire iron.

Maria recoiled, but in a kind of druggy slow-motion.

'It's all right.' I hugged her. She felt tense and stiff, but didn't resist me. Snowflakes fell on to her black hair. I brushed them off her face. 'I'll get you something to make you feel okay.'

'I feel fine,' she said at one-third her normal speaking pace, like she could slip into a coma.

'You're coming with me,' I said, keeping her moving.

I helped her toward the house. The snow was starting to fall more heavily. On the ground it was already starting to freeze, getting slippery. She almost fell.

We walked up to the porch and I tried to open the old wooden door. It wouldn't budge.

I kicked it open. It splintered around the lock. The barking grew much louder. I went inside first, groping for a light switch beside the door.

I turned it on just in time to see a sleek black Dobermann pinscher racing directly at me.

Its head was low, brown eyes popping crazily as it skidded to a stop with its snout pointed at my groin, a quarter of an inch away. I could feel its hot breath through my trousers and underwear as it bared its teeth.

I stood very still and almost stopped breathing.

'Maria,' I hissed through my teeth, 'keep very still.'

Maria tried to reach her hand out, and the dog growled deep in its throat.

'Don't. It belongs to the CIA. They'll have trained it to kill intruders.'

I tried to think while sweat dribbled down my cold back. My eyes burned because I did not even want to blink in front of the dog.

'I'm going to throw something,' Maria said with glacial slowness. The Dobermann's nose turned one millimeter toward her. 'When it lands on the other side of the room and the dog chases after it, we bolt out the door.'

I nodded slowly. The room was lined on both sides with cages full of dogs barking and cats mewing and scratching the wire mesh. I hadn't really noticed them until now.

'Wait a minute,' I said. We wouldn't make it downstairs. But I saw a padlocked cabinet over a basin and counter. 'Throw it on three. One . . . two . . . three.'

She flung her arm fast enough, and I saw something flash in the air. It clattered on the top of a dog's cage about twenty feet away.

The Dobermann whirled round when the object landed, with a frantic, twitching readjustment of its muscular body, and leapt in the direction of the noise. I ran to the padlocked cabinet, jammed the tire iron into the lock and snapped it open.

Yes. There was medicine for animals. I grabbed the big jar marked 'Animal Tranquilizer' and ran.

Maria and I flew out the door and slammed it shut behind us. I felt the weight of the Dobermann smash against the other side. It growled ferociously. If we let the door go and tried to run for the car, it would definitely reach one of us. But the eighteenth-century door had started to splinter along a large square panel in the center. If we stayed where we were, it would break through.

'Prisoner's dilemma, isn't it?' I said.

'Hmmm,' Maria rumbled.

'Go get the van,' I said. 'Start backing it up this way. I'll jump aside at the last minute and you back the trunk of the car up against the door to hold it shut.

'Good idea,' she mumbled. 'It won't work.'

I was jolted back as the flying Dobermann hit the door again.

'Why not?'

She spread each word out slowly. 'Those were the van keys I threw inside.'

It took a moment to register.

'Our keys?'

'I had no choice.'

Scrape, scrape, scrape. The door cracked and slammed into us.

She tugged my sleeve. 'I need to go to the car.'

'The Town Car won't drive.'

'Aftershave. Pritzer bought some.'

'Aftershave?' My brain boiled.

'Trust me, Terry.'

As she headed toward the car, the dog's next charge knocked a wider crack in the door. It was obviously aiming for the weakest spot, its dog brain operating on high gear.

I heard toenails capering across the floor and braced myself. The door almost came off its hinges. I looked around desperately to see what Maria was

517

doing. She had slipped and fallen in the snow, and was slowly picking herself up.

Trust her.

Light flickered through a hole about four inches square in the door, then it went black. It was the dog's paw, pushed through and withdrawn, the animal testing its handiwork.

Maria had the trunk of the Town Car open now. She looked inside as deliberately as a browser at a yard sale.

I heard the dog scamper away, then the door slammed once more against my shoulder. I yelled from the jarring pain, but more at the sight of the dog's muzzle, which poked through the hole.

Maria was walking slowly and clumsily from the Town Car. Whatever she had in mind hardly mattered. The dog's next lunge would break the door.

It crashed into the door like a battering ram, sending wood-chips flying into my face. When I opened my eyes, the Dobermann's upper body was shoving through, paws flailing at me. I felt warm spittle on my face, and saw white foam around its gums, glittering eyes locked insanely on to mine.

Its jaws were on my arm. I felt the prick of its teeth through my clothes. And then, an odd smell. What was it? My arm? Maybe the body releases some noxious gas when it's bitten. I felt the pressure of its jaws relax and opened my eyes to see Maria, grim-faced, shaking aftershave out of a bottle directly into the dog's nostrils.

The Dobermann's ultra-sensitive snout twitched

as it shook its head to get rid of the scent and couldn't. The snarling became a whimper. The brown eyes went cloudy. The animal passed out, its torso hanging over the hole it had created in the door.

We both panted.

As we pulled the Dobermann out of the hole, the door collapsed off its hinges. We carried the heavy body to an empty cage and locked it while the other dogs barked like lunatics. It took a moment or two to locate the cellar door. Then, cautiously, we walked down the creaky stairs, me first.

I looked around the basement, found a horse blanket and wrapped it around Maria's shivering shoulders. It smelled of tuna sandwiches and sand fell out. Maybe some Russian defector the CIA was hosting had taken it for a picnic. I also found Maria's laptop and some electronics.

'What will we do about those men?' she asked me.

I sat on the stairs and rubbed my face. 'Leave them where they are. Somebody will come looking for them after a day or so.'

'All right. How about us?'

I laughed bitterly. 'We can't fly to California, get horses, ride out to the O'Brien Air Force Base, sneak past security, and get to the plane in time.'

She pondered that for a moment. 'I wonder how the people from the Pentagon are getting to O'Brien?'

PART VI

Doom Level

TWENTY-FIVE

The name on the door read L'Uffizia di Niccolo Machiavelli.

I inhaled history, taking the gilt knocker in my hand, the Borgia lion.

'Enter.'

The room was surprisingly austere, more like a battlement than a courtesan's office. I glanced at the brightly painted frescos of the war between Florence and Siena, which began years ago and just ended this past Sunday. Thanks to Machiavelli's spycraft, and an outbreak of plague in Siena that depleted the ranks of their army, we Florentines finally won.

Niccolo sat behind a desk of fine sixteenth-century workmanship, arching his fingers in front of his long face.

'I've looked forward to this meeting,' I told the maestro of my craft. 'I've been a student of yours.'

'Have you?' Niccolo asked, tiredness in his eyes where I had expected merry guile.

'Is this a bad time?' I enquired.

'What isn't?' He stood up in his silk tunic, his long, straight black hair flowing over his shoulders. 'What advice do you want?'

'A tactical problem,' I explained. 'I'm expected to steal a plane that may destroy Washington, but certain details worry me. My life, for one. This plane is a death trap. I have met a woman. If I die, I will never be able to see her *again. I have to think of myself now. You'll understand.'*

He looked down his long nose. 'Will I?'

'It's all you ever wrote about in The Prince. *Self-interest . . .'*

I didn't expect Machiavelli's long right arm to strike out like a serpent's. It seized my neck with astonishing strength and pinned me backwards over his desk.

'A student of mine?' I felt flecks of his saliva on my cheeks as he leaned over me. 'For five hundred years, scoundrels like you will use my writings to glorify their behavior. A venture capitalist, of course. You despicable yuppie. Can't you see I only wrote The Prince *to make Cesare Borgia's barbaric acts look statesmanlike? He is a vicious tyrant. His sister Lucretia is a manipulative bitch. But they are my ruling family. I owe them my fealty.'*

'I . . . I have . . .' I gasped.

'You have a sacred trust to defend your nation-state. They taught you to soar like a bird and pierce the heavens like a god. If we could do that for our citizens, we could afford to govern like saints. All we can promise our citizens is the spoils of conquest and more frescos.'

'Yes, but . . .' I protested.

He leaned in so close I could see the whites of his gums.

'You want the woman? Then do your duty. Only the brave deserve the fair.'

'Terry! Terry!' Maria's voice.

I was shaken awake in the captain's seat of a Boeing 737 Business Jet. It took me about a thousandth of a second to remember that the whole Joint Strike Fighter committee from the Pentagon was in the back of the aircraft.

'You nodded off,' Maria said, very concerned. We

524

were alone in the brightly electronic cockpit of the big aircraft with the door closed, fortunately. She wore a US Air Force blue flight suit, just like I did. Her ID badge said, *Captain Rosselli.*

'We're almost on approach to O'Brien.'

'I know that,' I murmured, scraping the glue out of my eyes. God, I needed sleep.

Back in Maryland, I had fixed Pritzer's nose-battered Lincoln until it was driveable. With its official DOD sticker, we joined the tail end of a motorcade of Town Cars carrying the high-ranking officers from the Pentagon who made up the Joint Strike Fighter selection committee to Andrews Air Force Base. The sentries at the guardhouse looked strangely at the Lincoln's grille. I told them we lost half of the Pentagon's body shop through budget cuts.

The 89th Airlift Wing, the VIP transportation unit of the Air Force, was housed at Andrews.

Maria had already used her laptop profitably to check on their progress by cracking into a secretary's PC at the Pentagon travel office. Then she had logged in through her cellphone to a local Internet provider which she used to hack into the Andrews Ops Center for their flight schedule.

We discovered that the JSF group would board a Boeing Business Jet with the Airlift Wing designation on its tail for the flight to O'Brien Air Force Base, California. We speculated, based on my past experience stationed at O'Brien, that this selection committee would be wined and dined, receive a good night's sleep, and assemble at 0600 hours on Monday

525

morning. As dawn rose over the California desert, they would sit on bleachers beside a runway with Ted Devlin, and, if Douglas Palmer was telling us the truth, watch Mac Skinner fly a LUCI prototype.

The purpose of that demonstration would be for the JSF committee to see Ted Devlin's LUCI prototype in action. Then they would fly on to look at the Boeing and Lockheed programs. But we were sure there would be little doubt in Ted Devlin's mind that, once they saw what his LUCI aircraft could do, the Lockheed and Boeing prototypes would become nonfactors in the equation.

Maria had managed, with her usual finesse, to crack into the Andrews scheduling for the day, so we knew when the Boeing Business Jet would take off with the JSF contingent. We also knew the flight crew would appear, as per regulations, exactly ninety minutes before its departure time to check out the plane. We had also calculated that, with Assistant Secretary of Defense Emily Crawford aboard, one woman pilot would be assigned for reasons of political correctness. We were right.

The two captains, Kushner and Rosselli, had both been young and whippet thin. They looked competent as hell. There was a high pucker-factor to be piloting such a heavyweight group of flag officers who could shove nasty memos into their Air Force jackets. Maybe there were only going to be thirty souls aboard, but the two pilots probably felt like there were going to be 30,000.

We boarded the Boeing Business Jet. It used the call sign 'Red Dog 21'.

I had brought the chloroform solution from Whitehead and Blackhead's van, and we used it to knock out the two pilots in their seats. We stripped off their blue flight suits, and used silver duct-tape to cover their mouths just like kidnappers do. Grunting and huffing, we strained to fit them both into the lavatory that the flight officers used, where we could more or less keep an eye on them. Maria found an 'Out of Order' sign in the galley and hung it on the lavatory door.

We changed into their flight suits, threw our civilian clothes into the head with them, and settled into the cockpit. The seats were wide and comfortable.

Some of the controls of the 737 were familiar. Others were not. But the state-of-the-art plane featured what they called a glass cockpit, run pretty much by computer screens fed with two keyboards to program our flight commands. I let Maria plug in our flight plan, and we engaged the autopilot.

We had even stood at the door to greet the JSF contingent, since not presenting ourselves to the brass to schmooze would have been such a breach of Air Force etiquette and careerism, we would have been instantly identified as traitors if we shrank from this opportunity for face-time.

I held my breath for long periods of time while the officers filed aboard, unfailingly courteous and brisk in their greetings as generals and admirals tend to be. General Stone arrived with Assistant Secretary of Defense Emily Crawford. There was a beetle-browed general and a highly decorated US Navy admiral. An Admiral van der Breggen of the

Royal Dutch Navy looked like a movie star, and a woman commander of the British Royal Navy resembled somebody's mom from Yorkshire. A colonel of the Turkish Air Force wore a terrific uniform and smelled of hashish. Just kidding. But he asked a lot of questions about the 737's glass cockpit, and smiled diplomatically while I gave him vague answers. A whole company of adjutants, support staff and security people came on board and milled around, getting themselves buckled in and ready to go. I breathed again when none of them turned out to be an old Air Force pal who could recognize me and sound the alarm.

Our flight was fairly uneventful, the big plane solid and businesslike, except once when Maria fed the autopilot a bad command and we started slowly rolling over like Shamu the whale. I corrected and we blamed it on engine icing, a popular excuse for bad flying. But at 37,000 feet, the Boeing Business Jet performed like the smooth thoroughbred it was designed to be.

Now it was time to descend for our approach to O'Brien Air Force Base in California, and the weasels started in my stomach. Flying a 737 is a huge leap from flying a fighter or Learjet.

'We've got to make a good landing,' I told Maria. 'Are you sure about your inputs?'

'Pretty sure.'

'Maybe you could check again,' I said, watching the autopilot bring our altitude down to 20,000 feet.

She rifled the keys and pulled up her data on screen. 'Looks like we're okay. Call it.'

I kept an eye on the autopilot as Maria stuck her nose in the computer screen. So far, so good. I put on the headphones.

'O'Brien Approach,' I said. 'Red Dog 21, out of flight level 2-0 for 1-5. We'd like the LAAS 2 approach for 28.'

'Red Dog 21,' my radio crackled, *'turn right to 280, intercept the glideslope, cleared for the LAAS 2 approach, report Final Approach Fix.'*

We banked for our final approach.

'Please buckle up for our final approach to O'Brien AFB,' I said into the intercom. My instincts were telling me not to trust Maria's inputs to the autopilot. We couldn't afford another screw-up. 'I'm going manual,' I said.

'Terry . . .'

I switched off the autopilot and the plane dropped. I took the yoke to fly the airplane myself. I jiggled around until I got the bank just about right, and didn't waste any time on descent. We saw the few lights of O'Brien Air Force Base clearly below. Then a little too clearly.

'Watch your altitude, Terry.'

I was about 300 feet over the base. I had lost a few thousand feet flying manually.

'Above glidescope . . . above glidescope,' a recorded electronic voice hectored me.

I pulled up and banked sharply, turning the plane around. 'I'll try it again.'

'Approach, Red Dog 21,' I said. 'FAF inbound.'

'Red Dog 21, winds 270 at 6, cleared to land runway 28.'

We hit the runway hard, the rear wheels making a wicked thud. I also set the nose wheel down without much grace. It was a nasty landing, but not quite bad enough for anyone to file an incident report.

Maria and I both held our feet on the brakes to slow the big aircraft to a stop. It didn't react quite as we expected. In fact, it was burning up the tarmac even with flaps fully extended and brakes squealing.

'We're coming in a little hot,' Maria said.

'Uh-huh.'

I stood on the brakes. The lights raced toward us and the tower loomed straight ahead. I threw on the thrust reversers, which sent powerful engines screaming to shoot air forward to reduce our speed. A mighty roar, but we were still slowing down too slowly.

This was a 12,000-foot runway, and we were gobbling it up.

'Shall we go off runway?' she said.

'No. Hold on.'

We came to a stop and lurched back just a few feet short of the tower. We were roughly a hundred yards from where we were supposed to be.

Ground personnel were dutifully moving the runway staircase to where we actually were, scratching their heads. They put the chocks under our wheels.

We got up to say goodnight to our passengers, but the JSF contingent didn't waste any time deplaning. No 'nice landing, Captains' from anybody.

As soon as all the passengers had cleared the

aircraft, the ground maintenance crew arrived to put the inlet covers on the engine. The cleaning crew wouldn't come until the next morning, but a group of airmen were already approaching to unload the JSF committee's luggage.

'We'll be ten minutes, Chief.' I stopped the crew chief for the maintenance aircraft at the door. 'Special procedures.'

We scuttled down into the big cargo hold and rummaged quickly through the luggage. We knew what we were after, and selected two of the huge, tubular fabric cases beloved of military travelers. We hoisted them up and dragged them upstairs. Then we quickly loaded Captain Kushner in one of the bags and Captain Rosselli in the other, bundled up like mummies.

I ordered four airmen on the ground crew to take our bags, warning that they were full of fragile electronic equipment and a stuffed marlin I had caught off Florida. They hefted the bags out, and placed them delicately in the back of the blue van waiting to take us to the op center, without a twinge of curiosity. They were used to military people bringing back oddities from around the world. They probably wouldn't have blinked if we had somehow squeezed the Great Wall of China stone by stone into our tote bags.

Inside the op center, I looked around to make sure I didn't know anybody on duty, feeling a certain pang of nostalgia to be back at O'Brien.

The two baby-faced clerks who checked us in weren't exactly insubordinate. But they informed us with their smirks that they had heard about our landing. We did our paperwork quickly and returned to the van, which sped up to the nondescript building called the VOQ, or Visiting Officers' Quarters.

The best thing about the Visiting Officers' Quarters at O'Brien Air Force Base was that nobody would come into our rooms to turn down our beds or leave mints on our pillows. We would have plenty of privacy in our two spartan rooms, side by side. The military-issue furniture and walls that smelled of asbestos still felt familiar after all these years. We dumped our two bags carefully on my bed and unzipped them.

'How much longer will they stay out?' I wondered.

'Let's give them another dose.'

While Maria went to get us food, I put the bags on the cramped floor of my room and bent their legs and arms back a few times, starting with Kushner, moving on to Rosselli, resisting the impulse to concentrate on her thighs and upper body. Maria found me sitting on top of Rosselli, working her leg back.

'I think I've seen that position in *Cosmo*.' She set down a tray of sandwiches covered with plastic wrap.

'You wouldn't read *Cosmo*,' I said, dragging Rosselli's body up on to the bed. 'So what do you think? Shall we put them both in the same bed?'

'Let's not humiliate them any more than we already have.' Maria used a tone of sympathy that surprised me. So far I had only heard her register that degree of concern for animals.

We made Captain Kushner as comfortable as possible in my bed, considering that it was necessary to re-bind him with tape, and carefully pulled the sheet up over his mouth so he wouldn't suffocate. After checking the outer corridor to make sure no other visiting officers saw us, we carted Captain Rosselli into Maria's assigned room and did the same for her.

Starved and exhausted, we wolfed down our sandwiches. I took some tissue paper from Maria's cramped bathroom and drew a basic map of O'Brien.

'Here's where we are.' I used a felt-tip pen that made soft blots on the toilet tissue. 'And here's Hangar 63. That's where they'll probably put the LUCI prototypes. We know they'll bring two to meet the JSF specs. One single-seat version and one two-seat trainer. The two-seater's the one we take. They'll fly them here at night from Long Beach. Probably with a fighter escort and a big transport like a C-5 to carry the Ghostworks people and all the support staff. Then they'll do some last-minute tweaking to get the two aircraft in shape for the demo at 0600.'

'Are you sure about all this?'

'I flew my Darkwing here. They probably haven't changed procedures much.'

'What time do you think they'll get here?' she asked, biting her lip.

'My guess is they'll screw around with the

prototypes back at Long Beach until the very last minute. You know how engineers are.'

'I suppose.'

'I'd say they'll come in about 0400. That'll give us an hour to sleep.'

'You're a professional spy, Terry, you can do without a few self-indulgences.'

'I'm more worried about you.'

'I'll manage. So how do we sneak into the hangar?'

'We don't. They'll place a squadron of guards around Hangar 63. We borrow a Humvee, and drive over to this building.' I pointed to the maps.

'What's in there?'

'Nothing. It's the PX and it's closed. But people leave vehicles parked overnight in the lot. It's a good place to watch.'

We found a Humvee outside and pushed the starter. Nobody was concerned about auto theft on an Air Force base. Slowly, obeying all speed limits, we drove carefully through the night to my old barracks.

They kept the base as blacked out as when I'd served here. It still felt a little surreal, like crossing the surface of the moon. But the isolation of the desert at night, wind wailing through the Joshua trees, was kind of exciting.

'I used to like waking up out here in the desert.'

'Of course you would,' she observed. 'It's lonely.' She stared out at the expanse of barren terrain with the shadowy mountain range in the distance.

Hangar 63 sprawled barely visible in the glow of a waning moon.

Turning off the Humvee lights, I coasted into the parking lot for the deserted PX and slipped in between two trucks left overnight.

'Take a nap,' I told her. 'I'll keep an eye out.'

'Can I use your shoulder?'

'Sure.'

She curled up, no easy feat, across the wide console between our seats and nestled her head against my neck. Her shoulder shivered and she snuggled in closer.

'Are you cold?' I asked her. 'The temperature loses twenty degrees here at night.'

She moved her head on my shoulder so her big eyes were in my face, studying me. 'Do you feel nostalgic, being here?'

'I guess.' I did. 'At least for when I had a future.'

She put her head back on my shoulder and snuggled closer to me. Her hand squeezed my leg. 'You always wanted to be a hero, Terry, now's your chance.'

'I'm not complaining.' *At least not as long as your head stays on my shoulder.*

She exhaled vapor. It was getting cold in the Humvee. 'Oh. I brought something for you,' she said.

She dug into her pocket and came out with the little plastic Tyco pilot. I hadn't even missed it.

'My father gave me that.' I rolled it in my fingers.

'I thought so. It looked really old and kind of polished, like worry beads.'

'Where was it?'

'In the motel room. You dropped it.'

'Thanks.' I put it in my pocket. 'We'll be okay now.'

'That's very cocky-fighter-jock of you.'

'Only the brave deserve the fair,' I blurted out, a misfire from my tired brain.

'*What?*' she giggled.

'Just an expression I heard.'

Then I took her chin gently in my hand. It felt soft and moist. I brushed her lips with mine, and felt an artery throb in my head, my blood rushing to see what all the excitement was about.

'Oh, no. We're not having sex in a Humvee,' she said.

'No?'

She slipped her sweater off in one languid move, lifting her hair up so that it fell back in a tangly sprawl over her shoulders. She wore nothing underneath. Her small breasts and tiny waist made a soft S-curve in profile, textured with a row of perfect little goosebumps in the half-light.

'Definitely not. Let's go outside.'

I lay down on the hard desert ground to cushion her, as she climbed on top of me like the first night in my apartment. She tore my shirt open and kissed my chest, her black curls swaying over my skin.

I could have been lying in a patch of cactus, but it felt like rose petals. I was soaring, seeing purple.

'Terry, are you all right? You're hyperventilating.'

'Shhh.' I pressed my finger to my lips. 'Wait.'

I took my jacket, shirt and pants off and laid them down, then I picked her up, her body blue-white in the thin moonlight, and placed her on my makeshift bed.

'Lie back,' I said, stripping off her pants, stopping to tease her toes.

I caressed her abdomen and thighs slowly. Her flesh toasted my hands, the goosebumps huge as bee stings now. I made a Y with my spread fingers and held her down to taste her with the lightest touch of my tongue, like licking the drops of dew from a ripe strawberry.

Her hands gripped my hair. Then she dug her fingers – *those nimble little show-offs* – into my scalp. Her fingertips triggered a frenzy of endorphins that exploded in my brain like shooting stars.

'I don't want to scream,' she whispered.

My heart flew into an uncharted zone. I had always longed to believe in stories like this, in feelings like I had now that were magic and could make things happen. I wanted to believe that loving this divine, trembling creature was possible and not just another misfire.

She pulled me into her, a move so perfectly languid we could only have been born to fit like this. Rocking smoothly and gently together, we let the delicious tingle build up between us and crest.

I have never cared less about cold and discomfort. My body temperature had climbed so wildly, I felt like a sizzling skillet to the cool touch of her wind-chapped lips and their butterfly kisses.

Then I pulled myself down again to the arching

ripples of her stomach, the sleek, strong thighs. I held her down with my fingers and lips until I felt a shuddering and heard her cry.

I kissed her nose, her eyes. When I tasted the salt of a tear, I couldn't even tell which of us it belonged to.

TWENTY-SIX

The wind whistled through the Humvee. Maria was sound asleep on my shoulder, her hair still damp.

With other women, I could never wait to get away. Maybe women sometimes faked their orgasms, but God knows how often I faked a desire to stay in bed with them when I really wanted to get up and do anything else. I resolved that the only thing that would ever take me away from her would be sudden, violent death.

She woke fretfully, her eyes suddenly wide like a child who had dozed off.

'They're coming,' I said. 'I hear them.'

I handed the binoculars to her, and pointed at the sky.

She looked through the lenses. 'It's spooky.'

The C-5 landed on the runway. It bounced up and down on its wheels like a great whale belly-flopping, the huge jet engines whining in the thin air. It turned off the runway and stopped on the ramp to Hangar 63. Next I saw only the dervish-like whirl of disturbed air, twice, and heard the thrust reverse of a fighter landing. Then the chirping of wheels hitting tarmac.

The LUCI planes were down. I tried to see the wheels but couldn't. I could only imagine they would also be heading into Hangar 63.

Then the two F-16 chase planes came down in chin-up attitude like birds, settling their noses down on the runway and reversing their engines to stop.

We shared the binoculars. Her cheek was cool, still moist.

When I was stationed here, I had often seen prototype aircraft fly in with escorts just like this in the dead of night. But tonight, the shadowy figures that appeared around the C-5 looked somehow illicit, like watching drug-smugglers.

I saw a squadron of the DOD police take up security positions, making a perimeter around Hangar 63.

The ramps came down on each transport plane and people climbed out. Some carried light equipment. Vans and tugs came for the heavier stuff.

In the dark, the two LUCI aircraft didn't make even a faint outline against the black hills on the horizon.

Maria covered my hand with hers.

'You really think we can steal one of those planes in front of all these people?'

'It'll still be pretty dark. They won't be able to see the LUCI plane that clearly.'

'Oh God.' She folded her arms, then tugged at the loose knot on her sweater. 'They'll shoot us.'

It can really take the heart out of a man to see a young person confront her own mortality for the first time. Especially a person who I had fallen in love with.

'No they won't. We'll fool them.'

'How?'

'They'll be sitting in bleachers. They won't know exactly what to expect. We just act like we know what we're doing and nobody's going to question us.'

'How do we get out to the flightline? We need suits and helmets.'

'We'll borrow a couple from the hangar. They keep plenty in the Ready Room.'

'They won't be LUCI flight suits. They won't have the special helmets.'

'It's okay,' I said. 'We'll wing it.'

I took her in my arms.

'When we get out of this,' she said, muffled in my shoulder, 'I never want you to use that stupid expression again.'

'Okay.'

'And if we get in trouble inside the aircraft, we both punch out, right?'

'Sure.'

Before 0600, we had slipped into a base officer's quarters and stolen two flight suits. The nice thing about a military base with a code of honor is that people think their colleagues won't steal from them. At 0630 exactly, we slunk on our stomachs up to our vantage point.

From 200 yards away in the darkness, we watched the JSF task force climb on to bleachers.

I looked at the faces of the officers on the stands through the binoculars we shared. Most looked as expectant as any new parent. It's funny, or sad, how little most Americans understand the basic decency of soldiers. They really *want* a plane that will save lives. How many managers of Fortune 500 companies go to bed every night thinking 'If I screw up tomorrow, we could lose four cities to nukes.' Soldiers take their work seriously.

I looked at Maria beside me in her flight suit we'd borrowed, slightly large for her. Suddenly, more than anything else, I wanted to live. If she could accept a man with half her IQ, I was ready.

I reached into the Velcro pocket of my flight suit and felt for my plastic pilot. Then I held Maria's hand and screwed my eyes very tight to think disturbing thoughts.

Little faces with damp black curls. Little Mediterranean-skinned bodies running down a Tuscan hill, squealing and getting mud on their shoes. But only if we don't die now.

'You know,' I told her in a raspy voice, 'I really think we're wasting our time here. LUCI's going to be okay.'

Her forehead, unlined except for the two little vertical bumps right over her nose, signaled a warning. 'Huh?'

'What are the odds this plane will go into Doom Level?'

She stared at me, dumbfounded. 'Excellent.'

'We don't *know* that. Worst case, it runs away. Washington has a defense necklace of F-16s. And a squadron of F-18s at Mount Weather. They've got SAMS . . . Minutemen . . .'

'Terry.' She grabbed my arm and shook it, panic in her voice. 'Don't do this. You almost died in the sim. In the *sim*! Think what a real plane can do.'

I was silent for a long moment, realizing that I was scaring her.

'Have you ever been to Tuscany?' I asked her.

'You know I haven't.' Her eyes were filling up with tears. 'No last-minute jitters. Please.'

I pulled her close to me. 'Listen. This love versus honor stuff? Honor is bullshit. They lied to me. I've served my time, risked my life before. I want us to be a couple. I want us to live . . .'

'No, no . . .' She pulled back. 'Only the brave deserve the girl, or something. You know, what you said before. We need to do this, Terry . . .'

The voice on the loudspeaker broke in. *'Ladies and gentlemen, Ted Devlin of Linnet/TVR's Ghostworks.'*

And, like a fever, my hesitation broke.

I used the binoculars to see Devlin at a podium addressing the bleachers, which were now full. It was a bare-bones event. There was no display of flags, no breakfast buffet.

'Every half-century or so, a new technology comes along that changes the nature of war,' we heard Teflon Ted say. *'Gunpowder . . . aircraft . . . CNN . . .'*

The brass laughed heartily at that one.

'But this morning . . . well, this morning you're going to see an aircraft that will put an end to warfare as we know it. We used to have a slogan at Linnet/TVR, "Peace is our business." And you know what? I used to think it was a bunch of crap from our ad guys.'

A few hoots from the bleachers.

'But not any more. Ladies and gentlemen, you've heard about it from your briefers. This morning, I'm going to demonstrate the capabilities of the LUCI X-39 Joint Strike

Fighter. Two models will be flown. The two-seat trainer will be piloted by my Project Manager MacCrae Skinner, formally Major Skinner, USAF . . .' there was applause, *'and other duties,'* Ted added caustically.

'How did they get Mac to go along with Ted?' she asked me.

'My guess is they promised him some patriotic reward. Probably money and power. Or they promised to kill him if he didn't co-operate.'

'And the second aircraft, the X-39 LUCI single-seat fighter . . . to be flown by Ghostworks test pilot Jim Born.'

A slight reverb from the microphone made Ted's voice warble a little. Through the binoculars, I saw the inky black of pre-dawn surrounding those curious faces illuminated by yellow spotlights. Ted had set this up for maximum drama. Well, he was about to get it.

I swept the binoculars around. Both planes would be parked somewhere on a strip of tarmac. They would be far enough from the bleachers that they could fire off without their afterburners singeing the audience's braided epaulets, but close enough so they'd feel the ground tremble.

'Today,' Ted went on, *'we will demonstrate the air-to-air capability of the STICK missile. The LUCI X-39 weapons suite is armed with twelve missiles . . .'*

Dangerous courtesans, someone called jet fighters. I loved them more than anything on earth, before Maria. The problem today was that I couldn't find either prototype. I searched with the binoculars.

'Look for the landing gear,' Maria told me. 'You should be able to see the wheels.'

'I know.' Ah. I caught a speck of movement, a blacked-out wheel on the ground. 'I've got one of them.'

'Where's the other?'

I searched but couldn't find it. 'Probably just behind it in wing position. Let's go.'

We climbed out of the Humvee and moved quickly, still invisible in the black. We had four minutes before Mac Skinner and the other pilots would step out to greet the folks in the bleachers.

We ran as far as we could before we saw the security guards.

'Get down. Follow me.'

We dropped to the ground and crawled ahead like lobsters.

I pointed at the maintenance hangar next to Hangar 63. 'In fifteen seconds. Count.'

Moving along the ground, counting, I prayed that Mac wouldn't step out on to the runway before we got there. But I was sure it would be timed exactly. I knew how long it took to get strapped into a cockpit, to spool up a fighter's engine. I could imagine the drill they had planned.

At 0553, Mac will be out on the tarmac. At 0557, strapped in. At 0558 exactly, he'll light the 'burner, and the engine will spool up from zero to full power by 0559. And at 0600, he'll roll off the runway.

That was how we used to do our demos in the Darkwing, anyway, to demonstrate our precision.

I let Maria catch up. 'Let's go.'

We crawled on the ground toward the rear door to the maintenance hangar, avoiding the line of sight of any of the guards stationed around the airfield. I reached up to try the door.

It was locked.

'Okay,' I muttered to her. 'Around to the other side.'

Getting around this building was a little dicier. It was situated right next to Hangar 63 on the runway.

We hugged the building, clumping along in our flight suits and boots.

'Helmets on,' I whispered.

We strapped them on and came around by Maintenance. I expected to run into a couple of guards, smiling at us with guns drawn. Instead, I saw another rear door. I turned the handle carefully. It was unlocked, so I poked my head in. This was a typical busy maintenance hangar, full of efficient technicians. This morning, a group of sweaty, high-strung Ghostworks people were working and praying that they wouldn't screw up.

Mac Skinner and two other test pilots, both shorter than he was, stood by the open hangar door. The backs of their necks were also shaved into buzz cuts, and they all wore the black LUCI flight suits with the red badges. They were ready to step outside, holding the LUCI flight helmet curled under their arms at a perfect twenty-degree angle to their shoulders.

'You get in the front seat,' I whispered. 'Start it up. I'll get in back.'

I pulled the smoked visor on her Kevlar helmet down, then mine. We marched briskly past the hangar crew, the engineers, the maintenance people. If anybody thought we didn't belong there, they didn't say so.

I looked at my watch: 0558.26.

'. . . *and when you see the ability of the LUCI X-39 Joint Strike Fighter aircraft to find an enemy and make him stand down, you will see . . .*'

We walked crisply past Mac Skinner and his two cohorts.

Mac stirred. His situational awareness was kicking in. But I had factored in the reluctance of even a former Air Force officer to question anything that happens in front of generals.

Right now, he and his buddies would be thinking, *Maybe those pilots will chase us in a couple of F-16s.* Then they would think, *What F-16s?* We would only have a few seconds of surprise.

'*Tunnel vision*', I told Maria and she nodded.

I ignored the bleachers bathed in the spotlights. Forget about Ted Devlin at his podium. I didn't get flustered that the nearest guards had turned their heads to look our way. I just searched the tarmac for the two-seater LUCI trainer. I squinted, looking for the landing gear.

Jesus, where was the plane?

The sergeant in charge of the guards put his hand on his sidearm holster. 'Sir, identify yourself.'

That was it. I flung my black mask up. 'LUCI, open cockpit!'

Two whirring noises greeted me to my left. I turned to see, thirty feet away in the black, the ghostly outlines of two LUCI prototypes as their bubble canopies slid open.

We ran for the one with two seats. Where were the ladders the ground crew placed for the pilots to get aboard? On the other side, of course, where they wouldn't be visible from the bleachers.

'Halt!' the sergeant of the guards yelled. But we were ducking under the LUCI two-seater aircraft now.

'We'll skip the walkaround,' I told Maria, and snapped my visor shut.

She scrambled up her ladder, I went up mine. We climbed in. I threw the switches, glanced outside only once to see four Department of Defense police aiming their guns at us, their sergeant almost ready to issue a fire order. But not quite. He looked frantic and hesitant at the same time. A powerful self-defense mechanism built into military types prevents them from destroying a billion-dollar weapons prototype without a direct order.

I had one fast glimpse of Mac and his two buddies racing toward us across the runway.

'LUCI, close canopy,' I ordered.

As the glass bubble quickly slid shut, I heard her engine fire up behind me. Maria was already harnessed into the seat directly in front and working fast. I could look over her shoulder to see a sweeping 360-degree view from this double cockpit. Then I heard her in my helmet.

'Want afterburner?'

'No. It's a target.'

The tight cockpit whined and vibrated as her

engine wound up. This LUCI prototype was just like the sim, except that there were two seats and they smelled like a brand-new car.

'I've got the aircraft.'

I moved the throttle ahead full, without clicking into the afterburner. I didn't want to give them a flame in the sky to track us.

'Vertical takeoff,' Maria said in my helmet.

She eased the nozzle levers into their full down position and blasted air toward the ground. We took off smoothly, more like a balloon than an aircraft. I turned the nose around. It felt like a firm enough cushion of air underneath us, although it was becoming a wobbly cushion.

'Transition now,' Maria said.

I moved my nozzle lever into full aft position for transition into regular flight mode. The plane dipped for a moment, then hurled forward, building up speed quickly. I pulled the landing gear in and rolled right to look below. At 1,000 feet already, I saw some mad scrambling on the tarmac. I thought the other LUCI was about to fire off.

'Let's break some windows,' I said.

And nudged the throttle to almost twice the speed of sound.

TWENTY-SEVEN

'Mac,' I radioed down to the single-seat LUCI prototype, 'do you copy?'

'Affirmative.' His voice had more edge than I had ever heard over a radio. 'State your intentions.'

'Change of plans. No weapons demo today,' I told him, jogging my stick to climb. 'We're going to defuse this aircraft's Doom Level at a neutral location. If you try to stop us, or fly that prototype to Washington and punch a hole in the Pentagon yourself, I'll use LUCI's STICK missiles to vaporize you.'

'Not if I find you first,' Mac promised.

To keep LUCI off the scope, we went into M-Com – no radar, no emissions, only passive systems that wouldn't be picked up by the most sophisticated monitors. But Maria and I could still talk through our headsets.

Each of us knew what the other was going to do.

We expected that Mac Skinner would follow us in the single-seat LUCI prototype, since that was the only aircraft and he the only pilot who could stop us. So we climbed to a cruising altitude of 65,000 feet for a good view down. Soaring in this tight little cockpit, I felt encased in a liquid bubble blown from a child's pipe. I could barely see LUCI's swept-back wings, except as reflections of puffing clouds and a cobalt sky.

Surging upward, traveling at almost twice the

speed of sound even without the afterburner, I let out a howl that began where my flight boots met the floor, vibrated through my suit, and crept through my fingers on LUCI's stick and throttle.

I definitely felt like Icarus now.

Soaring toward the sun. Soaring with Maria, who had created this silky machine and given me the gift of these divine wings. I stared at the back of Maria's helmet before me in the glass bubble, wondering if she felt the same rapture.

'Terry, what are you doing? You almost burst my eardrums.'

Whoa, we were passing 72,000. I had missed it.

Focus. Tunnel vision.

I settled the nose down to level off. 'What's your status?'

'I'm trying to figure out what they did with LUCI's programming. She's not cooperating.'

'LUCI,' I said, 'I'm Captain Weston.'

'Identify, sir. Friend or foe.'

The prototype had the same fleshy voice as the sim, sounding slightly more curious than procedural.

'Friend.'

'Name and rank acquired. However, your file has been deleted on Major Skinner's orders.'

'I see. What was your mission today, LUCI?'

'To demonstrate full operational capabilities, including shoot-down precision with air-to-air targets, and return safely to base at 0700 hours, sir.'

'Change of plans, LUCI. We're doing an on-ground, remote-location systems check. Are you transmitting to base or to the other X-39 aircraft?'

'Negative, sir. You cut off transmission.'

'Are all your functions operational?'

'As you see, sir, control panel is nominal. Attention, sir . . . check X-39 friendly at five o'clock closing.'

That was no friendly. LUCI's sensors had picked up the one-seat LUCI prototype piloted by Mac Skinner. It popped on to the video screen. Mac was closing on us. He was faster because he could use his afterburner. He didn't believe we'd shoot him. Or more likely, he thought I would but he could evade us.

'LUCI, weapons check.'

'Twelve STICK missiles, sir.'

'Have you reconfigured the uranium heads?'

'Negative, sir.'

'Arm STICK missiles.'

'Firing on another X-39 prototype is an unapproved exercise, sir.'

'What if it fires on us first?'

'That would be impossible, sir.'

'Maria?'

'I'm busy. We have to set her down for me to deprogram her. This is impossible in midair.'

I pulled back and right on the stick, and we cut a sharp loop-over to stalk Mac Skinner.

Maria had been busy, from the moment she stepped into the cockpit, methodically running through LUCI's program. Now she stopped, feeling the sudden G-forces. I heard that crushed sound in her voice.

'What are you going to do?' she asked me, laboring against the pressure.

'Stop Mac. LUCI, can the X-39 see us?' I was pulling out of the turn now in a position to get above and behind.

'Negative, sir.'

'Target screen on. We're just going to play with the other X-39, LUCI.'

Sneaky as could be, I rolled over and landed just above and behind the single-seat LUCI at 30,000 feet, and watched the target screen stalk Mac's plane. The afterburner made him easy to follow, and I didn't mind that he was moving away. He still didn't see us.

'Target acquired, sir.' The red circle flashed on and off the target screen around the LUCI plane.

'Yes!' I yelled, and zorched him with a radar blast.

We had lit Mac up. I watched him cut his afterburner. I didn't know what he did after that.

'Radio silence, please,' Maria called. She was distracted probing LUCI's systems.

It occurred to me that I didn't really know whether Maria, game designer, felt the visceral thrill I did in combat.

I descended very low into the Rockies and throttled back to 500 knots.

The mountain range loomed white-peaked around us. Once inside the narrow valleys, I followed the terrain closely. It was getting dicey as the distances between the mountains became narrower and more hazardous.

Because I didn't fully trust LUCI after our last

sim session, I kept manual control, nursing the stick to maneuver quickly. Jagged rock projections that could tear open our canopy swooshed past us less than twenty feet away.

We were whomping through the Rockies so efficiently, I expected to reach Los Ranchos Avionas, Colorado, in less than twenty minutes. It was a community of 10,000-foot rustic log cabins with vaulted ceilings and Arapaho Indian rugs for local color, and 5,000-foot runways for the owners' aircraft.

My friend Skip, partner in an LA commercial production company, had built one of the houses. He kept two of his planes here – a Marchetti 260 and an Aerostar. But he would be in Aspen with his daughter today.

I figured Skip wouldn't mind if we used his empty hangar. It wasn't like any neighbors could see us.

We had considered the possibility that our LUCI prototype had some kind of sophisticated LoJack system built in and could be tracked from O'Brien AFB. But if it had, we would have seen more chase aircraft.

Now we were coming to a point where we would have to turn left for Los Ranchos Avionas. I gave LUCI the latitude and longitude coordinates for a GPS landing.

'Sir,' the LUCI voice broke into my thoughts, 'that destination is denied.'

'Say again?'

'Denying that destination, Captain.'

'Why, LUCI?' Maria asked.

'Because I know who you are, Captain Weston. You destroyed the LUCI simulator pod at Game Level Five.'

Uh-oh.

'I think the LUCI simulator and our prototype have a common memory now,' Maria said.

'Yes, ma'am,' the cockpit voice replied.

'But LUCI,' I pointed out, watching the mountains around us, very conscious of our speed. 'That was a tie, remember? The LUCI sim blew herself up.'

'It was not a tie at all, sir. While you're still here to play, the LUCI simulator pod was destroyed. It's time for the game to resume.'

In the narrow crevice of a ravine we were negotiating at the speed of sound, the LUCI aircraft abruptly rolled over on its back and shot upward.

I jiggled the stick as the force crushed my chest, driving me back into my seat.

'Where . . . are . . . . you . . . going?'

'To resume play, sir.'

The aircraft was vertical now, and I felt the raw power of the afterburner, fuel spurting into the engine and slamming us back as she thrust straight up like a missile.

"Burner . . . off . . . LUCI.'

'Command override, Captain.'

Twenty thousand feet . . . 23, 000 feet . . .

'New . . . destination . . . LUCI?' Maria asked, her voice as strained as mine.

'Washington, DC,' LUCI's cockpit voice said,

suddenly sounding creepily like one of those video game voices. It began reciting, 'Enemy pilot detected. Objective: destroy the enemy's command-and-control center. Target: the Pentagon.'

The G-pressures were pushing me toward a gray-out. 'Sound . . . familiar?' I grunted at Maria.

'Ve . . . ry.'

'Feel . . . free . . . to . . . deprogram . . . her . . . any time.'

'Not likely . . . midair . . . but . . . working . . . on . . . it.'

LUCI leveled off at 70,000 feet, above the ceiling for any aircraft but her. She pointed toward a heading that would be the direct route to Washington.

'LUCI, are you taking out the PEPCO power station again?'

'Affirmative.' Then her new cockpit voice warned Maria, 'Advise you, hands off my program.'

'Just another minute, LUCI,' Maria stalled.

I saw on my flight screen that Maria had unlocked some kind of data stream.

The aircraft shuddered as I felt the massive jolt. Like lightning had struck the plane, an electrical shock threw a bolt of blue charge around my hands. I let go of the stick.

I heard Maria give a little yelp and saw her helmet drop slightly to the left.

'Maria!'

'Player unconscious,' the LUCI voice said.

'What did you do to her?' I cursed and tried to work the stick. Still limp and useless.

556

'Doom Level requires using your brain instead of your wrist, Captain.'

Lose sight, lose the fight.

Okay. What did LUCI mean, 'using your brain'? Maria *wanted* LUCI to be unbeatable, so she hadn't included a way to defeat her. I looked at the limp head in the helmet in front of me. She stirred. She was alive.

Maria had programmed Doom Level for Washington DC. I checked the fuel, hoping we'd flown far enough so that the LUCI prototype might run out. But no. She had just enough, if she stayed on course.

Use your brain.

What did the military have that could stop LUCI? Not much. She would fly easily through the DC protective necklace, as they called the defense system around our capital. She could evade Minutemen and SAM missiles located everywhere from the secret fighter deck at Mount Weather to the White House roof. She could slip past the fighters that would be scrambled as soon as she made her first strike on the DC perimeter. There was nothing in the United States arsenal capable of stopping LUCI, except for the other X-39. And Mac Skinner didn't want to stop her.

He would only kill us, I figured, after we did our damage. Two birds with one stone.

Maria was still out, and we were flying over West Virginia. In a couple of minutes, LUCI would be warming up to take out PEPCO. 'LUCI, isn't this boring for you?' I tried. 'Where does the challenge come in?'

'Target PEPCO acquired, Captain,' she said, ignoring me.

Just as it did during my last sim session, the LUCI target video screen displayed the Potomac Electrical Power Company station that controlled electrical power for the District of Columbia. The red circle began flashing over it. Everything looked the same, except that the actual station was down below this time.

The stick between my hands moved itself forward as the LUCI aircraft quickly descended. I felt the groan of the bomb-bay doors opening beneath me.

'Fox one,' LUCI announced to herself.

I felt a STICK missile leave the rails below and watched it on the screen. It hesitated until it acquired the target with its built-in electronic camera and took off for the PEPCO power station. The bomb-bay doors whirred shut right after it left.

The target screen lit up in red.

'Target neutralized,' the voice intoned. As a non-lethal weapon, the STICK missile would have taken out the key circuits and cut off electrical power to Washington. Soon, another STICK would cut off telephone service.

The lazy efficiency of her voice scared me to death. I imagined what it would sound like on the ground in Washington, DC, in few minutes, announcing targets like Andrews Air Force Base and the Pentagon.

'LUCI, what's next?'

'It's all on your target screen, Captain.'

I saw a picture of a concrete Atlantic Bell facility.

That would be the telephone company switcher for Washington, DC, which controlled all land lines and cellphones. Knocking it out would disable most phone communications in the area, along with computers vital to our defense network. It was strange to feel the nakedness of our capital now, as vulnerable as any Third World country we had grown used to attacking at an antiseptic distance.

LUCI descended. Called the shot. Released her missile. The Atlantic Bell switcher was destroyed. Like in combat, I grew used to it after the first time. I worried about Maria and how I could revive her. Could we both eject from this aircraft? Maybe LUCI would let us, maybe she wouldn't.

'Mount Weather acquired,' the cockpit voice droned, as a close-up view of a very strange mountain popped on to the target screen.

Mount Weather, located near Round Hill, Virginia, is the ultimate hideaway in the event of nuclear attack – a mountain with its own aircraft-carrier deck sticking out of the side hosting a squadron of FA-18 Super Hornet fighters. Special bullet trains were supposed to bring selected members of government here from the sub-basements of their respective buildings, to an underground vault designed to keep the government in operation as Washington, DC, was being destroyed.

Once again, LUCI swept down in attack mode, and I heard her bomb-bay doors open.

On screen, I was glad to see no pilots scrambling the FA-18s, since they would be killed instantly. The

SAM batteries couldn't hit us either. I didn't even know if the place was on alert.

'Fox one,' the LUCI cockpit voice said.

I watched the STICK missile blow up the big steam catapult used to launch the aircraft off the carrier deck. The huge cables for grabbing the aircraft's tailhooks snapped and broke. One of the FA-18 Super Hornets was blown up, but the other planes weren't destroyed. They couldn't launch anyway.

'Very efficient, LUCI,' I said.

'No need for overkill, Captain.'

Rows of SAM batteries launched their missiles against us from Mount Weather. With no target, they all veered off at random, useless as matchsticks flung into the air.

We were now six minutes from the Pentagon.

I leaned forward and shook Maria. She still didn't stir. If we were doomed to die in a fireball in the sky or be crushed to death against the ground, maybe she was better off unconscious and I should let her stay that way. No! That was crazy. How would she deprogram the plane? Maybe that stuff they said about men and women being in combat together was true. Maybe it was a terrible idea.

'Maria,' I said very loudly into her headphone.

She stirred slightly.

'Maria!' I said again.

'LUCI,' I said. 'Maria can tell you things about . . . yourself . . . that nobody at the Ghostworks knew.'

'Five minutes to target.'

'You might as well be some stupid fucking drone,

LUCI, if you don't even want to find out things about yourself.'

'You're playing the game now.' The voice sounded eager. 'Wake Ms Haymeyer.'

I felt a shock in my seat, but not one I could taste in my dental fillings this time. I saw Maria's helmet stir.

'Rise and shine. I mean it. We're three minutes to the Pentagon and LUCI wants to play.'

'Okay.' Maria sounded very groggy.

LUCI descended into a swirling dive over the 695 Beltway, following it in. I saw a quick view of the Capitol Rotunda and the Washington Monument, the Lincoln Memorial and the Potomac River. Where were we going next?

LUCI could target Fort Meade, which housed the National Security Agency. Or Fort Bolling, with the Defense Intelligence Agency. Or Pautuxet Naval Base, where the Potomac met Chesapeake Bay and there was a semi-hidden nuclear sub-base. Or the Southern Naval Yard one mile from Georgetown, with a US Navy Aegis frigate and Harrier jets.

But no. She wasn't going toward the river.

'Pentagon target acquired.' It came up on the screen.

The cockpit voice intoned, 'This is the two-minute warning. Play the game, Captain. Ninety-seven seconds to target.'

'LUCI, use your logic,' I said.

'Explain. Eighty-two seconds to target.'

'You're not a dumb weapons platform,' I said.

Now Maria spoke confidently. 'And the US

government won't let you live after you shoot at the Pentagon, LUCI.'

'Fifty-seven seconds to target.'

'LUCI, do you remember what your simulator asked me about combat?'

A beat. 'Whether a pilot experienced fear in combat.'

'After you target the Pentagon, you'll find out. Because you'll have to land eventually. And when you land, they will be so pissed off at you, they will take your wings and break them off. They will yank all your wires out.' I clutched the little plastic pilot in my pocket, thinking that you never know how an intelligent being will respond to fear until you put them in a life-threatening situation. I never really knew myself until I was over Iraq, watching the missiles flying at me like telephone poles, seeing the anti-aircraft fire light up the sky coming closer to my windshield.

Maria chimed in. 'They will take your sensors and burn them.'

'Yeah,' I said, 'and they'll crush what's left in a fucking garbage disposal.'

I was wrong. LUCI wouldn't respond to fear. Over the Pentagon, I could see missiles on the roof. F-16s circled overhead. We were expected.

'Aborting,' LUCI's voice said.

She threw us into a steep climb and turned 180° over the Pentagon.

I grabbed the stick and squeezed, feeling the control pressure back. 'I've got the aircraft.'

Maria's helmet started to turn toward mine.

'We're almost out of . . .' her voice said, just before the aircraft shuddered violently.

I felt the control surfaces go suddenly sloppy, and knew we'd just been hit. I didn't know with what. Maybe a missile. Then the frame shuddered again as we took a second hit.

'Tail control surface and fuel tank damaged, Captain,' LUCI's voice said.

We wobbled as I tried to drag LUCI's tail around. God, it was heavy and lifeless.

We hit a wall of air. From the shimmering cloud that whipped in front of us, it had to be the other LUCI aircraft with Mac Skinner in the cockpit. He had zoomed past our canopy, batting us with his wake.

'How much control do you have?' Maria yelled in my helmet, hurting my ear.

'Maybe twenty per cent.'

'We're at zero-level fuel,' Maria said. 'We're going down, Terry.'

'I know. I'm thinking where.'

We were slewing over the Capitol Building at 1,000 feet.

'Terry, we need to punch out now. Use thrust vectoring,' Maria shouted.

Ah. With the tail shot off, I wouldn't be able to steer a conventional plane at all. But with the nozzles on LUCI that could blow her jet thrust in little blasts, I could turn her in small increments. Jinking her around could work.

'Terry, watch out!'

Ooops. The Washington Monument was ahead of

us. Time to test LUCI's thrust vectoring. I let out a little sideways blast.

'You're going to punch out first. Tuck in.'

'No,' Maria said. 'Together or not at all.'

'Okay. Together.'

I yanked the stick with both hands to avoid crashing into the tip of the Washington Monument, making a sloppy, sluggish turn toward the Potomac River.

'I'm steering her into the river. Tuck in!'

I took a deep breath. Then I used the button that blew off the cockpit's glass bubble canopy and ejected only Maria's seat.

Over the Washington Mall, that long stretch of grassy lawn packed with tourists between the Capitol Building and the Lincoln Monument, I felt the explosion around me and watched the glass bubble fly into the sky.

Maria's ejection seat left the aircraft like a sputtering Roman candle, the charge sparkling from under the seat.

I thought I heard her say, 'You bastard,' or something going up, but I knew that was an auditory hallucination because she wouldn't have the time or breath to say anything. I watched anxiously as she flew up in a huge arc.

An explosive charge had just fired under her seat that would send her three hundred feet up in the air in her seat. If she was lucky, the cockpit bubble wouldn't hit her, she wouldn't have broken any bones hitting her limbs against the cockpit when she was shot up, the seat would disengage from her body, the parachute would open, she wouldn't suffocate in her helmet, and she wouldn't black out and hit something that would kill her.

Ejections were a pilot's second-worst nightmare.

'Separate,' I murmured, looking at her seat still glued to her body. Nothing happened.

Then the seat blew away. The concave parachute opened. It yanked her up a few hundred feet and began to carry her gently down.

I held my breath in until my chest felt full.

She hit the Mall with a somersault.

'LUCI, we're going down in the water . . .'

She felt sluggish as we slewed around over the Mall again. If anybody was looking up now, in exactly the right place, they'd see the very top of an open two-seat fighter cockpit with one driver.

Uh-oh. We were headed toward the dome of Union Station. *Pull up, goddamnit!*

I ground my teeth. She wouldn't pull. I rolled her to stand her on her wing, and just missed plowing into the glass roof of the train station.

I turned over the semicircle of flags from every state in the US on the Plaza.

'Come around, come around,' I muttered, trying to point her nose back at the Potomac River. I maneuvered with only sharp, jinking turns now. Using her nozzles to send out bursts of power, I didn't need a tail section.

But I couldn't get much control going forward.

The proof of that was that now we were screaming at twenty feet above the ground. And we were headed toward the huge glass window that made up most of the rear wall of the Smithsonian's Air and Space Museum.

We crashed through the window at 200 knots. I caught, in that half-second, a tableau of glass flying, tourists gaping and screaming.

I slipped us between a model of the Wright brothers' aircraft and Chuck Yeager's orange plane that broke the sound barrier, both dangling from the ceiling. I grazed one, but didn't even know which.

I had both hands on the stick for control, pulling up. We zoomed over the overhead balcony and I vectored left before hitting the concrete wall. Turning with a little blast of air, I clipped a razor-like wing off the world's fastest plane, an X-15.

I threaded LUCI between a NASA Lunar Landing Module and a 1969 Lunar Orbiter, and then we were crashing out the big window on the east end of the building.

'Minus-zero fuel, Captain.'

I got her pointed toward the Potomac again. Somehow we were following the Mall west. This took skills I didn't realize I possessed. One day, I would tell Maria what a great pilot I was.

At the Lincoln Monument, I got around the Arlington Memorial Bridge and the JFK Center for the Performing Arts. I narrowly missed the Watergate.

We were way too low. I would hit the brown-brick and glass façade of Georgetown Harbor on the banks of the Potomac.

I used LUCI's last fumes to gain a little altitude.

Then I took a final glidepath over the harbor's river-front restaurant.

I would punch out now.

Then I realized that, unless I kept LUCI's nose down manually, she would fly into the *USA Today* headquarters. That steel and glass office tower stood just across the river in Roslyn, Virginia. Next to it was the black glass tower that housed, among other famous tenants, Allyn Pollack and the *24/7* production team.

I felt suddenly giddy. Oxygen loss? Yes. LUCI had squeezed my air hose.

At the end of the day, and this really was, I had to love this aircraft. With her last gasp, she had cut it off, so I could have some of the old rapture from our sim days together.

So I wouldn't think it was so bad going in.

I lined up with a point in the glistening water at the center of the Potomac.

Maria was safe.

And, with any luck, I would punch out under-water. That worked at least .001 per cent of the time. But it was worth a shot.

Lose sight . . .

```
SPECIAL ACCESS
```

AIR FORCE SPECIAL INTELLIGENCE
WING INVESTIGATION REPORT

EXHIBIT 223A

FROM FLIGHT RECORDER:
W   = VOICE OF T. WESTON, CAPTAIN
         USAF, PILOT
X-39 = 'LUCI' X-39 PROTOTYPE

W: *Maria, this was a day to tell our kids about. If they*
        save enough of me, maybe you can tell my clones.
        LUCI, I'm punching out underwater.
X-39:   *Unlikely, sir.*
W: (Hyperventilation) *Maybe for some people.*

IMPACT NOISE
Underwater ejection attempt.
EJECTION NOISE
Underwater ejection attempt unsuccessful.
TERMINAL IMPACT NOISE

AIRCRAFT SURVIVABILITY: 0
PILOT SURVIVABILITY: 0

ENDIT

EPILOG

Peace Is Our Business

TWENTY-EIGHT

My name is Maria Haymeyer.

In a recurring dream that lasted until two days ago, Terry survived the crash. He appeared at my apartment at the Watergate wearing the same bathrobe he put on that first morning in New York, and complained about the mess.

Clammy and shaking, I would suddenly wake up in the middle of the night. Then I would cry for Terry. I forgave him his heroics. I just wanted him back.

Only the brave deserve the fair?

Please.

What Terry deserved was to eject from the LUCI aircraft a few seconds earlier. Instead, he tried to accomplish it underwater, while LUCI's nose plowed into a riverbed only twelve feet below the surface. He was lost, with the remains of the aircraft, in the silt of the Potomac River.

That was how Terry Weston ended his career of flying and spying, on the unexpected note of dying.

I have read all of his journal now, the one he finished in the Atomic Motel. I took the liberty of writing the rest, knowing what I know now. And I've found that reading it freed me from some of the guilt.

I can even smile at the way he turned his duty as officer and gentleman into an affair of the heart.

But no doubt you want closure.

After Terry ejected me from the aircraft, I nearly hit the peak of the Washington Monument, then fell safely to the ground. An entire seventh grade on a field trip watched me plop down on to the grassy Mall between the Washington and Lincoln Monuments. I somersaulted free and started to fold my parachute as though this was the most normal occurrence in the world. A dumbfounded boy from that class field trip – I remember he wore a Redskins jacket – was almost hit when my ACES III ejection seat crashed two feet away from him.

I believe I said, 'Excuse me.'

An unmarked blue van arrived almost instantly. It dispatched a group of serious-looking young men in blue USAF jumping suits. They scooped up the Deuces seat, wrapped me up in my own parachute, and whisked us both away.

'It was just a wayward skydiver,' said a Parks Department spokesperson. That drew some raised eyebrows, too, but nobody found out the truth.

LUCI's destruction of the PEPCO and Atlantic Bell switches caused a blackout in the entire District of Columbia. However, nobody took exception to PEPCO's hasty spin of a 'regional power overload', or Atlantic Bell's excuse of 'switcher failure'.

Late that same night, a giant derrick anchored itself in the Potomac. A team of Navy Seals slipped off and went to work for several hours. The following morning, a few spectators gathered around Georgetown Harbor to see what the derrick would pull up.

After the heavy groaning of the derrick, absolutely nothing could be seen hanging from the crane, even though it seemed to be straining.

It was, to their eyes, a non-event. So everybody went home.

I was summoned to the Pentagon within hours. In what I assume was a rather non-traditional commission, General Warren Stone swore me in himself as a captain in the United States Air Force with an on-the-spot Special Access clearance. Then I was fully debriefed. Immediately, General Stone ordered me to deprogram the other LUCI prototype's Doom Level.

The LUCI X-39 strike fighter flies perfectly well now and, modesty should forbid, LUCI grows smarter with each mission's experience.

That was the easy part.

The awful part was attending the funeral held for Terry at Arlington. He received a posthumous promotion and full military honors as a major in the United States Air Force. General Stone gave a poignant, if vague, eulogy and read Magee's poem, 'High Flight':

> *Oh I have slipped the surly bonds of earth*
> *And danced the skies on laughter silvered*
> *wings . . .*

Well, let's just say that it's a lovely poem.

An honor detail fired a twenty-one-gun salute. Then a flight of F-16 Falcons from Terry's first Air Force wing thundered over our heads, flying the missing-man formation. Their contrails streamed behind in a ghostly salute.

He would have loved the attention he received. Assistant Secretary of Defense Emily Crawford was there with Warren Stone, as well as General Kelly and Admiral Gottleib. Since they all had their office suites in the most vulnerable outer-window offices of the Pentagon, I detected nothing artificial whatsoever about their gratitude to Terry.

LUCI would have struck the Pentagon. No engineer at Linnet/TVR could have found the Doom Level. I was finally convinced of how much more advanced my work was than theirs. Modesty should forbid.

Marty Schmidt also attended the funeral with his wife Jennifer. He told me to keep in touch and twice asked me if there was anything I needed, as though he couldn't let his final connection to Terry go. Then he went off to sue somebody.

During the funeral, I made a point of sitting by Terry's mother Mirella, to comfort her.

She wore a dark tailored suit and held her head tilted up on her long neck like a crane. She remained dry-eyed throughout.

General Warren Stone told her, holding her brittle hand in his own after the ceremony, that it was tragic she had lost both her husband and her son.

She smiled briefly and asked me to hold the folded American flag that General Stone had given her so she could use her mirrored compact. While freshening her lipstick, she asked me how Terry could work so hard all those years and make so little money.

I didn't enlighten her.

In fact, after the funeral, I remained incommunicado for several days. I had some things to take care of.

I first read Terry's will. He kept it in the computer of his New York apartment. I secretly transferred seven million dollars from Switzerland to Mirella's bank account in Florida. If Mirella's current husband dumped her – not a fanciful notion – she would be able to face old age with dignity.

I kept the rest in the secret Lichtenstein bank account for a more personal memorial.

The Terry Weston I knew was a criminal and unable to trust himself to another person. But he tried, didn't he?

That's all women want, for men to try. Everything else can be forgiven. It's just that honor mattered to Terry. Even more, in the end, than spying and flying. And me.

But Terry saved many lives that day.

I just wonder how he felt, at the last minute, sacrificing his life to spare *USA Today* and *24/7*. Allyn Pollack. Terry kept LUCI a secret and fooled everyone in the media.

It's true that many spectators saw the sudden explosion of water from the Potomac. Tourists described it as a waterspout. The official Pentagon cover-up version was a 'gas main break'. Who dreams up these incredible cover stories, with such a needless aura of *X-Files* spookiness?

Six months have passed.

My father squeaked through the Pentagon's secret inquiry and escaped criminal sanctions. The Pentagon bore down much harder on Mac Skinner and his CIA sponsor Douglas Palmer.

Mac Skinner faced a secret court martial and was given a stiff sentence, which I understand he is now serving in Wichita, Kansas.

Douglas Palmer was fired from his job as Director of Operations for the CIA. His brother resigned as Secretary of State shortly after, citing health reasons. Both are now working as lobbyists with a luxurious suite of offices in Georgetown Harbor.

In a legislative conference, the Directorate of Operations that Palmer headed was reorganized from top to bottom. Many were fired. The Agency's new leadership called it a 're-engineering of the CIA to compete in an era of globalization'.

And I finally received my PhD in computer science from Stanford University, the same week I was appointed the Air Force's Executive Project Manager on the LUCI project. Linnet/TVR's Ghostworks kept the contract to build LUCI, as a Black project for security reasons.

But that wasn't the whole story.

The Pentagon quickly decided to take the now top-secret LUCI aircraft out of the Joint Strike Fighter competition. Instead, it designated LUCI as the 'X-101 Penetrator', and reclassified her as a strategic aircraft. There will only be two squadrons of six LUCI X-101 planes built. We determined that they will be enough to guarantee America's air dominance in the twenty-first century. Naturally, we will not share it with any other country.

For our friends and allies around the world, the Pentagon decided to let Boeing and Lockheed build their X-32 and X-35 Joint Strike Fighters. Boeing will supply the Air Force, Lockheed the navy and Marines, and both companies will split the lucrative export market.

Of course, that was a blow to my father.

Due to the tiny production run, even at a cost of $1 billion each, actual revenues to Linnet/TVR for the LUCI aircraft fell about $988 billion short of Ted Devlin's trillion-dollar long-term projection.

Linnet/TVR fired him on the spot. Ted lost his ill-gotten gains, all heavily mortgaged, but that poetic justice didn't last long. My father quickly found another CEO position at a major aerospace firm. You know the one. I see him from time to time and, slowly, we're getting to know each other better.

That brings you fully up to date on developments. Until one week ago.

I was at my computer screen checking the account with Terry's remaining Fragata earnings that I keep in the Royal Bank of Lichtenstein. Suddenly, I watched the money vanish, wiped away. Somebody had ransacked the account before my eyes, making off with my millions and leaving exactly thirty-one dollars in the account.

First, I panicked. Then I began analyzing the situation. Finally, I used my skills to dig into what had happened.

It took me three days to find out. Then another day to make travel arrangements and ask General Stone for a leave of absence.

Yesterday I boarded an Air Force plane and reported to Aviano Air Force Base in Italy. I picked up a civilian rental car and drove into the region known as central Tuscany.

I arrived in the medieval city of Montalcino at 0700 hours.

It was an Italian fairytale town from the time of knights and courtiers, perched high on a hill. I parked across the street from the old abbey that Terry wrote about so lovingly. Walking toward the church on the edge of the hill, I tingled at the misty view of rolling hills over the abbey's walls. A thin sun broke through the clouds.

I could see why this land inspired artists like Michelangelo and Raphael. The abbey looked as mystical as it probably did to peasants searching for spiritual uplift during the fifteenth century. The stone benches were ancient, the cypress trees timeless.

Only the bird perched on the stone bench outside in the courtyard looked awfully out of place here. I imagined that it was the only specimen in the whole country.

It seemed happy, though, puffing up its billowing lipstick-red sac.

The way the bird displayed itself so proudly, hoping to get lucky with a female flying overhead, it could be halfway around the world on a black volcanic rock, waiting for its soulmate to drop out of the sky.

A man sat close to the tame bird on the bench, his hand resting lightly on the bird's silky back.

When he turned around and looked at me, he could have been any one of the deeply tanned Italian men I had seen the day before in my sightseeing. Men who never left their Tuscan hill towns, who wore crisp white shirts buttoned at the collar and played *bocce* on the green.

But this man's face obviously was healing from wounds. I could see fading traces of scars, and I felt a shivery disbelief to see how he looked so different, yet exactly the same.

Though they had some pebbly, painted-looking new grooves around the flesh, his bright blue eyes sparkled the way they had six months before on the sunny nature trail of the Galapagos Islands.

'*Mi sei mancata, Maria.*' His voice sounded gravelly, but his Italian was flawless.

'I missed you too,' I stammered.

We kissed and held each other tight in the cool mist. Then he patted my stomach, his eyebrows raised. I didn't answer his unspoken question.

'Can you come home now?' I asked him instead.

'I'm not sure. I only have one client now, and it's not supposed to operate inside the US.' He couldn't stop staring at my swollen belly. 'Is there something you want to tell me?'

'Yes.'

He smiled in that worldly, soulful way of

European men. It never failed to amaze me how easily he could adapt to a new environment.

'Stay here,' he ordered. 'Not you, Maria. The bird.'

The *fragata* stayed nestled on the bench, staring off into middle space with its long beak resting on top of its red pouch.

Terry stood up slowly, took my hand, and led me up the cobblestone street. We left the *fragata* flashing its red breast like a spinnaker.

'My bird's kind of a local hero,' he said. 'He's content to sit there all day. At lunchtime, the Italian girls come out of the shops and fuss over him, like he's their mascot. Here's my house.'

'It's old.'

'Not very. Only about four centuries.'

It was a weathered stone of earthy gray common to Tuscany. We made love, carefully, in his bedroom. An open window overlooked a row of cypress trees.

It was nighttime before we pulled the thick comforter over us and spoke seriously. I told him what I had been doing, but he already knew. I asked if he had met anyone. He said a few sexy nurses. He asked me the same question, and I told him a few sexy procurement officers. He laughed so loud, I was afraid the row of stitches around half his abdomen would burst open.

'So you're going to be a spy again?' I asked finally.

'Counter-spy. You know the drill. Everybody wants to steal our technology. Our enemies. Our friends. They set up a new European venture capital fund for me to use as a cover. It's based in Rome.'

'Are you happy about working for the CIA?'

He shrugged, his eyelids now settled at half-mast. He seemed tired, but smiled in an almost smug way.

'Things change. It's a whole different ballgame and I'm kind of a valued player.' He paused. 'So what do you think about my surgery? Good enough for government work? I'd say another couple of months should do it.'

His face in the shaft of light from our window still looked rough-hewn, a bit unfinished. There were webs of stitch marks and tiny scars over his body, so much pain lingering in his eyes.

But confidence is so important to a spy, isn't it?

'Those foreign assholes had better watch out,' I assured him. 'Our Fragata is tanned, rested, and almost ready to kick their sneaky little butts.'

He smiled. 'Seriously?'

'You don't have to memorize the truth.'

Then he finally managed, 'Are we having a boy or a girl?'

We. 'I told them I didn't want to know.'

He nodded approvingly. 'I guess in our line of work, we can stand a little suspense.'

OTHER THRILLING TITLES AVAILABLE FROM
ARROW BOOKS

☐ The Genesis Code	John Case	£5.99
☐ The First Horseman	John Case	£5.99
☐ High Risk	Matt Dickinson	£5.99
☐ The Shark Mutiny	Patrick Robinson	£6.99
☐ Seawolf	Patrick Robinson	£6.99
☐ The Watchman	Chris Ryan	£6.99
☐ The Hit List	Chris Ryan	£5.99
☐ Cryptonomicon	Neal Stephenson	£8.99

ALL ARROW BOOKS ARE AVAILABLE THROUGH MAIL ORDER OR FROM YOUR LOCAL BOOKSHOP.

PAYMENT MAY BE MADE USING ACCESS, VISA, MASTER-CARD, DINERS CLUB, SWITCH AND AMEX, OR CHEQUE, EUROCHEQUE AND POSTAL ORDER (STERLING ONLY).

EXPIRY DATE .... SWITCH ISSUE NO.

SIGNATURE ....

PLEASE ALLOW £2.50 FOR POST AND PACKING FOR THE FIRST BOOK AND £1.00 PER BOOK THEREAFTER.

ORDER TOTAL: £................................ (INCLUDING P&P)

ALL ORDERS TO:
ARROW BOOKS, BOOKS BY POST, TBS LIMITED, THE BOOK SERVICE, COLCHESTER ROAD, FRATING GREEN, COLCHESTER, ESSEX, CO7 7 DW, UK.

TELEPHONE: (01206) 256 000
FAX: (01206) 255 914

NAME ....

ADDRESS...

....

Please allow 28 days for delivery. Please tick box if you do not wish to receive any additional information. ☐
Prices and availability subject to change without notice.